UNWAVERING

UNWAVERING

The Fallen Guardians

This is a work of fiction, created by an exhausted human without the use of AI. Any names, characters, places or incidents are products of the author's imagination and used in a fictitious manner. Any resemblance to actual people, places, or events is purely coincidental or fictional.

UNWAVERING

COPYRIGHT © 2025 by Cassie Laelyn

All rights reserved. Without limiting the rights under copyright reserved above, no part of this publication may be reproduced, stored in or introduced into a database and generative artificial intelligence system or transmitted in any form or any means (electronic, mechanical, photocopying, recording or otherwise) without the prior written permission of the author, except in the case of brief quotations embodied in critical articles or reviews.

Cover Art by Diana Carlile

www.cassielaelyn.com

For you,
for making me feel like enough after a lifetime of feeling
unworthy

PROLOGUE

CURRENT DAY, HELL

BLAINE

Power surged from deep within him, tearing apart each cell, molecule by molecule, splitting him open from the inside. A scorching hot tidal wave crashed on the shore that was his body, paralyzing him on the burning earth. Shards of power, lightning bolts shooting through his skull, sliced open his flesh as visions, memories, flashed in his mind.

Warm sun. Blinding white light. Bright, brilliant stars shooting across a pitch-black night.

Golden hair. Crystal blue eyes.

Her.

His heart raced, his head swimming as dizziness clutched him in its grasp. Never could he have imagined an energy, a force, so great, so all-consuming. So binding.

The power swelled, expanded, snapping his wings open in a heady rush, as he threw his head back with a roar. Flames licked his feathers, curling smoke into the stale, hot air, but the burn didn't register. No. The essence consumed his senses, his mind, his entire body.

Memories flashed in his mind faster, brighter, making it almost impossible to catch a single snippet in full detail. *Wavy golden hair...his fingers digging into soft flesh...words whispered on panted breaths...promises made in heartbeats...*

Bolts shot through his chest, light and dark colliding in his soul until it felt as though the entire realm would shatter with his next inhale.

Darkness flashed before his eyes as memories of his past collided with visions of his future, overwhelming him until he succumbed to the intensity.

His knees hit the ash covered dirt.

His head bowed.

What felt like hours raced by in mere seconds. Days, weeks, months.

Millennia.

Gradually, the turbulence subsided, ebbing to a dull tremble that left him breathless. Sweat rolled down his temples while an ache sharpened at the midpoint between his wings. He focused on the prickling sensations, the heat from the looming sun scorching his bare torso as his pulse steadied and he dragged in a deeper inhale with each subsequent breath.

Rolling his shoulders, he straightened, and for the first time, inspected his new...accessories. Because they were no longer just wings. No longer wings of an angel who once resided in the pristine Heavens. No, this new version carried more than his past on their pointed tips. More than the vows he'd made. These new wings would carry him into the future he envisaged on the day he Fell. Over the past hundreds of years, he'd become accustomed to crimson replacing his previously black Guardian wings. Now though, those same wings mimicked the unholy fires of Hell.

Ash fluttered from his feathers, falling to the already sooty ground, yet the feathers didn't burn. They didn't ignite or incinerate. Instead, they...glowed.

Before he fully caught his breath, heaviness settled on his head, clawing into the side of his skull, securing itself to his flesh. Lifting his arm, he brushed his shaky fingers over the jagged surface, following the twists and dips as the splintered texture weaved back on itself in the shape of a crown.

Retrieving his fallen sword, he examined the masterpiece atop his head in the glint of the untarnished blade. Shards of obsidian woven with twisted bones and charred feathers, dripped with flames that vanished before reaching his shoulders.

Quite the crown for the new king of Hell.

Zath, his predecessor, had never possessed enough power to create such a masterpiece.

But Blaine did.

When his new power finally settled, fizzling through his body, a triumphant smirk curled on his lips.

Well, that was...unexpected.

Something the angelic version of himself could never have dreamed of back in the Heavens.

The thrill of his transformation. The rush. The...overwhelming desire.

Sudden clarity rolled through him on another powerful wave, accompanied by a memory so clear it rivaled the crystal blue skies he remembered from the Heavens.

Her.

Her plea. Her vow.

Her lie.

His path, the one destined for him long before this journey began, unveiled in his mind. His mission. The one he'd vowed to complete and the lines he'd cross to fulfill that single objective.

The smirk widened as dangerous thoughts lifted his chin to glare at the flaming sun, heavy and low in the ash filled sky. She looked back, he knew that with every fiber of his newly transformed body and the thought sent a renewed thrill through his heated blood.

"Watch out, my love," he whispered, words only for her. Always for her. "I'm coming for you."

Chapter 1

Current day, mortal realm

RIVER

The situation went to Hell on a hotdog faster than River could say "hold the onions." The Guardian mansion was in full chaos mode, and common sense told him it probably wasn't wise to stand in a corner eating candy watching the events unfold. Some would say impolite. His sister, Raine, would for sure roll her eyes at him, but she was currently too busy twirling a Kiel around her finger itching to stab something. Or someone. Poor bastard. She was even more trigger happy now that her soul-mate, Slater, considered misting to Hell along with Cole to save Evie after Blaine had kidnapped her only moments ago.

Again.

See? Absolute chaos.

River tossed another red frog in his mouth. The chewy, sugary goodness calmed him a notch so he could think of an action plan. Once things chilled, that was. And once someone actually needed his help, which was...never. Well, not for anything super important. Not for the fighting skills he'd trained millennia for, nor for his unmatched knowledge of Australia's most dangerous snakes, and definitely not for his badass dress sense.

No one ever needed him.

Maybe he should simply accept that?

"River!" Willow beckoned him. "Can you help me lift Jemma onto the bed?"

Okay. He stood corrected. Occasionally, someone needed his muscles.

Across the room, Willow crouched beside Jemma unconscious on the floor. The mortal they'd invited into their home alongside Cole's soulmate, Evie, a few months ago. The same woman who they'd, moments ago, found out that Blaine had possessed for the entire length of her stay. Maybe even longer. Uncovering this treachery had caused the second bout of chaos tonight. Right after Cole watched Blaine mist away with his soulmate like the villain he was.

Talk about a turn of events. One he did not see coming.

"River!"

Oh, shit. Right.

Shoving the empty candy packet into his pocket, he kicked into action, rushing to help Willow lift Jemma onto her bed.

"Will she be okay?" he asked, carefully maneuvering Jemma's head onto the pillow while keeping one ear tilted toward the remaining Guardians arguing in the hall. Something about needing to storm the gates of Hell...which was never a good option.

Willow sighed, meticulously tucking Jemma in bed as though she were a sleeping princess. "I don't know. We can't tell if or how much damage Blaine has caused. I tried to rejuvenate her mind, to see if there was anything I could heal, but it's beyond my abilities. Even if I could help with her mind, I don't think that's the problem here. It isn't broken. It's as though her entire body is swarming with... darkness."

He straightened, itching for a fresh bag of candy even though he knew it wouldn't ease the unsettled feeling swirling in his gut. Swarming with darkness? When Blaine had possessed Jemma's mortal form, had he also possessed her soul? Was that even possible? And if so, could a mortal recover from that?

Again, if so, surely there'd be lingering side effects from such trauma.

"This is a complete mess," Willow murmured, before she joined the others in the hall, leaving him alone with the mortal.

Sinking into the corner reading chair, he tuned into the heated discussion in the hall, where the Guardians debated what to do next. Some argued hunting down Blaine would give them answers and save Evie. Aric thought Raine's Raziel magic would heal Jemma as she'd done with Slater's soul, now that Willow's magic hadn't worked. Nope. Raine's powers wouldn't work, not that he had any proof. Just a hunch. Ever since she decided to heal Slater's soul using her magic, something had been...well, off. At the same time, something had shifted in him. Once, his sister could use her powers to imbued weapons, to amplify the *Purah* to end life, yet now, he suspected that may have changed.

Along with other significant abilities.

Mainly his.

Tayla slipped into the room and placed a glass of water

on the nightstand. "Everyone is so frantic. I wish we knew how to help."

She wasn't the only one.

"Jemma is mortal. What would you have done in this situation before Fate granted you immortality?"

Tayla shrugged, a tight expression on her face. "Take her to the hospital, I guess. But...I don't know. We don't even know if it's a mortal issue."

Bingo. That option was out of the question given they didn't know the extent of the damage Blaine had caused and if a mortal healer could easily identify immortal intervention. Imagine that. Someone finding an unidentifiable shadowy substance infecting Jemma's body, right to the depth of her cells. Something told him Evie wouldn't approve of the mortal government shipping her bestie off to that classified facility where they prod and probe alien lifeforms.

Which meant, neither would Cole for that matter.

As Tayla returned to the hall, leaving him alone with Jemma again, he mentally sifted through their current predicament. Darkness in a mortal's soul wasn't the end of the universe. It would likely align their soul with Hell instead of the Heavens, which wasn't ideal, but not a dire issue. Except for the fact that said mortal was the best friend of a Guardian's soulmate. They couldn't exactly let her slip down to Hell.

Which left healing her soul the only option.

And he only knew of one way to heal a soul.

How much trouble would he be in if he told them about his...other ability? The one no one, except his sister, knew about?

The one Fate made him vow never to mention in the mortal realm.

"Sunshine."

He jolted when EJ beckoned from the doorway. "Meeting in the war room. Stat."

Just as quickly as the Guardian appeared, he darted off again.

Well, at least that was one thing. If they weren't ever going to need him, at least they were polite enough to keep inviting him to their meetings and including him in their sparring sessions. He was like the cute, stray puppy they couldn't quite leave out in the rain.

After raiding his emergency candy stash, River sat in his usual seat at the long boardroom style table in the war room and nestled the packet on his lap for easy access. These meetings could go for hours, and one always needed sustenance.

Everyone was here today which was how he knew chaos still reigned in the household. Another indicator? Hailee already sat beside EJ and there were no cupcakes on the table. Not one.

Luckily, he'd grabbed that extra bag of candy.

Aric and Willow, plus Tayla across from them, were deep in conversation, and as usual, his sister leaned by the cabinetry running along the side wall. Her favorite spot where she thought she slinked in the shadows.

He chuckled to himself. With platinum blonde hair, his sister stood out like a ninja with a glowing halo.

She caught him smiling and curled her lip. Which made him smile wider.

"Why do you eat that shit?" Raine's words appeared in

his mind just as he popped another soft candy in his mouth. This time a purple snake.

He cocked a challenging brow. "*Why do you stab things?*"

She'd asked him that question countless times during the past four years since they'd lived in the mortal realm together and each time, he responded the same. Why not indulge? Why deprive himself of sugary sweetness when his teeth wouldn't decay? He couldn't contract any mortal ailments or gum diseases, and only Fate knew how long he'd have left here. So, why the Heaven's not?

Raine shook her head, but he caught the tiniest lift at the side of her mouth. Enough to prove she enjoyed their sibling banter as much as he did.

Raven strode into the room with an air of authority that silenced the conversations at once. "I've summoned Gabe, but he hasn't responded. How long do we expect Slater and Cole to take in Hell?" he asked, sitting at the head of the table.

Twisting slightly, he gave the boss his full attention, ready and keen to step in where required. Surely this was his chance. His time to prove he was more than a sidekick.

EJ braced his forearms on the table. "When I ventured to Hell with Reaper, we were gone for a few mortal days, I think. And that felt like we were only in Hell for minutes."

"That was a simple snatch and grab mission," Aric added. "This time, Cole and Slater have to make it to Zath's lair, use him as bait, and *then* rescue Evie. It's gonna take a few days longer, if not weeks."

"Right." Raven leaned back in his chair with a heavy sigh. "This latest stunt from Blaine is fucking bullshit. Any new ideas on how to help Jemma while we wait for news on Evie or for Gabe to pay us a visit?"

"Yeah, River, any ideas?" Raine's snark resonated in his mind. Not the first time today she'd asked him. His sister was nothing if not persistent and feisty.

How did he end up with all the sunshine?

A little swirl of guilt churned in his stomach for not having told her about his...issue. She was his sister, after all. She should be the first to know. And while he was at it, he should probably come clean and tell the others. But would it make a difference? They already overlooked him for countless missions. Telling the Guardians that something felt off with him would only make him appear less capable.

Plus, there was the whole threatened-by-Fate thing, and he wasn't the rule breaking kind.

Raine teased him about that all the time. But what did he have if not his loyalty and stunning fashion sense?

As the Guardians resumed brainstorming ways to help the mortal still unconscious upstairs, he continued to toss candy in his mouth until he emptied the packet. Mainly to prevent injecting himself in the conversation every second to tell them why that option wouldn't work. He didn't want to be a Debbie Downer, but he only knew of one way to heal darkness from a soul, and it wasn't easy. Or without consequences.

When the meeting concluded after Willow suggested Raine try her magic and if that didn't work, they would wait until Gabe responded, River shoved the empty candy packet in his pocket and pushed back from the table to follow the others. At the door though, Raine snagged his shirt.

His new shirt.

The audacity.

"There's no need to take your frustration out on my cool

threads, sis. This is new. And the first time I've worn it. Have some respect."

"River, stop calling material covered in pineapples wearing sunglasses cool threads. You're embarrassing yourself."

He lifted one shoulder, unfazed by the insult. "No need to be grouchy. I offered to buy you the pink version, but you declined. Rather rudely, I might add."

Her lethal eyes narrowed.

He smiled and stepped aside, but she held him back again.

"Why won't you help Jemma?" she whispered in a too harsh tone.

"Since when do you care about an injured mortal?"

Raine's top lip twitched, the tiniest little bit. "She's... grown on the others."

That was code for how much that particular mortal, and everyone else in the Guardian residence, had grown on *her*. Raine had developed these things called "feelings" and still didn't quite know what to do with them. And it amused the Heavens out of him. Of the two of them though, he was positive he would've caught the soulmate bug during their time in the mortal realm, not his hardcore sister. But alas, love wasn't in his future even though he had plenty to share. Instead, he harnessed that love by obsessing over decades old, heartbreak songs and the gooey smiles on the couples around him.

"You know why I can't tell them." He peeked out the door to make sure the others weren't within earshot. "Fate will..." He made the motion of slicing his neck.

Raine snatched a Kiel from her belt and spun it around her index finger. An action he figured gave her emotions an outlet.

"I don't know how I managed to imbue my magic on Slater's soul, something I wasn't meant to do, and Fate didn't throw a bolt of lightning at me. In fact, I think she approved of it. You'll be fine. Rules are meant to be broken."

He shuddered. "I beg to differ."

He quite enjoyed the mortal realm and all its colors. He wasn't about to piss off Fate.

"For fuck's sake, River. Just help the damn female. All the moping around the household is giving me hives."

He patted Raine's shoulder, holding back his grin at the second time she'd admitted having feelings in the past few minutes. "Hives. Sure it's not concern? Worry? A feeling of helplessness for someone you care about?"

She deadpanned him. "Don't be ridiculous." She slipped the Kiel back into her weapon belt. "You're the only one who can do this. I know how much you want your own mission. Well, here it is, dumbass."

Ooh, Raine knew exactly what candied words to dangle in front of him and he couldn't hold back the sense of purpose igniting behind his ribs.

You're the only one who can do this.

Purpose. Maybe this was his purpose? This was officially the second time someone had called upon him for help. Him. The second time someone had laid out a mission for him. And Heavens, the warm rush of someone needing him felt too good. Right even.

Perhaps this was his destiny, his individual mission that Fate had neglected to mention during her your-sole-purpose-is-to-ensure-your-sister-achieves-her-path speech before he'd departed the Heavens. Maybe helping Raine was his practice mission and this was real?

Giddiness fluttered his pulse. Could this be it? The moment he'd been waiting for?

How could he say no when he was the only one? And his sister was right, he had been wanting a mission of his own. Desperately. Aching for the others to take notice of him, consider him an equal.

A mission. A duty.

A chance to solidify his worth in the Guardian household before Fate recalled his soul.

CHAPTER 2

Fire burned through her. A volcano spewing blazing, molten lava into her veins, forcing it into her body, blistering her flesh. The agony. The nightmares. The torture tearing apart her soul thread by thread. White-hot pain scorched her throat, stealing any air she'd managed to inhale.

Having long given up, she awaited death. Welcomed it.

"Go."

Voices argued, fading in and out like her consciousness. Some muffled by the roar in her ears, others swallowed by the blackness encroaching her mind.

Familiar. New. Close. Distant.

"Once I figure...hell to...with her."

Deep inside, a strange pull lured her to the surface. She recognized this voice.

Help.

Safety.

But he was too late. She'd already given up.

Death had already come for her.

"Damn duty…Why do I…fuck it."

As darkness encroached from the corners of her mind once more, weightlessness lightened her chest. Floating. One side of her body pressed against something hard and warm. Hotter than her burning flesh. Fueling the fire not only from inside, but now outside, too. Her skin flamed. Panic clawed at her chest, and she tried to push away, to flee, but her limbs wouldn't respond.

Tingles erupted deep within, tearing her body apart molecule by molecule. A silent scream ripped through her, stretching her consciousness to the edge like an elastic band, right before it…snapped.

Blackness.

Shadows flooded her. Dragged her farther beneath the surface, toward the fiery lava.

Images flashed in her mind as one thought replayed before the nothingness swallowed her whole: I failed.

Coldness pressed against her cheek, seeping into her skin, fighting against the raging heat in her blood. Fire and ice. Two eternal forces at war inside her. Shards of pain shot through every part of her body, not a limb unaffected.

Make it stop. She sent the mental plea to anyone close by, whoever could hear, anyone.

Please…make it stop.

No one responded. No one came.

No one saved her.

Drawing on her last reserves of energy, she tucked her

legs up despite the roaring pain and curled on her side, spreading the coolness along her shoulder, down her hip and thigh, while her chest quaked with silent, tearless sobs.

Alone.

Always alone.

CHAPTER 3

Riverperched on the side of the bed, while Jemma still slept. He'd stood by and watched the others try to help her for nearly a fortnight without success. Now it was his turn. He hoped this was it—his mission. His chance to shine. He hoped to the Heavens this was the secret calling Fate had neglected to mention because he was about to summon magic he'd vowed not to use in the mortal realm.

He'd never flown a wing out of line, so surely Fate wouldn't retaliate. Especially, if it was his true mission. Right? Besides, this way, he still kept his magic a secret. Fate had sworn to recall his soul after Raine completed her mission, yet here he was. Still in the mortal realm.

The way he saw it, he was on borrowed time anyway.

Logic worked for him. Raine was the one who broke rules. She ignored rules like they were bright pink flip-flops. He, on the other hand, had always prided himself on being a star angel, one who followed Fate's rules to the letter and never stepped out of line for the good of the Heavens. Hoping one day, she'd grant him that mission. Reward him.

And now, he was about to break the only rule Fate gave him before he left for the mortal realm...to save a mortal.

This was what it felt like to rebel.

He didn't much care for the quivering in his belly.

Raine paced at the foot of the bed, her pointy heels clicking on the hardwood floor, but he knew better than to ask her to be quiet even though the action made him more jittery.

"Hurry up," she hissed at him. "Before someone comes in."

They should have told the others what he was about to do. What happened if it failed? What if it wasn't his mission? What if the weird glitch he'd felt when Raine had healed Slater corrupted his magic? What if he made Jemma's condition worse?

What if, and here was the kicker, this wasn't his mission and Fate recalled his soul to the Heavens?

He'd never recover.

He'd never taste candy again.

But...if this truly was his purpose, then he couldn't worry about any of those what ifs. Not when he was the only one who could help eliminate the darkness inside Jemma, at least enough for her to wake.

The Guardians would praise him, consider him an equal. Finally, he'd have found his place in their brotherhood.

The clicking paused. "River? Did you hear me?"

He tossed a candy in his mouth. "I'm immortal, just like you. I have spectacular hearing."

"Then hurry the fuck up."

"No need to be...snappy."

Raine glared at him, and he held back the urge to laugh. Instead, he shuffled closer to Jemma and gently held her hand between both of his. Possessing Raziel magic and using it were two completely different things. For instance, he'd had the magic his entire existence. But calling on it now took more energy, more concentration. It didn't come as easily as when Fate had called upon him to use it for her in the Heavens.

A nice little obstacle in his mission.

Nothing he couldn't overcome.

Still cradling Jemma's hand between his, he closed his eyes and summoned the beacon of flickering light flaming deep inside his soul. What started as gentle tingles across his skin, progressed to a tremor in his blood, until pale teal light beamed from his fingertips, streaming from his hands into Jemma's. Pulsing light bled from him, encasing Jemma's hand in a mystical glow before slipping beneath the surface of her skin and up her forearm, disappearing when it seeped into her veins. He kept his eyes closed, tracking the magic through his mind as it raced toward the shadows surrounding her soul.

Readying himself for the first clash, he yelped as his magic collided with the darkness. He entwined his fingers through Jemma's, steadying their connection, as he flooded her veins with power.

Another jolt slammed into him as the next waves collided. Not enough to make him lose his connection, more like...a warning.

Willow was right. The darkness lurking around Jemma's soul was unlike anything he'd ever experienced. It was...darker. Thicker. More twisted. Layered with a murky omen that screamed for him to retreat.

But this was his mission. He couldn't back down.

Needing more power, he drew on his reserves. His magic was usually strong enough to eliminate the darkness in one cleansing blast. But now...he struggled.

Pushing forward in his mind, he poured all his magic, tangling with the darkness, fighting for the upper hand. Two forces battled, dark versus light, good versus evil, until an invisible hand clenched his throat. It squeezed, blocking his airway.

Dots flashed before his eyes.

His ears whooshed.

Right before he passed out, he jerked back from Jemma, tumbled off the bed and landed with a thud on the floor.

Blinking, he found Raine glaring down at him. "What happened?"

"The power..." He cleared his throat, sitting up. "My magic didn't...it felt weird. Different. Not like it did in the Heavens."

Wrong.

But he didn't say that out loud. Because if his magic felt wrong, then maybe this wasn't his mission. And if that were the case...Heavens help him. He couldn't deal with his name falling into Fate's BBBA. Her Black Book of Bad Angels.

Raine waved off his concern. "It's because you haven't used it in the mortal realm. It's fine. Takes a bit to get used to."

Maybe. But...

"What if when—"

Jemma gasped and jolted upright. "What happened? Where am I?"

Raine threw her hands in the air. "Thank fuck you're awake. Now the moping can..." She stilled and tilted her head as though someone spoke in her mind before she turned to him. "I'll send Willow up. Slater's back...and has the evil twin."

Without another word, she strode from the room.

Thank Heavens. Because really, Jemma didn't need Raine's grouchiness right now while she recovered. And she'd been particularly grouchy while Slater had been in Hell helping Cole rescue Evie. He bet her stormy mood had nothing to do with the others moping around the house. She missed her soulmate. Not that she'd ever admit that to anyone, including herself.

Now, Slater had returned with the evil twin. Hailee's evil twin? What a plot twist.

Turning his attention back to Jemma, he jumped off the floor and offered her a fresh bottle of water from the night-stand. "Sorry about Raine, she doesn't do people well." He perched on the side of the bed. "How are you feeling?"

She winced a little as she swallowed. "Weird. I feel strange. How long have I been out?" Jemma peered around the room with a slight frown as though seeing everything for the first time.

"On and off for a long while. A fortnight I guess." He set the bottle back on the nightstand. "What do you remember?"

"The last thing I remember is finding out that the Beast stole my bestie after he stopped using my body as a human ride share." She gasped, hand on her chest. "Have you found Evie?"

That was a loaded question. Raine said Slater had returned, but nothing about Cole. Jemma didn't need bad news right now, not after she'd just woken from an extra-long hibernation.

"I'm sure Evie is fine. Cole will do everything he can to keep her safe because they're meant to be together."

Someone softly knocked on the door before it opened, and Willow entered. She smiled at Jemma, moving to the other side of the bed. "It's so good to see you awake. How are you feeling?"

He was about to tell Willow she was fine, and that he'd just asked the same question, when sudden queasiness sloshed in his stomach making him break out in a sweat. Had he eaten something bad? Too much candy?

Impossible. No such thing existed. Yet...

Bile rose in his throat, and he slapped a hand over his mouth.

"River? You look...pale."

He stood, backing away, still covering his mouth. "Uhh..."

Tingles erupted at his nape, and he panicked, mentally searching for the nearest bathroom before he emptied his stomach in front of Jemma and Willow.

Willow stepped closer, but he held up his free hand to stop her. "All good," he said before he hightailed it out of the room, bolting to the hall bathroom praying he made it on time.

Just as he darted inside, the nausea vanished as quickly as it came. The tingling, the sloshing in his stomach, the queasiness, all gone.

He splashed water on his face, trying to recognize the sickness, but came up empty. He'd never contracted mortal ailments, nor had any food affected his stomach. Was Raine right when she'd accused him of eating too much candy? Had it gradually made him...sick? Did he need to slow down? Pace himself? Try another brand?

After patting his face dry, River exited the bathroom, drawn to distant voices down the hall. On the ground floor, he paused by the stairs leading to the basement as a sharp tugging sensation flared in his chest. Unlike his earlier sickness, this force almost pulled him down the stairs, toward the armory where Raine forged weapons for the Guardians. As his foot hovered over the first step, his sister's angry voice diverted his attention enough for him to continue to the living room where other Guardians had converged. Raine stood on one side, fists curled in a face-off with Slater, while Aric, Raven, and Tayla held back by the leather sofas watching the scene unfold.

He approached with practiced caution.

"My queen, listen to me," Slater lowered his voice, bravely closing in on Raine.

"You brought a Fallen," Raine growled. "A known enemy of the Guardians, inside *this* house knowing how to bypass the Raziel spell *I* placed for our protection." She reached for a weapon at her hip but came up empty.

The collection of metal littering the wall behind Slater was proof she'd already thrown her stock. Not that it made them safe. Her heels were just as lethal.

"Yes." Slater stepped closer, hand out. "And I did it for a good reason. Would you have preferred me let her burn in Hell?"

Raine opened her mouth to reply, but Raven held up his hand. "Don't answer that. For the love of Fate, do not answer."

Creeping into the living room, he sidled up to Aric. "What happened? Where are Cole and Evie?"

If those two didn't get their happily ever after, he'd never watch another rom-com for the rest of eternity.

Keeping his gaze locked with Raine, Slater answered him instead. "Cole took Evie to the Heavens. She's badly injured."

Whew.

He had no doubt Fate would help heal Evie, and if not, the cleansing power of simply being in the Heavens would do the trick. Relief tumbled through his belly, releasing his earlier worries of the mysterious sickness and his new mission. Evie would be fine, and he'd cured Jemma. Movie night could go ahead this Saturday after all, and he'd make sure to have extra popcorn on hand to celebrate.

His unexpected mission—albeit a short and simple one—was complete.

But when Slater's reply didn't defuse the situation in the living room, he frowned. "Should I ask what else is wrong?"

"He," Raine's gaze shot to him, fury steaming from her ears. "Brought not just any Fallen here. He brought Ebony."

"Oof." He grimaced at Slater, recalling Raine's run in with the Fallen. "Good luck getting out of that one, buddy."

Slater grumbled a response then addressed Raine. "I couldn't leave her there. You know that don't you? If I left her there...she's so wounded, she wouldn't have survived. I couldn't."

Raine's fists loosened...slightly, meanwhile that tugging sensation returned to his chest. From the mysterious illness or something new?

"Will Ebony...be all right?" he asked because no one else had and despite her being a Fallen, she still deserved to have someone query after her wellbeing. Which was him. He was the designated carer this week, by the look of things.

"Regardless of how that Fallen is fairing," Raven answered, "until we know whether she's a threat, or if Blaine is still in contact with her, or Hell, if Blaine is controlling her, she remains in the cell Raine forged in the armory. No exceptions." Raven swept his gaze around the room, looking at each of them. "Understood?"

He nodded.

Ebony was captive in the basement. That explained the strange tug. His soul's natural reflex to warn him of a nearby Fallen.

Slater slowly reached for Raine, pulling her into his arms. And just like that, the living room chaos dissolved from all-hell-breaking-loose to let's-comfort-one-another. It should've eased the tension, now that his sister was no longer at risk of throwing more weapons, instead, that unsettling feeling in his gut intensified. This time though, instead of sloshing in the background, it gripped him in a vise, slamming into him with the force of a truck load of candy. Whatever was happening wasn't over.

Maybe, it was only the beginning.

Chapter 4

Ebony

Humming to himself, the strange angel glided around the deserted dance floor once again as she watched from afar. Hips swaying left and right, he closed his eyes and tipped his chin to the exposed metal beams and leaf covered sky lights. Yet to notice her, he moved with rhythm and grace, a stark contrast to his tall, athletic build. With wide shoulders and a narrow waist, wearing a ridiculous Hawaiian shirt covered in a confetti bomb of bright colors, she watched him for the third or fourth dream in a row. Slightly captivated, slightly annoyed, as he lost himself in the music right there in the center of his silent rave party for one.

Not her usual clientele.

But intriguing all the same.

Even though his tone was slightly flat, and his humming way off beat, she recognized the tune. After all, she'd played it as part of her final set at the end of every party she'd ever DJ'ed. The song that guaranteed to lure people together on the dance floor and lift the roof off the warehouse. A decades old song that still managed to capture the hearts of generation after generation. Or in this case, an immortal angel.

Not the funniest thing she'd seen, but damn close.

Music had always been the one medium which brought people together regardless of race or background. And her part, her sole objective in those precious minutes right before dawn rose and the magic of the night faded away, was to facilitate that congregation of humans. Encourage people, even for four minutes, to lay their troubles aside and surrender to the emotion. Lose themselves in lyrics written by strangers, in haunting melodies or sweaty baselines crafted by musicians miles across the ocean.

The magic of music had been her lifeblood.

Until it wasn't.

Now, it had been far too long since the simple pleasure of a song had soothed her. Any pleasure if she were honest.

As the angel tucked his hands in the pockets of his ripped black jeans, continuing to enjoy his silent serenade, she took the opportunity, from her hidden spot behind the DJ booth, to figure out why he seemed so familiar.

A niggling thought told her he resided with the Guardians, that she'd heard of him. But she couldn't recall his name. Once again, he flopped his unruly, black hair out of his eyes, but it spurred no memories. Nor did the straight set of his freshly shaven jaw, or his strong, square shoulders.

If only he'd open his eyes.

As though sparked by her single thought, the angel paused and spun her way. For the first time, his gaze collided with hers and his excited, almost mischievous unearthly green eyes stole her breath. Moss green. No, lighter. The color of new, young undergrowth hidden deep on the forest floor.

The color of the rarest fern.

Rather than speak, he held her gaze, assessing her as much as she did him, while he slowly withdrew a bag of candy from his pocket and opened the crinkled packet. The noise bounced off the corrugated tin walls in the eerily silent warehouse, almost as loud as her thumping heart.

Hand out, offering candy, he approached the DJ booth slow and cautious, the smile on his face growing with each step closer.

Who was he? And what did he want with her?

How did she know he was an angel? Had he invaded her dreams as a peace offering? To coax her back to the living?

A trick?

Despite her mouth watering at the mere thought of a sweet treat and the urge to snatch it from him, to have something which made this dream feel real when so many others felt like nightmares, she wouldn't accept. Wouldn't tempt herself.

Wouldn't ever put herself in a helpless position again.

Until she knew, she couldn't risk it.

Dreams were not aways what they seemed. They could connect, bring hope, restore faith.

Kill.

Explosions...hellfire...screams shrieking as lava fell from the sky...

She shook her head, banishing the nightmares that had plagued her almost constantly until...this angel.

Still, the angel gravitated closer, despite her back off vibe.

In the corner of her vision, a shimmering, transparent

teal wall caught her eye a few feet from her DJ booth. The same shade of wavering light that had appeared in her dreams for the past...week? Month?

Time moved differently in her mind with nothing but loops of her sister's soothing voice and strange dreams of this angel. She had no idea how long it had been since Blaine defeated Zath, triggering a change of reign that made her shudder.

Had she even survived? Was this...the Heavens?

No. She didn't belong there. These weren't dreams. They were hallucinations. Yet, another trick of her subconscious, dreaming of a life beyond the one destined for her.

Though, this one felt...different. The dull flutter inside her veins was new. So was the frantic thrumming of her heart.

The shimmering teal wall of light flared brighter as the angel glided through. Definitely hallucinating.

No dream had ever felt this...real.

His slightly narrowed, unearthly gaze roamed her face again, sparking heat beneath the surface of her skin...

No.

Not again.

Claws tore at her chest. She couldn't endure more flames. Not when she'd only just started to wake.

She stumbled backward, knocking over a stool.

The angel gasped, on high alert, searching left and right for potential threats. Did he not feel the burn? Feel the temperature in the warehouse spike? The fire licking at his skin?

But unlike the hellfire blisters along her arms that pulled taut when she moved, the heat as he neared even closer, reminded her of the...morning sun. Warm and comforting. Soft. Healing. Cleansing energy that chased away her fears.

It felt like forever since she'd basked in the sun's rays without a care in the world. Had that ever been the case? Yes. Before, when she'd been naïve to the horrors of this world. Now though, her eyes were wide open.

Directly in front of her, the angel paused on the other side of the DJ booth, merely an arm's length away as her trembling fingers righted the stool. Encased in a shimmering teal magic box, the colors danced in his bright eyes. He'd ventured closer than her other hallucinations.

In this alternate reality, did he not know she was a Fallen?

Did it even matter?

This time she should ask his name, but she couldn't bring herself to burst their magical bubble. A moment when nothing hurt. The blisters coating her arms no longer stung, her contorted muscles and broken bones no longer ached, and memories of that horrific fight in Hell no longer haunted her. In this stolen moment of time, in a deserted warehouse where she'd once found joy, everything was peaceful.

If she was dead, she welcomed it.

Softening his gaze, the angel reached forward, breaching the safety of her booth and tempted her again with the open bag of candy.

If this were real and if the roles were reversed, she'd think he was a Fallen luring her into darkness, not the other way around. But in this scenario, she was the Fallen. She was the evil one.

Just like moments ago, she shook her head.

Not deterred, he dug his hand into the bag and popped a candy in his mouth. "Well, you're missing out. These are the best strawberry and creams I've ever tasted. Except for that little shop down in Tasmania where Willow misted to last wildfire season. They were to die for. All soft and chewy with a gooey, creamy center."

Lighter green specks illuminated in his eyes when he spoke of the memory as though it truly was one of his favorites. But she couldn't focus on anything except his voice. How it soothed her yet sparked a need from deep within. How it eased the fire. Quieted her mind.

Ceased the nightmares.

"But alas, she won't mist there every week for me. Apparently, I need to ration them, otherwise, they're not special. Which is the most ridiculous advice I've ever heard. But until she mists back there, I make do with these." He jiggled the packet. "Still, a solid second."

Her reluctance to engage didn't deter him. In fact, it seemed to make him talk more. His constant babble of useless information about candy made her mouth twitch at the corner. Maybe she wasn't dead after all. Maybe he was an angel in her pain-fueled hallucination, sent by her subconscious to keep her hanging on.

Keep her alive.

The angel placed the candy packet on the DJ booth, conveniently facing her, and peered around the warehouse. "What is this place anyway? It's got a warehouse vibe, but I can't quite figure out why I'm here. Or how I got here." He frowned again. "No way am I telling Raine about this... she'll take away my candy."

As he continued to speak, his rich baritone swept over her like a soothing, weighted blanket she wanted to wrap herself in forever. On instinct, she reached for the treat...or him, only to snap back her hand. Now wasn't the time to indulge or falter. Right now, she had to summon the strength to snap out of this hallucination before her mind drifted deeper.

Would anyone miss her if it did?

Her sister, Hailee?

An uneasy sensation in her belly made it clear her powers were declining at a rapid rate. Her mind had held this hallucination together for far longer than the previous ones. In fact, this one felt more dreamlike than all the others since the explosion. Colors, details, smells, were more vivid, even down to the dials on her mixers and turntable. But that couldn't be right. Unless, however unlikely, she'd dreamwalked to an actual angel. Which was beyond impossible.

Just as she opened her mouth to ask him something, anything to distinguish between reality and dreamscape, the landscape wobbled.

"Whoa." The angel's eyes widened as he spun back to her. "What's happening?"

The hallucination began dissolving. She stepped back from the DJ booth with a heavy, defeated sigh. By now, she almost welcomed the hallucinations, the escape, they at least made her feel something besides the agonizing pain of her burns.

They made her feel...alive.

And soon, they would fade, too.

As though in slow motion, the warehouse folded in on itself, silently collapsing around them, falling away to nothingness in her mind. With a heavy heart, she braced for impact. For the moment when reality stripped the hallucination, and her mind reminded her of the state of her body.

The DJ booth fell apart, falling in a dark pit, as the concrete below her feet collapsed—

"Watch out!" Wings unfurled, the angel swooped

forward, catching her by the wrist to yank her to his chest while he hovered in the air. Sparks flashed through her blood right as the hallucination snapped.

Breath punching in and out, her eyes shot open to darkness, a faint teal glow a few feet away.

What the hell? None of her previous hallucinations had ended in a heart-pounding, panicked way. Like they were real. Like they *were* in a...dreamwalk.

Impossible. Yet...

Uncurling her body, she tried to sit up but cried out as a wound at her ribs re-opened. Silent sobs wracked her, while a cool, soothing blanket, much like the one in her hallucination, draped around her shoulders as though the angel were still there comforting her.

If only it were real.

CHAPTER 5

RIVER

River woke with a start, tumbling out of bed landing on his ass on a plush rug. What the actual drug-loving dragon? Had he dreamed of... Ebony? Hailee's twin. A...Fallen? For Heaven's sake, maybe he had ingested poisoned candy? Or too much as Raine feared. That would explain the tummy episode the other day, too.

For the Heavens. He'd better lay off, for today at least. He refused to give up sugary treats and couldn't fathom the idea of developing one of those terrifying mortal intolerances to his favorite sweets.

How could he live in the mortal realm without candy?

Yet, as he stood and straightened his plaid pajama pants, an undeniable tingle still hummed beneath his skin. Like when Raine's magic collided with his each time he walked through the Raziel protective spell surrounding the Guardian's property. Surely, he hadn't sleepwalked. Had he? How else would he have encountered power that strong?

Unless...

No. If he'd sleepwalked to the basement and entered the cell he'd heard Raine talk about, he would've woken there, not in his bed, or more correctly, on his ass in his own room. He peered around the room and recognized his bright orange shirt tossed on the chair in the corner. Yep, definitely his room.

He'd eaten too much candy. The only explanation.

Damn it.

He hated when Raine was right. Especially with something so important to him.

Right. An overload of candy equaled bizarre dreams. No need to panic. He just needed to cut back.

Someone banged on his bedroom door. "For fuck's sake, River. Wake up."

He had an uncanny ability to summon his cranky sister.

Launching to his feet, he opened the door and Raine barged in. "What took you so long? Were you dead?"

He cocked a brow. "Uh, not that I know of."

She grumbled under her breath. "The mortal is unconscious again. You need to cleanse her. Let's—" She eyed his pajamas with a horrified look. "What the fuck are you wearing? You know what, I don't even want to know. Let's go."

He had only enough time to grab his shirt before Raine took off down the hall.

His mission was back on.

Or more accurately, Jemma had suffered another setback and needed him again. Over the past six days, she'd slipped in and out of consciousness as though the darkness regenerated after each cleansing. Not the best news. But not all that surprising. His mission had seemed too easy at first, over and done in a matter of minutes, so it was no wonder he had more to achieve.

Jemma needed his magic. And he would deliver it in secret again.

With the halls quiet and dark, he loitered outside Jemma's room, tilting his ear toward the door to see if she was awake. Beyond the walls, her breathing was steady and even. Although he struggled with doing what Raine considered was right for the sake of his mission and healing Jemma, a twinge of uncertainty still made him pause at the door for longer than necessary. Completing his mission as assigned by Fate was one thing, but using his magic on another without their consent? Without their knowledge? That warred with his moral compass. He wasn't like Raine. He actually had one.

Despite that, he still twisted the knob and slipped inside Jemma's room for the fourth time while Raine held back, keeping watch from the hall.

Silvery moonlight spilled across the hardwood floor from the uncovered windows, landing on Jemma's sleeping form, curled beneath the covers in her oversized bed. One of these days someone was going to catch him, and he'd have to reveal the magic Fate made him vow to keep hidden. Thankfully, tonight was not that day.

Sinking onto the mattress, he placed his hand on Jemma's cheek and closed his eyes, quickly calling his magic. Light pulsed within him, burning with an intensity that would scare him had he not experienced it each time he used his power in the mortal realm.

On his command, bright teal magic erupted behind his lids, racing through his veins. Heat ignited inside him like a furnace. Fast and furious. He gritted his teeth, anchoring the magic in his mind, controlling the skittery tethers as they whipped left and right. And when he gained the upper hand, he slowly lowered the mental shield, allowing the heavenly light to stream from his fingertips into Jemma.

His arm jolted, wanting to recoil but he held steady as he searched for the source of the darkness, concealed deep inside her soul. Sweeping his magic over the black blemishes, he pulled, sucking the darkness inside him, swirling it with his light, weaving and blending the two together as he cleansed the tendrils.

His stomach twisted.

Bile rose in his throat as he retched, struggling to maintain hold of the power and his connection to Jemma. Nausea washed over him in a sweaty rush. The heat inside him boiling to a new level.

Chills skated down his spine.

Hold on. Keep holding on. A mantra he repeated inside his head as he continued to draw the darkness from Jemma. *More.* He needed to pull more than the previous time and ensure he left nothing behind so Jemma could fully heal.

So he succeeded in his mission.

Again and again, he drew the darkness into himself, swirling it with his magic before pouring the cleansed light back through their connection.

Black dotted his vision as his body swayed, the contents of his dinner threatening to reappear all over Jemma's bed. Still, he pushed forward, determined to help the mortal and achieve his mission.

Another wave of nausea crashed into him, snapping his connection with Jemma, throwing him sideways off the bed. On all fours, he heaved and retched, trying to catch his breath as the sickness dragged him under. Over and over, his stomach roiled. It took all his remaining energy to maintain consciousness and not collapse on the floor.

Movement beneath the covers in the corner of his dotted vision snapped his attention. Jemma groaned. He needed to get out of the room before she saw him. Before she asked questions he couldn't answer.

When Jemma rolled onto her side facing away from him, he forced himself to move. Lifting his head, he crawled around the bed, straight to the door, standing just before he slipped out of the room.

After giving Raine a thumbs-up, he used all his remaining strength to stumble back to his own room, where he threw open the door and collapsed at the foot of his bed, his body convulsing and burning up with a feverish sweat.

In all the centuries he'd had this power, all the times Fate had summoned him to use it, it had never affected him.

CHAPTER 6

Warm tingles lured River awake and he found himself back in the abandoned warehouse. The one from his dream with Ebony a few nights earlier.

Once again, she stood behind the DJ booth on the opposite side of the warehouse like a wild animal, caged for mortals to gawk at. And once again, despite her being a Fallen and every instinct ingrained in him warned him to flee, something about Ebony in this dream state called to him, drew his feet closer. He should simply go and see her in the basement, put his curiosity to rest so these strange encounters could end.

Until then, he slowly approached, scanning the warehouse for any further clues. Flames still licked the glass from outside, but this time, he couldn't feel the subtle heat on his skin. Nor did smoke filter through the cracks in the walls, curling around the exposed beams as it had before. The main difference was the absence of music. In this dream, no music bellowed from the handful of speakers positioned around the space ready for hundreds of partygoers. Which he instantly missed.

He didn't know a lot about the mechanics of dreaming, but this seemed eerily like how Hailee described dreamwalking. But that couldn't be right...could it? Dreamwalking? He didn't possess the gift...but...Ebony did.

According to Hailee's updates though, her Fallen sister still hadn't woken since Slater returned her from Hell. Could Duhamael dreamwalk when unconscious in the mortal realm?

He could ask Hailee or even EJ to better understand what dreamwalking felt like and how it worked, but a niggling sense of loyalty prevented him from mentioning it. Besides, what more could he learn? From what he already knew of Duhameal twins, the light angel had the power to dreamwalk with angels, and the dark, dreamwalked with Fallen. Ebony was a Fallen. He was an angel. Dreamwalking to him should be impossible.

Yet, here they were.

Unless this dreamwalk was a trap? After all, Ebony was in league with Blaine. But even as the thought formed, he dismissed the idea. Ebony was Hailee's twin. Despite her previous indiscretions, that counted for something. And if Hailee was concerned about her safety, she wouldn't spend all her time in the basement tending to her sister's wounds, and hoping she woke.

This mystery was up to him to solve.

It felt good to be helpful. To have another purpose.

Pausing in the center of the deserted dance floor, he peered at the sleek edges of the metal beams in the industrial ceiling as they sharpened, coming into focus before dangling, multi-colored strobe lights formed out of thin air.

Over by the DJ booth, Ebony fiddled with dials and in an instant, music blared from the speakers. This time the song was one of those beaty versions EJ listened to at SubZero. He wouldn't complain about the choice though, not when this encounter felt stronger, more real. That he'd somehow made progress in a challenge he had no idea he'd signed up for.

With a grin on his face, he continued toward the DJ booth. Ebony had one hand over a headphone ear, the other on the dials, her eyes closed as though lost in music only she could hear. A pastime he also loved. They had that in common.

Ebony had aligned herself with Blaine on the wrong side of this war, but did that make her his enemy? How could he fault her for choosing to follow her father, her family into a battle she knew nothing about? Just because she was a Fallen now, didn't mean she was bad. Did it?

He didn't know the answers just yet, nor why not knowing bothered him so much. All he knew was he had the urge to find out more about Ebony.

As he neared the DJ booth, Ebony lifted her gaze, locking with his. His heart stalled. Her pale crimson eyes narrowed, assessing him just as he'd done to her when he'd first appeared in the warehouse. He didn't blame her. She had as much reason to be wary of him as he did her. But that earlier sense of allegiance he'd felt proved they were kindred spirits. Perhaps because she loved to create music, and he loved to listen to it. Simple as that.

But maybe, it wasn't.

Maybe it was more. What if the pull between them that kept luring him to this dream was deeper than a superficial love of music? Fate had created them both for this realm to fulfill a destiny, regardless of what side of the war they fought on. And he sensed Ebony, like him, was a little misplaced. Lost even.

Tentatively, he pushed on with careful, unhurried steps, so as not to frighten her and have her lose control and collapse the dream like last time. In the last dream, she hadn't acknowledged him until he'd walked beyond the shimmering teal barrier surrounding the DJ booth. Now, he hovered a step outside it while her gaze roamed over him, from his eyes all the way to the tips of his toes and back up, giving him a heated shiver.

He stepped forward.

The teal barrier tingled his skin as he passed through and once again, he recognized the strength of its magic. Raine's? How? How could his sister's magic enter a dream with a Fallen?

And why did he have so many questions?

Beyond the barrier now, he saw Ebony more clearly. Her rich, almost black hair tumbled over her shoulders, and he had the sudden urge to run his fingers through the strands to see if they were as soft as they looked. Surely, they were. On one side, a thick, violet streak stood out like a defiant "fuck you" to the universe and he had to hold back a giggle. Maybe she wasn't lost. Maybe she hid herself on purpose so no one would find her.

"Violet is my favorite color," he said by way of greeting.

The color reminded him of the Aura Quartz lining the gates of the Heavens. Beautiful and stunning, yet equally as deadly. Much how he considered this Fallen.

Unconsciously, his hand slipped into his jean pocket to pull out a bag of red frogs and he didn't miss the way Ebony's gaze tracked every movement. Tearing open the packet, he held out his arm and offered her a frog. Her skittish gaze darted left and right as though she truly were the caged animal he'd likened her to when he first arrived, and he had the sudden urge to fight off all those gawking mortals and shelter her from the harsh reality. To protect this rare beauty.

He wiggled his hand, and her gaze dipped to the candy—

The warehouse wobbled.

"Wait." He rushed forward. "Don't end the dream yet, please."

Her dark brows furrowed.

A screeching noise ripped through his ears as though someone had scratched the needle on a record, while the strobe lights flickered out of control. Panic seized him. He didn't know how many more dreams they would have or if Ebony's corporal form would wake to answer his questions.

Ebony's hands shook, gripping the DJ booth until her knuckles turned white, her chest punching in and out in short, sharp breaths.

Glass shattered from somewhere behind him, and he spun just as flames burst through the broken windows. They shot to the ceiling in record time, engulfing the ware-house. Pops of glass rained down around them as metal groaned and creaked under the heat.

He reached over the booth for Ebony, searching for an exit. "Take my hand. We have to get out of here."

"*Leave me.*" Ebony's voice begged in his mind.

Leave her? No. "Never."

Heat singed his back as the fire surrounded him and the beam above groaned a second before it fell.

"Get down!" he shouted as he darted around the booth to sweep Ebony beneath him and braced for impact.

CHAPTER 7

Nightmares plagued her. Fires. Burning buildings, crumbling cities, the pits of Hell reaching up to drag her into their abyss. Through it all, she laid helpless, watching the world fall around her.

Endless. All-consuming.

"Leave me."

She pleaded with her mind to anyone who would listen. But only one voice replied.

"Never."

Yet no one came to her rescue, no one saved her. She'd been the one who put herself on the line for those she loved and now, it had been for nothing.

Until now, the nightmares had all been the same. But that voice, the one who kept drawing her back to the surface, forcing air in her lungs suddenly had a face. An angel. The one who'd called to her, whose mesmerizing eyes had captured her and promised her safety. Whose energy and mischievous grin had made her want for more. More adventures, more hope.

More time.

Did she survive when Zath's realm imploded? Was she still there, on the sooty ground while the earth crumbled beneath her?

It felt like she'd been trapped in this ash and fire waste-land forever, with glimpses of the angel sent to confuse her subconscious. To terrorize her?

To punish her.

She should close her eyes one last time...he would understand—

"Ebony, wake up," the angel murmured.

She stumbled forward, not quite here nor there in a dreamscape of her own creation. Once, she'd mastered controlling dreams, but now, her ability lacked...power. Strength.

A safe anchor.

"Leave me."

She remembered enough to know what had happened in Hell. What had happened to her. How Blaine had become King. How he'd abandoned her.

Like everyone else.

So would the angel.

The landscape wobbled again, sulfur once more lacing the heavily sooty air. She trembled, suspended an inch above the ground. Once this dream ended, so would she.

"Wake up," the angel repeated, his voice soothing amid screeching and groaning metal.

Why would he care?

"Leave me."

Waking up hurt. She'd tried to over and over only to end up tangled in the same fucking loop. Waking up meant fighting harder and right now, she had no strength left to give.

A heavy weight laid over her, protecting her from falling debris.

"I've got you," the angel repeated in her ear. "I won't let anything happen to you."

Even without realizing it, he'd somehow lured her back to the surface for one final breath. Granting her peace in these final moments with his deep, reassuring voice. As the fires blazed and the warehouse collapsed around them, she was thankful he'd come to her, that he was with her in the end.

That he'd protected her.

CHAPTER 8

River launched out of bed and bolted down the hall before his eyes had even fully opened. That time he hadn't eaten too much candy. After his bizarre dream a few nights ago, he'd made sure to ration himself and even changed the brand—despite his reluctance—in case that was the issue. But it hadn't made a difference.

He'd dreamed of Ebony again. The Fallen currently imprisoned in their basement. And it felt as though she was in danger.

He didn't stop to consider how or why the dreamwalk occurred, or even why he should care, not when urgent fear clamped around his lungs, expelling his last pulls of oxygen. Heat still singed his cheeks as though the explosions had been real, while the sounds of the warehouse crashing down around them would haunt him for decades if he didn't save her.

Leave me.

Down the stairs, two at a time.

Someone shouted at him, but he kept running, the churn in his gut screaming that if he didn't get there in time, Ebony would never wake. Hailee would lose her sister, her only remaining family. Guilt would eat away at Evie for the rest of eternity for her role in taking down Zath.

And him? He'd lose the sudden sense of purpose he hadn't realized simmered in the background.

At the basement door, his fumbling fingers incorrectly punched in the code twice before he managed to unlock the door and shove it open. He raced around the corner where he skidded to a halt.

A transparent, shimmering barrier surrounded Ebony's small quarters, as though sectioning it off from the rest of the basement. But that wasn't what tightened his chest. The color of the magic, the unique signature he sensed even from a few feet away. Raziel magic.

His sister's power.

An exact replica to the one he'd walked through in the dream.

Moving closer, he found Ebony lying on a simple cot. Her chest rising and falling with each breath. No flames. No warehouse crashing down around them. No need to protect her from falling debris.

Now that he'd made it to the basement and the adrenaline had started to drop, the sudden urge to reach Ebony, to save her, seemed...silly. Foolish. His mind had created scenarios where someone needed him, just to give him a purpose. Ebony had dreamwalked to him. Maybe even tricked him for all he knew. The dream wasn't real. In fact, maybe he needed to lower his sugar intake even more, despite his recent changes. Heaven forbid, maybe he should switch to—he shuddered—savory?

Asleep on her back, he took a moment to compare this

Ebony with the one in his dream. Bandages covered most of her limbs with dark patches staining the fabric. Her thick hair was faded, damp strands stuck to her forehead, while that "fuck you" violet streak still brought a smile to his face as he imagined her glaring at him for simply admiring it. Beside the bed was a single chair that Hailee probably sat in each time she visited, or Aric when he changed Ebony's dressings. And beyond that, an open door leading to the small basement bathroom, which he figured was useless considering Ebony had yet to wake.

Despite the sudden urgency having dimmed, a strange sensation tingled in his blood, urging him beyond the Raziel spell, closer to Ebony. Why? He had no idea. She was fine. Not that he was a healer or mortal doctor, but she wasn't burning alive beneath collapsed rubble, which is what he'd feared when he'd jolted awake.

"River?"

He jumped, spinning around as Hailee entered the basement, so lost in his head he hadn't even heard the door open.

"Oh, hey!" Why was his voice so high pitched?

Carrying a tray with bandages and a fresh bottle of water, she paused beside him and frowned. "Are you...is everything all right? You look...pale."

That tightness in his chest returned. How did he answer that? He couldn't exactly tell Hailee he'd had a horrific dream of her sister burning in a warehouse fire then bolted here to make sure she was safe. No, that would sound...ridiculous. But any other story or version of the truth would be a lie. He *had* run down here to save Ebony. He *had* panicked that she had no one to protect her, to save her. And even though Hailee would comprehend the whole dreamwalking thing, he still didn't understand how it had happened.

A Fallen. Dreamwalking to him.

Raine would punch him for coming up with such a stupid idea.

Leave me.

Dread roiled in his stomach at the two words Ebony had repeated in his mind when he'd tried to protect her. Had... any of it been real?

Heavens, why was this so confusing?

When he didn't reply, Hailee gave his shoulder a light squeeze before gliding through the Raziel barrier to place the tray beside Ebony's cot. Once again, a mystical tug called him closer. A spike in his pulse eerily similar to the feeling he'd had when he leaped out of bed.

Curiosity drove his feet forward until he breached the barrier. Just as he suspected, his sister's magic washed over him, her unique signature recognizing his own as he entered the...cage. A cage. Just how he'd described Ebony's situation in the dream. And the niggling sensation in his gut told him, like the dream, this cage was to keep Ebony locked in while others remained safely outside the barrier. Free to gawk at the rare and beautiful creature within its spelled walls.

Sudden, intense urgency to extinguish the barrier roared through him until he had to force himself to stop. Desire for someone to need him in a dream was one thing. Breaking rules for a Fallen he barely knew was entirely different.

"I didn't expect you down here this late," Hailee said as she meticulously unwrapped the bandage on Ebony's arm closest to her.

He held back. Not because he was squeamish, more so

he didn't try to take over. This bizarre yearning to tend to Ebony's wounds messed with his head.

"Dreamwalking must be a cool ability to have," he said instead, shoving his hands in his pajama pants.

Smooth, River. Not weird at all.

Hailee glanced at him over her shoulder frowning, because clearly, he was making a fool of himself, then resumed unwinding the bandage. "Sometimes. Though, it's pointless when I can't even reach the only person I desperately want to dreamwalk to."

"Ebony."

Her name flowed through his veins like rich hot cocoa on a cold, snowy night.

Hailee didn't need to confirm it, he already knew she'd tried several times to dreamwalk to her sister since Slater had brought her here, which baffled him even more. How had he reached Ebony? Or more accurately, how had she reached him?

Again, unless it was his candy overdose issue. But the longer he remained in her presence, within the magical barrier, the more he doubted that theory.

A soiled bandage fluttered to the floor by Hailee's feet, and he stared at the blood stains. How had Ebony survived? Would she recover? Without the healing power of the Heavens, could she?

"Can you pass me that powder please?"

He grabbed the clear vial filled to the brim with white powder and passed it to her.

"Have you tried to dreamwalk to Ebony recently?" he asked, to distract himself from the angry blisters covering Ebony's arm.

Hailee puffed white clouds of powder over the wounds, it sizzled for a few seconds before seeping into the skin.

He almost gagged.

"I tried earlier tonight but still no luck. It's no surprise though." She motioned to the intricate dreamcatcher bracelet on Ebony's wrist, strangely unaffected by the burns as though secured by a magical link directly to her soul. "I think it's a modified version of mine, to block unwanted dreamwalkers. Which also means only Ebony can take it off."

That made sense. Kind of. But he kept going around in circles. If the dream was real, how? If Ebony wore a dream protection relic, how had he reached her?

If his dream wasn't real, why was he standing in the basement?

"Can you control who you dreamwalk to, or can someone, like, hijack your dream without that protection?"

Hailee returned the vial to him, and he placed it to the tray before passing her a fresh bandage.

"Usually, I choose who I dreamwalk to. But in the beginning, when I didn't have control over the ability or an anchor to stabilize the power, I somehow locked onto EJ before I knew him." A soft smile lifted at the corner of her mouth. "Of course, I didn't know at the time, but it makes sense now. My soul recognized his long before we'd even met."

He remembered how confused EJ had been when a random woman entered his dreams, and he'd kept waking with the strange sense that he'd experienced the scene rather than dreamed it. "Yeah, but that was because he's your soul—"

Wait.

His cheeks tingled as the blood drained from his face.

If Hailee dreamwalked to her soulmate before she'd

even met him, did that mean Ebony.... Holy shit. No. Could she...Was she...

Surely not.

"What's with all the questions?" Hailee's eyes widened. "River? What's wrong?"

Soulmates?

Was Ebony his...soulmate?

By now, he was positive that path wasn't paved for him. That his destiny was exactly as Fate had described before he'd departed the Heavens. *Ensure your sister recovers... Ensure she locates the Empryen...*blah, blah, blah. He'd replayed the words over in his mind so many times, examined them from every angle, and still came to the same conclusion. His only purpose in the mortal realm was to ensure Raine succeeded. And ever since, he'd been stuck in waiting mode. Not wanting to hurry Fate but feeling out of place in the meantime.

But if he...if Ebony was...connected to him, was that the proof he needed? The dream had been real. He didn't need to stress about eating candy. In fact, he could eat as much as he wanted forever.

What had he done for Fate to bestow him with such a favor? A mission crafted for him *and* a soulmate? Could he be that lucky? Just as his excitement heightened, another thought ground it to a screeching halt. If the dream had been real...had the fire? The collapsing warehouse?

Urgency reared inside him. "Can you hurt yourself in a dreamwalk?"

Hailee frowned, no doubt trying to figure out why he was acting so weird. "Yes. While in a dreamwalk, it's real, which was why Raine made me the dagger ring for protection." A comforting hand squeezed his shoulder, but it only made him itch. "River, what's going on?"

His gaze darted to Ebony, lying deathly still on the bed. Her chest rose and fell with shallow breaths, but every few seconds, it shuddered then...stilled, before sucking in another shorter, sharper breath. Her body was struggling. Was she dying in the dream, and he was the only one who knew?

Was the warehouse fire burning her alive while he stood here mindlessly chatting with her sister?

Panic clawed his chest. He darted around to Ebony, landing on his knees beside the cot. "We have to wake her. Now. Hailee, it's urgent."

"River, you're scaring me. What happened? Did she... dreamwalk to you?"

He ignored the questions. His only focus, waking Ebony before she died. Could she die? Would her soul return to Hell?

Did Hell still exist after Zath's demise?

Or someplace worse?

Without thinking, he cupped Ebony's clammy cheeks and drew on the magic he'd so flippantly used over the past few weeks to cleanse darkness from Jemma. The magic he swore not to use when he departed the Heavens.

"Wake up, Ebony," he urged her as his palms began to tingle seconds before power erupted from his fingertips.

Metal clanged on the floor behind him. Someone barged into the basement. Another shouted. He blocked it all out. Concentrating on pure tendrils of light, he weaved power from his fingers directly into Ebony's soul. This time he wasn't searching for darkness he was searching for life. Heat billowed from his side, just like in the warehouse, yet he pushed on until his mind collided with a weak tendril of life, blinking in and out. He locked onto it and transferred his light into her soul with a burst of energy.

He flew backward, landing on his ass.

Hailee sucked in a breath. Someone else cursed.

But all he cared about was the cool relief rushing through his blood when Ebony's eyes shot open.

CHAPTER 9

Light assaulted her eyes, flickering between darkness and sharp brightness sending a jolt of pain through her skull. She blinked over and over, trying to clear the blurriness as her vision adjusted. Swallowing, her throat burned while a thick taste of smoke coated her tongue, reminding her where she'd been. What had happened.

The warehouse. The fire

How had she...survived?

Where was she?

After all she'd been through, anyone would forgive her for wishing her soul had been transported to someplace magical. Beyond the Heavens. Far from a world of pain and regret. One where she could start over.

"Ebony?"

Hailee's voice croaked by her ear, followed by a choked sob. Real? Not real? Had she found her twin for a fleeting moment before her soul crossed over?

"Open your eyes again, Eb. Wake up. Please."

No, this wasn't a dream or hallucination. It was real. She was...alive. And Hailee, her sister who she'd tried for so many years to protect, was by her side. Here with her. Instead of relief, her stomach twisted. If Hailee was here, if they were together, then her sister was in danger. They both were.

"River, help her. I don't know what you did, but she needs you to do it again. Please."

Her sister's voice cracked as though holding back tears. More than anything, she wanted to tell Hailee to run, to leave her be, let her go, but when she opened her mouth to speak, only a strangled sound escaped.

"There's nothing more I can do. She has to *want* to wake up."

That voice. The gentle caress over her mind, washing through her soul, jerked her back to consciousness faster than any threats in her dreams.

I've got you. I won't let anything happen to you.

The angel.

Forcing herself to blink a few more times, her eyes adjusted to the light and gradually, second by second, her vision cleared to reveal a smooth, slate-gray ceiling staring back from above. Her entire body protested, aching, and throbbing even though she lay on what she assumed was a cushiony mattress, her head supported by a lush pillow. Warm tingles danced along her skin as each limb, each muscle slowly came back online as though awakened by an unfamiliar power. Wounds that had haunted her dreams, blisters and hellfire burns, healed in seconds, her flesh tightening and stitching back together with each new breath.

The overwhelming sensations threatened to drag her

under. But the visions of the angel holding her, protecting her, continued to close the gap between her and reality.

Movement to her side made her head turn as Hailee appeared. "Hey. Welcome back."

Hailee crouched beside the bed with tear tracks down her cheeks. Less than a foot behind, her sister's soulmate had one hand twitching on a sheathed dagger as though Ebony was a threat.

If her lungs would work properly, she'd laugh. Her? A threat? She wanted nothing more than to flip him off.

She wasn't the enemy.

She never had been.

"How are you feeling? Any pain?"

Hailee, always the carer. Always the one who worried, who took it upon herself to ensure they had food on the table. That their mother was tucked into bed. After Hailee had found her soulmate and was under the protection of the Guardians, her sister was meant to live a long and happy life. She was meant to be safe.

That had been Ebony's only goal.

Yet, here they were.

"Like...shit." She coughed as her throat remembered how to form words.

Everything felt...different. She'd been happy, content in her halfway land. Where the pain didn't hurt as much while she drifted in and out of neither here nor there. A place where she forgot all the failures, all the times she'd trusted the wrong person, all the people she'd disappointed in this life.

All the people who'd abandoned her.

But once again, someone had ripped even that small peace from her. Paved her another path for her own good.

What good would that do if they all ended up right where they started?

She rolled slightly onto her left shoulder, testing the joint and skin. "Where...am..."

"At the Guardian mansion. You're safe here."

A scoff caught at the base of her throat. Nowhere was safe. Not after Blaine had claimed her as his greatest weapon before she suddenly vanished. He'd come for her. He'd find her.

Hailee dabbed a cool, damp wash cloth over her forehead. "Any pain?"

Everywhere.

"The light will heal you, give it time." She startled when the angel's voice, the one from her hallucinations, spoke directly into her mind. Looking behind Hailee, past her sister's soulmate, she found the angel standing on the far side of a shimmering transparent wall.

Memories rushed back hard and fast. Not hallucinations. Dreams. The angel in the warehouse, the way his unearthly green eyes peered at her across the dance floor as though he not only saw her but saw through her. Inside her. Beyond the walls she'd so heavily constructed over the past few years. He still wore a stupid colorful shirt like the ones he'd worn in the dreamwalks, but his features lacked the softness, the playful grin she'd come to look forward to. Through the transparent wall, his jaw was set in harsher angles, his midnight black hair scruffier and a little longer. But those eyes, they called to her just as they had each time she'd unknowingly connected with him.

Until the fire...

"Here, try to drink some water." Hailee held a straw to her lips, but she turned her head away.

She didn't need her sister's help before, and she definitely didn't need it now.

"You need to hydrate," the angel said, as though he had every right to invade her mind with his own thoughts and opinions.

"Get the hell out of my head," she mentally screamed back.

With what little energy she had left, she slammed shut the narrow gateway connecting their minds and rolled over to face the brick wall.

Pain flared, making her yelp as she rolled onto her right arm, the one wrapped in countless blood-stained bandages, forcing her back to the opposite side. Images of the hell she'd endured flashed behind her closed lids. *Blaine... Dreamwalking to Zath...The magic-welder casting a spell to destroy the king of Hell...Expelling power beyond her imagination...Maintaining the most intricate dream in Zath's mind.*

The protective bubble of her power faltering...Hell collapsing...

She forced back tears, willing everyone to leave. To leave her. To let her drift back to the halfway land where nothing hurt. All she'd tried to do was protect the one person she loved more than anything in this Hell forsaken universe. Now, it had all been for nothing.

"Leave me." The words left her lips on a strangled exhale.

Hailee sucked in a sharp breath.

"You keep saying that, Violet, and one day someone will believe you."

She had half the urge to give that dumbass angel a piece of her mind and tell him to fuck off. How dare he push into her mind whenever he damn well felt like it.

"I told you to stay the hell out of my head."

Her eyes snapped open only to see his unflinching, unforgiving emerald-green eyes staring back. Unaffected by her glare. Unconcerned by the venom in her mental words. The only hint he'd even heard her was the slight upward curve at the corner of his lips.

"Don't say that." Hailee touched her hand, sending a jolt of guilt roiling through her stomach, but she held tight. Kept her gaze on the angel just beyond the shimmering wall. "I know you're hurting, but everything will be okay."

Okay? Nothing was okay. Not now, and it definitely wouldn't be when Blaine discovered she had survived. But she couldn't warn Hailee. How could she when ever since their father came for them, she'd played the part of the bad twin? Followed by countless lies, betrayal, heartache. Even if she told Hailee the truth now, her sister would never believe her. No one would.

"Hails." Her sister's soulmate stepped closer, wrapping his arm around Hailee's shoulder. "Maybe you should let Ebony rest."

Hailee nodded. "Yes. Of course. You need to rest, you've been through a lot."

Ebony chanced a look at her sister and wished she hadn't. The hurt in Hailee's eyes burned hotter than any fires in Hell.

As Hailee stood, guided away by her soulmate, Ebony's lids began to close. She fought against the weight, trying to keep them open but lost the battle seconds later.

Someone squeezed her hand, probably Hailee again. "I'll come back and check on you in a bit."

Quiet.

After the shuffles of footsteps, and heavy thud of a distant door, the room fell deathly silent, save for the strange energy hovering in the corner. The angel. Maybe he guarded her, tasked with the delight of taking her out should she attempt to flee. Maybe they'd sent him to simply end her while she lay defenseless in their home. Her only true weapon was the ability to dreamwalk, which, given the circumstances, was a shitty ability.

The absolute worst.

She curled up on her side. Well, he could have at it. Kill her for all she cared. Death was better than once again bringing horror to her sister's doorstep.

The angel neared. Before she opened her eyes, a soft blanket draped over her body, and she couldn't stop herself from sighing from the warmth.

"Nah, you're way too pretty to kill."

This time, she didn't have the energy to tell him to fuck off. After waking and existing outside the halfway land, exhaustion tugged her deeper, tearing down her mental walls quicker than she rebuilt them. If the angel wanted to invade her mind and read her thoughts, he could go ahead and do it. It wouldn't matter. If she miraculously made it through this, Blaine would end her anyway.

CHAPTER 10

RIVER

"**W**hat the frickin' hell, sunshine?" EJ's voice boomed from the other side of his closed door, followed by four heavy thumps. Likely from his fist. Loud enough to wake the entire household, especially River if he'd been asleep. Which, he hadn't been, much to his annoyance. Who knew it was so hard to fall asleep when he actually wanted to?

Really, it took the Guardian longer than expected to bang down River's door. Ever since he'd barged into the basement and performed the party trick that would get him banished from the Heavens if Fate found out, he'd been wondering how long it would take for Hailee or EJ to demand answers. But when they'd both left him down there with Ebony, he'd thought he was off the hook.

They obviously hadn't seen his use of power.

Now, he wasn't so sure.

"Open the frickin' door, River," EJ barked again.

Lying in bed, he considered his choices. One: open the door and face EJ's demanding list of questions he didn't have answers for. Or two: fly off the balcony in his pajamas.

There was a third option. He could pretend he was asleep.

EJ banged the door again. "I know you're not asleep, dumbass."

There went that plan.

Groaning, he threw off the covers and stood, not bothering to grab a shirt before yanking open the door. "You rang?"

EJ loomed in the doorway with a scowl to rival even Aric on a moody day. "What the actual fuck? You wanna explain what happened in the armory earlier?"

He mimicked the Guardian's stance by crossing his arms. "Not really."

If smoke could billow from an immortal's ears, it would happen right about now.

"I rushed to the basement 'cause I sensed Hails freaking out, but when I got there, I found her and you in an intense three-way stare-off with her frickin' evil twin."

A little dramatic, but fairly accurate.

"Evil is a rather strong word, don't you think?"

EJ threw his hands in the air. "Ugh. Why are you like this?"

All right, that was enough chit-chat. He had a dream to get back to, or rather, commence. When he finally managed to fall asleep. The look on Ebony's face when he'd woken her would haunt him until the end of his days. Her bloodshot eyes darting left and right like the timid creature he imagined she was in her dreams, imprisoned in that magic cage of his sister's making. In all the chaos, he hadn't even had the opportunity to make sure she was well. Especially after he'd unintentionally abandoned her in a burning warehouse during the dream. How long had the nightmare continued for her after he'd woken?

Did she blame him for leaving her there?

He grated his teeth, irritated as EJ continued to spurt questions River had no intention of answering. Not when he still wasn't sure what had happened between them. Besides, he couldn't exactly tell EJ that Ebony had dreamwalked to him without revealing that she might be his soulmate. What other explanation was there? Unless, telling the Guardians everything ensured her safety within these walls? Made them release her from that barbaric cell?

He sighed to himself. No, they wouldn't believe him. Not yet anyway. They'd probably think that Ebony had possessed him just as Blaine had possessed Jemma. Naming her the evil twin only proved that point.

No, this secret stayed with him for the time being.

"I'm busy trying to sleep, it's been an eventful night. Do you need a candy restock?"

EJ raked his fingers through his hair and muttered a curse. "Be straight with me. Have you...dreamwalked to Ebony?"

Son of a sultana. There went that idea. EJ was clearly more intelligent than he portrayed. How did the Guardian stay one step ahead and foil River's plans before he had a chance to execute them?

"Frickin' Hell. Don't bother answering. It's written all over your pretty face. You did. Fuck."

Back to the hair raking and pacing outside his room.

He could deny it, but...could he? Maybe this was a sign from Fate that he could trust the Guardian? If he did, EJ could answer River's own questions given the Guardian had firsthand experience in the matter of dreamwalking to soulmates. Huh. Did that make them in-laws? Like when two mortals married sisters. Were they now family?

Grabbing EJ's shirt sleeve, he tugged him into his room and lowered his voice. "Technically, she dreamwalked to me, but I don't think it makes a difference."

EJ looked like he was about to cry. Or faint. He couldn't tell which with only filtered moonlight streaking through the windows. "When?"

"Why does it matter?"

"Because Hailee has been trying to reach Ebony through their dreams since Slater brought her here. And suddenly you can? I wanna know how and why. My soulmate is going out of her mind not being able to talk to her sister. Did you use your," he waved his hand in the air. "Raziel power?"

River shoved a hand in his pajama pocket for his candy stash and came up short. He must've dropped it in the basement with all the commotion. Damn it. He hoped Ebony wasn't a little candy thief otherwise they'd have serious relationship issues in the future.

"I don't know how we connect, but it started about the same time Slater brought her here."

EJ narrowed his ice-blue eyes. "Is she a threat to Hailee? To the Guardians?"

Something hot flared in his blood, hitting him square in the chest like nothing he'd ever experienced. Heartburn? The mystery illness? Could be the fact he'd just used magic, though he hadn't felt the same immediate side effects, like he had when healing Jemma?

EJ flicked his shoulder. "Are you even listening?"

"Sure." He paused. "What did you say?"

"Focus, this is important. Is she a threat?"

He crossed the room to snatch his shirt off the floor. This conversation was longer than he anticipated, and his fingers were twitching. "Are we a threat to her?"

EJ stared at him for the longest time, and the scrutiny made him itch. But he could handle a little passive interrogation from the Guardian. After all, if Fate entrusted him to carry out a secret mission *and* care for a soulmate at the same time, he could face down anything.

"River," EJ lowered his voice. "Have you...is Ebony—"

A terror filled scream ripped through the air, followed by Raven's voice booming in his mind. *"Living room. NOW!"*

He and EJ exchanged a quick confused look before darting out of the room, veering left down the hall toward the living room. Glass smashing, followed by Raven's shouts, urged his legs to run faster as he descended the stairs behind EJ, trying not to tumble into the Guardian. At the bottom, he didn't even pause to figure out what in the Heavens had happened because the living room had turned into an instant battle ground with Raven and Tayla at the center.

With Tayla tucked behind Raven, the boss fought off as many...holy smokes. Gray-toned skin. Sunken black, soulless eyes. A high-pitched screech he'd recognize anywhere. Devoid. Four of them surrounded Raven as he circled, trying to move Tayla closer to the exit. Closer to safety. But without a weapon, the Guardian struggled to hold them off hand to hand.

There was no time to dart upstairs for backup or weapons, instead, he threw himself into the fray. Flipping over the banister, he beat EJ into the living room and landed on the back of a Devoid. The soulless creature snarled at him, snapping teeth in a zombie like fashion but with more speed and a heck of a lot more accuracy. He punched the side of the Devoid's head, squeezing his other arm around the neck. It wouldn't kill the male, but it would at least buy them some time.

"Sunshine, catch," EJ shouted skidding around the corner into the living room.

A dagger sailed through the air, landing in his free hand a second before he stabbed the Devoid's neck in one quick strike. The creature howled with pain, thrashing his head back and forth as black blood burst from the gaping hole. Gross.

From his piggyback position, he couldn't get a clear shot at the heart, so he continued stabbing the neck until the Devoid wobbled on his feet and stumbled forward. Right as the Devoid beelined for the floor, River slipped off his back, flipped around and struck from beneath, lodging the dagger right in the heart. Bingo. The Devoid fell to the floor beside him, the body slowly shriveling up as though something sucked all the water out of it until it was nothing but a slimy outer skin of gooey gel.

He gagged. One down.

Bouncing back onto his feet, he spun as Raven, with his soulmate fighting back to back, took down another. EJ had divvied out his stash of daggers like candy, giving them the upper hand. For a split second, he paused to admire all the training Raine had given to Tayla, turning her into a warrior in her own right. But just as he opened his mouth to shout out a compliment, two more Devoid vaulted through the broken window to attack.

"Frickin' hell. How many are there?" EJ called out, sliding across the wood floor to slice the ankles of a newcomer. The female Devoid buckled, falling to her knees, where EJ lodged the dagger straight in her heart. Poof. Another slimy mess coating the floor.

River spun, facing two as they stalked toward him in tandem, far enough apart he couldn't fight them at the same time but knew without a doubt they'd attack together. The one on the left snarled, her tattered dress barely hanging on by a thread. Bite and scratch marks marred their skin with blackish bruises, matted hair half torn from the skull. He shivered. He thought Raine was scary when she raged, but this creature took scary to new heights.

The one on the right had all his clothes intact but missing an eye. That didn't hinder the male's sight though as he charged, running at him with teeth bared like a vampire, only with blunt canines. He easily ducked, leaning his weight on his back foot so he spun and popped up behind the Devoid to slam his dagger in the male's thigh. Not enough to take it down but enough to slow him. Bad Dresser attacked next. He didn't have the chance to straighten before they leaped onto his back, the weight shoving him forward as they viciously snapped at his neck.

He'd encountered Devoid before, of course he had, plus he'd heard countless stories in the Heavens of their soulless, zombie-like nature, but this...this was unlike anything he'd ever heard of. He'd never seen Devoid attack in groups, nor try and bite his jugular like they wanted to feed from his angelic blood.

They needed to end this fight before one of them turned him into a snack.

He stabbed at the leg wrapped around his waist, but it didn't distract Bad Dresser. Cyclops took River's momentary panic as a sign to re-attack, coming at him head on. He didn't shout for backup, even though he probably should have. No, he'd fight these two on his own. In the Heavens, he'd trained for centuries preparing for battles like these. Battles where he'd need to protect Raine to ensure she achieved her mission. Where he'd fight off Fallen to protect the Guardians. And as of late, he yearned for battles to prove himself as an equal to the Guardians. An angel they could count on, someone they considered a worthy member of their brotherhood. Someone they depended on when the shit hit the fan.

And he'd prove that today.

With his hand shoved against Bad Dresser's chin, angling the Devoid's head away from him, he used his free hand to swipe the dagger at Cyclops. The Devoid ducked and weaved his quick strikes, fighting way too lucid for a once mortal creature now destined for Hell. Still, River pushed on, backing the Devoid into the corner of the living room so their only escape was through him. Sharp pain exploded in his bare feet where glass from the broken window littered the floor. Cyclops didn't bat an eyelash at the blood pooling by their own feet, nor did the wounds slow down the attack, continually ducking River's strikes with attacks of their own. His arm began to ache, holding off the snapping jaws of Bad Dresser and fighting with the other. Another quick stab to Bad Dresser's thigh made no difference, as though this unique breed of Devoid was immune to pain.

Just his luck.

Seeing an opening, River darted forward to stab Cyclops in the chest. When he missed, his left hand slipped and Bad Dresser's mouth took full advantage, sinking their teeth into the fleshy part of his palm.

"Fucking fireball," he cursed, switching positions to

shove his forearm beneath the Devoid's chin to minimize the bite.

Fire erupted in his hand, sweeping across his wrist as though a Fallen talon had struck him. Which…couldn't be right.

"River!" Raven shouted.

River looked up just as Cyclops came at him. Still with Bad Dresser freeloading on his back, he sidestepped the strike, spun, and lodged his dagger in the back of Cyclops, between the ribs, straight into the heart.

Poof.

The Devoid shriveled up on the floor by River's feet.

Not a second later, the weight from his back vanished in an explosion of slime. Tayla appeared in the wake with a proud as punch smile on her face.

He heaved a breath, one hand on his hip while he shook the other in pain from that Devoid bite. "You're training has paid off."

"Can't say I enjoyed using my skills though."

He understood that.

Training for battle and being in battle were two different skills.

Thundering boots barreled toward them as Aric bolted in from the back door at the same time Raine slammed open the front, both of them skidding to a halt when they spotted the situation under control. He paused, taking in the room from their point of view. Towering windows shattered, torn apart couches, toppled furniture, patches of Devoid goo, and someone had spilt blood on the rug. The boss was going to lose his shit once he caught his breath.

"The place looks like a bomb hit it. What the fuck happened?" Aric, the first to react, gaped at them from the top of the landing.

"Nice of you to show up, Ric." EJ swiped the back of his hand over his forehead, wiping away a splatter of Devoid blood. "But the cool kids have already handled it."

He wouldn't go that far. Cool kids, sure. But those Devoid were...not normal Devoid. The four of them had barely held their own.

"What the actual fuck?" Raine said, re-sheathing her Kiel.

Raven righted a side table then inspected a broken lamp before dropping it on the floor again. "Fucking Devoid, that's what. At least ten of them. If EJ hadn't come down with daggers, you would've been walking into an entirely different situation."

"Devoid?" The shock in Aric's voice was no surprise. They were all shocked.

"Mutant Devoid," EJ answered, raising his arms in a monster like fashion to emphasize the fact.

River wiped his bloody dagger on the thigh of his pajama pants before passing it back to EJ. Great. These were his favorite pair and now they were ruined. He sank into the nearest couch and stuffing puffed out from a tear in the leather. "Did they...smash in through the window?"

Raven nodded. "We were sitting here one second, and the next, they launched through the windows. No fucking warning. I don't know how the fuck they managed it, but it can never happen again." He lifted his gaze to Raine who hovered by the front door. "I don't care what it takes, extend the Raziel spell on the grounds to include Devoid, not only Fallen, and do it now."

Raine gave a sharp nod before returning outside.

"Aric, you help EJ and River secure the window before any more decide to fucking sail through. I'm gonna help Tayla clean up and then summon Gabe again. This is fucking bullshit. Since when are Devoid outside Hell and when did they start attacking like trained assassins?"

Secret missions from Fate, wonky powers, unexpected soulmates, and now mutant, assassin Devoid. He didn't have any of those on his mortal realm bingo card, that was for sure.

CHAPTER 11

In the entertainment room, seated on the pool table with a bag of candy in his lap, he should've felt at ease. Comfortable. Relaxed. In under twelve hours, Raine had the Devoid situation under control after she amended the Raziel spell on the grounds surrounding the Guardian estate to prevent Fallen *and* Devoid from entering. Plus, EJ hadn't questioned him any further about his connection to Ebony, which meant the Guardian had likely forgotten and River was officially off the hook.

Yet, this morning—today? What in the Heavens was the time? Those wins only swirled in his stomach, feeling like bugs crawling beneath his skin. Something wasn't right. Something was off. Way off. But he couldn't figure out what.

"Quit fidgeting," Raine grouched from beside him.

"Like you can talk, spinning Kiels around your finger like miniature wind turbines responsible for powering the entire realm."

Raine scowled at him. "You say weird shit."

He shrugged a shoulder. He'd been told worse, especially back in the Heavens. "You still love me."

"Hardly."

He snickered to himself as Raine rolled her eyes and resumed spinning the tiny weapon on her finger. Before long, the Guardians and their soulmates filed into the room and settled into their usual spots. He remembered back when Raine and he had just arrived in the mortal realm and they met with Raven, Aric and EJ for the first time, and how expansive he thought the Guardian residence was compared to his tiny abode in the Heavens. How he couldn't fathom having a need for so much space and countless bedrooms. Just over five mortal years later and the entertainment room was overflowing with...family. Bonds tied together by choice rather than blood, and loyalty given rather than demanded. Even though he knew Raven or Aric or any of them would tell him he was stupid, that it was all in his head, he still didn't feel like one of them. Like he belonged. Like he was meant to be here. Many times, he'd considered asking Raine if she felt the same, but his sister wouldn't admit to having feelings if they stabbed her with one of her own weapons.

Would he ever feel like more than an outsider looking through the glass? Was the cause of all those unsettling feelings the recent Devoid attack? Or did it revolve around a certain Fallen currently in "protective" custody in the basement?

If she truly was his soulmate, then protecting her should be his priority. But how did Fate expect him to do that when his family had locked her in a cell? What happened if Devoid attacked again and somehow made it to the basement? How would Ebony defend herself locked in a box of his sister's power?

How did the Guardians cope with this pressure?

The chatter quieted as Gabe entered the room with Jemma in tow looking way sicker than when he'd seen her last. River studied her as she hobbled in, everything from the slight limp on her right side to her sunken cheekbones, and the new greyish undertone to her skin. When the Heavens had that happened?

"Why does she look worse?" Raine snapped in his mind in her most grouchy tone ever.

He didn't answer.

Jemma hadn't healed. Well, duh. He saw that for himself. But why? After four secret sessions of cleansing the darkness in her soul, she should have healed by now. She should have been back to her normal self after the first session, let alone three subsequent ones. Sure, she'd managed to get out of bed and regain her appetite, but right now, she resembled one of those walking half dead corpses that had attacked last night.

Given the amount of darkness he'd cleansed from her, to the point he still felt the remnants at the back of his throat, there should be none remaining in her soul. Yet, each time he secretly swirled his power through her veins, the process felt like the beginning. As though the darkness... regenerated. And today, it had doubled.

What was up with that?

Was Blaine still possessing Jemma from afar? Was he still pouring his darkness into her soul via some magical link River didn't know about? Or were the glitches in his power to blame? A problem he knew would eventually catch up with him. Not that he held a grudge against Raine for saving Slater, but...well, he was a touch annoyed about it right now. Especially when Raine refused to listen to his concerns, blaming them on his lack of wielding power in this realm. If only she knew how much practice he'd truly had.

Raine elbowed him in the ribs, and he jolted, mouthing "what?"

She replied with a lethal narrow of her violet eyes. *"You need to fix this. You're that mortal's only hope and I fucking hate all this drama."*

He turned back to face the room while Evie helped Jemma settle into the sofa. *"I'll cleanse more tonight."*

Raine grunted. He ignored it, instead focusing on Raven. The Guardian nodded as Gabe stepped forward ready to address the room. Ooh, that angel could dress. Today, he wore an immaculate three-piece navy suit, complete with burgundy check pocket square and matching tie. His pointed dark brown dress shoes shined so much River could use them as a mirror. The only thing out of place was the slight frown that disappeared a split second later. But really, they all looked a little worse for wear today.

There was a reason Gabe didn't mingle with the lower angels back in the Heavens, and it was a damn shame.

"Listen up," Raven raised his voice over the soft murmurs, bringing the room's focus to him and Gabe. "Gabe has information that might link to the attack and you'll wanna pay attention."

Gabe adjusted his already straight necktie. "I'll get straight to it. There have been reports from the gatekeepers of several mortals presenting with similar symptoms to Jemma."

Jemma curled into Evie's embrace.

"I haven't confirmed the accounts, as all the affected

mortals so far have ventured past the fiery gates before I've reached them. But I suspect, there is a wider problem at play with some, if not many, Fallen. One that Fate is...shall we say, not pleased about."

Hopefully, that was all Fate wasn't pleased about.

"Exactly what symptoms are we talking about, Gabe?" Aric asked from the barstool.

Gabe's gaze darted to Jemma before answering to the room. "Skin with gray undertones, sunken, vacant, or lifeless eyes. According to the reports, some have presented with darkness in their souls. Poison. Similar to Fallen darkness but more...catastrophic."

Someone gasped. Possibly him.

Dark poison in their souls? Like Jemma's?

"Until we know more, I've asked Raven to put together a team to investigate the occurrences in the mortal realm. Discover what is happening to these mortals *before* they arrive at the gates. And..." His golden eyes floated back to Jemma. "Who is responsible."

"You think the poisoned souls are linked to those mutant Devoid who attacked? Because they were in a league of their own," EJ asked.

"Perhaps," Gabe answered. "Something is happening to the mortals and redirecting their path."

"Could it be linked to what Blaine did to Jemma?" Evie asked, clutching her friend's hand.

"It's likely."

Slater shifted beside Raine. "You're blaming Blaine?"

"Tone, Slater," Raven warned, but Gabe seemed unoffended.

"Blaine has positioned himself as the new king of Hell, and with that, has acquired undefined powers. Something this realm was not prepared for."

Uh, that didn't answer the question, Gabe. Why was the Archangel being so cryptic? Did he know something the Guardians didn't?

"It's not his style," Slater continued. "He wouldn't infect mortal souls. He looks down on them as though they're annoying, fragile creatures. He wouldn't waste his time."

Jemma waved a hand. "Umm, hello."

Still, Slater pushed on, "I've known Blaine for centuries. He retrieved my soul from the Infernal Pits, he saved Raven by sending Tayla before it was too late. He protected Ebony when her father tried to end her. He fought with us when Asher attacked."

"Only because he wanted the fucking sword," Aric added, his tone dark and moody. "I don't wanna believe it either, man, but he also manipulated Willow to Fall, and kidnapped Hailee *and* Evie at separate times."

Slater shook his head. "He's the Sarael."

Ah, River had forgotten about that. The Empryen sword had revealed Blaine as the Sarael, the true protector of the Heavens. If that were correct, why in the Heavens was Blaine in Hell adding a fiery crown to his list of accomplishments?

"Allegedly." Raven perched on the side of an armchair. "Just because he activated the sword and used it to end Zath, doesn't mean Fate intended the sword for him. She could have intended for Raine to kill Zath, as Raine first thought, but Blaine intercepted and became the Sarael when he activated the sword."

All valid points.

River tossed a fruity, soft candy in his mouth, and chewed while considering the possibility that Blaine was involved. One hundred percent. But something still didn't add up.

The pieces to this puzzle were all laid out on the table but wouldn't connect. The grayish undertone of Jemma's skin, her sunken eyes, how she hadn't fully recovered even though she should have. Despite his attempts to heal her, the residue left inside her from Blaine's possession kept rejuvenating. As though slowly draining her soul of life until she'd become a shell of her former self, like the soulless Devoid who'd attacked.

Had something else affected her? Infected her?

If other angels had the ability to cleanse like he did, then Fate wouldn't have needed to summon him all those times back in the Heavens. More than ever, he sensed this was his path. He was the only one who could save Jemma, and even though he'd repeatedly cleansed the darkness inside her, it hadn't been enough. Clearly, he'd only skimmed the surface of a never-ending pool.

Because it was...poison?

He needed to do more. Try harder. Eat less sugar and use more power.

Whatever it took.

Because he'd achieve this mission if it was the last thing he did. And if the situation with Jemma somehow connected to those creepy Devoid, even better. Solving that would make the Guardians take notice of him. Then he could convince them to release Ebony.

Unless...What if Fate was testing his loyalty? Making him prove how much he wanted his own mission, for someone to need him, and instead of gifting him a soulmate, Fate served him a distraction. A temptation. Upped the stakes with a wicked choice that made him follow the path he desired more.

Prevented him from achieving either path until he chose one. Was that why Jemma hadn't healed? After all, Fate could pave a destiny down to the second, but she couldn't control freewill. And that right there was his biggest problem.

Which path.

The mission he'd craved for thousands of years...or a soulmate he'd only just realized he longed for?

CHAPTER 12

The angel wearing the colorful shirt plonked his ass on the concrete floor with a grunt, just inside the barrier, followed by a long-contented exhale. Back against the wall, he stretched out his long, jean covered legs, crossing them at the ankle, as though completely comfortable invading her space even after he'd avoided her for six days.

Six. Almost an entire week.

And now he'd strolled in like he fucking owned the place.

What fueled her anger even more was recalling her countless failed attempts to pass through that same barrier. Hailee walked straight through it, now this angel did, too. But not Ebony. No, clearly the ward wasn't to keep others out. It was to keep her in.

A prison with shimmering unbreachable bars.

The Guardians had swept her from one prison to the next.

"It's hot out there today," the angel remarked, all bright and cheerful.

Really? That was how he greeted her? After six nights?

Did he expect her to answer? Because he could go choke on his candy for all she cared. He hadn't even bothered to connect in her dreams, not that she'd admit to trying.

"Real scorcher," he continued, unfazed by her mental daggers spearing at his head. "Melted my candy right to the wrapper when I was outside this afternoon with Raine. I had to toss the entire packet in the trash. Never buying that brand again."

Served him right.

He was absolutely delusional. Why was he sitting here, inside her personal Hell, talking to her like...a friend?

And why had she missed...Nope. She refused to finish that train of thought. Not because she hated angels, or this one in particular, but because his absence over the past six nights had...well, rattled her. She should have been relieved. An immortal with the ability to access her mind despite her fortified mental walls, who also hijacked her dreams without even trying, was dangerous.

Shifting her weight slightly, she huddled in the corner of her space, by the doorway to the small bathroom, in case she needed a fast escape.

Despite her cold shoulder, he kept chatting away. Entirely too trusting with every piece of information he revealed about himself. Which in a world like theirs, would get him killed.

"I like the heat, summer in particular, but it seems much hotter than it was last year."

Out of the corner of her eye, she looked him over more thoroughly. In her dreams, he'd been so...angelic. Mystical. Everything about him had seemed unworldly beautiful. His body sculpted to perfection, with wide shoulders and dreamy eyes. A strong, angled jaw covered in a dusting of dark scruff. To say the angel in her dreams was handsome would be an understatement. But in person, outside the dreamscape created by her mind, his ridiculous hotness skyrocketed. As though the magic of her dream had muted his features rather than amplified them. In person, he was somehow less perfect, yet more attractive at the same time. She couldn't spot one defect in his smooth, bronzed skin. Not a single scar, uneven brow, or crooked nose. Even his fingers, adorned with silver and black rings, were...flawless. Long and slender, the ideal length for his big, sword-roughened hands.

Hands she now imagined gripping her hips as he yanked her toward him, his warm breath skating along the sensitive flesh of her neck while his lips tasted her skin.

Wow. That escalated quickly.

Just as quickly, she turned away to stare through the shimmering wall, mentally counting the endless supply of weapons stacked in the armory. No more losing herself to the sight of this angel, no matter how alluring. She needed to escape, not tie her panties in a knot over a Guardian.

Panty-knotting, although fun, wouldn't save her life.

"Willow said the heat is seasonal, all normal ebbs and flows, but it seems too early for summer. I mean, my candy *melted!*" He paused. "I know I shouldn't be here, I know I should have chosen a path by now, but with all the shit we've dealt with this past month, melting candy just sent me over the edge. I didn't know where else to go."

For fuck's sake. He's still talking.

Despite her intentions, she chanced another peek. From his lap, he tore open a bag of candy, digging in to remove a handful of individually wrapped treats. Her mouth watered at the thought of something other than the nauseatingly wholesome meals Hailee insisted on leaving beside her bed, along with a bottle of water and wooden utensils. Not even a proper fork. Like her twin considered her an enemy and wouldn't risk arming her with a potential weapon.

Figures. Locked in this cell like a prisoner, the Guardian's aim was probably to lull her into a false sense of security so she spilled all her secrets.

The first few days she'd silently protested, not eating a single thing on the tray, but that backfired when her energy levels plummeted so low she could barely open her eyes. Since, she'd eaten the food and drunk the water, trying to regain her strength in order to escape.

"I wonder if Ariel can influence an early summer or change the climate? Or is it mortal related? I see their concerns on the daily news and have to wonder if mortals really do affect the changing climate. If their big factories and overpopulated cities contribute to the mortal realm slowly dying."

From the stash in his palm, the angel slid a single wrapped candy across the concrete floor toward her. She watched it slowly glide along the smooth surface until it halted with a light tap on her bare foot.

"Personally," he continued, as though he hadn't just tried to sweeten her with a treat.

She wasn't a disobedient animal requiring training.

"From what I've seen since leaving the Heavens, I think it's a little of both. Mortal and divine."

Spellbound by some unknown force, she tracked the movements of his steady, sure fingers as he unwrapped one candy and plopped it in his mouth, chewing the treat before continuing to speak.

"If Fate created all this," he motioned to somewhere

beyond the stone walls of her confinement. "Then why can't she correct climate change? Why can't she undo what has been done? Or...is she leaving it up to mortals to fix? She can influence their destiny, but maybe they need to *choose* to heal their realm."

Why wouldn't he stop talking?

Although he made some valid points in his one-sided conversation, she still didn't engage. Engaging with this angel led to him potentially invading her mind again. Instead, she wrapped her arms around her bent up legs, reinforcing her mental walls while she prayed for silence. Not that anyone ever listened to her prayers.

She was officially fresh out of allies.

And friends.

"I remember last year," the angel said between mouthfuls. "When the bad wildfires happened, and Willow needed to help regenerate the earth, there was so much devastation that I wondered if it was the result of a changing climate or a natural cleanse of the realm."

Why was he still here? Couldn't he yap to someone else about the weather? Such a trivial conversation given the entire realm would eventually burn if Blaine had his way.

Hell, what she'd give for her noise cancelling headphones right now. The expensive pair she'd saved long and hard for, that blocked out useless chatter and let her drift away in her own world. More than her headphones, she missed the pleasure of music. Not only the compilations she made when she used to DJ, any music. Something to make her *feel* anything besides the utter helplessness gnawing at her insides. Something to drown out the dark clouds circling her mind waiting to pounce, or the dread roiling in her stomach when she thought of what Blaine would do once he found her.

He would find her.

He'd vowed to.

The angel grabbed another handful of candies from inside the bag and this time, slid two different colored ones along the floor to her. Once again, she stared at them as though he'd poisoned them.

A merciful death?

When she lifted her gaze to his though, the endless pools of emerald in his eyes seemed to darken with the slight lift at the corner of his mouth. He wanted her to have the candy. Free of charge. No expectations for favors, no trickery.

Just...for her.

Prickles of heat burst along her skin like goosebumps the longer she held his stare, as though he challenged her to look away first. To concede. To submit. But if he wanted those things from her, he didn't know her at all. She hadn't stayed alive for twenty-eight years by giving up. By following the easy path.

And despite her current accommodations, now was no different.

As though sensing her decision, the angel broke eye contact first, letting his lids drift shut as his head lolled back to rest on the stone wall. He looked paler today, tired, as though he hadn't bathed in enough sunlight. Which seemed completely wrong for an angel like him, who constantly dressed as though vacationing on a tropical island in the height of summer, minus a straw hat. Actually, now that she thought of it, even his Hawaiian shirt was more disheveled than usual. Less vibrant than the ones she'd seen previously on him. Something wasn't right. From what she knew, immortals didn't suffer from mortal sickness, but as a relatively newbie immortal herself, she didn't know everything.

Sure, she healed and no longer caught the common cold, but she could still die. Decapitation was a sure winner, along with sending her soul back to the Infernal Pits for a few thousand years.

But this angel was here in front of her, with his head intact.

He began chatting about the weather again, but she didn't register the words as she turned her attention back to staring at the three colorful individually wrapped squares of candy within arm's reach. Her mouth watered dreaming of the possible flavors, the sugar rush, the trip down memory lane to a much simpler time when she'd thrown a few hard candies in her mouth before kicking off a rave party. Or when she'd eaten them in secret beneath the covers of her bed while her mom was amid one of her turns.

As an invisible fist squeezed her ribs, she diverted her attention to the chipped stone wall rather than face candies taunting her with "eat me" vibes.

The tiny beeps in short succession she'd become accustomed to on the outside of the armory sounded before the heavy door swung open. She didn't bother turning to look when a female angel entered the basement. The immortal's magic whispered in the air, and she recognized the power as well as the warning for Ebony to back off.

This time, she didn't challenge it.

"River, what are you doing down here? I've been looking everywhere for you. We're waiting to start the movie."

River.

Just knowing his name swept a soothing, sense of calm through her blood, easing the tightening coil around her chest.

River.

"It's cool." A packet scrunched, followed by a shuffling noise, and she imagined him, River, shoving the candies back in his pocket as he stood. "Everyone wanted to watch that movie with the blond, hunky Australian dude in it. But he reminds me of an angel I once had a fling with back in the Heavens and that turned out to be worse than contaminated candy. He also ended up a Fallen, so...there's that."

"I see," the angel replied. "That would be bad."

"Toxic isn't the word for it."

Without moving her head, she peeked at River again out of the corner of her eye. Even though he didn't give her a single glance while he spoke with the red-haired angel, the tingling sensation at the back of her neck intensified, as though he stood right behind her with only a sliver of air slipping between their bodies. Blasts of heat darted down her spine, weaving in and around her flesh as she imagined their clothing brushing while he loomed behind her. In her mind, he'd lower his head until his mouth hovered by her ear, still managing not to touch her flushed skin. A mouth-watering combination of anticipation and neglected tension pooled low in her belly. All she'd have to do was lean back the slightest bit for his wet lips to skate over her neck—

Someone coughed.

She startled as River slammed a fist against his breastbone, choking and spluttering. "Sorry." Still facing the other angel, he coughed again before inhaling a ragged breath. "I should focus on chewing not...daydreaming."

He slid her the most discrete glance, and the burning darkness in his eyes made it abundantly clear that he'd read her thoughts. Again.

Bastard.

Couldn't she have a private fantasy without some angel invading it?

"Well," the female opened the basement door. "You'll be happy to know Tayla talked us into watching that vampire series instead."

"Awesome." River started to follow. "She hasn't stopped raving about those books. I hope she doesn't ruin the show by blurting out spoilers. No one likes a spoiler-blurter."

She sagged against the wall as River disappeared around the corner, heading out of the armory. But that didn't stop him from whispering in her mind right before the door shut with a resounding thud.

"Eat the candy, Violet. It's...mouthwatering."

CHAPTER 13

RIVER

"I'm not comfortable sneaking in anymore," River grumbled in a hushed tone. "We should tell her what I'm doing."

Raine shoved his shoulder, pushing him closer to Jemma's bedroom door. "Just go in there so we can get this over with."

His gaze slipped back to his sister, standing behind him like an ominous, gloomy cloud. A storm cloud strapped to the hilt with weapons. Or one of those scary monsters who snatched mortal children if they didn't eat their vegetables.

He couldn't blame them. Broccoli was gross. Who even liked that shit?

Raine whacked him on the back of the head. "Oww."

"Focus. The quicker you get this done, the quicker this problem goes away."

That sentence made him frown and spin to face his sister in the dark hallway of the Guardian mansion. "Which problem? The current issue with someone turning mortals into soulless Devoid and releasing them across the realm? Or the problem that one of our *friends* could be next on that list? Or...and here's a twist, that despite my best efforts, my power isn't cutting it."

The corner of Raine's top lip lifted in an almost sneer. "Why do you have to be so frustrating? Take your pick. I don't care. You're the only one who can cleanse her and you're stalling."

He almost giggled. Seeing his sister uncomfortable and awkward about having feelings was the highlight of his day. Even the slightest feelings looked good on her, and he had Slater to thank for that.

Slater. A former Fallen.

Much like Ebony who the Guardian's had locked in the spelled prison for nearly three weeks now.

Honestly, there were at least ten places he'd rather be than standing by Jemma's door arguing in whispered tones with his sister. And nine of those revolved around him being in bed trying to dream. Healing Jemma, his mission, should be his priority. Yet, he couldn't stop thinking about Ebony. Despite having avoided the basement for the last four days, it didn't stop him from yearning for her to enter his dreams. Sneaking candied treats on the trays of food Hailee took to her sister didn't ease the ache. But he'd seen the way her mouth had watered when he'd left candy last time he visited, and he never wanted her to be without again.

Raine grabbed both of his shoulders and turned him back to face the door. "Get this done. Then you won't have to do it again."

His stomach roiled and the cause stretched beyond feeling wrong about their covert midnight rendezvous in Jemma's bedroom while she slept. Sure, he was saving the mortal's life by cleansing the darkness in her soul. But did that make it right? In the beginning, he'd rationalized it as being the hero of his mission, finally being able to help someone rather than sitting on the sidelines. A mission, one tailored for him that would elevate his status to more than Raine's brother. The hanger-on-er to a kickass, lethal Raziel. He was so over being overlooked.

He'd never feel underutilized again.

But after at least seven cleansing sessions, he'd kind of lost count, without Jemma's knowledge, the knots in his stomach told him he'd gone too far.

"River," Raine snapped in an angry-hushed tone again.

He turned around, back against the door while she spun a Kiel on her index finger. A definite sign he'd tested her patience enough tonight.

"I...don't you think by now we should at least tell Jemma? I know Fate prevented me from telling anyone about my ability, but don't you think I should try and scoot around the truth for Jemma?" He leaned in even though the hallway was quiet and empty, save for them. "Don't you think I should, you know, get her consent."

"Consent to save her life?" Raine screwed up her face.

"Well, more, consent to touch her. To use my powers on her, even though we both know without it, she'll die."

"Really?" When he didn't back down, Raine huffed an annoyed breath. "Fine. What do you suppose we do? March in there and wake her—"

The door swung open startling the bejeezus out of him. A high-pitched squeak escaped his mouth as he jumped to find Jemma standing in the doorway, hair ruffled from sleep, wearing a pair of matching short sleeved pajamas covered in donuts iced in different colors.

Why weren't they besties yet?

"Can I help you?" she grumbled.

She didn't sound angry at the intrusion, more half asleep, verging on annoyed that they'd woken her.

"Ah, well, actually…"

Raine shoved him aside. "River wants your *consent* to touch you."

Jemma's eyes widened, her gaze snapping between him and Raine. Trust his emotionless sister to deliver a serious message with a healthy dose of slap-in-your-face.

He elbowed Raine out of the way. "Can we please come in? I'll explain everything."

Jemma's gaze settled on him before she nodded and widened the door for them to enter.

"You don't need to stay if you have something better to do," he said to Raine over his shoulder.

She grunted and followed him in.

Great.

An audience.

Once inside, he motioned to the bed for Jemma to sit and dragged over the single armchair for himself. Raine, of course, hung by the door, spinning the Kiel around her finger.

Holy smokes. Now that he'd had the opportunity to see Jemma awake and up close, the weariness on her face shocked him. Gone was the usual playful glint in her eyes. Dark, grayish circles were now a permanent feature beneath her eyes, and her cracked lips held a slight blue tinge. Not good, not good at all.

If he didn't figure out a way to help her ASAP, he'd fail his mission. What would the others think of him then? He gulped as his heart gave a few heavy thumps.

What would Fate think of him?

He couldn't even consider that right now. If he started

to panic, he wouldn't be able to concentrate or summon his powers.

Leaning forward in the chair, he braced his forearms on his thighs. "How about I fill you in from the start, and then you can ask any questions?"

"And this conversation is necessary in the middle of the night because...?"

"Your soul is dying," Raine not so helpfully added.

He shot his sister a "what the fuck" look before trying for a friendlier, less doom and gloom approach. "What Raine means to say is, the darkness inside you from when Blaine possessed your soul is taking a long time to heal. And as you heard from Gabe, if the darkness continues to poison your soul, you *may* end up a Devoid."

Jemma shuddered, pulling a blanket around her shoulders. "And hangout in Hell."

"I won't let that happen."

It didn't matter how he did it or how long it took, he'd save this mortal. He wouldn't fail.

"How will you stop it?" Jemma asked.

He fumbled with words in his head, sentences he could say to convince the mortal he considered his friend that she could trust him, without confessing the specifics of his power. "As you know, Raine and I are both Raziel," he began.

Jemma nodded. "You cast spells and cool stuff, kind of like Evie-Eve but different."

The mortal made him smile every time they spoke. Their energy matched on so many levels that he'd known they'd be great friends the second Jemma stepped into the Guardian house. He couldn't lose that.

"Yes, but my power is next level."

Raine scoffed and he slid her another "shut it or get the Heavens out of here" look. She glared back.

"Think of my powers like a...dishwasher."

Jemma leaned forward, the blanket falling from her shoulders to pool around her waist. "Say again?"

"You put dirty dishes in, and they come out clean. I have been dishwashing you while you're asleep."

Felt good to free that off his chest.

Jemma's eyes widened, her mouth falling open. "You used your dishwashing ability on me while I slept?"

Well, when she put it like that it made him seem like a weirdo. A stalker like in the books Tayla read.

Uh, that wasn't good.

"Explain your way out of that one, Dishwasher." Raine's sarcastic voice rang in his head, no help whatsoever.

He ignored her, as he did eighty percent of the time.

Instead, he nodded to Jemma. "Yes, and I'm sorry for not seeking your consent beforehand. The first time I did it, you were unconscious, and my only thought was saving your life. And when I discovered it might work, I repeated the process until you were able to wake and rejoin the living."

"Oh." Jemma's shoulders relaxed. "I guess that's fine. You did it for a good re—" Her gaze snapped between Raine and him. "Wait. Were you about to sneak into my room and use your power on me while I slept? Again."

He grimaced. In hindsight, he really should have knocked on the door and asked her, told her the plan and his concerns about why it wasn't working. But forcing her to keep a secret held him back. Not to mention Fate's potential wrath. Neither were a burden he wanted to share.

"Yes?" It came out as a question even though they both

knew it wasn't. "Because no one can dishwasher like me, which is why it's important that no one knows."

"Fine." Jemma pointed a finger at him, looking mildly scary. "Don't ever do that again, okay? I'm happy for you to do your power thingy to save my life, but now that I'm up and about, no doubt thanks to you, I'd rather you tell me before you go all dishwasher on me."

"Understood," he replied to Jemma, while mentally sending a smug *"told you so"* to Raine.

Jemma wiggled to the edge of the bed, the blanket forgotten. "Okay. Let's do this."

Chapter 14

Ebony

The angel was passed out on the floor beside her cot, where he'd been since he stumbled in like a drunk idiot at some ungodly hour during the night. The sound had jolted her awake when he tripped through the door, beelining to her prison cell before he toppled to the floor without even saying a word.

So out of character from the angel she'd come to know.

To be fair, she hadn't exactly given him the impression she'd been awake, and she sure as hell hadn't helped him. Peering through the tiny slit in her eyelids, she'd laid on top of the covers, watching him make a fool of himself until he'd fallen asleep.

Hours later, he still hadn't woken.

At one point, when he'd groaned, twisting onto his side in what looked like pain, she, for some stupid reason, sat beside him on the floor as though her nearness would somehow aid him. The concrete was neither cold nor warm, a neutral temperature barely noticeable through her leggings, because every damn thing in this magical prison cell was so...mundane. The cell was neither too hot nor cold, with a subtle breeze of fresh air even though she saw no vents or open windows, and a constant dim flickering light as though a few lanterns hung on the pale gray walls. Some would love it, a quiet, peaceful space to retreat to when the world outside became too much. But not her. Each additional day she spent imprisoned here, made the delusions and nightmares close in until she struggled to tell the difference between real and unreal. And right now, she'd give anything to feel something real. Anything. Something that reminded her that she hadn't died in Hell like she thought she would. That Slater had dragged her from the fires. Some tiny slice of hope that she wouldn't be a prisoner forever.

That she'd escape.

Free herself of all the shackles around her neck so she could live out her immortality making peace with her sister. But, instead of answering her prayers, whoever was in control of her destiny now sent this chaotic ball of sunshine wrapped in the body of an angel.

Instead of elbowing River to wake him or even worse, continue to stare at his unnaturally long, dark eyelashes flutter as though lost in a nightmare, she closed her eyes and slipped into a more familiar landscape. The only power still within her control. A dreamscape where she could avoid answering hard questions like why the angel kept visiting her even though they barely knew each other. And, even more so, why she felt a sudden dull ache in her chest each time he didn't.

Gradually, the dreamscape materialized around her.

The same scene she'd conjured in times where the real world had failed her, and she needed to regain control. If only for an hour. She'd retreated here countless times during the past few weeks since she'd aided Blaine to take down the king of Hell. Though, that title probably belonged to Blaine now. Even more of a reason to escape the Guardians' prison as quickly as possible. No one had any idea the level of power Blaine possessed now that he'd killed Zath, and she certainly didn't want to be the first to find out. Nor the first one he tested it on.

The DJ booth began to take shape in front of her, the equipment so familiar it created an excited flutter in her belly, thinking of times when everything had seemed so much simpler. Days when Hailee had grouched at her for not doing the dishes, or for stumbling in at four in the morning after a late rave and waking her. Or even before that, the years when their mother used to smile and enjoy life before the shadows began haunting her.

These days, she understood her mother's fears more than ever. Dreams were a powerful weapon, but nothing stood a chance when the shadows closed in.

Multicolored strobe lights pulsed in the deserted warehouse, flickering to silent beats as she fiddled with the dials and turned on the music. Nothing too heavy, a soft remix of one of her favorite eighties rock ballads. The one she always played for herself at the end of the night when her brain was too wired for sleep. If only she had access to music in her cell, it might make the long days a little less...lonely.

Lost in the lyrics, her hips swayed in time with the music while she closed her eyes and let the emotion wrap around her. The singer's voice rose and fell through the chorus along with her heart until the song faded out and began again. It wasn't until halfway through the second time that she felt warmth bloom along the back of her neck. A whisper. A beacon lit within her heart, knowing he'd arrived before her mind had even caught up. And when she slowly opened her eyes, and lifted her head, her breath stalled. River stood by the far end of the warehouse.

His hand stilled, halfway through his thick unruly hair, a split second before his gaze collided with hers. Those eyes, more vivid than ever, captured her. They reminded her of an endless cave of emerald fireflies, drawing her closer, promising her the world. Eyes that offered comfort and reassurance, but also a hint of mischief. Hell, something she couldn't explain happened each time she peered into them, and this was no different. The urge to run to him surged through her veins. To sprint across the empty dance floor and leap into his arms, knowing he'd catch her. Knowing that he'd hold her for as long as she needed.

Stupid, right?

Not only had they just met, but he was an angel. In fact, he was part of the brotherhood who held her prisoner. But each time she tried to group him with the others, one of the many villains in her story, a distant voice hinted that she was wrong. How could she be? How could things be any different? He was an angel, she was a Fallen. He was a rainbow of sunshine, she was a storm cloud. He was heavenly and she...she was in Hell.

Her heart thudded when he took a slow step toward her, his gaze still locked with hers. And when she didn't protest, he took another. And another. Until he stood just outside the teal barrier surrounding the DJ booth, which she now knew replicated the one encasing her cell. Preventing her from escape even in the dreamscape.

"You thinking about me again, Violet?" A cheeky smirk lifted at the corner of his mouth.

She could ignore him, as she'd done each time he'd visited her cell or wandered into her dreams, but this time felt different. He hadn't come to her prison to complain about the weather. A rising ache behind her ribs told her he'd stumbled there for comfort. For a safe place to lay his head while he recovered from whatever had hurt him. And despite the candies she suspected he purposely left on the trays of food Hailee brought her, this was the closest he'd come to proving that he just wanted her company.

And that was a little too real for comfort.

Fiddling with the dial, she switched the music to a remix with a stronger beat, increasing the volume slightly. "You crashing my dreams again, Maui?"

His eyes flared before that playful smirk took over, lighting up his entire face. God. He was way too beautiful for a male. "Hi."

One ear covered with her headphones, she pretended to be unaffected by the intensity of his gaze while she switched dials, blending one song into another in a smooth transition. But her heart wouldn't stop thumping, faster than the beat, so out of time it made her dizzy.

Slowly, River sauntered closer, gliding through the barrier as he approached the DJ booth, stopping less than a foot away. He seemed lost for words, which was a stark contrast to his usual visits where he practically never shut up, going on and on and on about whatever rolled around in that pretty head of his. Now, though, he looked...dumb-founded. Stunned. As though he'd never heard her speak before, which was stupid. She'd spoken plenty of...wait. No, she hadn't. She hadn't uttered a word to him, not even in the dreamscape.

She held back a smile, so he didn't trip over his feet and crash into her booth. To put the poor guy at ease, she turned up the music a little more and focused on the mixer rather than drowning in his eyes. "Any reason you felt the need to sleep off your hangover inside my cell? Pretty sure I don't possess any magical healing properties you can take advantage of."

He straightened the hem of his shirt. Another one of those Hawaiian prints that made her want to flee to a deserted island to lay in the sun all day, drinking cocktails in coconuts with colorful umbrellas. A dream she'd never had in this lifetime and the sinking realization refocused her back on the music.

"A cell?" River scanned the warehouse before returning that intense gaze to her. "Aren't we in a dream?"

Not too smart this one.

"Now we are. But in the real world, you're passed out on the concrete floor beside my cot. Did you drink too much angelic elixir tonight?"

The corner of his lip lifted in an almost smile. Actually, she wished it was a smile because whatever this smirk was did twisty things low in her belly. It confirmed that this angel was a little dangerous and a lot cute. Both of which could be her downfall.

"I don't remember how I made it to your cozy abode in the basement, but I can assure you, I wasn't drunk."

She narrowed her eyes, studying him a little closer. Angels couldn't lie, she knew that, and from what she'd already figured out about this one, she doubted he'd even twist the truth. The welcoming, openness in his eyes, the way he effortlessly slipped inside her personal space, was way too trusting. He might pretend to be a warrior with the other Guardians, but she could tell in the short time she'd spent with him, this angel wore his heart on his sleeve for all to judge.

Unlike her.

"If you weren't drunk, then what's with the..." She motioned to his disheveled appearance. Striped socks with no shoes, his thick, dark hair poking in all different directions, and a few popped buttons on his colorful shirt. Not that she complained about capturing a glimpse of the smooth bronzed skin of his chest. A girl had a right to fantasize. But the longer she studied his appearance, the more something felt off. His shirt for instance, how it was faded compared to the others he usually wore. Maybe this was his favorite and had been through the wash a million times. Hers was a Gallium tour shirt she'd worked her ass off to afford after she'd seen them live at the Grand Myer music bowl when she was fifteen. But she'd lost that shirt, along with all her other keepsakes, when she'd left for a rave party the night her father had tracked her down.

The same night he'd killed her mother.

River casually draped an arm on the DJ booth with a heavy groan. "The last thing I remember was helping Jemma."

Jemma? She'd heard Hailee mention the name but never asked. "Why did this Jemma need help?"

He groaned again, more of a sigh this time while he glanced to the vaulted ceiling. "Blaine infected Jemma with darkness when he possessed her but it's different to standard Fallen darkness. More...corrupt. I think it's poisoning her soul. So, I'm trying to cleanse it. Though, it's not going so well." He jolted, suddenly alert. "This is a dream, right? I'm not saying anything out loud?"

Her hand slipped causing the song to skip. "Not unless you talk in your sleep."

He relaxed again.

"You're syphoning poisonous darkness? Are you insane?"

Clearly, he was. Unhinged at best. Already, she knew he was too trusting with spilling information and lacked a working danger-awareness meter with how he constantly entered her cell without a care in the world. But this propelled his issues to the next level. Confessing he had such a sought-after power...to her. Was he an angel who didn't get out often? Had no experience beyond the heavenly gates? He knew she was a Fallen, right? That she could use the information against him.

That she could tell Blaine.

"Cleansing. Not syphoning. There's a difference." His eyes widened, darting left and right as though expecting an ambush and when none came, relaxed once more. "I don't ingest the darkness. Besides, Jemma needs help and I'm the only one who can help her. It's my...privilege."

Something wild and unrestrained ripped through her blood making her fists clench. She wasn't emotionless, like others seemed to believe, and she definitely wasn't heartless. In fact, her life, the remainder of her immortality, would be a shitload easier if she was both of those things. If her heart had dried up and turned into a piece of stone when she'd chosen to become a Fallen.

But it hadn't.

Which meant here she was, worrying about a naïve angel who talked too much and would probably get himself killed in the near future. She shouldn't take this on. Self-preservation needed to be her priority. But...that buzz in her blood, the smile that had split across his face when she'd spoken to him...He needed someone in his corner, someone to watch out for him. And if that was her, then so be it.

Hopefully, in return for her favor, he'd help her escape.

Forcing her hands to relax, she curled her fingers over the edge of the booth. "Darkness that eats away at a soul will create Devoid, you know that, right?"

He lifted one shoulder. "Sure. But I'm an angel, so I'm safe. The last thing I want is for Jemma to join their quest for evil. There's now even new super Devoid popping up all over the realm, so someone out there is boosting them with something extra."

"Because Jemma is your..."

His eyes snapped to her. If she hadn't been looking so hard, she would've missed the shadow pass over them and the slight frown on his brows. "My friend."

As much as she wanted to, she couldn't hold back the small, quiet exhale that burned all the way from her lungs and out her lips. River helping a friend made the situation a lot less complicated, that was all. It had nothing to do with... well, nothing to do with anything else.

"And until the Guardians get this Devoid situation under control," River continued. "I have to keep cleansing Jemma's soul, so we don't lose her."

Blaine.

No one else would bother to create a stronger breed of Devoid beyond the gates of Hell. What purpose did it serve? All they did was blindly follow simple commands, not clever enough for much else. Besides Blaine, she couldn't think of anyone who'd have a need for such mindless creatures to destroy so many souls. Unless...

No. Surely not. It wasn't possible.

Was it?

Her skin tingled, a thin layer of sweat slipping down her spine to pool at the dip in her back. Her heart thumped, but this time to a different rhythm. A frantic one. An invisible force wrapped around her chest. Smoke curled its way into her mouth, swirling down her throat, filling her lungs with a thick, inky darkness, stealing her breath. Hands grasped her throat, squeezing and squeezing. Tighter and tighter.

It's not real...it's not real...

It made no difference what she told herself, what she repeated in her mind. She'd lost the battle. The nightmares had once again captured her in their claws. Flames surrounded her, billowing heat from all directions, leaping closer with every second. Ropes tightened around her lungs as blackness dotted the corners of her vision.

"Ebony?"

River's voice was a muffled sound in the far corners of her mind as the panic took hold. The warehouse toppled. One second, she stood behind the DJ booth making fun of him for being too trusting, next the ground rushed toward her.

Strong arms softened her fall right before she hit the floor. "Ebony, what's happening? Tell me how to help."

Those same arms wrapped around her torso from behind, lifting her into his lap. But it didn't stop. Her lungs screamed for air. She clawed at his arms, one around her upper chest, the other over her waist, both immovable forces she lacked the strength to overpower.

The dreamscape wobbled. Lights on the opposite side of the warehouse popped one after the other, spraying glass over the floor. The arms tightened.

"Breathe, Violet. Breathe."

River's voice. His warm breath at her ear. Soothing. Comforting.

Safe.

"In...and out."

Her fingers relaxed a notch, enough to withdraw her

nails from his arm, while the bands constricting her lungs loosened each time he spoke. Each time his voice entered her mind, coupled with the steady in and out of his chest behind her, the shadows choking her lungs retreated.

Closing her eyes, she focused only on him. The warm hint of summer days drifting through her nose, of salty breezes and sweet candy at the fair. Of sunshine and happiness bundled together in a late afternoon swim by the lake. He reminded her of it all. All her happiest memories rolled into one cleansing sun shower.

"That's it," his voice a low murmur by her ear. "You're doing so well, Violet. Keep going...in and out."

The prickles on her skin faded with each word, each puff of breath at her neck. The hold around her waist gradually eased but never vanished. Slowly, the dreamscape steadied, her mind slowly rebuilt the scene until the warehouse looked exactly as it had when River arrived. Music played in the background while the lights reformed new glass.

Next, her mind focused on the heat at her back, or more accurately, the body encasing hers. How his arms not only comforted her but protected her. Suddenly, new tingles sprouted, only this time, much, much lower. River's steady breath hitched, sharpening and quickening in time with hers.

Oh, Hell. Was this really happening?

His breath exhaled at the sensitive junction of her neck and shoulder, and she bit her lip to hold back a moan. A low rumble trembled from his lips as he hovered millimeters from her skin. Heat exploded through her blood, a foreign urge calling to her, begging her to lean back against him, to angle her head so he could finally kiss her. So he could taste her. The power so consuming it chased away the final icy tentacles of her panic, morphing into a delicious ache.

All she had to do was lean back. Give him the permission he silently asked for.

"Ebony..."

The rasp of her name on his lips snapped the elastic pulled too tight, flinging them from the dreamscape so quickly she stumbled forward. River's arms tightened around her middle once more, catching her.

"I've got you. You're safe."

She opened her mouth to yell at him, to demand he let her go, but nothing came out.

I've got you. You're safe.

No one had ever said those words to her. *I've got you.* No one had ever guaranteed her safety, not without a hidden agenda or a plan to exploit her in some way.

And now...an angel made that vow to her?

But they were no longer in a dream, a fantasy world where she could create whatever her mind desired. She was back in the cell, held prisoner by the Guardians.

This time when she pushed away, River dropped his arms and let her go. On her hands and knees, she scrambled to the edge of the teal barrier where there was enough distance between them for her to breathe. Only...here, in the shadowy corner, the sudden loss of his comfort and the coldness seeping into her blood made her chest tighten once more.

"Are you okay?"

She couldn't look at him, not yet. What the hell just happened?

Had River entered her dream, but also protected her in the real world? How? When her mind had flung them from the dreamscape, he'd still held her, arms wrapped tightly around her. But even more shocking, how had he blended their dreamscape with reality?

Also, when was the last time someone worried about her? *Really* worried. Not like how Hailee worried about the mistakes Ebony had made or the people she'd embarrassed. Or how her mother worried that the darkness had already taken her, long before she even knew about the immortal world. Or how her father...Hell, he'd only worried that her powers weren't strong enough.

Having someone care for her felt so...foreign. And he was an angel for fuck's sake. But this angel, he worried about...her. And it was suddenly too much.

On his knees, he crawled closer, until he was a breath away, tentatively lifting one hand to her cheek, moving in slow, even, strokes. The pressure around her lungs eased at his touch but that torniquet around her heart pulled tighter.

"Tell me what happened," he said, his voice as tender as his fingertips. Such a contrast to the hard, muscular body which had protected her like an impenetrable shield only moments ago.

It was too confusing. His words, the sincerity in his voice, the tenderness in his touch. She needed air. Space to figure out what had happened and how to prevent it from ever happening again.

"I..." she cleared her throat. "I think you should go."

That quirky smirk lifted at the corner of his mouth again. "You pulled me into *your* dream remember? Why do you want me to leave?"

I need to think.

"Thinking is overrated," he replied in her mind, startling the hell out of her.

She recoiled. "Get out of my head."

His fingers slipped to her chin, lifting it so she looked

him in the eyes. Those emerald-green pools bored deep into her soul, latching onto a dormant spark. One look and he woke it, igniting an out-of-control fire.

With a playful tap on her nose, he stood. "If you didn't want me in your head, Violet, you'd have blocked me already."

CHAPTER 15

Guided by his growling stomach, River followed the smell of food through the repaired living room, along the narrow hall, and into the dining room where the others hovered around the oversized table, setting cutlery and glasses for dinner and chatting about their day. Probably trying to guess what concoction EJ had come up with given it was Wednesday. The night each week where Hailee taught EJ how to cook. So far, it had been hit and miss, and dinner went one of two ways. River would either leave with his belly full and content, or he'd flee to the nearest fast-food outlet in Summit Creek before swallowing the first mouthful.

Odds were always on the latter.

Besides food, his latest dream with Ebony had also muddled his thoughts. How, after cleansing Jemma, he'd taken ill again and after throwing his guts up, had wandered to Ebony's cell before falling asleep by her cot. Also, how she'd slipped him into a dream again, like they'd practiced it for years. That last dream though was unlike any other because finally, she'd spoken to him. The way her voice had carried through the dream-warehouse like a delicate tune to his ears, was better than any chimes in the Heavens on arrival day.

And just when he thought his existence couldn't get any brighter, she assigned him a nickname. A real nickname! He didn't know what it meant but hearing her calling him "Maui" made him all giddy. He'd asked Cole this morning if he knew the meaning of the mortal word, but the Azrael had come up with zip. At this point, if Fate had sent Ebony to distract him, he was well and truly screwed. Because completing his own mission was a dream come true, for sure, but hearing his soulmate tease him after so openly proving she wanted him nearby? That was a feeling he could become addicted to.

How could he ever choose between the two paths?

Sweeping into the dining room on a blissful cloud, he spotted Aric and Raven by the wet bar at the far end of the room, speaking in hushed tones. The boss's brows drew tight as he slowly sipped his drink. The two of them had been investigating the mutant Devoid situation for almost two weeks and from their limited updates, had found no solid leads. Probably because no more Devoid had attacked since they'd busted through the windows in the living room and Gabe hadn't provided any more information. In fact, the Archangel had been non-existent. But that didn't mean Devoid weren't out there lurking around, waiting for an opportunity. And it certainly didn't mean everyone was safe.

"What's with the pathetic grin?" Raine grouched in his mind.

He couldn't help it. This past month had been his

favorite time in the mortal realm, even with the random attack and mishap involving melted candy. *"What does Maui mean?"* he asked his grumpy sister.

She rolled her eyes at him, but before she answered, the door leading to the kitchen swung open.

"You better eat every bit, assholes," EJ announced, strutting into the dining room carrying a tray of what looked like turkey legs. "I slaved in that frickin' kitchen all afternoon for these bad boys. My back hurts more than when Raine throws a dagger at me."

"Doubt it," Raine countered with a cock of her brow.

EJ laughed it off, but the Guardian no doubt kept one eye on Raine as he slid the tray into the center of the table.

Following the others, he took a seat, choosing to squeeze in beside Evie who was deep in conversation with Cole. He couldn't help but overhear something about cupcakes were dessert not the main dish, followed by a grumble from the Azrael. Hailee wouldn't leave Cole hanging long, she always had a few treats ready for him after dinner.

"How's the super Devoid hunting going?" River asked, once settled at the table.

Sitting beside Tayla, Raven relaxed in his chair, opting for a liquid dinner for now, most likely until everyone had taste-tested the food. EJ cooked it, after all. "No reports of them anywhere. Willow misted us around half the realm this week. It's like they appeared, attacked here, and then vanished. Aric thinks they might have been testing our defenses. Almost like a trial run. Testing the protection spell's limits." Raven took a long draw of his drink. "Which fucking failed."

Aric grunted in agreement, piling food onto Willow's plate like her stomach was an endless pit. "We questioned a Raziel gatekeeper who said there'd been unexplainable mortal deaths over the past fortnight that whispered of poisoned souls. But the authorities blamed it on drug related crimes and that their clean-up hadn't been required."

Figured. The Guardians had no clue mutant Devoid existed; how would the mortal authorities?

"That's what the police thought happened when they took Ebony from that rave party," Hailee added, perched on EJ's lap.

Forgoing the steamed greens, River grabbed tongs and opted for turkey legs instead. He wasn't kidding when he said he didn't like vegetables. "But it was Fallen, right? Not Devoid." He looked at Slater, who despite now being a good boy, had been part of the crew who'd hunted down Ebony. Thinking of how terrified she must've been when Slater and that drop-kick father of hers had appeared in the warehouse and stole her to the dark side, made little rage bubbles boil in his stomach.

Wait. The warehouse. Was that the same warehouse Ebony crafted in her dreams? Did she take him there each time? Was it more a nightmare for her?

Slater draped an arm over the back of Raine's chair. She batted it away, but he lifted it right back up there. Those two were so damn cute. "It was Asher who found Ebony, not me. I went to the second location to save time. No Devoid at either as far as I know. I doubt the situation with those mortals this week was even remotely similar to the shit Asher pulled."

Huh. Well, that didn't help them. "Maybe the attack here was a one-off?"

Raven slowly shook his head. "Something is brewing, I can sense it. Devoid in the mortal realm, the poisoned souls Gabe spoke of, the shit Blaine pulled possessing Jemma. If he is involved in creating these new Devoid, we won't know why until he's picked the shittiest time to announce it. We have to get on the front foot for once."

River held the juicy turkey leg up to his mouth and took a decent bite—

Fire scorched his tongue, ripping the breath right out of him. He coughed, shooting a chunk of turkey across the table in Aric's direction. Tears flooded his eyes. Tiny hairs lining his nostrils caught fire as he tried to suck in a breath, only for the fire to blaze hotter and more intense. Flames tore apart his mouth, propelling down his throat.

Suddenly, the fire engulfed his belly. A whirling, scorching tornado of flames.

He was going to die. Death by turkey leg.

Frantic for help, he leaped out of his chair, bellyflopping on the table as he reached for the water jug. Someone shouted. Plates clanged; chairs scraped. He didn't care. All that mattered was getting that sweet savior down his throat to release the fire demon setting his esophagus alight. Snatching the jug, he flipped onto his back and poured. Water sloshed his face, gushing down his throat, making him gurgle and gag, but it wasn't enough. He needed more.

He stretched a hand to the nearest glass—Raven's drink —but the Guardian snatched it away.

"Dy...ing," he rasped, clutching his throat.

Someone shoved a glass in his hand. He didn't even care what it was, downing the liquid in one gulp.

Gradually, the flames subsided, easing to a smolder. The fire demon in his throat slowly retreated with each subsequent gasp of air. His vision cleared.

Holy firecracker.

"What the fuck is wrong with you?"

Blinking, he took in the chaos. There he laid, spread out

on the dining room table like an angelic offering, covered in scraps of food, with water dripping down the side of his face. An empty glass of something milky in his hand.

"The turkey...is...possessed." His voice sounded horse. Had the turkey leg damaged his voice box? Would he ever talk properly again?

What if he never spoke to Ebony again? Just when she'd started talking to him, he lost his voice.

EJ glared down at him. "No, it's frickin' not. I spent hours cooking that and put exactly a cup of chili in the marinade. Just like the recipe called for."

Beside EJ, Hailee gasped and covered her mouth. "A cup?"

"Yes. You said a cup, sweetness."

"No." A giggle burst free from Hailee's lips. "I said a *touch*. As in, a tiny bit."

Someone snorted. Probably Aric. Someone else complained about the lack of cupcakes. They all knew who that was.

River sat up, picking broccoli and purple onion off his shirt. "Well, those legs should come with a warning label. That heat level isn't even suitable for Hell."

The room exploded with laughter.

He was simply thankful he'd live another day.

Hailee stretched on her tiptoes to kiss EJ's cheek. "It's okay, we can try again next week."

Raven, already standing, downed the rest of his bourbon in one go before slamming the glass on the table. "Right. Who wants fucking pizza?"

Chapter 16

"**Y**ou better have candy for me, Maui," Ebony called out as he entered the basement.

Heat flashed through his blood, hard and fast, making him a little crazed. Just as well she couldn't see inside him, it no doubt looked like a spinning carnival ride with cotton candy streaming out the sides.

"That depends," he replied as calm as he could, sliding down the wall to plant his ass on the concrete floor beside her cot.

His favorite place.

Ever since the Devoid attack, he hadn't bothered rationing his visits with Ebony. In fact, he'd probably visited her more in the past few weeks than he had since she'd arrived. Not necessarily to protect her, no other Devoid had decided to bust through the windows, but because the attack had reminded him that they were in the middle of a war. Good versus evil and all that. The fact that at any moment, something as trivial as mutant Devoid could steal away everything important to him.

What then? He'd return to his mundane existence where he had neither a mission nor a soulmate. That sounded as dreary as watching Raine sharpen her daggers.

Looking over at Ebony, the challenging arch of her brow made him smile. She seemed better today, healthier. Sounded better, too. As though her immortality had finally kicked into gear and remembered how to heal her. Someone had removed all but one of the bandages covering her limbs. Rigid, pale pink scars were all that remained. They too would heal over time. He'd make sure of it. He wouldn't let her suffer for eternity because of Blaine.

Unlike the Guardians, he didn't have a vested interest in saving that Fallen. Only the one beside him.

Stretching out his legs, he crossed his boots at the ankles and gave her a smile. He could sit here all day and talk to Ebony, discover every tiny detail about her, everything she loved, her favorite candy, if she had hopes beyond this war.

Now that she'd spoken to him, he could listen to her for the rest of his eternity.

"Depends on what?" she replied, swinging her legs around to the side of the cot and wiggling her bare toes.

When he eyed her glossy jet-black polished toenails, desire ignited deep in his belly, sweeping through his blood in a rush. What he'd give to touch them. Not in a creepy foot-fetish way like when he'd accidently stumbled onto the wrong side of the internet. He wanted to pull her delicate feet into his lap and knead her tired arches until her eyes rolled back in her head, and she exhaled a breathy moan.

Far less creepy. Right?

Unless she wasn't into having her feet pampered. Every female was different. Take his sister for instance, if someone touched Raine's feet, she'd slice them open with the heel of her shoe.

Clearing his throat, he redirected his thoughts to the candy in his lap, where he withdrew his favorite flavor from the packet and dangled it in the air.

Lighter flecks of crimson in Ebony's eyes flamed to life, but her indifferent mask gave him no other hints about her mood. The thought of something happening in her past to strip that carefree attitude from her made his fist clench around the candy. And if it turned out to be *someone*, well, he could be lethal when the situation called for it.

"This is my favorite candy. The one from Tasmania. Willow misted there yesterday, so I thought I'd share some with you...when you tell me what Maui means," he said, his voice a little roughened with his own contained emotion. This was a monumental occasion. "I will admit to having asked around, but no one seems to know the mortal word. Is it a different language?"

The nickname had consumed his thoughts. How the name rolled off her tongue with playfulness, a fun teasing gesture, yet when she said it, he also sensed a hint of sadness as though it meant something to her. Which made him want to be worthy of the nickname even more.

Ebony held his gaze for a long moment until he thought she wouldn't answer, but then she surprised him with a laugh. Not a small chuckle, a full, belly laugh that echoed through the basement, coating his skin in a warm tingle.

He sat there watching her, enchanted by her smile. But clearly, he hadn't gotten the joke, because when he didn't join in, Ebony stopped and frowned at him.

"You really don't know?"

He shook his head, dangling the candy closer. "Tell me."

That same mask she'd worn earlier reappeared, clouding her smile, stealing the laughter as she shrugged one shoulder. "Maui is a mythical creature. A playful trickster."

"I've been called plenty of creative words in my existence and that one definitely fits." He paused, searching her eyes. "But something tells me there's another meaning. One more...personal."

Ebony quietly studied him, her pretty eyes staring into his while their invisible soulmate connection danced between them in the dimly lit corner of the basement. He'd lock this moment into his memory, storing it there with her smile and the sound of her laugh. If he didn't figure out a way to achieve his mission *and* keep his soulmate, at least he'd have those.

Did she feel the connection, the mystical tether drawing them together, the call of one soul to the other? Or because she was a Fallen, did she feel nothing? Slater had once confessed to him he'd felt the connection to Raine before they'd sealed the soulmate bond, but he hadn't realized what it was. Perhaps Ebony was the same?

Not for the first time, he yearned to be more than someone's favorite movie buddy, more than their favorite sparring partner, or favorite shopping friend. A favorite in all the trivial things that didn't matter. No one considered him their favorite immortal, *their* immortal, and no one ever considered him their favorite choice for Guardian missions. He wasn't bitter about it, more resigned to the fact that his role would always be the brother, the friend, the sidekick. The back-up.

Never the hero.

Never the *one*.

When silence stretched between them, Ebony shifted, adjusting the drawstring of her navy sweatpants.

"Maui is an island in Hawaii," Ebony whispered, gaze still on the drawstring.

Hawaii? Was she being cryptic on purpose? Was that word meant to mean something to him? He mentally ran the word through his vocabulary, coming up empty. "What is Hawaii?"

Tucking one leg beneath the other, Ebony swiveled to face him, hugging her pillow in front of her chest. "Oh, come on. Don't tell me you've never heard of Hawaii." She motioned to his new shirt. The one covered in purple hibiscus flowers that he'd purchased yesterday because violet was suddenly his favorite color. "Look at you. Your shirts. Hawaii. You know, islands in the North Pacific Ocean with volcanoes and stunning beaches? Tropical paradise."

He had absolutely no idea what she was talking about but made a mental note to discover everything about Hawaii, because the vulnerability in her eyes told him it was important to her. He'd even enlist EJ and his computer skills to help. And Willow. Maybe she could mist him and Ebony to this tropical paradise?

Ebony snorted a laugh, clearly at his expense but it didn't sting like when others did it. At least she laughed again. This realm would be a dark place without that sound.

"Did you hit your head, angel, on the way down from the Heavens?"

He gasped in mock horror, hand to his chest. "I'll have you know, Violet, I have excellent coordination while flying. In fact, I excel at all physical activities."

Pink bloomed over her cheeks, but she didn't shy away. Instead, she silently watched him again for a long moment, both of them caught in the centripetal force rotating around their souls, drawing them closer before she broke the spell with a soft sigh.

He tossed her the candy.

She fiddled with the wrapper in her hand but didn't unravel it. The glassy wash in her crimson eyes sucker-punched him in the gut.

"I didn't mean to upset—"

"Maui is one of Hawaii's many islands. It's my...favorite. Even though I've never been there."

Countless things to unpack in those three sentences.

Unconsciously, he slid closer until he could lean his forearm on the mattress. "How do you know that island is your favorite if you've never been?"

A soft, dreamy smile brightened her cheeks. "I just know. Like, when you meet someone and instantly know you're going to be friends, or when you smell food and know it's going to be delicious. Like that I guess." She fiddled with the wrapper again, opening and closing it. "I saw an advertisement one year in a mall travel agency window and fell in love with the glassy water and picturesque sunset." She rolled her eyes to herself. "There are probably a million places that have a sunset like that, but it doesn't matter. I want to experience it on Maui. Well...I wanted to."

Finished talking, she popped the candy in her mouth. The low moan that followed her first chew would've brought him to the ground if his ass wasn't already on it.

Distracting himself, he unwrapped his own candy and took his time devouring it. "Why not mist there? You know, before..." He motioned to the magical barrier surrounding them, which made him more uncomfortable by the day.

He held out the open bag of candy.

"I dunno," she said, grabbing a second one. "I guess it

felt like cheating. It was something I always looked forward to, a dream on the very distant horizon. One I never thought I'd realize and had made peace with that. And when all the shit went down with my mum, then Hailee, then Blaine and my dad, I...well, I guess you could say I chose a different path."

He carefully chewed the soft raspberry candy to stop himself from blurting out the first thing that came to his mind.

Let's go now.

Because that would be stupid. Reckless. And that was before he even considered the ramifications of breaking a Fallen out of the Guardian's holding cell to take her on a vacation to a tropical island.

Not any Fallen. His soulmate.

Would that excuse him from breaking the rules? Because he was almost ninety-nine percent certain she was his soulmate. Would the Guardians forgive him?

When she didn't provide any further details of this magical island, he broke the silence. "What you're telling me is, your nickname for me just so happens to also be your favorite place in this entire realm?"

She hurled the wrapper at him, and he laughed as it fluttered through the air before landing short of his lap. "Don't get a big head, angel." She reached forward, flexing her fingers. "Give me another raspberry one."

When he tossed her a purple wrapped candy, a million butterflies with tiny, delicate wings took flight in his belly. It seemed he and his soulmate had more in common than he first thought. It also seemed that, from this point on, he'd save all the purple wrapped candies for someone other than himself.

CHAPTER 17

EBONY

I t had been weeks, possibly even months, who really knew, since she'd stepped outside. Since she'd inhaled fresh air. Since Slater had done the unthinkable and carried her from the fiery inferno of Hell as it collapsed around them. Although she'd partly become accustomed to captivity, and the fact her sister refused to free her, didn't mean she'd accepted it. Nor that she'd forgotten about her plan to escape.

What she'd do for a bath right about now would make even the most evil Fallen cower in the corner. Not the small shower stall connected to her cell. A real bath. Neck high with floating bubbles, candles scenting the air, and all the girly bath salts and sponges she'd never had the opportunity to indulge in. Her childhood hadn't exactly consisted of fancy houses with hot tubs and clawfoot baths. She and Hailee were lucky if they stayed in one place for longer than a year before their mother took a turn, and the cheapest rent was always the most decrepit houses in some of the worst neighborhoods. Though, now she knew those turns were when her mother sensed Fallen hunting them.

Guess they won in the end.

Despite her doom and gloom mood today, strength rose inside her, healing her wounds, renewing her fight to live, her determination to finish what she started. After she escaped. Any day now, her sister would realize she wasn't worth the trouble and let her go. Until then, she indulged in small things, like dreams with the angel. Moments she began to look forward to. Moments when he behaved as though it was no big deal to befriend a Fallen prisoner. Because that was what had happened. He'd befriended her. She sure as hell hadn't befriended him. In fact, she'd ignored him in the beginning, pushed him away, but he'd kept chipping away at her walls until he sneaked through the smallest of openings with a burst of optimism. And somehow along the way, she'd begun to enjoy his company, the playful banter when he snuck her treats, and how, even if she didn't say a word, he listened. He sat on the floor beside her cot and listened. Not to only her words, but to her. Even if she didn't fully understand how, or even why.

Never before had someone heard her quite like River.

Not even Hailee.

Each time her sister visited, their limited interactions left her feeling hollow. Reminding her of how far she'd Fallen. That no matter her reason for doing so, no matter her intentions, she'd always remain on the wrong side.

A Fallen.

At the end of the day, when the dust settled and only the two of them remained, that choice would forever stand between them.

As though she'd projected her thoughts, the external

door swung open and Hailee walked in carrying her daily tray of food, with EJ trailing close behind.

Hailee shuddered as she passed through the barrier into her cell, while the Guardian hovered by the closed door, one dagger strapped to his thigh, another to his chest. She couldn't blame the angel for taking precautions, for wanting to protect Hailee. They shared that same instinct even if EJ didn't know it. Sure, she'd given the Guardians every reason in the past not to trust her. To label her the enemy. If only they knew Hailee never needed protection against her. Ebony would never intentionally hurt her own flesh and blood. Quite the opposite. There were worse monsters lining up for a piece of angelic soul or a Guardian to add to their collection, and Hailee was the perfect combination of both.

Protecting Hailee was a goal Ebony had always achieved.

Which was why she needed to escape before the true threat came knocking.

"How are you feeling?" Hailee asked as she slid the tray onto a small table near the foot of the cot.

Same question every day.

If Ebony wanted to escape, to free them both of this never-ending cycle, then the spark needed to come from her. She had to make Hailee want her to leave. Because a long time ago, she vowed to be the one who looked out for her sister because Hailee was always busy looking out for everyone else. To do that, Ebony needed to prevent further problems landing at Hailee's feet.

Allow her sister to live the eternity she deserved.

"Like a caged animal," she snapped harsher than she intended.

Though, maybe that was for the best. Hailee would get

the hint, and Ebony could leave without her sister hating her more than she already did.

Regret. Ebony had a lifetime of it.

Hailee winced. "It's for your own good, Eb. I know you don't think so now, but this is best for everyone."

"You're kidding, right?" She rolled her eyes. "You mean for *your* own good. Lock up the evil twin to protect all the precious angels until she either tears out her own soul from boredom or better yet, the bigger, badder Fallen hunts her down because, surprise, surprise, she knows too much."

Hailee stared at her as though Ebony had just sprouted horns and skipped off into the fiery sunset with Zath. Good. Maybe that would force her sister's hand. Because the longer Ebony stayed in this cell, the more opportunity Blaine had to track her down. And if that happened... nothing would protect them.

On her feet, she paced the small confines, clenching her fists rather than flipping the tray of food upside down. Which is what she wanted to do but afraid the move would only result in Hailee cleaning up yet another mess that wasn't her own. Her sister though, watched her pace with a keen eye, hands clasped in front of her and not a single strand of golden hair out of place. Angelic. Hailee had landed on her feet, on the right side of this shitty war and Ebony would do anything to make sure it stayed that way.

Together, their magic was unparalleled. Unstoppable. Apart, Hailee was only as valuable as the next angel. And she'd do whatever it took to keep it that way.

When Hailee didn't respond, she stopped right in front of her sister, speaking barely above a whisper. "Let me out."

Hailee's lips rolled inward as she slowly shook her head. "I can't do that. Not after where you've...been."

"Where I've been?" Anger barreled through her, overtaking logic. "You mean Hell? Is all this because I'm a Fallen? Newsflash, sis, I've been a Fallen for as long as you've been an angel. Nothing's going to change that now."

Hailee's gaze darted to EJ, still standing by the entrance, as though they communicated in their minds. Just like her and River. Did every angel have the power to mind speak or only a select few? She'd only ever had Blaine in her head and thought that was because of his abilities not any connection they might share.

When Hailee sighed and retreated a step, about to cross the teal barrier, she panicked, grabbing hold of her sister's sleeve. "Please. Slater brought me back from Hell, literally. I'm healed now, good as new. Thank you. You've done your job cleaning up my mess as per usual and I bet you'd like nothing more than to get me out of your hair."

"That's not true." Hailee's expression softened. "It's safer for you here."

"For real? You can't be serious. Listen to yourself." She released Hailee's jacket with a shove. "What are your plans? Keep me locked in this cell for all eternity? Until your Guardian boyfriend gets sick of ferrying meals with you and decides to drive a dagger through my heart?"

Hailee threw her hands in the air. "What will you do if you leave? Run back to Blaine?"

"Blaine?" Her voice rose despite every intention not to start a yelling match. "Regardless of what you think, I never stayed with Blaine because I wanted to. Not that you have ever asked for my side of the story."

EJ pushed off the wall about to barge through the barrier until she growled at him, halting his feet. "Oh, calm the fuck down, Guardian. Can't two sisters have an argument without everyone freaking the fuck out?"

"Not when one of those sisters is a Fallen and a threat to my soulmate."

"A threat?" She scoffed. Wasn't the first time she'd heard that. If only they knew the real story.

Hailee gave the Guardian a look that seemed to remind him that she could fight her own battles. EJ hovered closer though, just outside the barrier, but he didn't look happy about it. In fact, with a dagger now in his hand, his feet shoulder width apart, he looked every bit the lethal warrior she'd heard stories about.

Hailee leveled Ebony with an icy glare. "You didn't stay with Blaine because you *wanted* to? Really? Could've fooled me, Eb. You had plenty of chances to tell me the truth, to tell me where you were, to let me help you and you never took them."

Her sister marched closer until the backs of Ebony's knees knocked into her cot. Good. This fight had been brewing for years, long before either of them knew of the immortal world and the part they would play in it. This fight represented every double shift Hailee had worked. Every time she'd bailed Ebony out or came to the school when Ebony had gotten in trouble and their mother wasn't lucid enough to leave the house. This fight represented their transition from childhood to adulthood and every broken year in between.

"You tricked me." Hailee shoved her finger at Ebony's chest. "You lied to me, told me that you were sorry for what happened with mom. You begged me to save you from Blaine. And it was all a lie."

"It wasn't," she whispered. Even though the conversation propelled in the direction she wanted, she still couldn't stomach Hailee thinking that none of it had been true.

"I call bullshit. You chose our sadistic father and a

crazed Fallen over me. Your family." Hailee's voice cracked on the last word, and it tore a new gash in her heart.

But she slapped a Band-Aid over it. The sooner Hailee realized she was better off letting Ebony go, the quicker she could flee this place.

"Don't you dare cry, Hailee. Don't you fucking dare. This isn't your fault, this isn't your mess to fix or clean up. Let me out of here so I can deal with it myself."

"You're my sister," Hailee shouted, tears tumbling down her cheeks. "Stop asking me to let you go! You're the only family I have left."

Ebony softened her voice and reached out to take Hailee's hand. "Which is why you need to do this. It's the right thing. You know that. You said so yourself, you're done cleaning up my messes. So stop fucking doing it."

A long moment passed where Ebony expected love, compassion, even trust to wash through Hailee's watery eyes. Instead, hopelessness and bitterness flared in their wake. Would they ever mend the splintered bridge between them or would her choice to protect Hailee, to ensure she lived her best life, always come back to haunt her?

The second Hailee's eyes turned a cold shade of blue, her sister backed through the barrier.

Ebony's heart sank.

"No, Eb. Despite everything you've done, I can't hate you. I can't toss you aside and let you make your own mistakes, even if it's killing me. If this cell stops you from turning out like our father, I'll keep you locked in here forever. I'm doing this for you, and one day, I hope you see that."

Without another word, Hailee bolted out the door along with her only ticket to freedom.

CHAPTER 18

RIVER

Breath wheezing, River forged ahead, racing through the obstacle course at the far rear of the Guardian property, pushing his body harder than ever. Dodging strategically placed branches, dropping to the loose dirt to roll under fallen limbs. At one point, the course extended beyond a shallow stream, where he leaped over the flowing water, unfurling his wings at the final moment to propel his body forward at breakneck speed. Harder and harder. If only it would clear the nausea. Or even better, the constant chant in his head.

Free her.

Free her.

Free her.

Shining between the towering trees, the midday sun sizzled on his bare back, its power tingling through his limbs, renewing his energy as quickly as whatever was happening with his stomach depleted it. He could do this over and over, hour after hour, if it kept him from busting through the basement door to free Ebony.

He'd never wanted to break rules so much in his entire existence.

Was this what it felt like to have a soulmate? To form a bond with another living being? A connection so strong, even now, he sensed her. He couldn't explain it, but ever since Slater brought Ebony to the Guardian house, an essence, a life force unlike his own hovered near his soul. Never quite connecting, always drifting in the background just out of reach.

And it drove him insane.

Could their unsealed bond make him sick?

Sweat pooled at the junction where his running shorts kissed the small of his back, while the bow thumped his shoulders with each heavy footfall. He'd ventured into the forest over an hour ago for target practice yet never found the desire to nock an arrow. Instead, his legs and mind snapped into gear and propelled him along Raine's deadly course.

Racing around a sharp bend, the sound of voices made him skid to a halt. Up ahead, partly hidden by leafy shadows, EJ, Aric, and Cole gathered beside a towering pine... stuffing their faces.

The sweet scent of freshly baked goods laced the cool, mountain air, drawing him closer, and despite nausea still swishing in his stomach, hunger growled at him. There in the center, atop a blackened fallen branch, sat a container overflowing with baked treats.

"Is this some kind of weird Guardian ritual I didn't know about?" he asked, weaving around a trunk.

Aric snorted.

"You can join, Sunshine." EJ hitched his chin in greeting. "But if you breathe a word of this, I'll cut up all your flower shirts."

Good enough for him.

He snagged a cupcake with swirly pink frosting, chose a vacant spot nestled beside a sturdy tree, and dumped his bow and quiver on the dirt beside him.

"Hailee's stress baking," EJ said between mouthfuls. "And given the bakery is closed today, the food is piling up which is upsetting her even more, so we're...helping her out."

"By hiding in the woods eating her food?"

"Don't pick apart our logic." Aric curled his lip at him. "It is what it is. Take it or leave it."

He wasn't stupid enough to think Hailee's stress baking came from anything other than her sister's situation. Heavens, it had caused him enough stress for the two of them. Over the past few weeks, he'd spent countless hours trying to figure out a solution, one where everyone won. One where he didn't disobey direct orders. One where the Guardians no longer held Ebony captive in the basement. Where Hailee gained her sister back. Where he achieved his mission to heal Jemma *and* lived a long eternity with a soulmate. But the problem with all those scenarios was they began with him breaking the rules he'd vowed to uphold. Which in turn, broke his loyalty to the Guardians.

Did Fate have her hand in this proverbial cupcake?

"You good, Sunshine?" EJ asked, eyeing him a little too closely.

He swallowed his mouthful. "Why wouldn't I be?"

Evasive, but he couldn't exactly tell the truth right now, not until he figured everything out. Why did using his powers make him sick? Why couldn't he sleep as soundly as he had months ago? Why couldn't he rein in the urge to purchase all the raspberry candy across the realm and leave it by Ebony's cot?

Why couldn't he be like Raine and laugh in the face of rules and responsibility?

And then there was Jemma.

He'd run into the mortal at breakfast, where she'd looked the healthiest she had since Blaine's magic had departed her mind but by lunchtime, she was back to being a shell of her former self. Gray-ish skin tone, dull, sunken eyes. Freaking him the Heavens out.

Why weren't his powers working? Why was she still sick? How was the darkness rejuvenating faster than he could cleanse?

"You look a little pasty, man," Aric said, leaning forward on his elbows to study him closer. "You sure you're good?"

He nodded, shoving the remainder of the cupcake in his mouth.

"It's the lack of candy," Cole chimed in, sitting directly across from him on a small boulder.

"First, I don't eat candy that often. And second, sometimes I enjoy taking a sugar break. Well...from candy, not cakes, obviously. It makes me appreciate it more."

The Guardians gasped at him like he'd lost his mind until Aric laughed. "Bullshit."

"It's true." He reached forward and grabbed a cookie this time, one dotted with chocolate buttons.

"You look weird. Like...sick," EJ said, still frowning at him.

Cole pointed to the space beside River. "It's contagious. Even that fern is all sad and droopy from being near you while you're on a so-called candy break."

While EJ threw his head back and howled with laughter, River inspected the plant in question, brushing up against his thigh. Compared to the others surrounding it, this fern had indeed lost its luster. The outer edges of the leaves were brown and crinkled, the new undergrowth drooping toward the dirt rather than curling up to the patchy sun. But that had nothing to do with his mood... right? A plant couldn't sense these things. Could they?

He made a mental note to ask Willow.

With the three Guardians distracted, talking to one another and grabbing more cupcakes and cookies from the container, River studied the fern some more. His heart kicked up when little by little, the brown stained edges began seeping inward, slowly darkening the entire leaf right before his eyes. When it reached halfway, he dared a touch and trailed his finger beneath the stem.

He gasped, jerking back.

The leaf died. Right before his eyes. It shriveled up, snapped off from the main stem and fluttered to the forest floor to join countless others.

His gaze shot back to the Guardians, to see if they'd noticed, but they'd already moved on to other topics, rather than figuring out what was wrong with him. Clearly, more than he first thought.

Had this ever happened to an immortal before? Where their wonky powers affected the environment around them?

EJ caught his gaze. "Haven't seen you visiting your Fallen friend lately?"

River choked on a crumb.

EJ hadn't seen him because after last time, River had chosen to visit immediately after Hailee, so he avoided another run in with them. "And?"

Aric and Cole frowned, their gazes darting between him and EJ.

When EJ cocked a brow, no doubt wanting him to spill all his secrets, River changed the subject. "Speaking of visits, shouldn't you be inside helping your soulmate de-stress, rather than hiding in the forest?"

EJ knew too much. Sooner or later, the Guardian would blab, but he wished it wasn't in front of the others and not before he'd figured out a solution. How could he confirm or deny matters if he didn't fully understand them?

EJ whistled out a long breath. "I know better than to mess with Hailee while she's stress baking."

"And for that, I'm eternally grateful," Cole added with a tip of his cupcake.

Thankfully, his tactic worked, and their conversation ventured to safer topics, including Aric giving an update on the Devoid situation he and Raven had been investigating. Until it veered right back to Ebony and all his uneasiness returned.

"She begged Hailee to let her go." EJ sighed and leaned back, stretching his legs to cross them at the ankles.

Of course, Ebony wanted to leave. Yet, at the same time, the past few days she'd seemed happier. With him, anyway. Almost as though she'd accepted her situation and made the best of it. Maybe because he didn't treat her like a feral animal locked up for everyone else's safety. He treated her like a treasure.

He treated her like a soulmate.

At first, he understood the reason for holding her in the basement. Her injuries were significant, and her body wasn't healing as it should have, and they had no idea what would happen when she woke. But the more days that passed, the more he felt the crippling ache to free her. Not that he wanted her to leave, he wanted, no *needed*, her to be at peace. She deserved not only to live, but to thrive.

And maybe, above everything else, that was something he could grant her?

"Why keep her locked up?" he asked. "It's not...right."

All gazes snapped to him as though the others had only just realized he'd joined their forest binge eating session.

"Uh, because she's a Fallen inside a house of Guardians and their soulmates?" Aric said.

"Sure, but is she really a threat to anyone if she's Hailee's sister? Her twin even," he added, hoping to plant seeds of doubt without being too obvious.

"Frickin' Hell, Sunshine. You couldn't be more obvious if you had a neon sign on your forehead. You only want her out of the cell because you think she's your soulmate."

Welp. There went the hope of EJ holding onto his secret for a little longer.

Gasps followed. More than a few curses. A racing heart. Wait, that last one was his.

Well, he had two options here: he could deny it in a way that wasn't a lie. Choose his words carefully and continue on his merry way eating the cookie in his hand. Or he could...admit it. Confide in someone...or three some-ones. Sooner or later, the Guardians would connect the dots and honestly, it surprised him that only EJ had figured it out. Why he visited Ebony more regularly than Hailee.Why she had new bedding on her cot every few days. Why candy deliveries arrived at their door more often than usual.

"Is it true, man?" Aric again, the first one to break the silence.

Okay, moment of truth. Fall or fly?

He straightened his shoulders, mustering all the confidence he could so they took him seriously. In this anyway. "Maybe? I think so." He cleared his throat. "Yes?"

Well, that went as well as his sister befriending a pet fish.

What in the Heavens was wrong with him? Why did he suddenly have beads of sweat bobsledding down his spine? He didn't need to seal their bond to know she was his soulmate. The light sparking in his soul each time he thought of her was evidence enough. And how she was the first Fallen, the first immortal, who'd not only captured his attention, but also returned it for more than a fleeting moment.

If only in half smiles and playful taunts, she'd noticed him. Truly saw him.

"That certainly paints the picture in a new light." Aric's mouth twisted as he stared at him.

EJ pegged a cupcake wrapper into the container. "No, it doesn't. She kidnapped Hailee." His wide eyes swung to Cole. "Her and Blaine blackmailed Evie, and she nearly died for the final time."

Cole stayed silent for a long moment, his gaze lost in some sort of battle waging in the Azrael's mind. "I don't forget the role she played in forcing Evie to take on Zath, but...River's right. She's family. She's Hailee's twin. And potentially this angel's soulmate, which is the greatest bond we honor. Surely, at the end of the day, that counts for something?"

EJ threw a hand in the air. "Reaper, she tricked my soulmate into running to Hell to save her. I can't just forgive and forget."

"You don't need to," River interrupted. "I'm not asking you to forget all that's happened, all I'm asking is for us to show her some compassion. What if she, like us, did what she thought was right at the time?"

EJ leaped to his feet, tugging at his beanie. "This is insane."

Maybe. But he had to do something, because lately, he'd had urges that were shocking even for him.

"What do you suggest?" Aric asked.

A million ideas sparked in his head. Sure, he'd thought about having this conversation many times over the past few weeks, but he hadn't expected it to happen today in front of three Guardians. If he had, he would've prepared.

He joined EJ on his feet, addressing all of them. "Let Ebony out of the basement. Give her a room upstairs, there are plenty to choose from." When EJ swore, he held up his hand. "I'm not saying welcome her into your arms like long lost family, or that we leave her to her own devices, but she deserves to be treated better than a rabid animal locked in a cage."

"What if she crosses us and feeds information to Blaine?" EJ asked the question no doubt on everyone's lips.

If he were honest, the thought had crossed his mind once or twice. But he had to believe that he'd built enough trust with Ebony for her not to betray him. After all, last week she'd started calling him "Maui" because he reminded her of her favorite island. Her favorite! Surely, that meant something.

And, it was about time she had someone in her corner.

Looking EJ dead in the eye, he replied, "If she does, then you can hold me responsible for her actions."

"You're frickin' insane. She's going to eat you up and spit you out onto the coals of your smoking bones."

Maybe. Maybe not. At this point, it no longer mattered. He had to do what was right.

The instant he'd signed that deal with Fate and she whisked him to the mortal realm along with Raine, he'd vowed to live his existence here to the fullest, not knowing when she'd recall his soul. Which included embracing every challenge set before him.

"Take it to Raven," Aric said. "I'll back you."

Those words sparked the tiniest tingle in his soul, sending his heart fluttering. And for once, no one could blame it on sugar.

CHAPTER 19

EBONY

Fire encroached from all sides the split second she closed her eyes. Long crimson fingers reached for her from dark pits. Invisible claws held her tight while ice seeped into her veins, colliding with the heat flaming her cheeks. Before the smoke even split from the shadows, she knew Blaine had come for her.

She cursed herself for thinking he'd forgotten. That now he'd overthrown Zath he'd found new immortals to torture with his free time and no longer needed her unique talents. That he'd discovered another way to enact his revenge without using her and Hailee. But luck had never been on her side.

Her heart slowed to a sluggish thud as she mentally searched for an escape, knowing deep down there was none.

Her time was up.

Gradually, the flames died to a low burn, and the area beyond materialized. Patchy dirt, scattered, broken branches. A handful of large boulders forming a circle around a roaring campfire. The air heavy with brimstone and burning coals.

Standing, a few feet away, was the only Fallen who truly scared her.

Teaming up with Blaine hadn't been a necessity. It had been the only option to protect Hailee. A choice she'd make again and again even if it cost her everything.

"Ah, there you are," Blaine said with the familiarity of a long-lost friend.

Despite the panic clawing at her chest, she refused to show him any fear. She would face him in the same nonchalant manner she had during all their previous encounters, reminding herself they were in a dreamwalk. He wasn't actually here. And even though he could still hurt her, beyond this dreamscape, she was safe. As safe as one could be while imprisoned by the Guardians.

Blaine's dark, predatory gaze gave her a slow once over, lingering for a few seconds on her exposed arms and the pale pink scars that had almost faded from her flesh. "You're healed, I see."

She lifted her chin in reply.

Despite now being the king of Hell, he still wore the same black jeans and aged leather jacket, his unkept midnight black hair still falling in his eyes. The only noticeable difference in his attire was the twisted vine of charred bones and Hellfire adorning his head in a crown straight out of children's nightmares.

A slow and sinister smirk lifted at his mouth.

Stopping a few feet away, he snapped his fingers again and again, igniting a small flame before extinguishing it. Over and over. A power play. A reminder that he held her immortality in the palm of his hands and could snuff it out whenever he desired.

Just like the flame.

"Why are you here?" she asked, seeking the source of her magic.

Blaine surveyed the landscape still materializing around them. Blurred trees came into focus, leafless branch by branch until a thick, wintery forest extended for as far as she could see. Darkness blanketed the sky, no moon or stars, or any form of light beyond the flickering campfire to her right. Because this was his dream after all, not hers. And the power weaving through the air was more intricate, more potent than any she'd felt before.

Which terrified her.

"It's been a long moment between our chats, don't you think?"

Since Slater had extracted her from Hell, she'd lost track of time, the notches in the bathroom drywall the only indication of night and day. Thirty-eight days.

Thirty-eight days of helplessness, feeling like a target while she waited for Blaine to find her.

Escaping the Guardians was paramount, and this dreamwalk made that abundantly clear. Because Blaine's power would always be infinitely more powerful than hers. He'd find her anywhere. She had nothing left to lose. Whereas Hailee would lose everything.

"Not long enough, if you ask me," she replied, inspecting the remnants of her black chipped nails.

Blaine was silent for a few beats before he threw his head back and barked a laugh. "Oh, I've missed your snark, love."

Was this a game to him? A joke?

She pretended to wander the campground, putting the fire and as much distance between them as she could. Not that it would stop Blaine. He could destroy her with a flick of his wrist.

"Although," he said, gravitating toward the fire. "There is another reason for our exciting reunion."

Of course, there was. There always was. In the four years she'd known Blaine, he'd never acted without an agenda that served him and him alone.

Without slowing, the Fallen strolled through the campfire. Her breath hitched as the flames parted for him, curling up his legs, weaving around his unlaced boots as though assisting him across their path. Guiding him.

The flames...obeyed him.

That earlier thud in her chest morphed into a boulder sinking low in her belly.

Now standing before her again, he continued, "Word in Hell is that your father lives."

She recoiled but kept her mouth shut.

No way. Impossible.

The last time she'd seen her father was during the battle where he'd attacked the Guardians for the Empryen. Every immortal had wanted to lay their hands on that sword, and despite Slater's soulmate stealing it, it had somehow landed with Blaine. During that battle, Raine, River's sister, had killed her father, sending his soul to the Infernal Pits.

"When I ended Zath, I ended every realm he created. Which included the Infernal Pits. A move that benefited several immortals it seems, not only your father."

Holy fucking shit.

She'd assumed that when Zath's realm had collapsed around them after Blaine killed him, it had only affected that section of Hell. But it hadn't? How many souls banished to the Pits were now suddenly free? And how many of those were now gunning for Blaine? Or the Guardians?

Revenge was a powerful motivator.

Pressure pulsed behind her eyes as the gravity of the situation sunk in. If her father was free, she was also on his revenge list. He'd know, or at least suspect, that she was the one who'd fed Blaine information before the battle with the Guardians. He'd know she'd betrayed him. It wouldn't matter that she'd done it to keep Hailee safe.

Asher would end her.

Unless...she thought of another option. Was Asher the lesser of two evils? Was she safer aligning herself with her twisted father rather than placing her wings with Blaine? Would the lure of hunting down Blaine be enough to convince her father to keep her alive?

Was she cunning enough to pull it off?

Once again, she was treading water in treacherous seas between two jagged shores, neither particularly safe. But until this ended one way or another, until Hailee was safe, she'd continue to fight the battles.

Whatever the cost.

Mind made up, she lifted her chin and summoned the strength she'd once possessed. "What does my father being free have to do with me?"

Blaine's deadly black eyes darkened even further. "Do you think I don't know where you are? That you are playing house with those angels?"

She inhaled slowly through her nose to steady the sudden spike in her pulse.

Blaine prowled forward, a panther toying with its prey. "Or have you forgotten our deal to keep your sister safe? One which is null and void if your father walks this realm."

At the mention of Hailee, her fingers balled into fists. "If you touch Hailee..."

Blaine leaned in as tiny flames ignited in his pupils. "You'll...what?"

She couldn't threaten him, especially not in here where he maintained the control. Not when he could evaporate her soul so easily. But would he? If he truly needed her for his plan, would he risk losing her?

She needed to be smarter.

Blaine straightened and his cocky grin returned. "My angelic brother will no doubt discover this information shortly and begin his hunt for the Fallen. I'd find him first, but I'm a little...predisposed. Instead, you'll do it for me. You'll report their findings to me so I can end that traitor once and for all."

May as well add spy to her long list of treachery. It wasn't like she was aiming for a redemption medal or anything.

"One small problem. How am I supposed to give you information when the Guardians have me locked in a cell?"

"I'm sure you'll find a way to earn their trust...with the right motivation."

Blaine swung his arm in a wide arc, where a wavy fragmented version of her sister appeared. Wearing an apron, her hair piled on top of her head, the flickering version of Hailee looked confused for a second, before her startled gaze locked on Ebony.

"Ebony? Are you—"

Before Ebony could warn her sister, Blaine flicked his hand and snapped the connection.

Her heart sank.

Blaine not only now had the power to dreamwalk, but to also pull in...an angel.

"Do we have a deal?" he asked in a bored tone, as though bartering the price of fruit.

Once again, this Fallen had robbed her of a choice. Either she fed him information about what the Guardians discovered regarding her father or he'd hurt Hailee. Helpless had never looked good on her, yet she'd worn it for thirty-eight days. She wasn't about to wear it fulltime.

"Fine."

"Wise choice, love." Blaine turned to walk away but stopped before the tree line to look over his shoulder with a crooked smirk. "Oh, and if you get the crazy idea to double cross me with your father, I'll make you watch as your sister's life bleeds out at your feet."

CHAPTER 20

"**A**ric," Slater called out, marching into the entertainment room. "You know those four college kids you and Raven watched get arrested while breaking into that abandoned building up north?"

Aric swiveled on the bar stool to face Slater. "Yeah?"

"Well," Slater stopped by the couch and crossed his arms. "The mortal authorities are trying to figure out what drugs they've taken cause it's nothing they've seen before."

"Let me guess," EJ chimed in, pausing for the twelfth time from making the cocktails River had requested twenty minutes ago. "They're high on Devoid?"

"Bingo."

"Fuck," Aric muttered.

His heart sank. The Devoid situation was getting out of hand. First a few popped up here and there, then they sailed through the living room windows hellbent on sucking the life out of a Guardian or two. And since Aric and Raven had been tracking them, they'd found more and more. Groups masquerading as mortals, inserting themselves in cities in plain sight. Soon, mortals would discover that Devoid were soulless beings controlled by...someone. Who though? Because each time Raven had gotten close to interrogating one, they vanished.

"Does the boss know?" River asked.

Slater tipped his chin. "Just left him."

Which meant now wasn't the best time to approach Raven about the situation with Ebony. Since the forest cupcake shenanigans the other day, Raven had either been tracking Devoid or otherwise occupied, giving River no chance to petition for Ebony's release. Nor an opportunity to explain why.

It felt like once again, even though he was in the same room, the Guardians were on one path while he was on another.

He frowned at EJ lazily drying glasses behind the bar, still not preparing River's drink order. Surely, his was next.

"What purpose would a Fallen have for Devoid in the mortal realm? They're basically mindless puppets. All they do is destroy," Slater asked.

Devoid roaming the streets made him nervous. They hadn't roamed the mortal realm since long before Blaine Fell. Why now? And more and more appeared every day.

EJ shrugged. "Shits and giggles?"

"Given it only recently started happening, and in sporadic places, my guess is it's a Fallen who's already in the mortal realm." Aric took a swig of his neat whiskey. Meanwhile, River was officially dying of thirst. "It can't be Blaine. We haven't seen nor heard from him since his fucking showdown with Zath."

He tapped the bar top to gain EJ's attention. "Can you maybe hurry on that drink order? Please."

EJ stared at him as though he'd requested the Guardian shave his own head. "First, I thought you were frickin' kidding. And second, since when do you drink piña coladas?"

Since he'd discovered that mortals enjoyed tropical, coconutty flavored cocktails while relaxing on a tropical island. Not that he said that out loud. They'd only make fun of him.

"And third, which I just thought of," EJ continued, "Why do you need two?"

He didn't reply to that question either. But the look on his face must've given his intentions away.

EJ's hand stilled on a bottle of liquor, his eerily bright eyes narrowing. "Oh, no way, Sunshine. You're not serving my top shelf rum to that Fallen."

"Don't be a dick, EJ," Aric grumbled.

EJ only huffed. "Why are you frickin' entertaining this? She's a manipulative Fallen with a long list of bad choices."

Slater straightened. "What the hell is wrong with being a Fallen with a long list of bad choices?"

EJ threw up his hands and there went any chance of the Guardian making River's cocktails. "I'm not trying to be an asshole. I just don't wanna see Sunshine get his soul crushed."

Oh. Well...um...

He'd reassure the Guardian that no one could crush his soul, but the words wouldn't spill from his mouth. Countless times, Raine teased him for caring too much, for showing too much affection. For loving the idea of love more than air. But why was that so bad? He ached to have someone confide in him, depend on him, for him to be their one. And until recently, he thought that fantasy was exactly that. A fantasy.

Now, he had a chance.

"I'll be fine," he grumbled.

"Sure." EJ scoffed. "Look at your shirts. It's like her villainess is stealing all your sunshinery through your damn clothing."

Aric snorted.

"Sunshinery?" River squawked, tugging at his shirt. Somehow it must've faded in the wash because last week he could've sworn the palm trees were not...a dull shade of brown. Clearly, the detergent was faulty.

This was not his wonky powers at play again. He refused to believe it.

"C'mon. Don't tell me no one else has noticed. It's like you're becoming a dull version of yourself."

River's eyes widened. "Take that back."

EJ rolled his eyes and grabbed the bottle of rum, pouring some in a blender. "Someone needs to make you see sense. All your blood has clearly vacated your brain and is currently residing in your pants."

Before he replied to that outrageous insinuation, Raven stormed into the room. "Those college kids just self-destructed while in custody. Now there's Devoid goo on the floor instead of bodies. It's a fucking mess. I need someone on memory wipe, stat."

River stepped forward about to volunteer when Slater beat him to it. "Raine and I will go."

Raven gave a curt nod and Slater marched out of the room before Raven had even looked at River. "Aric, can Willow mist us to the Raziel gatekeeper again we spoke to last week? There must be something they didn't tell us. We need to stop whoever is creating these Devoid before the situation gets out of fucking control."

"Sure can. Have fun, man." Aric tapped the bar before leaving with Raven.

As EJ resumed making what River hoped were his cocktails, his mind drifted back to how the Guardian had accused Ebony, someone River was ninety-nine percent sure was his soulmate, of stealing his sunshine. He refused to believe that, too. He hadn't paid much attention to his clothes, but now that EJ had mentioned it, his favorite shirts had faded, more so in the past three weeks. At first, he thought someone had tampered with the washing machine as a joke, he wouldn't put it past them, but now other things were not adding up. Like the fern he'd touched yesterday. How it had died right next to him. The mysterious sickness he experienced whenever he cleansed Jemma's soul. His pale skin.

Was he actually sick?

Was his soul...poisoned? He sucked in a sharp breath then shook his head. He was being paranoid. Poison couldn't harm him, he'd never heard of that happening. What he needed was *more* sunshine, not less. All this focus on mutant Devoid made his brain imagine things that weren't there.

Fingers snapped in front of his face. "Heavens to River."

He blinked a few times, trying to clear his chaotic thoughts. "Yeah?"

EJ slid two tall glasses on the bar, full to the brim with a milky mixture, each topped with a colorful umbrella and slice of fresh pineapple. This was what tropical looked like. An exact replica of the picture he'd shown the Guardian.

"Peace offering." EJ braced his forearms on the bar top. "If she really is your soulmate, then, frickin' hell, you're in for a crazy ride. But if she deceives you, I'll have no issue with slipping a little Purah into her drink next time. Just say the word."

A smile lifted his cheeks as a warm, summery breeze swept through his lungs. Was this it? The moment where EJ accepted him as one of them? The moment he was no longer standing on the outer fringes of their brotherhood, peering in. He'd spent countless centuries in the Heavens waiting for Raine to wake, knowing she had a mission and that his sole purpose would begin once his sister's did. And not once, during that entire time, had someone offered to poison an immortal who had wronged him.

Giddy, his fingers curled around the chilled cocktail glasses. "I'm sure it won't come to that, but I appreciate the red-flag gesture."

EJ barked a laugh. "Red flag? Sounds like a term from Hailee's romance novels."

"I can't stop reading them. She has an endless supply and mortals have such vivid imaginations. Besides, heroes written by mortal females are seriously hot."

CHAPTER 21

EBONY

Shivers racked her body, long after the nightmare with Blaine, icy shards still sliced down her spine each time she thought of his words. His threat. If she didn't betray someone—her father or the Guardians—Hailee would once again suffer the consequences. Just when Ebony had glimpsed a sliver of hope, Blaine snuffed it out.

Could she trust anyone? At her last visit, Hailee had made it clear she wouldn't help Ebony escape. The Guardians would never side with her. Ebony had shown them no loyalty. Hell, all she'd shown them was manipulation and dishonesty at Blaine's behest. Trusting Blaine had come with a price, and more often, that price was steeped in blood. Her father? On more than one occasion, Asher had tossed her to the fires of Hell because she didn't comply.

Huddled on the floor of the cell, she pulled the light blanket up to her chin, resting her back against the wall. Never had she felt more helpless.

The heavy clunk of the door opening roused her from sleep right before the angel waltzed in, causing a warm, floating sensation somewhere in the center of her chest. A grocery bag dangled from the crook of one arm while his hands carried two creamy looking drinks. Despite River being a Guardian, his attention brought her comfort she'd begun to crave.

He strolled through the Raziel barrier without care, abruptly halting a few feet from her. Muscles along his beautiful carved jawline popped as his emerald eyes morphed into fierce darkness. "What happened? Did someone hurt you?"

The sudden surge of protectiveness nearly made her weep.

Unable to form words, she softly shook her head, clutching the blanket tighter. Was she hurt? Not physically.

River crouched, peering into her eyes with an intensity that stripped bare all layers between them. He tore down the walls and barriers she'd spent years erecting, and stormed through the gates until he cradled her soul in the palm of his hands. It unnerved her. How, she'd only known this angel for just over a month, yet, in that time, she'd begun to...trust him. Instead of hiding the vulnerable parts of herself, chose to let him see.

And that was scarier than facing any enemy.

With a grumble, River squeezed into the tight space between her and the cot, shuffling until he sat with his back also against the wall, the grocery bag between his stretched-out legs, and the two drinks somehow still balanced in his hands.

Finally, she found her voice. "What's all this?" She nodded to the bag and, well, how close he sat to her.

He'd never been this close before, nor had he...touched

her so casually. Like now, his side pressed against hers, so close she may as well be sitting in his lap. And that...that created all sorts of fiery sparks she shouldn't think of right now.

Sweet notes of pineapple and coconut, like the sunblock her mom used to rub on her, drifted in the air, making her heart sing with nostalgia. Happier times when she and Hailee were high-spirited kids living their best life, oblivious to the horrors of the immortal world. Times when they were not only sisters, but best friends.

"Well, my Violet, given you can't mist to Maui yet, I brought you a taste of it."

A sharp, jagged rock jammed behind her ribs.

"These are piña coladas, and in here," he placed one glass down to jiggle the grocery bag, "Is your very own Hawaiian shirt."

She bit the inside of her cheek to quell the rush of heat making her smile.

"Knowing what mortals call these shirts has unraveled an entire realm of colors and patterns I didn't even know existed. There's so many at the touch of my fingertips, now that I have the right keywords to search. And, well, you were the first person I wanted to share my new favorite with."

He grinned, a full and carefree version that made her heart stall as he offered her a glass. Without stopping to overthink, she took it. Condensation dripped between her fingers as the tiny umbrella and pieces of fruit decorating the rim, coupled with sweet coconut scents, transported her mind to a place beyond her dreams.

Right before the metal straw kissed her lips, River yanked the cocktail out of reach. "Hold up there, Miss

Eager. You need to put on a shirt first to enjoy the whole experience."

She glared at him. "I'm not wearing a Hawaiian shirt."

Wearing Hailee's hand-me-downs were bad enough.

"You haven't even seen the color yet."

A twinge caught in her chest at his pout. But before she opened her mouth to argue, River yanked the shirt from the bag and held it up. Beaming. He was positively beaming.

"Like it?"

My god. The shirt was a vomit of palm trees and coconuts all strangled together in a violet, pink and blue paradise. A laugh burst from her lips. "That's the most over the top Hawaiian shirt I've ever seen."

"Right?" He responded like it was a good thing. "And it's violet!"

Who was this angel? Did he hit his head when he left the Heavens?

River dangled the Hawaiian shirt between them, charging the air, lodging a grappling hook in her chest to lure her in until she snatched it from him with another laugh. She had nothing against people who wore these shirts, but there was a time and place. Like nowhere and never.

River's smile softened into one of adoration as he playfully nudged her shoulder. "I love hearing you laugh."

The smooth words glided from his mouth as effortlessly as always, yet these ones hit harder and a hell of a lot lower, reigniting those earlier sparks. This angel wasn't only cute, he was deadly, wrapped in devastating cheek bones and unruly midnight black hair. And that flawless, angled jaw... well, that was clearly Fate showing off because she'd never witnessed anything more beautiful.

Instead of acknowledging the compliment or the

sudden heat pooling between her thighs, she slipped the shirt over her tank, leaving it unbuttoned. "Happy?"

At River's gasp, she followed his gaze to the handprint-sized gray patch on the right side of the shirt. As though the color had seeped from the print in one spot.

"Not another one," he grumbled, helping her out of the shirt before stuffing it back in the bag. "I'll return it and get you a new one."

Guilt stirred her stomach at the hitch in his voice and his urgency to hide the shirt. "It's fine. Defects happen with material. I'm sure you can return it."

Without responding, he lifted the cocktail straw to her lips urging her to taste.

Heaven.

She'd died and been transported to some tropical paradise where the balmy breeze kissed her skin, while waves washed over her feet as she dug her toes in the cool, wet sand. Closing her eyes, she almost imagined sitting on a beach in Maui, nursing this same cocktail, watching the sunset over the tranquil water.

The scene, the scents, the fact she hadn't slept properly for what felt like years, and how a random angel in a house full of Guardians kept visiting her...Tears pricked her eyes, and she turned away to banish them.

River shifted the drink and bag to one side so he could drape his arm over her shoulders, drawing her close. Her heart stilled, fighting a silent battle between body and mind. Waves of emotions crushed her chest, leaving her breathless. Since discovering the immortal world and the dangers facing her family, she'd tried her best to make the right decisions. To choose the right path. But each time, each choice, felt as though Fate battled against her, kicking her to the curb like an annoying piece of trash.

She'd hit wall after wall.

Until this angel.

Until he stormed into her dreams like a blaze of sunshine on a cold, dreary day.

"Why are you doing this?" she whispered.

"Doing what?"

She blinked away tears, but one slipped through and trailed down her cheek. River swept it away with his thumb, his touch so tender it clenched her heart, stirring a fresh crest of emotion.

"Being nice to me. Why are you being nice to me?"

"I like talking to you. And spending time with you."

"Why?" The word came out as a croak.

Without missing a beat, River cupped her cheek, turning her to face him. "Because you listen, Violet."

Normally, she wasn't one of those girls who fell to her knees over romantic gestures or gooey words. Yet, when River did them, when he blurted truths without care for how someone received them, the ball of light inside her threatened to burst. Being swept away by someone's actions was...dangerous. Yet, she softened to his touch. Even drifted closer, little by little, until his breath tingled her lips. She could kiss him. Could imagine the burst of coconut cocktail on his tongue, the thrill of pleasure slipping low between her legs. But what good would that do? It wouldn't aid her escape. Only complicate it.

Hailee was always the hopeless romantic in their family. Always seeing the good in people, holding onto hope and the promise of a happily ever after. Even as a teenager, her sister always had a romance book within reach—in her bag, by her bed, in the bathroom. She lived for the idea of love and for the first time, Ebony understood why.

Still cupping her cheek, River brushed his thumbs

lightly over her bottom lip sending a jolt through her middle. *"Kissing you would be so sweet."*

The words whispered in her mind so softly she wasn't sure he'd meant to say them directly to her. Had he thought the words and accidentally projected them? Should she respond?

"Like tasting my favorite candy for the first time, over and over again."

When he guided her mouth until it aligned with his, her heart set off, bolting out of her chest and smashing through the magical barrier encasing them. Hell, she wanted to kiss him. If only once. Something for herself. To Hell with the consequences and secrets and wars between them, she wanted something she could hold onto in the dark lonely corners of her world after she finally escaped.

"Then...kiss me."

An almost relieved exhale slipped from River's mouth before he gently pressed his lips to hers. Heat slammed into her body. Balls and balls of fire swept her up in an inferno she couldn't, nor did she want to, contain. It consumed her, engulfed her, laid her bare and crushed her. It was too much. Before he'd even had the opportunity to deepen their kiss, to sweep his tongue over hers, it became too heightened. Too raw. Too...terrifying.

If she didn't stop now, River would be her downfall. Not Blaine, not her father, not any of the enemies she'd made since becoming a Fallen. This angel. The one holding her face so carefully in his hands, treating her as though she held the key to his world, would be the one who gutted her.

As River's tongue slipped over her bottom lip, urging her to open for him, she abruptly jerked back, forcing him to drop his hands. She grabbed her cocktail, silently cursing herself at the sudden loss of his touch but not willing to openly acknowledge it.

"Tell me what's happening on the outside today, Maui." She took a long sip of the creamy drink to quench the fire in her belly. "Enlighten me."

"Well." River cleared his throat and adjusted his position, seeming to compose himself. "We have a Devoid problem. They're not only ambushing the Guardian house, but now they're also popping up all over the realm in groups like soulless gangs. The boss thinks a Fallen is creating them."

She choked on the piña colada. "What did you say?"

"Devoid." He wiped a splattered drop of cream from her lip and licked his finger. "You know, those creepy soulless creatures. We need to find out who's creating them before the situation gets worse."

Memories from the earlier nightmare with Blaine flashed in her mind. *My brother will no doubt discover this information shortly and begin his hunt for the Fallen.* Her heart sank. Was her father...creating Devoid? Asher had attempted to years ago, when he'd first had the insane idea to overthrow Blaine, but every attempt had failed because he'd needed more power. Had he sourced it? Was this why Blaine wanted information about Asher? Why the Fallen blackmailed her into reporting the Guardian's knowledge back to him? Blaine knew. And now, she also suspected he knew that she'd try to contact her father if she escaped.

You'll report their findings to me so I can end that traitor once and for all.

Ice shattered any warmth that had bloomed with River's kiss.

"Do you know something?" River asked, studying her again with those keen eyes.

Once more, her loyalty whipped around like a live wire caught in a storm. Blaine demanded information on the Guardians in exchange for Hailee's safety. Asher no doubt still craved revenge, even more so after Blaine had gained more power while her father was in the Infernal Pits. And River, sweet, sweet River and his too trusting, too caring soul, wanted to know if she knew something.

What a loaded fucking question.

"About what?" she asked, slamming down her mental walls as a precautionary measure.

His green eyes narrowed, and she shifted slightly, not wanting to give away her secrets, but also uncomfortable at keeping them all to herself. Especially in the wake of his kindness.

"About the Devoid situation. Anything might help."

Anything? Could she give him a snippet of information to satisfy his curiosity? This was the first time he'd asked her for something in return. All the times he'd visited, he'd given in the form of one-sided conversation, candy, fresh bedding, devastating smiles, updates of the outside world. He'd never expected anything from her. Nothing. Holding back knowledge was the safest option. She couldn't trust anyone. But the tiny voice in her head whispered that was a lie.

Maybe she could trust one person.

Even for a heartbeat.

Lifting her gaze to his, she said, "I know some Fallen have tried to create them in the past."

River grunted, nodding as though that wasn't new information. "Do you know which Fallen might try to now?"

Yes. But did she know for sure? Suspected, yes, but that wasn't solid evidence. She assumed it was Asher because all the dots aligned. What she needed to do was escape this fucking cage so she could track down her father and find out one way or the other. Sitting here like an animal waiting for slaughter, giving information to Blaine, while her father built an army of soulless soldiers, hoping that the Guardians never found out was no longer an option. They would.

So would Blaine.

Then what would River think of her? Why did that even matter? When he discovered she'd betrayed him, Hell, just imagining it shredded her soul.

But...could she trust River? Really trust him?

Everyone had their own agendas and revenge plots, and every step in one direction had been the wrong one in the other. Yet, this angel had befriended her in the heart of a war, despite her being the enemy.

If she trusted someone at a time like this...it would be him.

Placing the drink down, she shifted to face him once more. "I think it might be...my father."

CHAPTER 22

"**W**ait. Your...father?"

Ebony didn't respond, simply stared ahead at the shimmering teal barrier surrounding her cell.

Her father? How? "I thought your father...well, I thought Blaine...Uh, you know."

Sent her father's soul to the Infernal Pits with a gaping hole in his chest.

Her head lowered while she fiddled with the condensation dripping off her cocktail glass. "I thought the same."

It took every effort not to startle her by jumping up and demanding answers, especially after that epic kiss. That kind of move with his precious, skittish beauty would get him nowhere. Instead, he casually sipped his own cocktail, waiting her out, even though a horde of tiny yellow minions ran around in his mind screaming. Eventually, she'd trust him enough to share her knowledge. Over the past weeks, he'd done everything to make her feel welcome, safe, and protected. Wasn't that his job as a soulmate?

As a potential lover?

Not that they'd progressed beyond talking, besides that heated press of their lips. The moment he'd never stop replaying in his head.

Ebony fiddled with the straps on the tote bag containing the Hawaiian shirt he'd gifted her, which he now needed to return because of yet another blend of faulty material. Just like the one he wore.

Slurping the last of his cocktail, convinced Ebony would beat him at their little game of break-the-silence, he opened his mouth to speak, but she cut in. "I think...he's free. My father. I think he's out there."

Free, as in no longer in the Infernal Pits? Impossible. From what he knew of that realm, there were only a few ways someone could free a soul from there and they all centered around Zath. Or was it linked to the king of Hell, which was now...

Blaine.

He straightened at that realization. Had Blaine contacted Ebony? Had she dreamwalked to him? The thought made the muscles in his jaw clench. If that Fallen hurt her...

Ebony swiveled to face him, placing her own empty glass next to his on the floor, a sudden urgency drawing her closer. "Can I trust you?"

"Of course."

Duh. He didn't even need to think about that answer.

"No, I mean like, *really* trust you. Trust you to get me out of here. Out of this prison."

"Wait." The warmth blooming in his chest suddenly vanished. "As in...leave?"

"I need to."

Okay, this wasn't how he thought their conversation would play out, but he could work with it. Maybe they could come up with a plan together.

Turning slightly as well, he gave her his full attention. "Where will we go?"

Ebony huffed, peering at the door to the basement with longing and a hint of sadness that made him want to shake the Guardians until they saw sense. "If my father really has escaped the pits somehow, then I need to find him."

So many red flags in that sentence. More than Hailee's latest dark romance book. "Let's process one revelation at a time. Starting with, why do you want to find your father after he..."

"Just say it. After he double crossed Blaine? After he kidnapped me? Or after he tried to hurt your sister? After he...killed my mom?"

He swallowed. "Well, any of those would work. Ladies' choice."

The side of her head leaned against the brick wall in a heavy sigh that he felt all the way to his bones. "It's not as simple as that."

"I of all angels know enough about complex situations to last a millennium. What I struggle to understand is why you would actively search for someone who has wronged you on more than one occasion. Someone who has harmed you and those you love."

Her gaze lifted, looking at him through long, dark lashes. "Because sometimes it's better the devil you know.

He crossed his legs, shuffling on the floor to face her fully so she listened carefully. "If you leave, Blaine might come for you. No, scrap that. He will."

A haunted laugh escaped her lips. "Don't you get it?"

She threw a hand in the air. "He'll come for me no matter where I am. It doesn't matter when or where, I'm not safe from him. Anywhere."

"I can protect you in here," he said it with such certainty as though her staying was the simplest solution.

He'd protect her until his very last breath.

"Sure, you will. You and your army of Hawaiian shirts." She rolled her eyes and all that sass sent a rush of blood south to long forgotten territories. "And who will protect the others?" She motioned to the door again. "Including my sister, while you're here protecting a Fallen?"

Sitting was no longer an option because the live energy igniting in his limbs made it nearly impossible to keep still. He'd come to the basement, to Ebony's cell, to gift her with a sensory trip to a tropical paradise. Now though, they'd somehow ended up in an argument about right and wrong, left from right, good versus evil. Protecting her was his priority, but even he knew the sensations drawing him to her were more than that. What he felt, through their soulmate connection, was a compulsion to be close to her. To cherish her. To fly her across this realm showing her every single palm tree lined beach until she'd had her fill. The idea of her father being involved in creating Devoid under the Guardian's noses, that he'd not once, but twice that he knew of, tried to harm her, had his hands curling into fists. Because history told him that Asher wouldn't hesitate to do it again.

Ebony needed more than protection. She needed someone she trusted to eliminate her enemies once and for all, so she no longer lived in fear.

A fear she hid behind her colored hair and hardened exterior.

He wasn't a Guardian, he wasn't bound by their code to

eradicate Fallen from this realm, yet he'd somehow found himself aching to be in their boots. Craved their sense of duty.

He stopped pacing and spun to face her. "What do you propose?"

While he'd been thinking, she'd moved to the side of her bed, the tote bag discarded and her Hawaiian shirt spilling on the floor.

"Let me go."

"Let you go." He stepped closer. "Let you go? To where? Tell me, Violet, where will you go?"

He closed in until she lifted her chin to maintain eye contact, causing a sudden flash of heat through his blood. For a hot second, the way she bit her plump bottom lip distracted the Heavens out of him. Hunger to seal their soulmate bond was one thing, but this all-consuming desire to press his lips on hers again was a fierce need constantly building in the background whenever he thought of her. How it ebbed and flowed through his veins. A rolling wave on the horizon, just out of reach, never washing to shore.

Her pupils darkened, a deep crimson, reminding him again that she was a Fallen. But...he no longer cared. That had never stood between them.

"Let me out of here. Let me find my father. Let me protect...Hailee."

Even though he suspected she didn't feel their bond, reminders like this still smarted. Reminders that his feelings were one sided despite the lust in her eyes moments ago. "I can't let you go." He turned away, shoving a hand through his hair. "The Guardians have said you are to remain here. Raven forbids it. I can't have the boss thinking that I...It's for your safety. The mortal realm is chaos out there."

She scoffed. "Oh, my pretty rule-following angel, nothing is always as black and white as it seems."

Wasn't that the truth.

He should say no. Tell her all the reasons why she should stay with the Guardians, why she should let him protect her, why it was safer inside these walls than out there where Blaine could reach her. But something about the way she said "my" made his brain foggy. What if she did sense the bond between them, but was too scared to acknowledge it?

Hope was a fickle emotion mortals relied heavily on. Now, it seemed, so did he.

"Convince me," he said before his brain talked him out of it.

"Sorry?"

He crouched before her, eyes locked with hers. "Convince me. Convince me to let you go. You have ten seconds before we go back to dreaming of summery cocktails and forget this conversation ever happened."

"What?" She sat up straighter, suddenly alarmed. Or shocked. He was still working out which was which.

"Nine."

"Wait. Okay, hang on, angel, you're flustering me. I wasn't expecting you to say that."

"Neither was I, so now we're even. Also, for the record, I like how your cheeks flush when you're flustered. Eight."

"Stop counting," she glowered at him. "I can't think."

"You can't think when I'm counting, yet you want me to release you from the protection of the Guardians so Blaine can hunt you down? I don't think so, my little Fallen."

Her eyes narrowed in a ferocious glare as she jumped up and stood toe to toe with him. "For your information, I protected myself just fine before the Guardians came along."

"Seven."

"Ugh. I don't even remember what I'm meant to answer."

He cocked an eyebrow, not backing down. "Six."

She threw a hand on her hip and the other against her forehead, squeezing. "Okay, hold on. Convince you..."

"Better hurry. You have five seconds left and I'm suddenly very hungry."

For what, he wouldn't say. But the fire in her eyes and the way she didn't back down made him a little antsy.

She shoved a finger in his chest, and he barely held back grabbing her hand to yank her flush against him. "You're counting down like my mom used to, so I know I really have more time because you're doing it so damn slow. In a moment, you'll start adding 'and a half' in between the numbers."

He grinned, which seemed to frustrate her even more. "Four...and a half."

She threw her hands in the air. "This is my life. Why do I need to convince you?"

"Because I'm your only hope of leaving."

She froze, staring at him as though he'd given her the missing piece of a puzzle. Her bright crimson eyes suddenly clear and focused.

"Four."

Her eyes narrowed, head tilted, searching for something. If she needed reassurance of his loyalty, his word, he'd give it to her. He'd give her the entire realm if it were within his grasp. But all he had was himself and his vow to protect her until the end of his days.

"Three," he whispered, his voice deepening as emotion

swelled in his throat. Would she trust him? She'd just asked if she could, and he'd assured her. Would she believe him? "Two."

Her chest rose with a shaky inhale as her eyes closed, and he held his breath waiting for her answer, unconsciously gliding closer, lifting his hand to brush the back of his fingers along her jaw. "Come on, Violet. Tell me." He paused, waiting for her lids to flutter open. "One."

"Because I don't want to die in here alone."

Chapter 23

RIVER

"This is ass turd," River grumbled, to whoever listened. Which was usually no one.

Why were they overlooking him again? Why was everyone else more skilled, more capable, more everything?

"You come up with the weirdest shit." EJ eyed him from the opposite side of the long table. "It makes sense for Reaper to go. He can track the souls."

Take that back. EJ listened. Not that it helped his cause.

"They don't have souls," River countered. "They're Devoid. Their souls have withered away to nothing. They're soulless."

Raine groaned. *"What's up your ass? You never give a shit about who Raven assigns. Why start now?"*

Is that what Raine thought? Is that what the Guardians thought? He might not give a shit about patrols, fighting random Fallen day in and day out to protect Summit Creek, but just because he wasn't a fighter didn't mean he didn't care about being chosen for a mission. Or that he didn't have an opinion. Or here was the cracker, that he wasn't good enough to send into battle to represent the Guardians.

Why did they always treat him like a third wheel?

He'd undergone more training than Raine, because his primary mission, the one Fate had bestowed upon him way back when, was much more crucial. More dangerous. Not every day Fate tasked an angel to ensure another angel, a deadly warrior with Raziel powers, completed her mission. If he failed, Raine failed. But she hadn't, and he'd like to think part of that was because of him.

Maybe he needed to be more obvious. More direct. Summon some of Ebony's sass.

Straightening his spine, he turned to Raven. "I'll go. And I'd like to bring Ebony."

EJ spat out his drink and droplets sprayed River's cheek.

Gross. He wiped it with a napkin.

"Ebony?" Raven leaned back in his chair with a deep frown, curiosity lightening his tone. "Why would you bring Ebony?"

For once, he had Raven's undivided attention. When Ebony had told him she didn't want to die alone, something shifted inside him. Determination. Purpose. And now, Raven gave him the chance to prove why they should choose him for this latest mission and why they should release Ebony from that barbaric cell.

Telling the Guardians about Ebony's father felt like a betrayal, even though he thought Hailee deserved to know. After all, Asher was her father, too. But, if Ebony wanted to tell Hailee, surely, she would have by now. She'd had plenty of opportunities. Instead, she'd told him, and he wouldn't destroy that trust at the first obstacle. It felt good to finally have someone confide in him. Choose him. Until Ebony, no one had ever trusted him with their secrets. Their fears. And if keeping them close to his heart proved his loyalty, then he'd do exactly that.

He chewed a soft candy while considering how best to convince Raven. An answer that would ensure the Guardians trusted Ebony. One that explained all his visits to the basement, and his subsequent happy moods. An answer no one could debate.

"Ebony is my soulmate."

A mixture of groans echoed around the table from the Guardians who were already privy to this information and still found it ridiculous. The most surprising, Raine, jabbing a dagger into the nearby window frame, the black hilt wobbling with the force.

Raven, undeterred by Raine's little tantrum and everyone's moderate annoyance, studied him. "You've sealed a soulmate bond with Ebony? She's no longer Fallen?"

"That's kind of a personal question, don't you think?"

"I don't want to be an asshole, River, but I think the answer makes all the difference." Raven crossed his arms. "Because if you don't trust your connection, the unmistakable bond you're positive you share with her, how can we trust it?"

Damn it. Raven had him there. In a very asshole kind of way, despite his good intentions.

The problem wasn't that he didn't trust the bond between he and Ebony. The problem was, ever since Raine did the crazy trick with her magic, he didn't trust himself. A soulmate bond, a vow exchanged and sealed, was forever. An eternity. Could he offer Ebony that? Each time he tried to cleanse the darkness inside Jemma, which had become a daily task now, the side effects hit him harder. Every encounter left him weakened and woozy. And don't even get him started on the bizarre clothing issue and the numerous times Aric had told him he looked pasty.

Something weird was happening to him, and if he didn't know better, he'd think it was related to the darkness inside Jemma. That his power had twisted or more correctly, reversed. But that was impossible. Right? Because if his power sucked in darkness rather than cleansing it, his soul would...

He shook away the thought. He couldn't think about that right now. Not with all the other problems he had. Starting with Ebony's earlier confession, her father on the loose, the fact that...

With his mind wandering, chasing thought after thought, Raven moved on, continuing to map out the Devoid situation, including the second group intercepted in the forest lining the Guardian grounds two nights ago. Once his mind settled, he attempted to listen but spent most of his energy reinforcing his mental walls against Raine's incessant prodding.

Before long, the meeting concluded and when everyone had filed out the door, he pushed back his chair.

"River." Everyone but Raven, who still sat at the head of the table.

His entire body itched to beeline to the basement. To Ebony. She hadn't dreamwalked to him last night, after her confession in the basement, and it made him antsy.

The Guardians refused to release her from the cell. What kind of potential soulmate was he if he didn't fight for her? Fight to free her after she'd all but begged him to?

A douchey one.

That needed to change. His priorities needed reordering.

He needed to make a choice.

Rolling his chair back under the table, he gave Raven his attention.

"I know there's something you're not telling me," Raven started, fingers steepled. "And I really don't wanna demand it of you. I respect your privacy, I do, but know that you can tell me. Hell, look at Raine and Slater. We know it's possible for a Fallen and an angel to be soulmates, I'm not debating that."

Slater was once an angel. Both Slater and Raine were, in the beginning, angels. Was that why their pairing worked? Was that how Raine healed him? Or was it because Raine had drawn on power that wasn't her own?

Power that had been his.

He and Ebony had none of those things. She wasn't once an angel, and his power was all haywire, barely functioning. What if his soul no longer…He couldn't share his concerns with Raven without sharing what had happened with Raine.

When Raine and him had arrived in the mortal realm, he'd been so hopeful. Not that he would achieve his mission, but that by achieving his mission, he contributed to saving this realm. That he'd make a difference. But year after year, that hope dwindled until it left him feeling empty. Hollow.

Lonely.

Then, as the Guardian house grew and soulmates bonded, that hope sparked again. And for a time, he'd convinced himself that it didn't matter if they chose someone else for the missions or called on only Raine for her power to imbue their weapons.

He lived here.

He celebrated their accomplishments. He rejoiced in their bonds.

Until Ebony.

Now, he yearned for more.

With Ebony, that fickle sense of hope had roared to life, grounding him while at the same time setting him free. More dangerous than hunting Devoid, or Ebony's father, or trying to save Blaine, hope grasped him in its claws refusing to let him go.

Had Fate foreseen his path colliding with Ebony's? Had she known?

Raven gave his forearm a squeeze. "Listen, my man. Your head isn't in the game. And that's understandable. I get it. I remember how confusing those emotions were in the beginning. Maybe it's best you stay here until you've figured it out."

That snapped his focus. "You're...grounding me?"

"No, dumbass. I'm saying let Raine, Slater and Cole handle the Devoid situation for now. You can help in other ways. This will give you time to focus on sorting this out." Raven pushed back from the table to stand. "Because if Ebony really is your soulmate, that's going to send this house into a fucking spin."

With a brotherly clap on the shoulder, Raven strode from the room leaving him in a complete state of shock.

If she really is your soulmate. Did Raven not believe him? Did anyone? Was it so impossible to imagine that Ebony was his soulmate? Had the Guardian expected him to find a different soulmate, or none at all? Or was their uncertainty because he was still the slightest bit hesitant?

He huffed a long breath, expelling the unhelpful energy. He didn't need to sort out his feelings for Ebony, he needed to prove he had her back. Otherwise, he'd lose her before he'd even had a chance to kiss her again.

What a tragedy that would be.

And if her father was involved, they needed to find Asher and end him before he created more Devoid. Before her father hurt Ebony. Before Blaine hunted her down. A few weeks ago, he was so sure his bonus mission sent by Fate to heal Jemma would take precedence over finding a soulmate.

But now, he saw everything so clearly.

The Guardians would never consider him one of them. He would always be on the outside looking in. Which meant they would never release Ebony, keeping her a prisoner for as long as Raven saw fit. She thought no one was on her side.

It was time he proved her wrong.

CHAPTER 24

EBONY

Days flew by in a blur, since the angel had last visited her cell. She'd lost count. No word. No Hawaiian themed deliveries, nor a single connection through her dreams, despite her numerous attempts. Nothing. River had drawn out her confession and then never returned.

Like everyone else in her life.

Abandoned her.

In the quiet days and nights since, the grouchy one, his sister, retrieved items from the armory, and Hailee brought meals and water, but Ebony barely held a conversation. As though River had broken something inside her and then left her to rot in the cell.

But she refused to break. Sure, River had weakened her resolve, tugged on long buried emotions until she confessed something stupid, but he hadn't broken her. She hadn't even meant it. Dying alone was a sacrifice she'd make, an outcome she'd accepted long ago when she'd vowed to protect Hailee. In that, she wouldn't give up. She wouldn't stop fighting.

She wouldn't surrender.

Because surrender was never an option. Not when facing her father or the other Fallen who challenged her, nor was it with Blaine. Surrendering got her killed. She was a Duhamel for fuck's sake. An angel with the powerful ability to dreamwalk, to manipulate an immortal's thinking, to change the course of their actions through their subconscious. That counted for something.

Except, what was the use of that power when she couldn't connect with anyone who could help her escape?

Pushing the food tray aside, her mind too worked up to eat, she swiped the wooden knife and began scratching another notch in the bathroom drywall like a true prisoner. Sooner or later, she'd figure a way out of this enclosure, and when she did, she'd hunt down her father before Blaine even discovered she'd escaped. She'd have the advantage for once.

Blaine blackmailing her into feeding him information on the Guardians was the most ridiculous bargain he'd ever executed. How could she possibly gain information when she never saw them?

The wooden knife snapped under her force before she fully scratched the notch, and she pegged it across the cell, screaming in frustration when it sailed through the magical barrier to land on the other side. Everything and everyone besides her could enter and exit. Next the tray suffered her wrath. She hurled it through the barrier like a frisbie, grinding her teeth when food splattered the opposite wall before sliding to the floor. The tray landed with a loud clang.

The pin code to the main door beeped before it opened,

and without bothering to look, she sensed River enter. The awareness at her nape was a dead giveaway and getting kind of annoying.

When his slow, heavy footfalls paused near where she'd thrown the tray, she couldn't stop from looking his way. If only to see disappointment on his face.

Instead, the tender caress of his eyes, the slight frown when his gaze roamed over her from head to toe, made her damn heart skip. Despite anger moments ago, her heart all but slipped into a stupid puddle because this angel had clearly come to check on her. To make sure she was okay.

Not to chastise her for being difficult.

When he stepped closer, her brain kicked into gear, noticing the backpack clutched in his hand, and bow in the other.

Why the hell was he here?

With a grunt, he bypassed the mess to stride through the barrier, apparently on a mission, and tossed the backpack at her feet. "I don't know what you had against your meal, but it no longer matters. We have roughly ten minutes before someone figures out that I skipped movie night and comes looking for me. This is our only chance." He pointed to the backpack. "Get dressed."

Uhh...what the hell? "Why? For movie night? Or so I can look pretty before you use one of those arrows?"

On me.

She hadn't said it out loud, but the insinuation hitched her voice.

He recoiled as though she'd told him his candy sucked. Which it didn't, for the record. "No. For our jailbreak. What in the Heavens? Why would I hurt you?"

Good question. Years of bitterness had trained her mind to jump to conclusions and at times, not the most logical ones. But if River planned to kill her, or hand her over for a ransom, he'd had plenty of opportunities in the past few weeks and hadn't. The time they'd spent together convinced her she could trust him, and until she had evidence contradicting that, she would.

As he unzipped the backpack, she studied this different version of River before her. Was it just her or was something off with him? The last time she'd seen him, he'd acted playful and silly, having brought her touches of Maui with a Hawaiian T-shirt and tropical cocktail. Now, he was all... bossy. Commanding. Lethal, dressed in Guardian black from top to bottom instead of those colorful shirts and pants. Everything from fighting leathers to a form-fitting black shirt snuggled his muscular body, with at least three daggers sheathed at his thighs, and a quiver strapped across his back with Purah-tipped arrows poking out the top. This entire look was a stark contradiction to what she'd witnessed up until now. Gone was the fun-loving, humorous angel. In his place, a version that made her blood heat.

Yep. She admitted that to herself. This version of River was freaking hot. With his hair disheveled in a harsher way, leather bands around his wrists and silver rings on his fingers, he still resembled the same angel she'd come to know, come to enjoy his company, but now he oozed power and masculinity rather than wholesomeness. And the smoking-hot burn in his emerald eyes almost undid her. Sure, she enjoyed their playful banter, but this guy reignited long forgotten desires. As though River would toss her over his shoulder if she disobeyed him and...Wow. That made her blood pump a little faster.

"Ebony."

God, even his voice had somehow become more. Deeper. Raspier. Had he been holding back all this time?

Get a grip. Clearly, imprisonment made her brain malfunction along with her libido.

The slightest smirk lifted at the corner of River's mouth. "Get dressed, Violet."

Again, he motioned to the backpack by her feet.

"Why?"

"Because you can't defend yourself in socks and sweatpants."

Defend herself? Random negative thoughts invaded her mind until she shut them down. Defend herself *with* him, not against him.

Crouching, she pulled out a pair of military style combat pants and a soft, cotton T-shirt from the backpack, along with a pair of boots like his. A weird style, but a fresh change of clothes was a fresh change of clothes, and she wouldn't complain. Eager to rid herself of Hailee's hand-me-downs, she gathered them in her arms.

"Does this outfit really work together?" she teased.

"Complain about my fashion choices when we're in the air. For the last time, get dressed."

"Okay, okay." She darted into the adjoining bathroom and made quick work of changing before returning to the cell. "When did you become so grumpy?"

A long beat of silence hung in the air before he answered. "When I started breaking rules for you."

Well...shit.

Something clogged in her throat, but she stuffed that unhelpful emotion all the way down. Regardless of this little escapade of theirs, and the fact this angel was for some reason helping her, she needed to keep her wits about her. Her list of enemies was long. A hell of a lot longer than her list of allies, which basically narrowed down to the one standing in front of her.

"Are you done?" he grumbled.

She tied the lace on the second boot and stood. "Yep."

Using his foot, he swiftly slid the empty backpack under her cot before grabbing her hand. Tiny sizzles of electricity jolted through her blood at their contact, heating, swirling around her body making her lightheaded. Given how his jaw clenched, she sensed he felt it too.

Desperate to distract herself, and perhaps him, from the tumbling sensation in her belly, she motioned to the teal barrier in front of them. "I hate to point out the obvious, angel, but someone weaved this to keep me *in*. And as much as I've enjoyed our time together, if I could've just walked out without it zapping me, I would have by now."

That slow smirk lifted again at the corner of his mouth and the gooey sensation restarted. "My magic connects to Raine's. Even after the...mishap which I'd rather not go into, I can still uncast every spell she casts and vice versa. We... balance each other. That's what Fate does. Creates balance."

What. The. Living. Hell?

Taking full advantage of her shock, he raised his free palm and faced it to the barrier. Teal magic erupted in a gust of brilliant swirls, tangling with the barrier before surrounding them. River's power weaved through the fibers of those already there until it was impossible to distinguish between the two. His magic was...mesmerizing. The glimmering threads, bright and pale contrasts of blues and greens blended into one. How he effortlessly wielded it without letting go of her hand.

When the barrier vanished in an explosion of light, she gasped.

River's shoulders sagged, as though the powerful blast

took its toll on him. Only now, did she notice the beads of sweat on his brow.

"Are you okay?"

He nodded.

"Are you sure? You look a little...green."

River tugged her hand, leading her over the non-existent threshold of the cell to stand on the other side. "That amount of power requires more effort. I thought I'd waited enough days but clearly not."

Before she asked more, the enormity of what happened dawned on her. She was free.

For the first time in what felt like months, she was...free.

River, the quirky angel who'd invaded her dreams more than once, who'd brought her candy and silly shirts, had set her free.

He'd...She yanked her hand from his and glared at him. "You." She shoved his chest. "You had the ability to uncast that spell all along and you didn't."

A flash of something resembling guilt darkened his usually bright green eyes, but it disappeared too quickly. "Yes."

"Yes?" She raised her voice. "Yes? That's all you have to say? Yes?"

She backed up a step. He'd had the ability to free her from the beginning and she'd blindly sat in the cell enjoying his company. Looking forward to it even. Yet, what pissed her off the most was that another person, immortal or otherwise, had controlled her. Had *used* her.

"Would you rather I deny it?" He lifted his hand and once more, power streamed from his palm in a direction behind her. "I can't lie, remember?"

Focusing on something over her shoulder, he waved his hand in the air, no doubt casting power she couldn't care less about. She was so stupid. Why did she think he was a kindred spirit? Someone she could trust?

Hailee was the hopeless romantic who'd always dreamed of a happily ever after with some dashing hero that swooped in to save the day. Not Ebony. She was a realist. And this...whatever connection she imagined between her and the angel, wasn't real. It was all a lie.

"I...trusted you." The words tumbled out her mouth before she could stop them.

Halting the power, River stepped closer, lifting his hands to cup her jaw. She wanted to retreat, to push him away, to slam her walls shut so he no longer invaded her mind, but the sincerity in his eyes wrapped around her like a weighted blanket on a blustery cold day.

"I had the ability to, yes, but I thought keeping you here was safer. I now realize the error in my thinking."

She swallowed the ball of emotion clogging her throat. "Because now you don't think keeping me here is safe?"

He should stop touching her, stop stroking his thumbs over her cheeks, because it weakened her. It splintered those walls. It...terrified her.

"No, I still think that. But I also know that if your father is involved in the Devoid situation, you are our best chance at stopping him."

Our.

As in him and her? Or him and the Guardians?

"Only after I stop your father, will you be safe."

She laughed, although it lacked humor, backing out of his embrace. "Safe? You think once I find my father, I'll somehow convince him to stop creating Devoid, if it's even him who's doing it? And then you think I'll be safe?" She shook her head in disbelief. "That any of us will be safe?"

"I'll do whatever it takes to make that happen."

He reached for her again, but she retreated, bumping into a wall that hadn't been there moments before. Spinning, she found the shimmering teal barrier once again intact. Everything looked exactly like before, with the addition of a hologram of herself tucked beneath the thin blanket, head on the pillow, facing the wall. The level of detail, including the violet streak in her hair, was...astounding.

And a little concerning.

Strong hands glided over her shoulders. "I said I'd protect you, Ebony. And I meant it."

She wanted to believe him, she really did. But anyone who'd ever vowed to protect her had either betrayed her or died. Yet, for some unknown reason, she wanted to trust that this angel was different. That this time was different.

Slowly, as though testing her, he slipped his hand in hers and stepped toward the door.

"Just like that? We're going to...walk out of this room?" Her pulse quickened. "What if your scary sister can sense that you ruined her spell? What if she comes in here and uncasts yours and figures out I'm missing?"

He squeezed her hand, and part of her hated the burst of reassurance it gave her. "Although unlikely, anyone who wanders down here, Hailee included, will only see you sleeping." He led her to the door. "As for Raine, she's out on patrol with Slater again, and tonight, should be far enough away not to sense the jolt. But if she does..." He paused by the door to look over his shoulder at her. "She'll probably assume it's me entering and exiting the cell. Which I think would cause a similar sensation and completely bore her."

Her brain almost exploded with the new information. "I have so many questions."

"And I'll answer them, once we make it outside."

Outside.

Hell, she'd almost lost hope of ever seeing the sky again, or feeling the change in temperature. Of being free. It surprised her how much she ached for simple experiences after the Guardians had stripped it all away.

River opened the military grade door before resting his palm on the small of her back to direct her out and up a set of stone steps.

He leaned in, right by her ear. "Be quiet and follow my lead."

She nodded. Not that she had much of a choice.

Ascending the curved staircase, they tiptoed to an upper level where River opened another door, glancing left and right before leading her down a long entranceway, past what looked like a sunken living room. Hand once again on the small of her back, he guided her out the front door and into the night.

A blast of air cooled her cheeks, but she didn't have the opportunity to appreciate it. River grabbed her hand once more and they hurried along a gravel drive before darting into the forest lining the property. She'd been to this forest several times now, to deliver messages from Blaine, to plead for her sister, to, well, do things she knew Hailee wouldn't agree to. Not once had she taken the time to appreciate the spectacular towering pine trees, and the woodsy scent heavy in the night air.

Once they were deep in the forest, River stopped and turned to face her. "Can you mist us?"

A tingle danced over her flesh at the thought of misting. Because if she could mist, that meant she could also escape. She could disappear into the ether right now and never return to the Guardians.

They'd never find her.

But where would she go? Where would that leave her?

And River? He'd trusted her enough to break her out of the cell. He'd broken some unknown rules that clearly meant a lot to him so he could help her. So, he kept her safe. And at the first opportunity, she contemplated ghosting his ass.

Would the Guardians punish him when they discovered his betrayal?

He'd become another person hurt by her actions. Another innocent soul caught between trying to protect her and doing what was right.

Hell, he'd even changed his entire outfit tonight and put so much effort into looking so...badass.

With a heavy sigh, she peered into those stunning green eyes and instantly regretted it. Because nothing made her weaker than catching how he looked at her. "Yes. I can mist."

It came out as a groan, as though the ability to poof from one place to the next in a blink of an eye was a burden. Right now, maybe it was.

"Good." He gave her hand a reassuring squeeze. "The last Devoid sighting was in Cape Thornton. Can you mist us there?"

"Hang on a second." Was she really doing this? Everything had moved so fast. Mere days ago, Blaine had threatened Hailee's life if she didn't give him information on the Guardians. And before that, he'd constantly held that threat above her head, controlling her every move. But this had all started when her father had kidnapped her and turned her into a Fallen.

She hadn't asked for any of this. Yet, here she was, at the mercy of another immortal, using her for their own agenda. How did she know this time was any better than all the others?

"I need to know why we're doing this. Why you're helping me. Why...you care about my safety."

River's confident and somewhat commanding armor faltered, revealing the softer side she'd come to know and... like. He lifted her hand, twisting it to kiss the inside of her palm, and she once again softened toward him. Swayed almost.

"You want to know why I care about you?"

"Yes."

"Because I see you, Ebony. The real you. You're not a Fallen hellbent on destroying souls, you're a sibling trying to survive. Someone who I know would do whatever she could to protect those she cares about. And...well...I can relate." His brows creased in a deep frown. "And I also want to ensure that you have a person like that. Someone who is protecting you and making sure your soul stays alive."

Goosebumps sprouted over her arms. But it wasn't enough to trust his words, to believe them. She needed more. "You don't get it. Here you are, a beautiful angel, not only being nice to me, but helping me escape. And you're telling me it's because you want to ensure my soul stays alive? That I have someone protecting me? You hardly know me."

"First, we'll come back to the part where you think I'm beautiful. Second," his jaw clenched as he tugged her closer. "Everyone deserves to have someone looking out for them, including you. And I would like to be that someone for you."

The hard tone of his voice promised retribution for anyone who dared to stand against him and that was the most surprising twist of the evening. As though slipping on that Guardian fighting gear had changed his entire demeanor. Unless this was a side he rarely showed. A part of himself he hid behind his fun-loving, candy-addict exterior?

Clearly, he trusted her to know all sides of him. Trusted her.

He shouldn't.

"Together, we'll find your father and stop the Devoid threat. It's the only way everyone will..."

Will what? She waited, almost held her breath for him to finish that sentence, but he never did.

"It's the only way to keep you safe."

There was a long list of problems with this scenario and countless dangers with River's plan, but for some reason, she had a sudden desire to say yes. For the first time in forever, someone wanted to help her. Had prioritized her safety. He hadn't chastised her for making bad decisions. Hadn't condemned her for being a Fallen. Instead, day after day, he'd shown her that he cared. Actually cared. He'd listened to her, comforted her, laughed with her. And she'd be lying if she said it didn't feel fucking great.

Maybe there was another reason he wanted to ensure her soul stayed alive, to make sure they stopped the Devoid and whoever created them, that they found her father, but she could address those as they came. Right now, it felt like someone truly had her back.

River muttered, glancing in the direction of the main house before looking back at her. "I hate to rush you, but you have about thirty seconds to mist us out of here before someone catches us."

Trust. Everything revolved around trust. And it was about time she gave it.

With a curt nod, she closed her eyes, envisaged the last location she'd seen her dad before the battle with the Guardians and...misted them.

CHAPTER 25

RIVER

By the power of Fate, he missed misting. The freedom. The thrill. How his entire body swelled with magic, dissolving his flesh and bone to minute molecules, transporting him to another location before reknitting himself back together.

The rush.

A power Fate revoked when he and Raine arrived in the mortal realm so they could blend with the Guardians.

Beside him, Ebony gave his hand a quick squeeze before slipping hers free and stepping back. He let her go. Earlier, he'd probably touched her more than he should've, more than the situation warranted. But the way she looked at him, really peered into his eyes, made that primal part of his soul hum with energy he struggled to contain. The thought of her whimpers, the breathy moans he hoped she'd make when he broke through her hardened exterior, had his body awakening in more ways than one. But confessing the soulmate bond to Ebony could go one of two ways: she'd admit to feeling the same or she'd call him crazy and flee.

Many had called him crazy before, which no longer bothered him, but he took a huge risk freeing her. The last thing he needed was for the Guardians to find out. Which they would if she misted away without him.

He shook his head to clear his thoughts and surveyed their surroundings. Stone monuments, narrow paved pathways leading between them, whispers of Raziel magic tingling in the cool night air.

Hang on. "Where are we?"

Ebony yanked open a centuries old stone door. "Lafayette cemetery."

He caught up to her in a few quick strides to grab her hand, twisting her to face him. "Why are we not at Cape Thornton?"

"First, angel, you're way too trusting. I could've misted you anywhere, including to Hell."

The thought had crossed his mind for a fleeting second, but he'd dismissed it just as fast. Would she have? Would Fate have let Ebony mist him to Hell...and if she did, would he have had time to flee? No. He lacked the ability to mist. If Ebony had transported him to the entrance of Hell, he would become a Fallen.

Like her.

Heavens help him. He *was* too trusting.

Ebony no doubt saw the horror on his face and took pity on him, playfully shoving his shoulder with a laugh. "Relax, I wouldn't have done that. Despite what everyone thinks, I'm not heartless. But you...you need to be more careful and a hell of lot less trusting. Not everyone is worthy of that trust. Angels included."

He knew he shouldn't push her, to seek answers to

questions he shouldn't ask, but the slight plea in her voice had him drifting closer until the tips of his boots kissed hers.

"And...you are?" he said in her mind. *"Worthy of my trust?"*

She lifted her chin, and the little defiant spark of crimson in her eyes sent a strange heat through his blood. "No one is worthy of it. Especially me."

He begged to differ. Though, the wary sigh in her voice hinted that if he pushed too far, she'd close the vault in her mind again after he'd worked so hard to open it. Instead, he changed the subject. "Lesson noted. And second?"

"Second, there's no point going to places where the Guardians have spotted Devoid. If my father is behind this, we need to go to where he might be creating them."

Pretty *and* smart. He'd sure hit the Heavens goals with his soulmate.

Ebony motioned down the dark, narrow tunnel. "This leads to a chamber where my father...met with other Raziel before he discovered your sister was the key to unlocking the Empryen."

Raine had told him about the chamber and how she'd found Asher torturing information out of an unsuspecting Raziel. Also, the same chamber where she'd saved Slater.

"You think he came back here?" He lowered his voice, even though he hadn't sensed anyone else in the tunnel. "That he could be using this same chamber to create Devoid?"

Ebony peered into the darkness. "I don't know. But we have to start somewhere."

Solid point.

Her logic made complete sense. Yet, it was her confidence. Her courage. How, even after the Guardians held her captive for over a month, she strode along the edge of the tunnel wall as though she'd been the one who'd captured a Fallen, not the other way around. Pride bloomed in his chest. This was his soulmate. Cunning, smart and pretty.

A warrior.

Sure, the soulmate bond drew them together, ensured they'd meet in this lifetime, but their connection was more than that. His attraction, how his body lit up every time he thought of her, that was all him. And the many dreams where she'd slowly opened up to him, allowed him to peek behind the fortress she'd built around herself, revealing a hidden world beyond. Those moments strengthened their bond more than he ever could have imagined.

After witnessing her determination, her compassion for her sister, no one could ever include her in the same category as other Fallen.

No, his soulmate was in a league of her own.

"You coming or what?" She hissed in his mind making him smile. Her instigating their mental connection was one step closer to her believing in their bond.

Quickening his step, he caught up to Ebony—

A dagger whizzed past his face, skimming his nose.

He grabbed the back of Ebony's shirt, yanking her to his front before shoving her behind him just as a shadow curled around the tunnel entrance. Correction: two shadows.

Raine and Slater.

And he didn't need to see his sister's face clearly to know she was pissed. Royally.

"What the fuck?" Raine waved another dagger in the air like a lunatic, standing at the threshold.

Much to his annoyance, Ebony refused to stay behind him, and instead, moved to his side. "Slater."

"Ebony."

Raine scoffed. "What is this, some sort of Hell reunion?" She pointed the tip of her blade at River. "I knew you were up to something. And I knew it involved..." She waved the blade at Ebony. "Her."

"Drop the dagger, sis. That's my soulmate you're referring to."

Raine's feral violet eyes snapped to his. For a second, he wondered if he could trust her. His own flesh and blood. The sibling he met for the first time only a few mortal years ago yet would lay down his soul for on the battlefield. Raine must've sensed his indecision, because the fierceness of her glowing eyes softened.

In the dead center of a creepy cemetery, his sister sheathed her blade and crossed her arms. "Start talking."

Chapter 26

Oh, shit. What was more startling than an ambush? Soulmates.

What the living Hell?

But before she even had time to comprehend the word, all Hell was about to break loose.

No way would she let River shoulder the blame for sneaking her out and breaking a stupid rule. Not to mention how he'd uncast his sister's magic before freeing her.

But the relaxed set of River's jaw threw her. He seemed...excited. Almost relieved to have a secret out. And damn if that didn't make him scale the hotness tree. With his playful demeanor, his head-to-toe black Guardian attire, and the bow over one shoulder, he oozed contradiction. Dangerous and fun. A guy who'd tickle her silly while they laid in the sun but would shoot an arrow in anyone who interrupted them.

The combination was...magnetic. And if they weren't about to have his sister and Slater interrogate them, she'd grab the neck of his shirt, pull him down and kiss the living hell out of him.

Because they were supposably...soulmates?

Was she...could River be...?

Did she even have a soulmate? She was a Fallen. Yet Slater...

So many questions she wanted to ask River, demand of him, but as she opened her mouth, he squeezed her hand. For the first time, she noticed the spark zipping between them. Had it always been there?

"Let me handle Raine. She can be a little grouchy."

"I heard that," Raine called out.

Slater's shadows still swirled over the ground in preparation for battle, while Raine spun what she assumed was a Kiel around her index finger.

River drew closer, her hand still clutched in his. Sure, she found him attractive. Fun and charming, with a calmness that called to her. And sure, she'd on more than one occasion found herself leaning toward him, soaking up his warmth as though it would heal her emotional wounds. But lately, she'd noticed finer details. How his emerald irises darkened when he neared her, how they lightened when he entered her dreams. How he playfully touched her at every opportunity as though he couldn't get enough. And she'd found herself...craving it. Missing him during their time apart.

Counting down the hours until he returned to the cell.

Because they were soulmates? Because Fate had destined their two souls to find each other. Or because he was kind to her in the face of so much hatred?

Proof of a Fallen and angel soulmate pairing stood thirty feet away in Slater and Raine. The bond had somehow healed Slater's soul, so he was no longer a Fallen. Which she'd had no idea was even possible. From the outside, the two of them were the most unconventional match. A scary Raziel soulmate with a shadow-wielding Fallen. Yet, the love and adoration in Slater's eyes when he spoke to Raine made her chest clench. She'd never been one to ache for happy endings, but that didn't mean she never longed for... someone.

As though in slow motion, River turned his head and caught her looking at him, giving her a cheeky wink that sent her heart fluttering. Hell. What was wrong with her?

"Gawk at me later, Violet, when no one else is around. It's distracting." River all but crooned in her mind.

She choked on air.

"Don't bother denying it."

Fine. She was gawking. But he didn't have to call her out.

Rather than wondering how River's stubble would feel on the sensitive flesh of her neck, she diverted her attention to the two angels standing at the tunnel entrance.

"I've been tracking your movements for days, you idiot." Raine flipped the throwing star in the air before catching it again. "I knew the instant you unraveled the barrier spell, but I had no fucking idea it was to sneak her out." She pointed the sharp tip at Ebony.

"Her name is Ebony, Raine, and I suggest you start using it."

Raine cocked a brow at her brother. "Possessive looks good on you."

River shrugged one shoulder, again, unfazed.

Possessive. Soulmates. How had she not figured this out earlier? Was he only helping her because she was...No. That was a toxic path to travel, and not one she wanted to entertain. Fate might have destined their souls to find each other, but over the past few weeks she'd bonded with him in other ways. Through his kindness, her attraction, his attentiveness, his protectiveness. His trust in her. The security he'd freely given.

Soulmate or not, one quirky conversation after the other, she'd begun falling for this angel.

Raine edged into the tunnel with Slater close behind. "If Slater and I have been hunting Devoid, what are you two hunting?"

"It's your story to tell, Violet." River peered down at her. *"But you can trust my sister."*

River could, sure, but could she? As she'd discovered earlier when she'd pleaded for Hailee to free her, her list of allies only contained one good looking angel. Could she risk adding two more because River trusted them?

Did she have any other options?

In Hell, Slater had been somewhat of a friend to her. He might not have thought so, but she respected him. Even when she returned after Blaine had sent her father to the Pits, Slater had convinced Blaine not to kill her on the spot. Instead, Blaine had offered her a place beside him. For a price, but that was neither here nor there now because she'd accepted.

If River vouched for his sister, then she'd trust her too.

Speaking to Slater and Raine, she said, "I think my father is creating the Devoid. When Blaine ended Zath, it dissolved the Infernal Pits, setting the souls free."

Judging by the stunned looks on their faces, they hadn't considered that option.

"Of course, he fucking is," Slater muttered, his jaw flexing as the shadows around his feet billowed outward, reaching for an invisible enemy in the tunnel walls. "He was creating while he was in Hell, wasn't he? Before Blaine sent his soul to the Pits?"

Trust.

They couldn't do it alone.

Even if her plan to find her father turned to shit, if everything backfired, at least she'd tried. At least she'd fought until the very end.

She loosened her fingers to let go of River's hand, but he tightened his hold, not letting her move an inch. That traitorous heart of hers skipped like a deer bouncing in a bright green pasture during the height of spring.

"Yes. He was building an army under Blaine's nose with the intention of using it against him."

Raine began flipping the throwing star again, but this time she recognized it as a frustrated move, rather than a preemptive strike.

"Fuck," Slater growled.

Startled bats flew from the trees beyond the tunnel entrance causing a ruckus.

"How is he in the mortal realm, Ebony?" Slater asked, his shadows growing in intensity, darkening and thickening, inching closer to...her.

River angled his body slightly, sending an unspoken warning to their new allies. "We're all friends here, so why don't you keep the accusations out of our conversations, yeah? And while you're at it, tell your shadows to back off." Once the shadows retreated to Slater's feet, River continued. "We're not sure Asher is in the mortal realm. We were about to start searching for him."

Slater's eyes narrowed. "He sure as shit won't be in Hell. Blaine would sense his presence and fucking obliterate him."

"Which isn't entirely a bad choice but won't solve the current situation," Raine added.

After Raine listed all the places she and Slater had searched for Devoid, Ebony found her gaze drifting back to River, who was already peering at her. That same devastating, soft smile curled on his mouth as he tangled his index finger in the thick stripes of violet weaved through her hair.

"Thank you for trusting them," he whispered in her mind.

"Someone once said I needed to trust more."

His smile widened into a stunning grin, making his eyes blaze in the darkness of the tunnel. *"Sounds like awesome advice. Your angel is a keeper."*

"Who said anything about my angel?" She bit the inside of her cheek, trying to contain her grin.

River's hand slipped to her jaw, his thumb stroking her cheekbone as his eyes dipped to her mouth. Those flutters in her heart morphed into a drum solo as her breath quickened and she found herself swaying closer, needing more. More heat, more of his touch. More connection.

"Can you two stop eye-fucking each other, so we can search the tunnels?"

CHAPTER 27

With Raine and Slater in tow, Ebony led them through the extensive tunnel network, lit every thirty feet or so with a single lantern. Enough light not to throw the tunnel into complete darkness, but not enough to spot the end.

Or the hidden gateway.

Magic rippled across his skin, making him pause. Shit. He'd totally missed the gateway. Had it transported them somewhere? Unconcerned, the others continued as though the magic hadn't fazed them, while he quickly assessed his new surroundings. Still in a tunnel given the damp, stale air. But where?

Around another corner, the tunnel opened to an expansive chamber, with several paths leading in different directions. As though this were the central hub for people to congregate.

Weird place but who was he to judge?

Ebony paused inside the chamber and peered around,

so he did too. Smooth grayish stone replaced the compacted dirt walls of the tunnel, the smell a lot cleaner and more pleasant given the non-existent windows. Positioned in the center was a large stone dais covered in what looked suspiciously like dried blood. Grimacing, he brushed his fingertip over one of the stains, feeling tingles of old magic react with his.

Raziel magic.

"That's where Asher tortured the Raziel before we arrived," Raine sneered.

Ick.

He shuddered. Turning away, he found Ebony across the chamber, and watched her inspect the area with a keen, assessing eye. Touching the stonework, trailing her hand along the walls, kicking loose dirt, clearly looking for something. Had she participated in the torture of that angel? Had her father forced her? Threatened her? Was she an accomplice, someone who, in the heat of battle, did what she needed to, to survive? Trusted those who should have protected her. Unlike Hailee, the Guardian's hadn't rescued Ebony until Slater brought her back from Hell. He hadn't found her until recently. And for that, for what she'd endured before he knew her, he'd spend his remaining days making it up to her.

To ensure she never suffered again.

On many occasions, immortals had referred to him as a compassionate lover. Yet, that didn't save his soulmate when she needed him most.

As though sensing his thoughts, Ebony glanced over her shoulder at him. And for the first time since they'd met, time seemed to halt. Air whooshed from his lungs. Her eyes, rimmed with crimson, captured him, knocked over the barriers to her soul and welcomed him. Drew him closer until he slipped into her orbit.

A feeling he'd never tire of.

Blinking, he regained his composure. "Did you find anything?"

He briefly felt the familiar tingle in his mind as Ebony slipped in, but she retreated just as quickly.

"No. I don't think my father has been back here since..."

Since he tortured that Raziel.

He nodded, letting her know that he understood and didn't expect her to rehash the events. Changing the subject, he pointed to the nearest tunnel, similar in opening to the one they'd entered.

"Where do the other tunnels lead?" Slater asked from the far side of the dais.

Starting with the one closest to her, Ebony pointed to each of the tunnels. "This one leads to Hell. That one is a one-way gateway from the mortal realm to here. That one is a gateway from Hell, and those two," she motioned to the ones either side of the first tunnel, "I haven't been down those, so I'm not sure. My father only ever took me through the other ones."

He inched closer, peering down one of the unknown tunnels, noticing nothing different on the outside. Like the others, the tunnel began with an opening just wide enough for them to walk side by side. But this one, he'd have to duck his head.

Just beyond the entrance, the cave-like formation along the walls changed from the smooth stonework to compressed dirt, extending until darkness closed in. He stretched his hand to the threshold, sensing a slight temperature change, and woven magic crisscrossing between the walls, preventing him from reaching beyond the entrance.

A pit of despair cracked open in his mind, making his stomach roil.

He yanked his hand back, severing the connection with a gasp.

Something evil was in that tunnel and he suspected it had everything to do with Ebony's father.

Was Asher in there?

And what would happen if they tried to disarm the seal?

Heat billowed at his side as Ebony approached, and every cell in his soul reached for her. His hand flexed to touch her, even for a moment. To caress her soft skin. To hover so close to her lips that he inhaled her air.

He was no stranger to lust, to the throws of sweaty passion. He was also no stranger to wanting more. To yearning for connection. But the feelings racing inside him, the raw need driving him closer to her at every waking moment, were so much...more. Stronger, clearer. So primal it made every ounce of lust he'd ever felt before pale in comparison.

Now he understood why the other Guardians constantly sought out their bonded soulmates. The urge undeniable.

Right before he lost his restraint and reached for Ebony, she stepped toward the darkness.

He snagged her wrist to yank her backward. She spun at the same time, face planting in his chest.

In that split second, her scent slammed into him. The subtle coconut of her shampoo, the toasted vanilla smell of her skin, flooded his senses and before he stopped himself, he leaned closer, inhaling a lungful, his eyes fluttering closed—

"What the Hell?" Ebony shoved his chest, glaring up at him. "Why did you stop me? Let me go."

Bright crimson flashed in her eyes, but it didn't repel him. In fact, it made his blood heat knowing that he'd affected her emotions.

He peered over her head, down the unexplored tunnel, once more sensing danger. An uneasy sensation. Something was down there, and the flare of his magic warned him it wasn't good.

"You said you don't know where this tunnel leads." He loosened his hold on her wrist but not enough to let her go.

She huffed like a little dragon puffing smoke from her nose. "And how do you suppose we find out? Stand here and...wait?"

The corner of his lips kicked up at her snark. So many sides to her personality and he enjoyed uncovering each of them and rising to the challenge. "It's sealed with Fallen power."

"What?" She yanked her arm again and this time, he let her go.

"I felt it on my hand as I tried to push past the threshold. And I'm not taking unnecessary risks."

Admitting that he didn't want to risk her safety was probably overstepping the invisible boundary between them.

"Oh, and I suppose you call all the shots, do you?"

"For now. But that doesn't mean I—"

She shoved passed him. "I've just jumped from one controlling asshole to the next. Why don't I ever learn?"

Her words punched him in the gut. Instead of grabbing her, he held still. "Violet." He softened his tone, waiting until she turned around to face him. "If you know me, even a little bit, you know I'm nothing like your father. Or Blaine."

She rolled her eyes.

"In fact," he slowly moved closer. "I have no desire to control you. I only want to keep you safe."

That was probably a line where rolling her eyes would be warranted, but instead, something eerily familiar to vulnerability flashed across her face. There and gone in an instant, but he latched onto it.

"So, what? We just pretend we didn't find the biggest clue in case we get hurt?"

This time, when he moved closer, he didn't bother restraining the urge to tangle a strand of violet hair between his fingers. The smooth, silky locks tied knots in his stomach. As always, she seemed to soften to his touch. "No. But we need to be smart about this, not just dive headfirst into a tunnel full of dark magic."

"For fuck's sake," Raine grouched, now also staring down the entrance. "Cleanse the darkness so we don't have to listen to your love spat any longer."

River stiffened.

He was afraid of this. When Raine and Slater caught them outside the tunnels, he suspected something like this would happen. That, now that he'd used his magic in the mortal realm, his sister would rely on it. But how could she rely on magic that didn't work? He couldn't cleanse it. Heavens, he barely uncast the spell surrounding Ebony's cell without passing out. Slowly, over the past few weeks, ever since he started using his magic to heal Jemma, the inky darkness had affected him more and more.

His power no longer cleansed darkness. It...consumed it. And if he continued, soon it would completely poison his...

He could no longer ignore the issue. Nor the signs that had crept up on him over the past few weeks. At first, he thought he was invincible given he was an angel. The fact that, to his knowledge, this had never happened before because angelic souls resided safely in the Heavens. But now...

Now, he had no choice but to accept the possibility.

"No," he whispered.

"No?" Ebony frowned at him. "Why the hell not?"

River flinched at her tone, but he couldn't look at her. She'd confessed a fear of dying alone, of being abandoned. Telling her the truth would devastate her. It would destroy the trust he had tried so hard to build. He needed more time.

When Ebony's eyes narrowed, he slammed his mental walls in place to prevent her from entering his mind, which made him feel a thousand times worse. She'd began to use their mental connection more frequently, and he fucking loved it. Now, he'd broken that too.

And that stung.

Muscles in his jaw flexed, as he stared at Raine, who also hammered against his mental walls. If he wouldn't let Ebony in, he sure as the Heavens wouldn't let anyone else in.

Just as Ebony slipped her hand from his, Raine yelled in frustration. "Why the hell are you blocking me?"

"Don't push this," River said, his voice so deep it was almost a growl. Gone was the fun-loving persona he'd let everyone see. Replaced with a deadly angel balancing on a dangerous slope.

Still facing off with Raine, he snatched Ebony's hand back, not allowing any distance between them. Not allowing her to retreat even though he should.

Moving into his line of sight, blocking the others out, Ebony cupped his cheek and gently lowered his head until he was eye level with her. "It's okay. You don't have to tell anyone why. We'll find another way."

For the Heavens, he wanted to cleanse the magic from the tunnel entrance for her. But more than that, he didn't want to disappoint her. He didn't want to lose her. "I can't," he whispered, speaking only to her.

"Bullshit," Raine interrupted, once again having no concept of boundaries. "You've been cleansing Jemma for more than a month now. That's what you do. It's your power. You can cleanse any darkness."

Ice tiptoed down his spine one vertebrae at a time. He *should* be able to cleanse the entrance. Yet, each time he summoned his power, it weakened him. Each time he used his power to cleanse, it stole his light. It drained him.

His eyes were paler. His skin colder.

He wasn't choosing to become a Fallen. To embrace the dark side instead of the remaining light pulsing in his soul. By the end of this, his soul wouldn't exist. The poison would have withered it away to nothing. Heavens, he never thought stripping an angel's life was even possible.

But here he was.

Finally, he'd found a soulmate, someone who chose him, someone who trusted him with their secrets. But he was damaged long before Ebony came along.

His gaze snapped to Raine. "I can't. After you saved Slater, my power broke."

Silence.

Deafening silence.

So silent that if he strained, he'd hear the ghosts of Lafayette cemetery roaming the grounds beyond the tunnels. He'd hear Ebony's frantic pulse, the heavy thump of her heart.

Broke.

Every day, he felt his soul slip away. Because he'd defied Fate? Because Raine had twisted his magic when she healed Slater? Because he'd strived to become someone he wasn't destined to be? Because he'd wanted to save a friend? Regardless of the reason, soon he would become just like the others. A shell of his former self.

There was nothing he could do about it.

Realization dawned on Ebony's face as she sucked in a breath. He shook his head, almost begging her not to confirm it. To forget he'd said it. To pretend they'd never had the conversation.

"No," she whispered, placing her palm on his chest, over his racing pulse.

"What do you mean it...broke?" Raine grumbled, her heavy footfalls rounding to Ebony's side. "You've been using it. I've seen you. Your power isn't broken. The mortal is still alive."

The torment in Ebony's eyes almost buckled his knees.

"No. It can't be," she said louder this time, more forcefully. Maybe in case she'd misunderstood, and he felt the need to correct her.

But she hadn't misunderstood. She hadn't misheard.

"River, answer me." Raine now stood beside them.

Ebony curled the tips of her fingers in River's shirt, over his heart. As though she had the ability to transfer his burden to herself.

His heart thumped against her palm as he peered down in her beautiful crimson eyes. "I'm sorry," he whispered.

Sorrow muted the flashes of crimson, tearing open his veins.

"If you don't tell me what the fuck is going on, I'm going to start throwing Kiel. At your head. And I never miss."

One beat. Two.

On the third, River twisted to face his sister. "When you healed Slater, my power twisted, became the opposite of what it was. Jemma is alive, but not because I'm cleansing the darkness inside her. Because I'm...absorbing it. The poison."

Saying it out loud made his eyes sting.

Ebony lifted their joined palms to place a gentle kiss on the back of River's hand, sending him silent reassurance. But he couldn't accept it. She'd need all his strength, and he wouldn't be selfish at a time like this.

Raine's eyes widened. "If you absorb the poison it will dissolve your soul. It will destroy it. You'll become..."

He steadied his voice, accepting the gravity of the situation. "A Devoid."

Chapter 28

The second River materialized beside her, she yanked her hand from his and bolted toward the front door of the Guardian house. River quickened his steps to keep up. Not that she cared. Why had she even come back here? Why hadn't she misted far away from him?

Since he'd dropped that bombshell in the tunnel network, she'd hadn't been able to look at him let alone think. Had recoiled each time he'd reached for her.

His power absorbed darkness. The angel who'd befriended her. The one who had shown her kindness and tenderness, who'd demanded Raine show her respect. The angel she'd fallen for, was becoming a Devoid.

Just when she'd let someone in, had depended on someone else, that same person would abandon her when his soul withered away to nothing.

She shoved open the front door, her mood darkening with each stomp of her feet.

Rounding the corner, she stormed toward the stairs to the basement, back to her cell. What was the point in talking to River when he would eventually leave?

He snagged her arm.

She spun, hissing at him like a wild animal. "Let me go."

"You're not going back to the cell."

She grunted, yanking her arm, which only made him tighten his grip a second before he bent and scooped her up, tossing her over his shoulder.

"Put me down."

Ebony unleashed her fists on his back, but it did nothing to slow his ascent upstairs to the second floor, where he briefly paused to unlock a door, before entering and slamming it closed behind them. Once inside, he lowered her feet to the floor to face him.

Air punched from her lungs as she zeroed in on his irises, challenging him to fight her on this. To let her go. To...tell her it was all a lie. A joke. His soul dissolving wasn't really happening.

"Why?" River softened his tone, his strong hands resting on her hips. "Why do you want me to let you go, Violet? So, you can go back to hiding in a cell? So, you can go back to avoiding interactions and confrontations? So, you can avoid...me?"

Those same eyes, the ones she'd dreamed of long before she knew this angel existed, peered into hers and the light sheen across them nearly buckled her knees. This casual, fun-loving angel had earned her trust with his kind and nurturing approach, which had claimed a piece of her heart.

Regardless of whether she believed in soulmates, or that they were destined for one another long before she was even born, she felt it. Felt it in his touch. In his words. In his unwavering commitment to visit and care for her.

To free her.

And now he'd...destroy it all.

As tears threatened, she turned to leave, but River pulled her against his chest. His free hand brushed down the side of her face, tucking beneath her chin to lift it slightly. No one would ever make her feel so protected.

"Let me go, River. Please."

He kissed her forehead, completely ignoring her request. "This is your room now. Our room. Not that cell. You're never going back there."

"Your room?" His hands fell to her hips when she stepped back. "You're kidding me, right? Why would I share a room with you?"

He flinched. "Because I will no longer allow you to be caged in the basement."

"Because I'm your soulmate? That you neglected to mention to me." Her voice rose as she wriggled from his grasp. "Why bother when you'll eventually abandon me like everyone else? Another important piece of information you withheld."

"Abandon you?" River's expression softened as he drifted closer. "I would never. I *will* never."

She scoffed. "As if you have a choice. Not if what you said is true. Not if destroying an angel's soul is possible."

Panic clawed her chest, she scanned the room for another exit, trying to control the raging emotions making her eyes sting.

"You...care about me."

She froze, staring at an abstract painting on the wall. A mess of deep, somber colors tangled together like her heart. Remaining silent, she sucked in a sharp breath when River moved behind her, his heat radiating down her spine and wrapping around her waist.

His mouth hovered by her ear, raising goosebumps along her arms. "Don't worry my little violet, your secret is safe with me."

"Is this some kind of joke to you?" She spun in his arms. "Because it's not funny."

He brushed the back of his hand along her jaw, staring into her eyes. "Nothing about this is funny for me."

Invisible bands squeezed her chest, compressing the air in her lungs until she could barely breathe. How could his voice sound so sincere? So, defeated yet determined at the same time? She'd never encountered a Devoid whose soul miraculously rejuvenated, nor had she ever heard of an angel turning into a Devoid. In her limited immortality, she'd also never encountered an angel with the ability to cleanse darkness. Why hadn't she learned more? Sucked up every piece of information available to her? If no other angel cleansed, how could River survive this?

Who would save him?

"Besides," he whispered, his mouth lowering, hovering an inch from hers. "How could I possibly leave this realm before we've even kissed properly."

A half scoff, half laugh cut through the tension in the air between their mouths. How could River talk of kissing at a time like this?

His eyes roamed her face, darkening. "After all the time we've spent together, the Hawaiian shirts you've enjoyed me wearing, the Maui themed treats I brought you, you still haven't kissed me properly."

Her heart fluttered like crazy. "*I* haven't kissed you properly?"

Slowly, he shook his head. "No, you haven't. And I've been here waiting, Violet."

Breath caught in her throat, she searched his eyes for a

promise. A vow that if she kissed him, he wouldn't leave her, his soul wouldn't die. That he made it all up. That she wouldn't lose someone she'd only just come to...like. Really like. But the signs, the shadows beneath his eyes and the weariness in his voice, were right in front of her. She couldn't ignore them any longer.

River couldn't make those promises, he couldn't guarantee her forever. Was now enough? Not forever, not years, but right now. Right in this moment. A tiny voice in her head wondered if she kissed him would he fight harder to find a cure? To survive?

"And...if I kiss you properly now, you'll..."

His thumb trailed along her bottom lip, pressing slightly harder at the edges. "Enjoy every blissful second."

The ball was in her court because he was right earlier. She did care for him. Maybe this was her punishment for pretending not to care about anyone or anything, or maybe this was always her destiny—to find someone who cared for her, who put her first, and then lose them just as quickly.

If that were the case, why waste another minute? Why cower from the fear of losing him? To save herself from heartbreak? Fine. But she'd never believed in happily ever after anyway. Why bother to start now?

As a smile curled at the corner of River's mouth, she lifted on her toes and pressed her lips to his. White hot power shot through her middle, fusing their mouths together. A heady rush of lust weaved down her spine, sending spiderwebs of heat through her blood, through every fiber of her body until she gasped.

The second her brain caught up, and she considered the implications of kissing this angel again, it was too late. River stole control with a demanding kiss. Claiming her, consuming her. Devouring her.

What she'd meant as a chaste peck, an expression of gratitude, died the moment his fingers tangled in her hair, holding her mouth to his. She didn't pull away, didn't stop. Instead, she fisted his shirt and held on for dear life.

River...moaned.

Fucking moaned. And her mind dived headfirst into the frenzied water surrounding them.

What began softly, quickly turned desperate. His hands glided down her neck to cradle her face, tilting it slightly, gaining better access. With another gasp, her lips parted, and he didn't waste time slipping his tongue inside, deepening their kiss.

Damn Fate for creating a soulmate bond that was destined to fail, destined for heartbreak. Damn anyone who tried to come between them.

Ripples of pleasure pulsed in her blood, sweeping through her body from the crown of her head all the way to the tips of her toes. Over and over, she succumbed to the bliss. The tragedy of their circumstances, the unfairness of it all. But when River's mind slammed through her mental walls, demolishing every brick with a single word, she succumbed to the passion.

"Mine."

No one had ever said that to her. Never inferred it or claimed it.

To be fair, she'd been his since the first time he'd ambushed her dream, appearing in the abandoned warehouse of her mind with his ridiculous shirt and endless supply of candy. She'd been his since the second he'd protected her when fire had erupted in the warehouse and he'd...saved her.

And for now...that was enough.

As though he'd read her thoughts, he tightened his hold

on her face, deepening their kiss even further. If this was their only kiss, the only one she'd have the pleasure of enjoying, then she'd damn well make the most of it.

But before they got carried away and clothes came off, River brought things to a dizzying halt. Their panting breaths collided between their mouths, and she blinked a few times as the world drifted back into focus.

"Right." River's heart pounded against her palm. "Now that's settled, let's get ready for bed."

Leaving her standing there stunned, he trotted to a dresser, pulling out a shirt and pair of sweatpants for her. "It's been a long day, I'm beat."

She eyed the clothes as though he'd drawn a weapon. "You can't avoid talking about this. It won't go away. We need to figure out how to reverse the damage."

"I know." He passed her the clothes before unlacing his boots and tossing them by the door. "But let's table it for later. Which side of the bed do you prefer?"

"Hang on. You expect me to...sleep in your bed?"

He frowned. "Why not?"

"I suppose you're going to do the gentlemanly thing and sleep on the floor?"

"Nope." His shirt came off as he headed into the adjoining bathroom gifting her with a downright sinful view of his tanned, sculpted back. "It's my bed and I'm partial to thousand thread count sheets. Besides, it's big enough to share."

Her heart wouldn't stop thrashing behind her ribs. Was she really going to sleep here in this angel's bed after he'd just devoured her mouth like that? What about the prison? What about the other Guardians' stupid rules? Her sister? What happened when they discovered River had freed her?

River exited the bathroom wearing a pair of plaid

pajama bottoms with no shirt, and she had to forcibly snap her jaw shut. *Holy hell.*

"I put a spare toothbrush on the vanity for you."

She opened her mouth to speak, but nothing came out. After one kiss, he'd rendered her brain to mush.

Needing a distraction, she washed her face in the bathroom, hoping to douse the flames in her blood, before changing and brushing her teeth. Reappearing in the bedroom, she found River settled beneath the covers on one side of the bed looking comfortable and relaxed, as though they'd shared a bed for years.

Was she really doing this?

He patted the empty space beside him. "Come on."

She'd accused him of being too trusting. What angel invited a Fallen into their bed? But she couldn't even summon a response. Because of all the angels in this realm, River was safe with her, and he knew it.

She'd shown him.

Gingerly slipping beneath the covers, she lay facing him. He reached backward to flip off the lights, plunging the room into darkness. It took until her eyes adjusted to find her voice.

"Why do you do this?" Her words were so soft she almost thought she'd spoken them in her mind.

"Do what?" River whispered just as quietly.

"Fight for me."

That clenching in her heart returned with a vengeance when he found her hand beneath the covers, entwining their fingers together.

"Because, Violet, I really, really, like you."

Chapter 29

EBONY

Early morning sunlight beamed through the windows, the soft golden rays stretching over the sheets tangled between Ebony's legs. For a few quiet moments, she laid there alone staring out the glass to the forest beyond. She'd had a dreamless sleep. No one had ambushed her dreams, no one had forced her to dreamwalk, and nightmares hadn't plagued her. She'd simply...slept.

Curled up in River's arms.

In his room. In his bed.

Would it be terrible to sleep here forever and ignore the difficult and awkward conversations she knew awaited beyond the bedroom door? Pretend, just for a moment, that Blaine wouldn't eventually come for her? Or that her father wouldn't, too? Pretend that River wasn't potentially the first angel to become a Devoid? If only for a few minutes more.

Rolling to the other side, she stifled the sting of disappointment at River's absence and instead focused on the folded clothes in his place, with a yellow and white plumeria on top. A smile grew, warming her cheeks, sending a rush through her blood knowing without a doubt that River had left them for her.

He'd thought of her.

Sitting up, she picked up the flower and found a note.

I hope I didn't snore! Come downstairs when you're ready. R

That earlier rush transformed into frantic, little butter-flies fluttering in her belly for three distinct reasons. One: the Guardians no longer had her locked in a cell, and clearly, she was free to move about the house. Two: River's ridiculous attempt at drawing a palm tree beside his initial. And three: *Because, Violet, I really, really like you.* The words he'd whispered to her last night before he'd fallen asleep. Would he remember them today? Had he expected her to reply? What would she have said had her brain not malfunctioned?

I really, really like you, too.

Now, that was an awakening.

With the sealed tunnel they'd discovered last night, on top of her growing feelings for a certain angel, it was no wonder her mind didn't have the energy to dream. It was a miracle she'd even fallen asleep.

No matter how nice the sheets were on River's bed though, she needed to face the day. Face River, and perhaps even the other Guardians. Her sister. Because one thing was for sure: she needed their help to figure out how to enter the tunnel. And if River trusted them, she would try to as well.

After changing, she peeked out the door and with no one in sight, found what looked like service stairs and tiptoed down in search of a kitchen. At the bottom, she slipped through the door and froze.

Hailee stood behind the counter, head down, concentrating on the contents inside the electric mixer. Before her sister noticed, Ebony turned to re-enter the stairwell. Then paused. Was this her life now? Avoiding every difficult conversation? Never facing her past, always running? River called her out on that last night when she'd fled toward the basement after she'd misted them back.

Because that was exactly what she had done. Instead of dealing with the news of being River's soulmate or the potential of his soul withering away, she ran. She wanted to hide. To flee. Yet, River had steadied her while he held her hand and listened.

He'd calmed her.

And then he'd kissed her. And hell, that kiss had been worth hanging around for.

Maybe that kiss was a turning point. A pivotal point where she had to change, something that forced her to face difficult situations instead of fleeing from them.

And maybe...she started now with Hailee.

Tentatively turning around, she placed one foot inside the kitchen. Hailee's head snapped up, her gaze darting to Ebony.

No turning back now.

The mixer stopped beating, throwing the kitchen into instant silence.

"Hi," Ebony said, giving her sister an awkward wave.

"Hi."

One more step inside the kitchen and the door latched behind her. "Are you baking again?"

"Yeah." Hailee glanced at the bowl, then back up. "I, um, started again when I...moved in with EJ."

Her heart thumped louder as Ebony took another step closer to the opposite side of the counter. "That's great. You were always so good at baking. Mom would be really proud."

Hailee's eyes misted before she once again peered in the bowl. More silence. Uncomfortable. Strangled.

For a second, she considered turning and running from the kitchen, bolting from this house, as pressure clamped her lungs, but she held her ground. Stood there, facing her sister.

Twin sister. Yet, they were nothing alike.

Hailee with all her goodness, golden hair and nurturing soul. The sister who had more than once dragged Ebony along to a birthday party when they were kids, or a trip to the mall, because no one had invited Ebony. The sister who'd given up school, her dreams of owning her own bakery, to care for their mother toward the end, working two jobs to make ends meet and put food on their table.

But who'd looked after Hailee?

Who'd made sure, in the end, Hailee lived her happily ever after with all the sprinkles and rainbows and book boyfriends she'd ever dreamed of?

After a deep inhale, Hailee lifted her head and motioned to the open bag of flour. "Add some in for me?"

A peace offering? A metaphorical olive branch? A truce in the war thrust between them without their consent. Or was this another moment where Hailee felt the compulsive need to keep everyone happy. To ease the tension. To make Ebony feel included.

Yes, yes, and probably yes.

But Ebony no longer wanted to play the loner part. She no longer wanted Hailee feeling sorry for her. For her sister to treat her as though she were about to break or as of late, some evil version of her past self. What she craved was something real. And for however long she had left before

Blaine called on their deal, she wanted that realness with Hailee.

With lighter steps, she rounded the counter to stand beside her sister, and sprinkle in the flour as the mixer restarted.

After a few seconds, Hailee spoke, "River came to see me early this morning."

Her pulse kicked up a notch at the mention of his name.

"He told me that he'd freed you from the cell and that you were now staying in his room. That you were free to come and go as you pleased. That you were his...soulmate. He didn't go into full detail, but he also said you'd protected me time and time again and that should count for something."

Ebony nodded, unsure how to feel. Angry that River had gone behind her back, or...honored that he'd sided with her?

Hailee paused the mixer again, her fingertips resting on the edges of the bowl. "I'm...sorry."

A silver charm on Hailee's bracelet caught in the harsh kitchen lights, snagging her attention. Although the dream-catcher charm was unique, the bracelet attached to it matched Ebony's before she'd modified it, given by their mother prior to them discovering its power or significance.

Guilt weaved through her stomach, twisting it into knots. "You don't need to—"

Hailee held up a hand, halting that train of thought. "No, let me get this out. Please."

After Ebony's slight nod, Hailee continued, "I'm sorry for not trusting your motivations. For not trusting *you*. I'm sorry I let the past couple of years cloud our history and what you mean to me. I'm sorry I wasn't there for you. You're my sister. My twin sister. I wanted you safe, and I was so scared of losing you, I went about protecting you the wrong way. You're the only family I have left, and I...let you down."

The rush of emotion was like a tidal wave drowning her with such fierceness it crushed her lungs.

Gripping the edge of the counter, she sucked in air. She wanted to correct Hailee, tell her sister that she hadn't let her down, but deep down, that was how she'd felt. Abandoned. First by her mom, for not preparing them for this world, but even before that, by their dad for deserting his family on his own selfish quest for revenge. By both their parents for not teaching her how to love, how to defend their home from the monsters. Because when those monsters had attacked, she'd stumbled through that on her own, learnt how to fight, learnt what really mattered, and protected that at all costs.

And after she'd lost her mother, when she'd fallen too deep, her own sister, like everyone else, had banished her.

Hailee had called her reckless, treating her actions as betrayal, and she'd never stopped to ask why.

River had hit that nerve when he'd vowed never to abandon her. Only now, the morning after that amazing kiss and the tenderness of their night together, did she truly understand how much he already knew her. How much he understood her. How much he saw the fears buried deep within her soul and vowed to vanquish them.

But he would too, intentionally or not, eventually leave.

Would she ever feel happy? Loved? Like she belonged?

Looking at her sister, the pressure began to ease. Maybe it wasn't about planning for a future or running from the past. Maybe life was about appreciating the present. Accepting the path Fate dealt her and trying her best.

Whatever that looked like.

She could still protect Hailee from Blaine and their father, and perhaps she could also have her sister back.

Reaching out, she pulled Hailee in for a long-overdue hug, sinking into her sister's embrace as she let go of the hurt and resentment she'd harbored for far too long. This was a fresh start. A new beginning. A chance to make amends.

Hailee eased back and smiled. "I've missed you so much. I've missed having my sister."

"Me, too." She gave Hailee's shoulders a squeeze.

"Maybe, when I put these cupcakes in the oven, we can sit down and chat. You can catch me up on what's happening. I'd like to help you however I can."

A balloon of warm air inflated in her chest. "I'd like that."

After another quick hug, Hailee resumed mixing while Ebony sprinkled in little dashes of flour. "What are you making?"

"Tropical cupcakes. River has been hounding me to make them all week."

Her smile returned and felt damn good after so many years without.

"Can you pour in that melted butter please?" Hailee lifted her gaze. "What are you smiling about?"

"Nothing." She shook her head and slowly poured the butter. "Where are the others? I didn't see anyone on my way to the kitchen."

Although, she did take the service stairs.

"River said he called an emergency meeting after he'd spoken with me. Maybe it's still going?"

The noise of the electric mixer hummed in the background as Hailee concentrated on mixing the batter. Several times, Ebony opened her mouth and closed it, wanting to talk about their father, of the possibility of him being involved in the Devoid attacks, but she couldn't bring herself to utter the words. Not when she didn't know for sure. Not when she didn't know all the facts.

And a part of her worried the conversation would only dampen the mood.

Everything could wait until they sat down to talk.

While mixing ingredients, with small talk at a minimum, her mind drifted back to happier times. Moments just like this, when their mom baked cakes and cookies when she and Hailee could barely see over the counter, all crammed into a box-like kitchen. Flashes of fond memories before their mother's nightmares began.

A beater covered in pale yellow cake mix appeared in her vision, with Hailee grinning behind it. "For old times?"

She snatched the beater and lifted it to her lips. "Abso-fucking-lutely."

The two of them giggled, licking the mixture off the beaters like children, and for the first time in a long time, the pressure eased, lifted off her chest, allowing the slightest relief.

Enough to know that maybe all hope wasn't lost.

The door to the kitchen swung open and River strode in, stealing what little air she'd managed to inhale. He was a sinful mixture of dark tanned skin and toned muscles, topped with a goofy attitude and colorful shirt that made her grin when she least expected it. His playful banter reminded her of times when she'd naively thought adventure hid beyond every door and that one day, she'd sink her toes into the hot sands of Maui.

"Hey, you," he drawled, rounding the counter to her side. "I've been looking for you."

His gaze dipped to the beater hovering in front of her mouth.

Before she realized what was about to happen, those emerald irises locked on her, and he leaned in to drag his tongue from the bottom of the beater, right to the tip.

"Mmm." His eyes hooded on a contented moan.

She opened her mouth, but nothing came out.

Did he just...

River grabbed the beater, his hand over hers, and twisted it to lick the other side. This time, the action unraveled something wicked inside her belly. How his tongue flattened and swept up the side of the beater in a slow, seductive motion, pointing slightly to dip in the corner, before he curled his tongue inward and sucked the end.

Holy mother of fucking Hell.

Without warning, heat flooded her core, followed by the urge to maul the guy right then and there in the kitchen. To beg for him to use that tongue on her.

Locked in an intense stare, she swayed forward, caught in his magnetic pull while she zeroed in on the smatter of yellow batter at the corner of his bottom lip. His mouth would taste like tropical flavors, mango and passionfruit and coconut and vanilla. Heavenly. So good that her knees wobbled at the thought of tasting him.

River's eyes darkened further, deep emerald pools calling to her, and she was fucking here for it. For every taste.

With his hand still over hers, River lowered the beater and leaned forward to—

Hailee cleared her throat.

Startled, they let go of the beater and it clanged to the floor between them.

Shit.

She'd totally forgotten they had an audience. So caught up in River, and the unmistakable electricity between them, she'd dropped her guard.

River recovered first, again showing no sign of awkwardness or guilt as he picked up the fallen beater then tossed it in the sink. "That mixture is exactly what I imagined. It's perfect, Hailee."

Having put the trays in the oven while Ebony had considered climbing River like a palm tree, Hailee set a nearby timer. "Wait until you try the cooked version with the icing I've created. EJ helped me replicate piña colada flavors. You're going to love it."

Her sister beamed with pride, and a stab of envy shot through her chest. Everything was so easy, so natural for Hailee. Would Ebony have had this life had she chosen a different path? Or was this Fate's plan all along?

"Well, I better make up an emergency on the other side of the realm, so Cole doesn't get his grabby hands on them." River slung an arm around Ebony's waist, pulling her close. "Come on, Ebony, the Guardians would like your input on the mysterious tunnel."

Chapter 30

RIVER

R iver couldn't stop staring at Ebony's lips. Surely by now, someone must've noticed. If not, they were bound to soon given he couldn't tear his eyes away. He wanted to devour her, to slip his tongue inside her mouth and see if she tasted as good as the still warm cupcakes Hailee just delivered to share with the Guardians. Including Cole, who hadn't fallen for River's fake emergency so the Azrael wouldn't hog the treats. Damn angel. At this rate, he'd have to wait another fortnight for Hailee to make the next batch.

He wanted to enjoy them in private, with only him and Ebony, so he could smear that delicious icing on her lips before he took her mouth.

Call him obsessed.

Rather than sit next to him at the long table though, Ebony had chosen to hover by the door, a few feet from Raine. Which had annoyed him at first. He'd wanted her to feel included, involved. After all, he'd met with everyone in the household before she'd woken so he could make sure they all understood how important she was. Not only to him, but to stopping the Devoid situation. And the look he gave them each time she spoke sent a strong message to be nice. Which they did.

The added bonus of Ebony standing by the door was it gave him the perfect opportunity to...admire her. Admire her eyes, all crimson-rimmed and fiery when she spoke about her father. Her long, slender legs when she crossed them to lean against the wall, and how the jeans he'd bought her made him want to sneak his fingertips through the holes at her thigh to brush her skin.

Oh yeah, obsessed all right.

Urges surged through him so strong it surprised him fireworks didn't explode from his body. He'd never felt this primal desire for someone. If he didn't get his hands on her soon, something might burst.

Most likely his zipper.

He snorted and all heads snapped his way.

"Something funny?" Raven asked.

Shit. He'd been in a fantasy bubble and had forgotten they were currently running over the last-minute preparations for tonight's tunnel raid. Maybe Hailee had slipped an aphrodisiac into those cupcakes. He wouldn't put it passed EJ to play a prank like that, but if that were the case, everyone would feel the effects, not just him.

"Nope." He bit the inside of his lip to stop smiling. "Sorry. My mind wandered a little there. I have a short attention span unless I'm, you know, fully invested. Which I absolutely am."

His gaze slid to Ebony's right as her cheeks bloomed with color. Her eyes widened. She'd look so pretty with her mouth open while he—

"Right, we're all set." Raven announced. "Cole, when does Evie need the blood?"

Wait a second. He jolted upright. "Blood?"

Aric frowned. "Were you paying attention at all?"

"Yes. Of course." They didn't need to know that River had focused all his attention on the single Fallen in the room rather than the discussion.

"Evie is going to use the blood of a descendant to amplify a spell, which will hopefully unlock the opening and let us inside," Cole responded.

"Ahh, that sounds risky, don't you think?" His gaze darted to Ebony and back to Cole. "Blood spells are dark magic."

Cole swallowed the last mouthful of his tenth cupcake, going by the wrappers piled in front of him. Hog. "Evie and I misted to the cave this morning. She's certain someone used blood magic to conceal the entrance, so it makes sense to use it when unlocking the spell."

He wanted to argue more, but Ebony straightened, stepping forward for the first time. "When do we head out?"

"The cemetery closes at ten. I suggest going after that to avoid running into mortals or ghost hunting enthusiasts," EJ added.

For a few more seconds, the Guardians confirmed meeting times and who would come along, while he tried to steady his restless legs. In less than twelve hours, he was about to run a mission for the Guardians. Sure, four others would join them, and he wasn't leading it, plus Evie needed to unlock the tunnel first, but he was going. He was actually going on a mission.

So, as the meeting concluded, why did it still feel like they'd overlooked him?

Reaching forward, he stole the last cupcake before

standing and pushing in his chair. He'd asked Hailee to make them as a surprise for Ebony, but he hadn't seen her try one. The least he could do was save his soulmate the last one. Hanging back, he waited for everyone to file out before jogging after Ebony, who'd turned in the opposite direction to their room.

Their room. That had a nice ring to it.

He quickened his steps, protecting the uneaten cupcake in a napkin. "Where are you going?"

Ebony dashed downstairs. "To my room."

"Uh, I thought we'd already agreed the basement isn't your room any longer."

Also, the word room was a bit of a stretch considering his sister had imprisoned Ebony in a Raziel cell which had taken him a considerable amount of power to break. All of which he didn't wish to repeat.

Ebony paused at the basement door, staring at the combination lock. "What's the code?"

He held back a step. "Not telling."

Her shoulders lifted and fell with a frustrated breath before her forehead dropped against the thick metal door with a thud.

The defeat in her movements urged him closer until his front brushed against her back and he wrapped his free arm around her middle holding her close.

She stiffened, only for a moment, before her body sank into his embrace. "Please unlock the door."

"Why?"

What could she possibly want in the armory that he didn't provide in their room upstairs?

"I just want quiet. It's been a morning. It's been a fucking decade."

Stepping back slightly, he twisted her to face him. "Is

my bed uncomfortable? Do you not like the view? Do I actually...snore? No one has ever complained of my snoring, but..." He grimaced. "Please tell me I don't snore."

What if no one had told him because it would embarrass him? This realm would end. He'd die.

Ebony shook her head, her gaze cast downward, pulling that tether once more in his chest.

With the crook of his finger, he lifted her chin. "Tell me."

"It's none of that. You don't snore."

Thank Fate. Relief had never felt so sweet. "Then what is it? Because I distinctly remember telling you that you no longer sleep down here. That my room was now our room. That you were never stepping back inside that cell."

She held his gaze for a long moment, until he almost considered lifting the cupcake between them just to make her smile.

"I...don't belong here."

A dagger speared his chest. Ebony felt like she didn't belong? With him or in the Guardian house? Or...both?

How had he screwed this all up so badly? All this time, he'd thought they were forming a bond, that he was chipping away at the walls she'd fortified around her heart so she could be herself with him. That he was letting her in. Yet, she still felt like she didn't belong?

He needed to do better. More.

Gently, he curled his finger around her pinkie and gave it a squeeze. "It looked like you were having fun with Hailee in the kitchen."

"I was." Her gaze darted to the stairwell before resting her head on the basement door. "Baking with Hailee almost felt like old times. Like nothing had come between us. I've...missed that."

His fingers drifted up her arm, over her shoulder, up the column of her neck, brushing her racing pulse. "Then what's wrong? Have I made you feel like this?"

"No. It's just..."

She shifted her feet, as though trying to sidestep him, but with the stairwell behind him and the armory door behind her, he'd effectively closed her in. And the sudden need to protect her surged through him.

He wanted to banish her fears. Obliterate them.

Since Ebony had waltzed into his dreams, he'd felt... seen. Not just Raine's brother or the eleventh wheel on movie nights. Really seen. And for the first time since Fate tasked him with ensuring Raine fulfilled her destiny, he felt as though he had a higher purpose. Something not linked to his powers or lack thereof. And not something linked to someone else's goals. And he'd do whatever it took, for as long as he had, to protect that.

"Surely you see it?" Ebony whispered. "The way the others looked at me. How Cole is no doubt plotting my death or counting down the days until someone does it for him because of my history with Evie. Everyone in that meeting was nice to me because you told them to be. No one wants me here, yet they also don't want to risk me leaving."

"Do you want to leave?" Even though the question made him physically ill, he had to ask.

Ebony's eyes squeezed closed before reopening. "I... don't know."

Not "no," so there was still hope.

Slowly, he lifted the cupcake and unwrapped the napkin, letting it flutter to the floor, before tilting the icing toward her lips. "I want you here. I don't want you to leave."

Her eyes softened as she reached for the cupcake, but

before she grabbed it, he smeared the icing on her bottom lip. Momentarily shocked, she jerked back. So he did it again.

"I couldn't concentrate during that entire meeting. All I kept imagining was this icing on your lips and how it would taste."

Colored coconut flakes, tinted to match a sunrise, dusted her mouth, and by Fate, he had the biggest urge to lick them off.

She beat him to it.

While staring into his eyes, her tongue slipped over her bottom lip, licking away the sugar in one slow sweep. "Tastes yum."

He groaned. "Do it again."

He dragged the cupcake over her lip again, only to watch her suck it off.

His blood roared to life, heading straight behind his zipper. The game, at the bottom of the basement stairs, continued as though they had all the time in the world. Him smearing the icing on her lips, her licking it off, until he wished he'd stolen the entire dozen.

Each slide of Ebony's tongue chipped away his restraint until he hummed with need.

When he smeared the last bits of icing on her lip, he couldn't hold back any longer. The cupcake fell from his hand as he took Ebony's mouth in a hot, messy kiss, sucking the icing off himself, reveling in her soft moans.

Fate, the noises she made when his sugar-coated tongue swept inside her mouth undid him. Passion, need, desire, collided together in a heady mixture that spun his head. Urgency roared through him, and he struggled to rein it in. To slow down. To savor this.

He wanted to worship her, to claim her, so bad, but he

had no right. How could he seal their soulmate connection when his soul was on the brink of dying? Only Fate knew how long he had left, and given his increased bouts of nausea, the end wasn't far.

But that didn't mean they couldn't enjoy their connection in other ways. Right now, though, he needed something, anything, to tide him over. To tide them over. To quell the chemistry between them so they could concentrate on the mission ahead. More than that though, he needed to prove to her that he wanted her here.

With him.

Still devouring her mouth, he dipped down to grip her ass and lift her legs around his waist, pressing her back against the door. Their kiss turned frenzied in a heartbeat, a boiling concoction of sugary lips, tongues and grabby hands. Her fingers tunneled through his hair, tugging on the longer strands, while he tightened the grip on her thighs, massaging and squeezing, holding her firmly against his hardness as she rolled her hips.

For the heavens, he'd never felt such fire scorch his veins in one rush. White and hot and he couldn't get enough.

Trailing his mouth down her neck, he nibbled and licked as Ebony's head fell back against the door with a low moan. He drifted down to her collar bone and the sweet spot at the junction of her neck and shoulder, never tasting anything so sweet. It almost sent him into a tailspin until he considered pinning her down and getting them both off right there in the stairwell.

But damn clarity burst through his subconscious, reminding him of what was at stake.

Slowing down, he lowered her feet back to the floor and rested his forehead on hers while their breathing steadied. "That was so hot."

Ebony wistfully sighed.

If only she knew what else he wanted to do.

When he drew back enough to see her face, her bright crimson eyes hazy with lust, her cheeks dusted with the prettiest shade of pink, a grin lifted at the corner of his mouth. "Hopefully, your head is clear enough to walk up those stairs and find your actual room, otherwise, I'll have to carry you."

That smile again. The secret one only for him.

"I want you here, Violet." He kissed her neck, jaw, cheek, mouth until she giggled. "Stay with me."

Chapter 31

Ebony

After their moment in the basement stairwell, Ebony gave up fighting River on the bedroom situation. His bed and those sheets he raved about were far more comfortable anyway. Hiding in his room meant she could curl up in the luxurious bedding and enjoy the quiet she craved.

If River ever stopped talking.

But if she never left this bedroom, she would never find her father. Despite the twist in her current situation, she couldn't afford to become complacent. She still needed to find Asher and, somehow, find a way to stop Blaine. Because that threat, the one Blaine placed on Hailee's life, was counting down in the background.

Dressed in what she would describe as Guardian fighting leathers, she opened the bedroom door and found River waiting in the hall.

His eyes lit up as they raked over her body. "You ready for this?"

"Sure." *Fake it until you make it.* "Why wouldn't I be?"

He frowned, but she tried not to read too much into it. What they did in the stairwell was exactly what he'd said. Hot. But how could he keep seducing her when he knew he'd eventually leave? His soul would dissolve into nothing if they didn't find a way to reverse it. And yet he never wanted to talk about it. Each time she had raised it this afternoon, trying to find a loophole, a solution, he'd shrugged it off. Sure, his casual and fun persona had attracted her at first, but sooner or later he'd have to face the truth.

And then what?

"Thanks for the clothes."

He searched her eyes for a moment longer, no doubt concerned about her sudden change of tone, but she slapped up those walls, blocking him. They had a job to do tonight.

"They look good on you." He took her hand, leading her down the stairs.

"You shouldn't say things like that."

"Why?"

"Because someone will hear."

He smirked back at her. "You didn't seem to mind someone hearing us in the stairwell."

She slapped his shoulder. "Shut up."

River only laughed.

Voices drifted up the stairs but at the bottom, when they rounded the corner into the living room where the Guardians congregated, the conversation ground to a halt. Her heart thumped faster, heavier, urging her to flee. More than one Guardian held a grudge against her or resented her for something in her past. The biggest from Evelina. Who right now, scowled at her from beside Cole.

River squeezed her hand. *"I've got you."*

Such simple words whispered in her mind, yet they somehow untangled a web of anxiety darkening her thoughts.

"Let's do this," was all Raine said before the Guardians filed out of the house.

Jogging ahead to talk with Raine, River exited before her, and she found herself swept to the back.

"I don't trust you," Evie hissed, coming up beside her.

Ebony ignored the angel and really couldn't care less if Evie trusted her.

"I'm here to help find your twisted father. But the second you step out of line, or hurt someone I care about, I'll come for you."

Hatred rolled off Evie in thick waves, tightening around Ebony's neck.

She didn't give the angel the satisfaction of a response. To the Guardians, she would always be an evil Fallen who'd betrayed her sister. It didn't matter that Ebony also nearly died in the attack against Zath, that she too risked her soul to aid Blaine. It didn't matter that her dreamwalking powers helped Blaine take down a Fallen far worse than anyone's comprehension.

No one remembered that.

Evie sneered before catching up to Cole, and once again, Ebony held back, taking a few seconds to steady her pulse.

River waited at the edge of the porch, the strong set of his jaw making it clear he'd heard every word. He didn't comment though. Instead, he slipped the cool hilt of a dagger into her hand.

A weapon.

"I had Raine make it for you."

Emotion clogged her throat. Once again, he proved that he trusted her. When everyone else pegged her as the enemy, he was on her side.

Flipping the dagger in her hand, she tested the weight and size, before strapping the matching sheath to her thigh. "Thank you."

He nodded then took her hand and she misted them to the cemetery. Once their feet touched the ground, she strode toward the crypt but stumbled. Her vision waivered, flashing between the dark, empty cemetery and a similarly isolated forest. Catching her balance, she blinked a few times as her surroundings blurred before coming into focus. The familiar rush of magic flowed through her veins, crackling along her skin.

A dreamwalk.

She'd stumbled into a fucking dreamwalk.

Before Ebony had a chance to switch gears and gain control, Blaine sauntered from between the trees. Fire flickered from the crown upon his head, licking the air in all directions, reminding her of flaming snakes.

Discretely, she touched the blade at her thigh, relieved to find it carried into the dreamwalk. It wouldn't hurt Blaine, but it would sever the dream connection if things went haywire.

"Hello, love," Blaine said, crossing the clearing to stand in front of her. "I hope I'm not interrupting."

Every fiber in her body screamed to run. To stab Blaine in the chest and release his hold on the dream. Instead, she held deathly still as he slowly circled her. "I thought you would have contacted me by now. It's been some time since we had our last chat. What is the benefit of being the king of Hell if I need to run my own errands?"

"Why don't you just torture me for information rather than—"

His hand shot forward, but it wasn't his fingers that clenched around her throat, it was hellfire. Pain ripped through her throat, stealing the scream building inside her.

"I expect better manners from you, considering I have spared your soul on numerous occasions."

The hellfire tightened. The scent of burning flesh made her eyes water. Could she die like this? Could Blaine's power sever her head in a dreamwalk?

An image of River appeared in her mind, making her heart sink. He trusted her enough to fight for her, to stand up to the Guardians and defend her, and here she was cowering in the face of death.

She was a fucking survivor.

Closing her eyes, she fought against Blaine's hold on the dream, summoning her own power to wobble the landscape. Not enough to change it and gain control, but enough to distract Blaine.

The flames vanished.

She was torn between two worlds. Earlier today, she had been honest with River when she'd admitted feeling like she didn't belong. Yet, he refused to see it. As his soul withered away, he expected her to play happy families with him, with Hailee, when the reality of their situation was far from happy. Long ago, she'd chosen to protect her sister.Now wasn't the time to forget that. Because one thing she knew with absolute certainty: Blaine never lied. He never gave empty threats. Everything he did served his own path.

Blaine wandered the clearing, tiny puffs of smoke billowed from a tree trunk as he brushed his fingers over the bark. "I seem to remember you agreeing to tell me of the

Guardian's plans, and yet, I have heard nothing." He moved to the next tree. "Has your dreamwalking ability failed you as of late?"

Quite the opposite. Lately, she'd found it easier to enter a dreamscape and lock onto her intended angel. "No."

He paused, the firelight from his crown flickering in the black abyss of his pupils. "I may have an endless supply of patience, but even I am becoming weary of this game."

Game. Funny how she considered it more akin to a death match.

"What do you want me to tell you? The Guardians don't let me in on their secret meetings."

Until now.

As he drifted closer, she reinforced her mental walls. With Blaine's increased power, she had no idea how boundless his abilities had become. Without the restrictions Fate had imposed on Zath, Blaine's power was likely infinite.

The entire realm was in danger.

"What's your plan, Blaine? Why do you need to know what the Guardians are doing when you're the king of Hell? You're Raven's brother. He'll never try to harm you."

Blaine resumed his meandering. "They are pivotal in my quest to remind her of what she destroyed. To make her feel it."

Her heart stilled. Did Blaine intend on hurting the Guardians to have his revenge? And...River?

"Oh, do not look so shocked, love. Fate is well aware of my intentions. That is, until I—"

"Violet?"

River's voice cracked through the hazy dreamscape, making the landscape ripple.

Blaine narrowed his eyes. "What a revelation. An angel,

a Guardian even, interrupting your dreamwalk. How... interesting."

She had to end this before Blaine put the pieces together. Then, not only Hailee would be in danger.

"The Guardians are also searching for Asher," she blurted out, hoping to distract Blaine.

"Why?"

"They're trying to stop the Devoid situation in the mortal realm."

Bile rose in her throat at the confession. But telling Blaine snippets of information wouldn't jeopardize the Guardians. It also wouldn't put them in more danger. And hopefully, it would keep him off her back for a little longer so she could somehow find her father first.

The dreamscape wobbled again, and a familiar tug edged her toward consciousness. River. She had to protect him. Inhaling a deep breath, she projected her own power to stabilize the dream, blocking him out. If River somehow entered, Blaine would discover their connection.

Blaine edged closer. "Where is he?"

"I don't know."

"Ebony?" River's voice boomed in the distance, barreling through her walls.

She fueled the dream with more and more power until her limbs trembled.

Blaine flipped the collar of his worn leather jacket. "Our catch up is coming to an end and you've given me no new information."

Yay her.

"Oh, wait. Yes, you did." He leaned in, flames alight in his irises. "It also seems not only your sister is important to you."

With a flick of Blaine's hand, the dream collapsed. The

landscape vanished so quickly she stumbled forward. Strong arms shot around her middle right before she hit the gravel.

"Ebony. What the hell just happened?"

River. The concern in his voice clenched her chest. Slowly, she straightened, and River twisted her to face him.

"What in the Heavens happened?"

She took a few deep breaths to steady her racing heart. "It's nothing. Sometimes that happens."

She couldn't tell him about Blaine, at least not yet. He'd only try to protect her more, which would put him in Blaine's path.

"Your eyes turned all...flaming, and when you started trembling, I freaked the fuck out." His hands touched her face, her shoulders, her arms. "Are you okay?"

She shooed away his concern with a laugh. "Yes. I'm fine. It happens more often than you think."

Instead of calling her bullshit, he yanked her in for a hug. "Thank Fate."

That torniquet around her heart tightened. How long could she do this? How long could she maintain this façade? The longer she played both sides, the more dangerous it became for everyone involved.

She shook off the after-effects of the dreamwalk and placed her hand over River's. "I'm okay. Now, let's catch up to the others. They're probably wondering where we are."

CHAPTER 32

RIVER

Ebony was hiding something from him. Was she right when she'd accused him of being too trusting? Surely, if there was one immortal in this realm he could trust, it would be Ebony. Right? When he'd seen the blank look on her face, flames alight in her irises, he'd freaked out. Yep. Totally freaked out. Knowing she was a Fallen was one thing, but seeing her eyes flip like that, like something had possessed her, had made him want to torture Asher for thrusting his daughter into the Fallen world.

Before he called for help, she'd startled back into focus. Just like her panic-stricken-self had jolted awake after the dream where the warehouse burned down. If she'd dreamwalked, why didn't she say so? And while he was on that crazy flight, who had the power to pull her into a dream?

Why keep it a secret?

As though reading his thoughts, Ebony tapped his cheek. "Stop worrying. Let's get this over with."

Easier said than done.

At the entrance to the spelled tunnel, Ebony held out her hand, and he shuddered as Evie sliced a thin cut across Ebony's palm, twisting it to direct the flow of blood onto Evie's waiting hand. When the first drop connected, wind whirled through the cave. A sudden gust whipped around Evie, encasing her in a tornado of power, her hair flying around her face in a tangled mess. Evie's head fell back, but he no longer watched. Instead, he lifted Ebony's hand and kissed the now sealed wound.

"Are you sure you're okay?

She smiled back at him, though it lacked her usual glow. "I'm sure."

The black symbols Evie had carved around the tunnel's entrance suddenly pulsed before a burst of magic exploded.

The wind ceased when Evie lowered her hands. "It's done."

"I love you so much," Cole announced right before he grabbed Evie's face and kissed the living hell out of her.

River swallowed the pinch of envy curling behind his ribs. Would he ever have the honor of openly declaring his love? Because the swell of his heart every time he thought of Ebony had progressed beyond like. For a while now, he'd imagined saying three words to her but worried how she'd react given his situation. Would he run out of time before he had the chance?

"Get a room," Raine muttered as she and Slater veered around the couple to peer down the tunnel.

Evie laughed, then summoned tiny bursts of light to hover above their heads as they all entered the tunnel single file—Raine and Slater taking the lead, and he and Ebony at the rear. Seconds in, the tunnel began a gentle decline and branched in two directions.

Slater spoke over his shoulder. "Raine and I will go left. Cole, you, Evie, River and Ebony take the right. Signal if you find anything."

Wait a minute. Wasn't this River's mission? Hadn't he brought the information to the Guardians and worked with Cole to devise a plan to unlock the tunnel? He loved his brother-in-soulmate and all, but he wanted to at least look capable in front of Ebony. To show her that he could protect her. That they were all on her side.

That he was a worthy soulmate.

"Wait up," he called out.

Raine paused, turning back. "Will you shut up? At this rate, you'll announce us to the whole of Hell."

"Sorry," he lowered his voice. "We should stick together. Isn't that the whole point of this mission? To combine our strength as a collective and use that to hunt down Asher?"

His sister stared at him. Correction: everyone stared at him. Had he spoken angelic?

A hint of crimson power slipped into the corners of his mind reassuring him, giving him the confidence to continue. "If Asher is creating Devoid down here in this creepy tunnel, we'll have a better chance of stopping him if we band together."

Raine cocked her brow and studied him for a long moment. "Which way do you propose we go?"

He turned to Ebony. "Can you sense anything? A connection? A hint of your father?"

The others moved aside as Ebony weaved to the front, peering down both tunnels. For a moment, he wondered if he had overstepped, if he was cut out to lead such an important mission. But this was what he wanted. His own mission. To prove to Raven and the others that he was capable. That he was one of them.

Ebony hitched her chin to the left. "I sense something dark that way. Not my father, more like...death."

Fireworks exploded in his chest. Not from sensing death, but from he and Ebony working together as a team.

Giving her hand a quick squeeze, he coaxed her forward.

The hovering torches, courtesy of Evie's magic, illuminated their path, and after what felt like hours of walking, they stumbled on symbols carved in the stone in a circular pattern. No idea what they meant, but he would bet his last packet of candy they linked to Asher and his band of cronies.

"There's magic in these runes," Evie murmured, running her hand along the stone, circling a marking that reminded him of swirling lines interconnecting at the center. Where had he seen that before? "I think I can unlock them like the spell at the entrance."

Cole's shadows intensified, curling around Evie's arms as her own power illuminated from her palm. Before leaving the Heavens, he'd never encountered Nuriel, only read of them in the many scrolls kept in Fate's personal library, while he waited for his sister to wake. From what he knew, Evie's bloodline reached far back into the history books yet only produced one Nuriel. Evie. The only one of her kind.

But that didn't stop him from blocking Evie's path when she pointed the dagger at Ebony. Sure, his soul was falling apart at the seams, but he would lay the good half on the line before he let Cole's soulmate harm Ebony.

"Relax, brother." One of Cole's swirly shadows tapped his shoulder. "Evie needs Ebony's blood for another spell."

"I knew that." Clearly, he'd forgotten that vital point. Also, how many times would Evie take blood? He turned to Ebony. "You don't have to do this if you don't want to. We can find another way. We don't even know if the runes connect to Devoid."

Ebony brushed his cheek again. "Stop worrying about me."

He held her gaze and mentally whispered, *"I'll always worry about you."*

Her eyes warmed for the briefest second before she stepped around him and offered her palm to Evie. He clenched his fist as the dagger sliced another clean cut and Evie lifted Ebony's hand to place it flat against the stone wall, in the center of the runes. "Hold it there."

Even with her back to him, he sensed Ebony's sudden nervousness in the quickening of her breath. She didn't have to do this alone. Edging closer, he moved to slide his arm around her waist when Evie shouted, "No!"

He recoiled.

"If you touch her, the spell could twist down a different path. This isn't a simple unlocking spell, River. We're attempting to *unveil* dark magic. Runes filled with it."

"Right. Got it." Holding his hands up, he retreated a step. *"I'm still here,"* he mentally said to Ebony.

As Evie began chanting, her power swirling like orange ribbons of light, he continued reassuring Ebony. *"You're doing great. I'm here. I've got you."*

When Evie grunted, Cole streamed more shadows to swirl with the Nuriel power until the stone surrounding Ebony's hand began to vibrate. It glowed, pulsing faster and faster, as Evie continued to chant, pouring more and more power into her spell. At the same time, the symbol beneath

Ebony's palm transformed, a dark inky substance seeping between her fingers.

Right as Evie's breaths labored, and her voice took on a harsher note, black smoke burst from the stone. Ebony fell forward, landing on her hands and knees.

Time seemed to halt. Evie's power vanished. Cole retracted his shadows. The air...stilled. Ebony stood, staring back from the other side of the wall.

"What the hell?" she muttered, peering at the arched entrance. "Did I fall through the stone?"

"That's why we couldn't see it," Evie said, more to herself. "It's a doorway through a solid object."

"Let's get moving." River stepped into action. "How long will it stay open?"

"I have no idea."

"We'll stay outside in case it suddenly begins to close." Slater motioned to himself and Raine.

Two out and four in seemed like good enough odds to him.

Stepping through the wall, he joined Ebony. "What is that smell?"

Turning in a circle, they found the source right as Cole and Evie entered.

Mortal blood.

Shelves carved into the dirt walls lined the chamber, a much smaller version than the entrance to the tunnels, stacked with various bottles and vials. Metal tables, strewn with a collection of hand tools. He gravitated closer and wished he hadn't. Covering his mouth, he pointed to the pieces of flesh, and buckets of blood collecting what looked like run off beneath the table.

He was going to puke.

"What the fuck are they?" Cole pointed down a narrow hallway to...

No. It couldn't be.

Dagger palmed, Ebony strode ahead before he could stop her.

He didn't want to follow. Instead, he wanted to turn around and pretend they'd never found this place of horrors. What kind of sicko operated an underground morgue with fresh mortal blood coating the floor? And the buckets.

He gagged again.

One thing was for sure, he needed to be strong for Ebony. If her father had anything to do with this, Asher was more deranged than they'd anticipated.

Forcing his feet forward, he caught up with Ebony, who stood frozen at the entrance to...cells. An entire row of them. And if he thought the stench behind him was bad, it had nothing on this.

"What in the heavens—"

Someone coughed, and he cursed when Ebony snapped into action. She rushed toward the sound and crouched by the opening to a cell. "Who put you here?"

A mortal male laid on the dirty floor, clearly malnour-ished, with visible outlines of his ribs, mattered hair, and sunken skin.

Sunken gray skin.

Panic tore through him. Was this his fate?

Ebony yanked on the metal bars while he scanned the remaining cells. Each one contained at least one mortal in a similar state: matted, dirty hair, exposed ribs, and sunken skin.

"It's a Devoid...farm."

Ebony gasped. "What did you say?"

"Whoever created this place is...creating Devoid."

Cole swore beside him, taking in the surroundings. "And I sense these have almost turned."

Ebony's face paled as she looked back at the male on the floor in front of her. "We have to help them."

Gripping Ebony's shoulders, he steered her away from the horror. "If your father created this place, we can't do anything that'll tip him off. If we help them, he'll know we've been here. He'll know we've found him."

"He'll already know. My blood opened the doorway, remember? We have to try harder. I need to try harder. I have to find him before..."

Something in the way she didn't finish that sentence set off alarm bells in his mind.

Before he could ask, Raine shouted, "Get your ass out now!"

Back in the main chamber, the opening in the doorway gradually darkened around the edges...closing.

After Cole and Evie rushed out, he spun to grab Ebony's hand.

She stepped out of reach.

"We need to go," he said, urgency in his voice as he pointed to the sealing doorway.

"I have to stop him." She shook her head, trembling as she took another step back. "This is what happens. People get killed. I can't protect everyone. It's not enough. I can't..."

He gravitated closer. If the doorway closed, locking them in, he had no way of knowing how long they'd be stuck here. "This is not your fault. You had nothing to do with this."

"He's sending a message...Blaine will..."

"Hurry the fuck up," Raine shouted again.

A quick glance at the doorway revealed their time was running out. Fast.

He kicked into gear. "Yell at me later, Violet."

Before the words were even out of his mouth, he dipped, wrapped his arms around Ebony's thighs and flipped her over his shoulder before bolting to the wall. At the opening, he all but tossed her at a waiting Raine, then dropped to his hands and knees to slide through at the last second. His boots slipped free right as the veil closed, leaving the stone wall whole again with intricate symbols in its wake.

Holy hotcakes. That was close.

Chapter 33

EBONY

Tremors wracked her body. Hot. Cold. Shards of ice sliced her ribs as constant shivers chattered her teeth. She'd been so naïve. So stupid. As reckless as Hailee always accused her of being. Only this time, nothing could stop the trajectory. Nothing would save them, and she'd put everyone at risk by once aligning herself with that monster.

This time, he'd gone too far.

Devoid. Innocent mortals, like her, caged and waiting. Counting down the hours before their soul withered and died, and they transformed into sickening soulless creatures. Puppets. What had they done to deserve that fate? And now River. An angelic soul as bright as his, potentially withering away just like those mortals. What had River done to deserve that? Nothing except live. Exist. Perhaps a small handful of those mortals in the cells had trusted her father.

Like her.

Because this had his name written all over it. The blood.

The mortal sacrifice. She'd seen it all before just not to this scale.

Acid rose in her throat.

Why? So her father could defeat Blaine? So he could seek revenge?

Was River an innocent bystander? Someone who tried to help a mortal but got caught in a vicious battle between two Fallen?

If Asher truly cared for Mom, or Hailee, or even on the slightest chance, cared for Ebony, he'd fight for them rather than continually putting them in harm's way. Continually using them as chess pieces in a sick game.

He wouldn't have killed their mom.

The tremors amplified and she squeezed her eyes shut as a piece of her mind splintered.

For once, she wished it would all end. That she could stop fighting and just breathe. Exist. Not continually live looking over her shoulder. To have someone want to spend their life with her. For there to be a life worth living. For someone to want her not as a weapon or a link to the Guardians or for her dreamwalking abilities.

For someone to want her for her.

Strong arms scooped her off the dirt and carried her. Voices argued, others shouted, never far behind, but only one penetrated her mind enough to make out the words.

"Just breathe, Violet. I've got you. Always. Just keep breathing."

River.

Her heart stretched and expanded, about to burst at the seams. River. When all the immortals in her life exploited her, bargained with her, forced her hand, he protected her. He held her, gifted her tokens, encouraged her dreams to flourish. Not the magic ones, the hopes and dreams she'd held so close to her heart she never imagined would ever come true.

Yet River sparked hope that somehow made her believe they would.

Light danced behind her closed lids, before darkness took over once more, but they never stopped moving. She didn't dare open them again. Images of that cave, of those helpless mortals, would haunt her until the end of her days.

Which, given the shit she'd tangled herself in, wasn't far off.

A chilly breeze whipped her cheeks before her body tingled and the familiar sense of misting overtook her cells, splitting them apart and fusing them back together. Then a more familiar scent, of pine and earth and a calming sensation seeped into her blood letting her know they'd made it back to the Guardian residence. God. How could this place feel so much like home when for most of the time they'd locked her in a cell.

River.

Urgent voices resumed behind them, but River continued forward, reassuring her in her mind, never severing his connection. Safe and secure in his arms, she almost believed someone had put her first.

When she briefly opened her eyes, as River stormed through the front door, her heart wept. The determined set of his jaw, the deep burrow in his dark brows. How when those emerald irises dipped to her face, the thundering of her heart stilled. For a single moment in time, the chaos surrounding them vanished. With quick and assured strides, he carried her upstairs like an avenging angel sent to rescue her from the pits of Hell, silencing the horror behind them when he stormed through the bedroom door and kicked it shut.

Quiet.

Calm.

Still in River's arms, she finally took a breath.

Tears pooled behind her lids when she thought about the conversations, the accusations she'd face from the Guardians now they'd discovered the contents of the tunnel. The looks that would accuse her of being involved. That she'd somehow known about her father's plans.

That she was a traitor.

Right now, she'd give anything to make it all disappear. For a force so strong to open and swallow the entire realm, leaving only those she loved. For River to whisk her away to Maui and lay with her on the hot, sandy beach watching the sun dip over a crystal blue ocean.

Her eyes fluttered open again at the sound of running water to find herself on River's knee beside the freestanding bath as he filled it.

After adjusting the taps, he twisted her in his arms, caressing her cheek with the back of his fingers. "I'm going to undress you, okay?"

Her heart swelled even further.

Too numb for words, she nodded.

With gentle hands, he lifted her to sit on the side of the tub and undressed her with so much care it made her eyes prick. Folding her clothes and placing them neatly on the vanity, he then undressed himself with far less restraint. If only she had the emotional energy to fully appreciate his male form. The beautiful dips and hard lines of his sculpted torso, the indentations at his hips, his strong muscular thighs, the smattering of dark hair over his chest. But all she focused on was his face. How instead of mirroring her spiral, the tenderness in his eyes gave her enough strength to inhale breath after breath until the tremors racking her body eased.

After scooping her up again, he lowered her into the steamy water and climbed in behind to nestle her between his legs. His comforting arms wrapped around her upper chest, holding tight as she continued to inhale and exhale. He didn't say anything. Not a single word. Just sat there, using his hand to sluice water over her body, the repetitive motion lulling her into contentment. At one point, he tilted her head back and washed her hair, combing his fingers through the strands until he unraveled every knot.

Just like her heart.

When the water cooled and her shivers returned, River lifted her from the tub and wrapped her in a heated towel, drying her before securing one around his waist, then led her into the bedroom.

At his bed, he tucked her beneath the covers and brushed a damp strand of hair off her forehead. "I'm going to go get you something to eat."

The tremors started again, clamping down on her chest, tightening her lungs. "Don't..."

"Shh. You're safe." The bed dipped as he sat beside her. "No one will hurt you here."

Safety wasn't a luxury she had anymore. If she'd ever had it. Sooner or later, Blaine would come for her. The naïve idea that she'd find her father first spiraled down the drain the second she saw how far he'd gone. Further than anyone had expected. It wouldn't take long for Blaine to stop Asher in the same way he'd ended Zath. Then, she'd lose her last bargaining chip. She couldn't hold either of them off forever. Suddenly, she felt like the splintered shard in the center of a wall of mirrors, ready to smash.

When River stood, a sob escaped her lips. "Don't... leave me."

In the end, everyone always did. Her dad, her mom, Hailee. River would too, eventually. But for a moment in time, she wished he'd stay. That he'd be with her.

Leaning down, he pressed a gentle kiss to her temple before he dropped his towel and climbed in behind her, wrapping her up in his arms to hold tight against his chest. The steady inhale and exhale of his breath slowed hers once more, floating her back to the surface.

Time and time again, he proved in actions rather than words. He protected her. That she was safe with him.

That he chose her.

As another tremor quaked her, River held her tighter, murmuring reassurance in her mind. She'd give anything to live in this bubble. To have more time with him. To grasp in her hands all the things she'd never known awaited her had she'd chosen a different path.

Before long, the warmth of River's bare chest, of his naked flesh against hers, eliminated the chill in her bones, shifting her thoughts to the angel behind her. How he'd taken care of her just now in the bath. How earlier he'd cradled her face in his hands and kissed her, as though he couldn't get enough. As though he was so hungry for her, he'd battle all her demons just for a taste. How he touched her at every opportunity from brief brushes of their skin to intentionally seeking her out for comfort. How even now, with his growing hardness pressed against her butt cheeks, he held back. Put her first.

He always put her first.

Even while she was locked in the cell, he brought her food, clothes, stupid Hawaiian shirts to make her laugh. He shared his favorite candy. Time and time again, he'd shared his secrets, his passions with her. Sudden clarity swept through her in a heady rush and instantly she craved more. Not more from him, more *with* him. She wanted to experience all of him. To kiss him, to touch him, to feel the sense of euphoria as he came apart. To witness undiluted hunger in his eyes as he sank deep inside her. To have him claim her until the stars aligned and exploded around them.

River adjusted his arm, slipping it lower to drape over her hips. Such a slight move yet it fired thousands of nerve endings over her heated flesh. With his chest flush against her back, she felt his breath quicken. The smallest shift confirming he'd sensed the change in her thoughts. Or maybe, she'd sensed him through the mystical bond that connected their souls. Either way, she wanted him to know. She wanted him to hear her most inner thoughts, the ones she couldn't formulate into words, the fears that haunted her, her long forgotten desires, so he knew all her secrets and continued to choose her.

His warm breath brushed over her exposed neck, sending tingles dancing over her limbs. "Violet..."

A warning? A plea? A gravelly temptation in the dark of the night? It didn't matter. He didn't need her words. He got her. He understood her in ways no one ever had. Despite their doomed fate, that would never change.

With an upward tilt of her chin, she offered him greater access to her neck, and he took it. Gently, his lips coasted along her exposed shoulder one kiss at a time. Heat bloomed in her blood, transforming her earlier panic into raw desire. She craved it all. The calmness he instilled in her mind, the rush he invoked in her body. She wanted to be selfish for once and put her needs first just like he always did.

She wanted to claim him for herself.

Placing her hand over his, she guided it down her stomach in the direction of her aching core.

"You should rest," he murmured by her ear, following with another kiss on her neck, shooting bolts of heat through her middle.

"I don't want to rest. I want to feel. I want to feel wanted and desired and chosen. I want you to strip away the horrors of tonight and replace it with something good. Something real." Still guiding his hand, they reached the junction between her legs and her back arched at that first whisper of his touch. "I want to feel you."

"I've ached for this, Violet. To make you fall apart beneath me."

Oh, god. Already their connection bordered on too much and they'd barely begun.

Untangling her fingers from his, she withdrew her hand, letting River explore at his own pace. First, his fingers trailed along the inside of her thigh as far as he could reach, before slowly travelling back up, cresting her sensitive hips, circling her belly. Again and again, he leisurely caressed her. Just when she couldn't take it any longer, River slipped a finger through her wetness, rolling over her clit, and she all but exploded with sensations. She'd discovered the entrance to the Heavens and hungered for the light.

As though he had all the time in the realm, River stroked her, building her higher and higher, as his other arm snaked beneath her side to knead her breast. His lips skimmed her shoulder, her neck, nipping and kissing as though he yearned to claim her, to mark her, as much as she did him.

When pinpricks of light danced before her eyes and she skipped toward the edge of release, River slipped a finger inside her.

"You're so beautiful," he growled beside her ear, adding another finger. "So ready for me."

His words, his voice, the way he somehow always knew what she needed, sent her grasping the release that danced just beyond her reach.

Gliding in and out with the same unhurried intensity, he brought her to the brink of madness. She rocked her hips, desperate for more. For release, for connection, for the cure to make her feel whole and loved. Once again, River anticipated her needs, lifting her leg to drape it over his to gain a better angle, before continuing.

She moaned. *"Oh, Hell."*

River would be the end of her, and she was fucking here for it.

"No, my Violet. This is the Heavens."

His fingers resumed their exploration, spreading her wetness, touching her, coaxing her back to the cliff, before slipping inside. The second he pressed his thumb on her clit, lights exploded before her eyes with a release so powerful it convulsed through her body, wringing her of every sensation.

Her heart exploded with a heavy beat as her core clenched and thrummed with energy, latching onto River's soul with a magical tether she could almost see dancing before her eyes.

Panting, she sank against River's chest as he withdrew his finger to lazily stroke her. "That," his lips coasted over her shoulder, "was the prettiest thing I've ever seen."

The hardness of his length nudged her ass, reminding her of its presence and the mere touch reignited her need.

"Violet..." His voice matched her desire, yet he still held back.

Thoughts of him inside her, of taking her, of careening

her to those heights with his cock, consumed her. His scent curled around her, mingling with her own in every breath she sucked in, and she couldn't seem to get enough. Once more, his fingers returned to her core, stroking and rolling, building and building the tension, the raw desire.

Reaching between their bodies, she brushed the head of his cock, making his hips jolt and his mouth lock onto her shoulder in a bite. "When I said I wanted you, angel, I meant *all* of you."

His following growl rumbled through her belly making it whimper.

"Doing this...It's forever. Eternal. I want it with you. The Heavens, I do."

Unease tempered her desire. "But..."

Dropping her leg, she twisted to lay on her side facing him.

He stroked her cheek and the hesitation in his eyes tugged her heart. "Right now, I can't guarantee you forever. Eventually, my soul...it will..."

The fact he still protected her, even from a future neither of them might have, made this more right. Fate never would have paved a path for this gorgeous angel, so full of life, to end up with a Fallen like her. But somewhere along the way, something shattered the equilibrium. In this moment, tonight, that neglected part of her craved for it to be true. For him to be hers. For her to mean more to someone other than a job, a hustle. A means to an end.

For him to want her.

"Take me, River." She draped her leg over his hip bringing their bodies that much closer. "Make me yours for however long we have."

His eyes flashed with a feral look. Wild, unhinged, an

emotion she'd never witnessed. She was his, long before they crossed paths, and now, they'd seal their destiny.

With a grunt, he rolled her over to straddle his hips where he lifted her slightly to nudge the head of his length at her entrance. Hell, the anticipation, knowing what was about to happen popped goosebumps along her heated flesh.

"You are mine, Violet," he growled as he edged inside, inch by inch, stretching and filling her, spreading a delicious wildfire over her limbs, through her blood, to her very soul. "You'll always be mine."

Too soon, she lost herself in the sensations, in the squeeze of his fingers on her waist, in the steady rock of his hips, in the sweet murmurs by her ear. For once, she opened herself to every feeling, every emotion clashing inside her, never holding it at bay. She allowed herself this freedom, this path, with this beautiful angel.

Tingles centered at her core when River quickened his thrusts, digging his fingers into the soft globes of her ass, rolling and rocking her hips. With her hands on the mattress on either side of his head, she reveled in how his irises darkened, how they locked on her and never once diverted.

"I've never felt safer than when I'm with you."

The thought exploded from her mind into his without restraint. If she thought River's eyes couldn't darken any more, she was wrong. Now they resembled the leafy ferns hidden deep within the forest.

"I'll always protect you," he replied before taking her mouth in a demanding kiss.

One hand moved up to her hip, while the other tangled in her hair, holding her head in place as he devoured her mouth. When her body erupted in heat and the rush of release barreled toward her, the emotion became too much, and she lowered her head in the crook of his neck.

In an instant, River rolled them once more, flipping her onto her back to nestle between her legs before gliding back inside her.

She closed her eyes as her chest squeezed, coming apart at the seams with the realization that by now, with the emotion bursting inside her, her eyes would've changed, showing their true colors. Reminding River exactly who she was.

A Fallen.

He cupped the side of her cheek, slowing his thrusts to a deep and intentional push and pull. "Don't hide from me, Ebony. Open your eyes."

She swallowed. How could she? How could she show him her eyes at a time like this? He'd despise her.

"I want you. Every part of your body and every part of your soul."

The words drifted through her mind as he leaned down to kiss her again. This kiss felt different to the others they'd shared. With the sweep of his tongue while he glided in and out, he branded her soul. Stamped his name on it for all eternity.

It should scare her. Instead, it...freed her.

When his thrusts deepened and her eyes fluttered open, she fell apart. Beneath him, with her heart safely in his hands, her soul ruptured, split, burst in an explosion of light until that same light captured every broken piece and stitched it back together. Her release came somewhere in the middle, clenching River inside her, wringing every last sensation. River peered down, and with three deeper, harder thrusts, careened off the edge of that cliff after her into the tangled waters below.

Her body sagged into the mattress and River wrapped her in his arms, tucking his head in the crook of her neck while their breaths steadied and returned to normal.

"That was..." She couldn't find the words. Magical? Earthshattering?

Terrifying?

River kissed her temple. "Destined."

Air punched from her lungs in one swoop. *Destined.* Nothing had ever felt destined, meant to be. That Fate had paved a path for Ebony that led to somewhere...good. Yet, curled up in River's arms, with sweat coating their heated flesh while his pulse thrummed in time with hers, she could no longer deny the obvious.

Fate had destined them for each other.

If only she'd destined them with forever.

CHAPTER 34

EBONY

Ebony jolted in the armchair when River burst through the door in a flurry of bright colors. "Get ready, Violet!" He tossed clothes on the bed before dashing to the adjoining bathroom. "We're taking a break from twisted Dad hunting."

Behind the closed door, he coughed and retched a few times before flushing the toilet.

"River?" She padded to the door, knocking before inching it open. "Are you okay?"

He stripped off his clothes and threw them in the hamper. "All good. Just a minor inconvenience. Nothing I do works and I hate the thought of failing at this mission." He turned on the shower, letting the steam fog up the glass. "Don't worry. Nothing can stop us from going to SubZero's annual beach party."

In the shower, he soaped and rinsed, and yes, she stood there openly gawking. The way he'd moved inside her body this morning, and every night for the past week, was nothing short of glorious. Her gaze roamed over his taut muscles, watching the water sluice over his flesh, slipping and falling in every groove and dip.

"Eyes up, Violet. You dozed all day. We don't have time for a repeat before we leave. Save it for after."

Not even caring that he'd caught her, she let her gaze gradually rise to meet his, where she paused on his eyes or more accurately, the dark shadows beneath them. How could she have forgotten about his soul, how it withered away because he ingested that mortal's darkness. Why was he still sick? If what she knew about soulmates was accurate, then shouldn't sealing their bond have healed him?

"Are you still cleansing the mortal?" She didn't mean to snap but couldn't stop the grit in her voice.

Why would he willingly choose to shorten his life?

His cheek twitched as he rinsed his hair. "Is that a hint of jealousy?"

She had never had a thing for throats, but River sure had a fucking delicious one she'd like to punch right about now.

"No." She pushed from the doorway to cross her arms. "Why are you still helping her when it's..."

Killing you.

The water shut off and River exited the shower to wrap a towel around his waist. He cupped her cheeks in his warm hands. "I'm only taking little bits to keep her alive. I won't let Jemma die before we find a cure."

"What about you?" Eyes wide, she shook her head. "You can't save her and yourself. Helping her poisons your soul and we have no idea if there's even a cure."

His thumbs stroked her cheeks before he kissed her forehead. "I'm fine. In fact, I feel awesome and I'm ready to party like a drunk coconut."

She tried to stay mad, but a snorted laugh burst from her lips. "A drunk coconut?"

"Yeah, you know, jiggling in palm trees." Using her shoulders, he turned her back to the bedroom and slapped her ass. "Now, hurry up or we'll miss the song request timeframe."

"What's that?"

"The DJ takes requests ten minutes before a set." He diverted to the dresser. "He never plays mine, but that won't stop me from trying. I am nothing if not persistent." He shoved on a pair of slim jeans. "Last time, he told me the patrons aren't from the last century and until I suggest something from this decade, I should go home."

River requesting songs from another DJ shouldn't make her jaw tighten. Yet, it did. More so that the DJ ridiculed River's requests. And now, she wanted to throat punch the DJ too.

She sank on the corner of the bed. "What song do you request?"

His eyes lit up like the sun and his excitement sent a bolt through her chest. "Not one song, songs. I've tried so many options, so many different varieties."

"Give me one, Maui."

It was cute to see him this animated, bouncing with excitement over a song choice. If she were honest, it made her miss DJing. Made her miss the simple days when she wasn't running from Fallen. When immortals hadn't torn her family apart.

A time she wished she'd known River.

"I'd take anything with a falsetto and decent amount of heartbreak. Oh! And a sexy guitar rift."

She chuckled. "You're a power ballad lover, huh?"

Why did that not surprise her?

His face exploded with delight, like when she'd given him the name for his Hawaiian shirts. "Power ballad." He nodded, saying the words to himself again. "Yeah, power ballads."

Lucky for him, she knew quite a few. Unlike other DJs her age, her style leaned more toward mixing hard rock songs with heavy beats that mortals belted out in the early hours of the morning. Ones that brought people together rather than isolated them. Many times, she sensed a gift with music, for choosing the right song for the right crowd, which was why her gigs sold out far in advance.

And right now, she knew the exact song for River.

Slipping on his canvas sneakers, he hitched his chin to the clothes thrown on the bed. "Come on, get ready!"

She eyed the outfit. "My usual club attire consists of a classic rock band T-shirt and ripped jeans. This is seriously against my style, angel."

He threw his head back and laughed.

When the battles ended, and one of them walked away with nothing, she'd miss this banter with him. How his emerald eyes brightened when she teased him, and how the slight lift at the corner of his lips told her just how much he liked it. But more than their banter, she'd miss...him.

"Wait." She peered down at the material. "You bought us matching Hawaiian shirts?"

The grin on his face was contagious. "Aren't they great?" He straightened the collar on his matching explosion of color. "This is the one time of the entire year everyone compliments my outfit, rather than makes fun of it."

Could he be any cuter? And since when did she want to kill everyone who said otherwise?

"Fine." She replaced her shirt with the one he'd given her. "But only because it has skeletons surfing on it."

While River tapped his foot, she finished getting ready. "Do the other Guardians go to this party?"

"Under duress. But I think EJ secretly loves it, except for the sand. He has an unholy grudge against sand."

She couldn't hold back the smile when another bolt of joyful energy swept through the newly secured link between her and River. Would it dull with time or forever be this vibrant?

Finished, she did a twirl for River. "How do I look?"

His eyes darkened as they moved over the length of her body and back up again. "Perfect."

Outside on the gravel drive, River gave her a rundown of who'd already left for the club and who would join them later.

"Hailee's not coming?" Although her sister and her still had a fair way to go before they mended the distance between them, she'd enjoyed these past few weeks of having Hailee back in her life. Of having their baking routine and quiet chats.

River motioned to the garage. "EJ likes to take Stella for a spin when we all head out. And Hailee was dropping cupcakes off at the store."

Yesterday, she had learned about the quaint bakery her sister owned in Summit Creek. A dream Hailee had had for most of her life.

River unfurled his wings, fanning them wide as he rolled his shoulders. "Let's fly tonight. I can't think of anything sexier than kissing you while we hover above the twinkling lights of town. I'm like obsessed with it. It's a newly unlocked kink I think."

Fly? Sure, she had wings she hardly ever used these

days, but now? In front of River? Did he not remember that her wings were...Fallen. Crimson instead of black, with poisonous talons capable of killing an angel. Surely, he forgot.

The thought of him seeing them, twisted her stomach into knots. He could overlook the change in eye color, but he couldn't avoid seeing huge crimson wings attached to her back.

Suddenly she wanted nothing more than to hide them. To tear them out and forever forget they existed.

If he didn't see them, he wouldn't remember, which meant they could continue pretending. Pretending that her father wasn't potentially responsible for creating Devoid, that she wasn't a Fallen. That River's soul wasn't withering away.

That they had a future.

If only for a little longer.

"Hey." River crooked a finger beneath her chin to lift it. "Have your wings not...healed. I'm a lover before a fighter, but even I would burn down Hell to avenge you."

Her heart clenched.

She could take the easy route and lie, but where would that end? Tomorrow, next week, next month, she'd be in the same position. Sooner or later, they'd have to face the truth.

Also, what was the point of planning that far ahead?

"It's okay. I can ask Willow if she can help rejuvenate them."

Fuck. After everything he had done for her, she couldn't lie. Not to him.

Swallowing, she looked away, but River wasn't having a second of it. He pinched her chin between his finger and thumb and turned her face back to him.

"I just..." She was a Fallen. Never had she even given a

shit what others thought, or how they reacted. But now, this damn angel made her feel things she never thought possible. Hopes and dreams she once thought were only destined for Hailee.

Looking him in the eye, she lifted her chin. "You haven't seen my wings. Maybe you've forgotten...my wings aren't like yours."

His gaze softened as he drifted closer, stroking the backs of his fingers along her cheeks. "I haven't forgotten. I was giving you time to show me when you were ready."

That damn heart of hers was at the breaking point.

"If you're not ready, it's okay. I now quite like the idea of flying you." A wicked grin curled on his mouth. "You know, with your legs wrapped around my waist."

She rolled her eyes but couldn't stop the laugh.

How did River always make her feel protected, so worshipped, even with only his words? Now she wanted to show him how much it meant to have him on her side.

"Alright, angel. You asked for it."

Stepping back, before she talked herself out of it, she willed her wings to unfurl. A sudden rush of adrenaline shot through her blood at the release, a buildup of tension from not having used them in what felt like forever. Why bother, when she could mist wherever she wanted in a split second? Plus, in the air, she became another target.

Lifting her gaze, she found River drinking her in, from the tip of one wing all the way to the other in a slow, perusal that made her belly tighten. His eyes hooded, just slightly letting her know her wings didn't scare him. They didn't repulse him.

They...turned him on.

She held still as he inched closer, his fingers gliding along the inside of her left wing, igniting a pulsing sensation through her blood. But it wasn't until he spoke, that her heart took flight.

"They are the most badass wings I've ever seen."

Not some cliché telling her she was beautiful or that her wings weren't that crimson. Nope, he stood in front of her, eyes smoldering, and described her wings as badass.

She couldn't hold back the smirk. "Badass, huh?"

"Oh, yeah." His fingers trailed over the top of the wing, up her spine to her neck where he gave it a squeeze. "They'd look fucking hot wrapped around me, just sayin'"

A laugh burst from her without warning and the grin on River's face undid her. All the times she'd run from one danger to the next, all the years she'd endured in Hell fighting to keep Hailee safe, being on the brink of death after taking down Zath had all been worth it to land here right now. With River. He understood her better than her own sister. Sure, they had things in common—they were both loyal to a fault, both would do whatever it took to protect those they loved. Their joy of music. Outside the Guardian mansion though, in the quiet of the night, the tether that pulsed between them now shone more vividly. It no longer simmered in the background waiting for her to acknowledge it. It barreled forward. It exploded with light and illuminated the path before her.

And all she saw was River.

The angel she'd fallen for over the past few months. Someone who, for the first time in her life, had put her first. What had felt in the beginning as a kindred spirit had morphed into something deeper. Something stronger.

And all she wanted to do was protect that feeling, protect their bond, at all costs.

Chapter 35

River

SubZero was lit. And the matching Hawaiian shirts he'd bought for Ebony and him were so epic. The little skeletons glowed beneath the colored strobe lights exactly as he'd imagined. Totally worth the express shipping. And despite the patches of muted color, curtesy of the darkness leeching from his pores, they were the best shirts in the entire club.

Music pumped through the speakers from the usual Friday night DJ, who he had a love hate relationship with. Before he'd met Ebony, he thought the mortal was good looking, but the DJ's refusal to play one single request lowered his attraction to below...well, zero. Sure, the guy had nice cheekbones and infectious energy, but nothing compared to Ebony's plump bottom lip or her voice when she begged for more each time he sank inside her. How the realm stopped spinning when she smiled.

And the fact the dude still hadn't played River's request, after more than three hours, made him touchy.

Tonight, he'd even chosen a more recent song, one released only twenty years ago that he thought the DJ would totally approve of. But nope.

Standing by the Guardians' table in the private sectioned-off area of the club, the only body his eyes sought was the female Fallen currently weaving through the crowd, heading to the traitorous DJ. Hopefully to give him a stern talking to. Although, more likely, Ebony was drawn to the booth. He loved her passion for it.

Almost as much as he loved her.

Her devotion to protect her sister, her endless resilience, her compassion. How her eyes lit crimson in the thralls of emotion. How this morning, after he'd taken her in the shower, they'd curled up in bed devouring a packet of their favorite candy.

He wanted to encase them in their own magical bubble for the rest of eternity.

As Ebony reached the DJ booth and waved for the mortal's attention, Aric bumped his shoulder.

"If you stare at her any harder, you'll incinerate her clothes, and that shit will get awkward fast."

A wistful sigh slipped out. "I can't help it."

"Yeah, I get it, man." Aric's gaze swung to Willow seated in a corner booth chatting with Tayla. "I really do. But all this isn't easy. Have you thought about what happens after?"

"After?"

For a second, he panicked, thinking Raine and Slater had spilled his secret, about him potentially being the first angel whose soul had an expiration date. But they wouldn't do that. If there was one thing his sister was good at, it was keeping secrets and finding answers. Tonight, and every other night for that matter, he didn't want to think about what happened once his soul ceased to exist. Why, when it would only bring him down. The mishap with his power had taught him immortality wasn't in fact forever and that his existence was too short to waste time dreading the future.

"Yeah, after we find her father, or what happens if she goes back to..."

Blaine.

Oh. That.

For the past week, he'd thought of little else. How right now everything felt so perfect, yet a storm brewed on the horizon. One that had the power to strip away all he cared for.

Countless times, he'd felt Ebony drift, caught the fear in her eyes, and he'd considered abandoning his mission to save Jemma, his quest to help find Asher, and whisk them both to Maui where they could live out their immortality until his soul became nothing. But then what? If he did that, he'd leave Ebony defenseless. Without someone to protect her. Thoughts of a different future took a backseat because she'd always gravitated back to him, back to his bed, back to his arms.

He'd suspected Ebony was his soulmate since he first laid eyes on her. Soulmates were supposed to be endgame and there was plenty of proof to support that here at the club. Raine and Slater. Cole and Evie. Aric and Willow. Raven and Tayla. He just needed to figure out how to make it work. How he could steal more time.

He gave the Guardian a reassuring nod. "I appreciate your concern, I really do. I know the risks. I know Ebony is a Fallen and the odds are instantly stacked against us, but I also feel like—"

The music switched halfway through a song causing the crowd to stir out of the corner of his eyes.

Hang on. That beat. That...voice...that guitar riff...

His gaze snapped to the dance floor where Ebony stood at the edge peering back at him. *"Get your ass down here, Maui, or you'll miss it."*

Conversation with Aric forgotten, he launched from his chair, all fumbling legs and tangled feet as he bolted toward the dance floor. If there was one time his previous ability to mist would come in handy, it was now. He zipped around the crowded bar line, through the sea of mortals congregating off to the side, until his feet halted in front of Ebony.

His breath hammered in time with his heart.

Ebony offered her hand, and he took it without question, too overcome with shock to do much else. She led him through the crowded dance floor to the center, pulling him closer to drape her arms around his neck.

His hands landed on the small of her back indecently close to her ass. "This...this is my song." His voice rose a notch with uncontained excitement. "The DJ is playing my song."

He was right earlier, when he said the realm stopped spinning when Ebony smiled. Because in this moment, everything around them halted. Flashing strobe lights faded to the background, mortals singing along with the loud music softened to a distant hum. All his worries for their future, of whether Fate would intervene or Blaine would come for Ebony, vanished. All that remained was her. His soulmate. In his arms, as broody bass and elegant power chords swept them away in lyrics about coming back to life. A song so perfectly suited to them.

"How did you...?"

"What?" She shrugged one shoulder. "Convince that

subpar DJ to grant your wish to play the grungiest power ballad of this generation?"

He threw his head back and laughed, welcoming the heady rush of joy. "You make it sound so romantic, Violet. I'm overcome with swoon."

Ebony spun in his arms, her body moving effortlessly in time with the heavy beat. "The mortal is lucky I didn't compel him to play it on repeat for the rest of the night. Believe me, I was tempted. He had the nerve to tell me the song was bad for his reputation." She scoffed. "If only he cared that much about his outdated equipment."

His eyes widened as he spun her in a twirl. "You... compelled a mortal?"

She flashed her crimson pupils at him for the briefest moment. "Yes. I compelled a mortal to play your song because it pissed me off that you've waited all night, and that lousy DJ still hadn't played it."

Giddiness bloomed in his chest. "You compelled the DJ for *me*?"

She hitched her chin, as though preparing for battle. Or to make her point perfectly clear. "I'm a Fallen, remember? Me compelling some shitty DJ should be the least of your worries."

Without another word, he grabbed the back of her neck and slammed his mouth against hers in a hard kiss. "No one has ever compelled someone for me." He kissed her again, lighter this time, small pecks over her face. "Thank you."

Caught up in the music, he held Ebony tight in his arms as the crowd around them pumped their fists in the air in time with the drums. Before long, his soulmate began belting out the chorus at the top of her lungs. He couldn't be prouder. And more in love. Despite his existence being shorter than expected, he wouldn't wish for anything else in this moment.

When the song faded, replaced by a more upbeat version of some new music he didn't know, Ebony drew back to see his face. "Happy?"

He cupped her cheeks and kissed her again, not seeming to ever get enough. "I love you."

In his arms, squished together by the growing crowd, Ebony tensed. "What did you say?"

Even if he could, he wouldn't take it back. Maybe he'd said it too early. Yeah, he'd definitely said it too early. But he'd never felt anything truer. And why hide? Why hide from the one immortal he could bear his soul to?

"I said I love you, Ebony. I've loved you since you screamed at me to get out of your head."

Beneath the lights, her skin looked a little pale. "Really?"

"Yep." He peered into her eyes, hoping she felt the promise weaving in their bond. "And I'll love you until my final breath."

CHAPTER 36

Her breath punched in and out as she took flight in the overcast night. She could have misted, but part of her wanted River to know where she'd gone. That she hadn't abandoned him. That she desperately wanted him to follow. Like he did. His majestic black wings soared through the patchy clouds, chasing her down.

But she didn't slow.

He'd told her that he loved her. That he'd love her until his final breath. Who did that? Who confessed something so beautiful knowing that their last breath wasn't far off? It was cruel. Yet she couldn't find it in herself to resent him for it.

They'd met each other at the wrong time. In the wrong life.

Something inside her heart had beat a little faster, a little heavier, when she'd compelled that DJ to play River's stupid song. The thought of his reaction, of the look on his face when he heard the first bars, had made her almost high with anticipation. And for what? A few more days? A few more weeks?

She'd never hated herself as much as she did right now.

Tears streamed down her face as River caught up with her, grabbing her hand, forcing them both to hover above the dark lake surrounding Summit Creek.

"Did I upset you?"

When a silent sob wracked her body, and her wings fell limp by her sides, River scooped her into his arms and lowered them to the shoreline. Curled up in his lap, River sat on a fallen log.

"I'm sorry for upsetting you," he murmured in her hair. "I knew it was too soon, but I couldn't help it. It just came out. No one has ever done something like that for me before and it...made me really happy. It made me realize how much I love you. And for that, I'm not sorry."

Wiping her tears, she sat up straighter, sucking in a deeper breath. "I didn't mean to freak out."

"I know everyone you've ever loved has abandoned you, Ebony. I know that. But I'm not going anywhere." Slowly, he wrapped his wings around her, banishing the humid breeze cutting across the lake. "I'm not leaving until this realm takes my soul. And even then, I'll fight it."

A familiar tug in the recess of her mind crept through the cracks in her mental walls, reaching for her. It reminded her of the first time he'd invaded her thoughts, and she'd yelled at him to get out of her head. The time when River said he'd fallen in love with her. In hindsight, she'd probably fallen for him then, too. Fallen for him because he'd shown unwavering persistence to break through to her. To never give up.

The second her mental walls crumbled, he stormed in.

"I love you," he murmured over and over thrusting countless images and emotions through their bond. The first moment he'd seen her lying on the cot, bruised and burned, and his overwhelming urge to help her. His panic when he'd woken from that dream where the warehouse had burned down, and he couldn't wake her. The moment he'd summoned light from deep within his soul and blasted it into hers to save her. Their first kiss. His eyes as he'd pushed inside her for the first time.

A thousand tiny moments in the span of seconds. Enough to back his words.

Despite being broken, despite being the wrong sister, the black sheep, a Fallen, River loved her.

When the seams holding her heart together stretched near the breaking point, she kissed him. And just like she'd come to expect, this kiss was different from all their others. Soft, delicate, a gentle connection of their mouths fueled by the bands of emotion streaming between them. The bond they'd formed over the past few months, anchoring her to not only him, but this realm. This path.

His mouth moved down her neck and she leaned back, giving him more access. Bright teal lights shimmered around them, fireflies caught in the stillness of the moment, and she recognized his magic. How it pulsed in the air, shining above them so captivating and heartbreaking at the same time.

Twisting her in his lap, he guided her to straddle his legs. Looking up at her with so much worship, so much adoration, it was hard to not believe his words. Believe that maybe this was her path. Maybe every bad choice she'd made over the past twenty-eight years had led her to this one splinter in time.

When River's hand dipped beneath the hem of her shirt and up her waist, she scrambled off his lap. She couldn't do this anymore. She couldn't pretend to be someone else, to play both sides in a war she never wanted to join. Not when he loved her.

Not when...she loved him?

How could River love her when he didn't know all of her? How could she sit here and cry that he had given a part of himself which he would eventually take away, when she'd held back this entire time. She'd withheld a truth because of what? Fear that he'd leave her if he knew? Because eventually, everyone always did. Parents turned their backs on kids that were too hard. Lovers turned their backs on partners that were too headstrong, too independent. Siblings turned their backs on sisters that were too much trouble. Everyone. And for a moment, she'd felt as though this angel, the one reaching for her, wouldn't be like the others.

That he'd hold her until daybreak.

But how could he?

She had wanted someone in her corner so badly that she had hidden the truth from him. And until he knew her entire past, all her horrible choices, and still accepted them, he couldn't truly love her.

Avoiding his inviting hands, she retreated further, turning toward the lake while trying to form words. Tonight, misty fog swept over the dark water, swirling and coiling. She'd never seen something so beautiful. How the mountain ridges, gloomy high rises in the distance reached through the earth to protect the lake. She'd forgotten what it was like to live in the mortal realm with all its wonders.

She'd forgotten what it was like to live.

"Ebony." River's arms snaked around her middle as he rested his chin on her shoulder. "Let me in."

Still peering at the water, she willed the words to flow from her mouth. "I like when you call me Violet. I like when you bring me gifts and your excitement to try new candy." Once the words started, she no longer held them back. "And I like how passionate you are about decades old power ballads, and how you want to slay my demons just to see me smile. I like you, River. Maybe it's love, I don't know. I can't say I've had a whole lot of experience with it. But I do know that love can't be based on lies. I owe you that."

His wings wrapped around them once more, cocooning them in feathery confines. If she didn't get this out now, she never would.

Turning in his embrace, she saw a reflection of what they could be in his stormy emerald eyes. "I...have to tell you something."

If she continued to keep secrets, they'd never move forward. She'd never start a new life, make amends with Hailee, escape Blaine's hold.

"Did you compel the drink waiter tonight, too? Because those blue cocktails were extra delicious. Don't tell EJ I said that."

That made her chuckle, easing the tension a notch. Trust him to know exactly what to say in a moment like this.

"No." She should compel him to stop talking because his low, raspy voice did things to her belly, making her want to resume their earlier undressing. "That's not it. I need you to be serious for a second and...listen"

"Okay. Serious mode turned on." He straightened, his hands landing on her hips. "Whatever it is, you can tell me."

"What if..." She paused, staring at her shoes before

finding the courage to lift her gaze to his. "What if it makes you...hate me?"

Her stomach whirled, swishing beneath the surface like dangerous currents.

This time when he drew her in, wrapping his arms around her shoulders, she didn't pull away. "Not possible. Nothing could make me hate you, Violet. Nothing."

She hoped that was true.

If Blaine knew, if Blaine even suspected, he'd retaliate. That Fallen might show a soft spot toward an angel or two, but never to her. No, he'd take her soul and destroy it for even doubting his intentions. His power. Yet, here she was, beside a lake, about to confess to an angel.

A fist squeezed her chest as she peered up at River. "Blaine..."

Here went everything. The cliff she stood on, about to leap into whatever faith remained in her soul. Because that was what people did when they loved someone, right? They believed, they trusted. They leapt without hesitation.

"Blaine has been dreamwalking to me. He...wants me to update him on the Guardians' progress with finding my father. He'll hurt Hailee if I don't and now, I'm also scared he knows about us."

For a long moment, River held her gaze. Not even a crinkle in his brow gave away his thoughts, and she refused to intrude on them. She'd accept whatever he said, whatever he chose. Because she'd jump off that cliff hoping he'd catch her, and if he didn't, she'd rather drown.

The air thickened, pulsing and thrumming with a current she couldn't quite grasp. One that weaved beneath her skin, searching for an anchor. The teal Raziel power River had summoned earlier once again glittered between the branches above their heads, the flickers catching in his eyes.

As though in slow motion, he cupped her face and dipped so they were eye level where she found sincerity in his gaze. It told her, even without words, that he trusted her. He had faith in her.

As her heart swelled with equal parts love and hope, River kissed her forehead. "Let me help you," was all he said, and she found herself nodding.

In that moment though, she truly believed he could.

Guiding her back to the log, River sat facing her, holding her hands in his. "Tell me everything."

And so, she did.

Everything from the moment Asher had found her at that fateful rave party a few years back, where she'd chosen to protect her family rather than send the monsters to her mother and Hailee's doorstep. Not that it had mattered. She hadn't known at the time, but they'd already killed her mom. She finished the story with the most recent visit from Blaine, where he'd threatened Hailee's life until she did what he wanted.

The entire time, River held her hands, his wings keeping them safe. Tears came somewhere along the way, where River silently brushed her cheeks, so they didn't linger for too long.

When the words ended, a sense of belonging, of calm, washed through her, made more secure by River's undivided attention.

"I might not be the strongest, kickass angel in this realm." He scooped her into his lap once more. "And I might not have the coolest abilities, but my loyalty and determination are epic. And for you, Violet, I'll do whatever it takes to protect you. Including figuring out how to fix this situation with Blaine. Because there is no greater reward for me than keeping you safe. And maybe even along the way, we can transform your like into love."

Taking her mouth with his, he banished all her fears, all her worries, all her unhelpful thoughts of abandonment, and swept her off to a mystical place where it was only the two of them against the realm.

CHAPTER 37

EBONY

"I can't believe EJ loaned you his car." Ebony slid the last batch of cupcake containers onto the back seat. "From what I heard, he treats this car like it's his own flesh and blood."

Hailee opened the driver's door. "Right? I was waiting for the fine print when he said I could finally use my spare key. Though, he did give Stella a talking to after he pulled her out of the garage, making sure she wouldn't go above the speed limit no matter how hard I pressed my foot on the gas."

Ebony laughed, shaking her head as she hopped in the passenger side. "That Guardian is something else."

"Yep." A soft smile lifted Hailee's lips. "And I'm so thankful I found him."

Ebony braced herself for the usual sting of want, of loneliness and longing, but it never floated to the surface. In its place, warmth and happiness spread through her chest while an image of River staring down at her as he twisted her violet hair around his finger, made her practically giddy.

Last night, she'd confessed to him about Blaine, and it had been almost two weeks since the Fallen had dreamwalked to her. She wasn't naïve enough to think that Blaine's absence meant he'd forgotten about his threats or the hunt for her father. Quite the opposite. Blaine's absence likely meant that he was preparing. Gathering the troops.

And nothing good ever came from that.

After buckling up, Hailee started the engine and Stella roared to life, a steady rumble beneath the seat. In the distance, the sky transformed from night into a dusky glow as hints of the sun speared upward from below the horizon, the last smattering of stars fading in the new light. This early, she hadn't run into any other Guardians, and the stillness, the peacefulness she found with just her, Hailee, EJ, and River made her heart swell. This was the life she could've had if she'd found River sooner.

As Hailee tore down the gravel drive, Ebony peered back at the house through the passenger window, and chuckled. "I expected to see EJ racing after his car or crying on the porch."

Hailee snorted. "I made him promise to stay inside, otherwise, he wouldn't have gotten out of the driver's seat." After a few minutes of following the gravel road as it weaved between the towering pine trees, Hailee pulled out onto the highway, heading down the mountain to the township of Summit Creek. "Anyway, I wanted it to be just us. A morning where we didn't talk about Devoid or how our father is potentially behind the attacks or how barbaric he's become. I feel like we don't get any time to ourselves, and I've missed that."

"Same."

Since she and Hailee had made peace, Ebony had joined her sister every other day to help with baking for the store. Between licking the frosting off the beaters, countless laughs, and a few flour fights thrown in for good measure, she'd started to feel like her old self. As though she and Hailee were on the right path, and their relationship had begun to heal. The feeling was addictive. Everything she thought she didn't need, that she'd forgone in exchange for keeping her sister safe, was once again within her grasp.

Would Blaine come to collect on his deal? No doubt. But this time, she didn't feel so isolated, so...lost in the darkness. This time, she had River on one side, with Hailee and EJ on the other. And something in the way Raven and a few of the other Guardians treated her suggested that they had at least warmed to the idea of her staying. For the first time since discovering the immortal world, she didn't feel powerless or alone.

"I can't believe you're up this early. The sister I knew would be just falling into bed right about now, not awake." Hailee teased. "Unless...you haven't slept yet?"

The cheeky grin lifting at the corner of Hailee's mouth made her giggle and she playfully shoved her sister's shoulder. "I slept...a bit."

Hailee's grin turned into a full-blown smile. "So River, huh?"

The car slowed, sweeping around a tight bend in the road before Hailee knocked it back a gear to accelerate once more.

She wasn't a girly-girl who blushed at the mention of her—boyfriend? Soulmate? Angel lover? What was the appropriate term here?—but even she sensed the sudden rise in her pulse at the mention of his name.

"Yeah. Me and River."

A rush of heat wove through her middle as though the angel stood behind her, wrapping his arms around her torso as he did every night. Welcome side effects of the soulmate bond swirled together with a healthy dose of love. She was still coming to terms with the feelings, but that didn't stop her from recognizing it. River had said he hoped to convert her "like" into love, but she suspected, she was already there. It had crept up on her over the months with his playful banter. In every sweet gesture and the attentive way he touched her. The way he joked with her. How he put so much thought into every word he whispered in her ear right before they fell asleep. And more than that, how he proved he had her back, time and time again.

And once she realized it, she called the feelings for what they were.

She loved that quirky, Hawaiian shirt wearing, candy addicted soulmate of hers with all her heart.

Hailee remained quiet until curiosity won, and Ebony glanced at her sister, seeing for the first time genuine happiness on Hailee's face.

"I'm so glad. He's a good one, Eb. He really is."

Don't I know it.

For the rest of the drive, Hailee chatted about the bakery, how it had grown over the years and how her initial vision expanded into something better than she ever imagined, and each breath helped draw them that much closer. She'd missed not only having a twin sister, but the feeling of contentment, of being home, which, in hindsight, she'd only ever experienced when playing music. How when she put on her headphones, the hours passed in a blur. Her troubles swept away in the beats. Music had the ability to convince her mind she could achieve anything she set her heart on. Much how River did.

When Hailee pulled into the back parking lot of the bakery as the sun's rays breached the horizon, Ebony turned to her sister and really looked at her. The twin connection they'd always shared roared to life. It didn't matter the physical distance, nor the realms separating them, or the fact she was a Fallen while her sister had an angelic soul, their bond remained. A thin tether linking them together as blood. As family. For the first time in years, she didn't try to lock it down or block Hailee from entering her thoughts. Instead, she unclasped the bracelet on her wrist, tucked it into her pocket and welcomed the release with open arms.

Damn River. He'd gone and made her all sappy.

Stacking the containers three on top of each other, Hailee balanced a set in her hands as she headed inside the rear entrance, while Ebony grabbed another.

A loud crash ricocheted through the still air, followed by a scream.

Dropping the containers, Ebony bolted into the bakery with a dagger in each palm. She skidded to a halt beside Hailee, who stared wide eyed at...their father.

"Good morning, girls," Asher said, casually perched on a nearby stool.

"What the actual fuck?" she spluttered.

Their father. The Fallen she and the Guardians had hunted for almost a month, sat right in front of her. As discretely as she could, she dodged the smashed cupcakes littering the floor to move closer to Hailee.

"Relax, Ebony. I'm not here to hurt either of you."

Yeah, and she was a unicorn.

"Then why are you here?" Hailee asked.

For someone who'd spent time in the Infernal Pits before having his soul released, their father looked...good. Healthy. Wavy blonde hair cut short with a freshly shaven jaw, wearing a long sleeve button up and matching slacks. The last time she'd seen her father had been when he attacked the Guardians, battling for the Empryen sword. When he lost, Raine unleashed her power and all Hell broke loose, leaving her at the mercy of Blaine and the others.

Asher had thrown her to the wolves.

"You bastard," she grunted, before charging at him with her dagger raised.

But she only managed three steps.

Asher uncurled his shadow magic, the tendrils squeezing her middle, halting her. "I don't have a great deal of time, so I suggest you listen rather than acting so rashly."

Hailee darted forward, trying to free Ebony. "Get those things off her."

"Acting rashly?" Ebony seethed, grunting as she tried to loosen the shadows. "You tricked me. Sent me into a battle you knew we wouldn't win. And now you turn up here acting like our father."

Fury pulsed in her blood until crimson tainted the edge of her vision. She wanted to kill him, to watch his body burn in the fires of Hell. But reasoning kicked in far too quickly. Losing her cool would get them nowhere. It also wouldn't yield any information on the Devoid he'd created or how to stop them. Losing her shit gave her no leverage when Blaine dreamwalked to her next, and it definitely didn't protect Hailee.

"Enough," Hailee shouted.

The shadows retreated in an instant. "Now, let's talk."

Asher motioned for them to sit. They didn't.

"You expect us to trust you?" Hailee hissed, twisting a silver ring on her index finger that looked suspiciously like a miniature dagger. "After everything you've done. After you killed Mom."

Asher's lip lifted in a sneer, making her stomach churn. "And yet you trust your sister after she sided with Blaine."

Hailee's gaze darted to Ebony, and she tried to send her sister a silent plea that said, "Don't fall for his bullshit," but Asher spoke first.

"I came to warn you and offer you a chance out of this."

She hated how her heart pounded in her chest, giving away how much she feared their father. "If you came to warn us about the Devoid, you're too late. We already know."

"I'm surprised you didn't find the site earlier, given I had taken you to the caves so many times." Asher laced his fingers together, laying them in his lap. "I came to warn you to leave this alone. If you don't step aside, you're both going to be caught in the crossfire."

How could he act so casual, so relaxed when he'd done nothing but cause endless pain? All those innocent mortals. The tens or potentially hundreds of souls that would never find peace. It sickened her. She'd like to think that out of all the mistakes she'd made, all the wrong paths she'd chosen in the hope of protecting Hailee, she had never stooped to his level.

She hadn't become her father.

"I hate you." The words like venom in her mouth.

Asher sighed. "This path has been in motion since before you were even born. It's bigger than a few measly Devoid following commands. It's bigger than the three of us."

What bullshit was this? From what she knew, her father Fell after Hailee and her were born, when he thought they had died. Gabe had given them bracelets spelled by Fate to hide them until they reached twenty-five. How had Asher been involved prior to that?

"What's the endgame? End Blaine? Throw over the new king of Hell?" she snapped. "Blaine knows you're alive. He won't let you finish him."

Asher lifted the lid on one of the cupcake containers that hadn't toppled to the floor. "May I?" he asked Hailee.

"I can't even look at you, let alone offer you a cupcake. You disgust me."

With a heavy sigh, Asher closed the container. "Blaine's time is nearing the end, and although he won't fall easily, he will fall. The cleanse cannot begin until he does."

What the fuck?

"Violet, you good? I'm getting a weird feeling. My stomach is churning like I ate too much candy, but I've only had two packets. What's up with that?"

Her breath hitched at River's voice in her head. She dipped her gaze, so Asher didn't clue in. She had two choices: Tell River the truth and risk him and no doubt EJ flying to them fast as lightning to fight Asher. Or she could lie and risk his disappointment after she brought Hailee home safe. Only one kept River safe, too. Asher might not harm her and Hailee right now, but he wouldn't hesitate if a Guardian busted through the door with weapons raised.

Now her stomach churned.

"We're almost done," she mentally replied as calmly as she could.

Asher's shadows once again shot out, this time wrapping around Hailee's throat. Hailee gasped for breath, hands scratching at the tendrils squeezing her windpipe as she swiped the silver ring through the smoke. It hissed and burned, but Asher held his ground.

"I don't know who you're communicating with, but I

know that look. I'm not fucking stupid. Stop it now or your sister pays for your treachery."

Hailee.

Hailee always paid the price for Ebony's bad choices. For her mistakes. Once again, she'd put her sister in danger because they'd come alone.

"Let her go," she lowered her voice, inching closer to Asher, the Purah dagger River had given her, tight and steady in her palm.

She didn't know where Fallen souls ended up now that the Infernal Pits no longer existed, but that was Asher's problem, not hers.

Her father loosened the shadows enough for Hailee to suck in a sharp breath and the scene threw her back to when Hailee had misted to Hell under the pretense of saving Ebony. But Ebony didn't need saving. She had tricked her sister into connecting Blaine and Fate in a dreamwalk. Blaine had no intention of ever freeing Ebony, she knew that now. But he'd kept his word not to call on Hailee again until the final battle.

Back then, Asher had almost torn Hailee's soul from her chest with his shadows, and if EJ hadn't stormed into the castle, if Ebony hadn't thrown that dagger to disarm her father, Hailee wouldn't be standing here today.

Her father had so much blood on his hands.

He'd never help her stop Blaine. He'd never choose her over his quest for revenge or whatever the hell this was. Her father would continue to hurt innocent mortals and watch them all die at his feet. He was no better than Blaine.

"Come with me," Asher gritted between clenched teeth. "Join me or risk dying a final death."

The entirety of her immortal life, she'd surrounded herself with villains. Bullies who promised not to harm her sister provided she did their bidding. Well, no longer. Now, she would protect Hailee herself. Not with a twisted deal, or some halfhearted scheming. And definitely not based on the word of the man who'd killed their mother because she hadn't given him the information he wanted. Their mother had shown true strength until her dying breath. Loyalty. She wanted River to remember her for those qualities, too.

"Never." In one swift movement, she threw the dagger, aiming straight at Asher's heart.

Everything happened in a blur as time seemed to halt. The shadows around Hailee's neck split, one branch diverted to the dagger. Ebony lunged for Hailee. Glass sprayed the bakery as Devoid burst through the storefront windows.

A foreboding figure, hovering in the doorway, struck a match.

CHAPTER 38

River

River rapped his knuckles on the open door. "You got a minute, Boss?"

Raven lifted his head and waved him into the war room. "Sure. I can't figure out this shit anyway." He closed the laptop on the desk in front of him. "What's up?"

That was a loaded question. At this very second, River had so many competing priorities on his mind he couldn't hear his own subconscious. Right? Wrong? Up or down? Who knew?

Last night at SubZero had been the best night of his existence, and it had ended in Ebony dropping the heavens of all bombs in his lap. Blaine. That Fallen had been dreamwalking with Ebony, and River wasn't entirely sure how he felt about it. Sure, he wanted to be civilized and confront Blaine, demand the Fallen back off so he could protect Ebony. But at the same time, he wanted to punch that male right in his perfect nose.

Soulmate emotions were confusing. Like now for instance, when his gut swirled like he'd eaten all the red candy right before flying in circles for three hours straight. At first, he had thought the weird sensations came from his bond with Ebony, that she was in danger, but she'd assured him everything was okay. He trusted her. Wanted her to see that he trusted her. He didn't want to be one of those overbearing soulmates who didn't let their other half out of their sight. *Cough-cough, Aric.* He wanted Ebony to feel safe and secure, giving her the freedom to spread her wings while knowing he always had her back.

"River?" Raven prompted, snapping River's attention back to him.

"Oh, right. Yeah." He pulled out the chair to Raven's left and sat, dumping his open bag of candy on the table.

Raven cleared his throat. "Is something on your mind?"

"Now that you mention it, yeah, there is." He tossed a soft candy in his mouth, grimacing at the bitter lemon. He forced himself to try new flavors these days because he saved all the raspberry chews for Ebony. Bitter lemon though, that took it too far. He shuddered as he swallowed, pushing the packet aside.

"River? Where the fuck is your mind wandering to today?"

"Shit stick. Sorry. I want to talk to you about Ebony." He shook off the weird sensations. "More specifically, how Blaine has been dreamwalking to her."

Raven cursed, leaning back in his chair to cross his arms. "I knew this would happen."

The insinuation made the muscles in River's jaw tighten. Another new experience for him. "First, Ebony hasn't done anything wrong. In fact, she told me about it so I could pass the information to you. So that we could help her." He tilted his head to Raven. "Second, I don't appreciate the accusation that you expected her to betray us."

"Fuck." Raven raked his fingers through his hair. "Sorry, my man. She's got a twisted history that's hard to trust but that's no excuse. I need to do better, especially for you."

"I want everyone to stop thinking the worst of her. She's my soulmate. You didn't treat Slater like this in the beginning. He just somehow weaseled his way in without anyone but Raine making a fuss."

Raven's cheek twitched with a smirk. "You're right. I guess because we knew Slater, *I* knew Slater before he fell. But you're absolutely right. I'm sorry. Ebony is your soulmate. We honor that bond above everything else, which means Ebony is now a part of our family. I'll do better to treat her as such."

A wild giddy sensation exploded in his belly at the thought of the Guardians including Ebony in their family. Even if he'd wanted the same for himself since he'd joined them a handful of mortal years ago, it comforted him to know that when his soul expired, Ebony would have them protecting her. She wouldn't be alone.

For the past few nights, he'd held out hope that their soulmate bond would heal her soul, transform it to angelic, and that would in turn, save his. He'd even slowed down on healing Jemma in case it hindered the process. But so far, all he'd noticed was the steady stream of light, of love, swirling through their bond. Back and forth. He wanted to ask Ebony if she'd felt a difference, maybe seen feathers change in her wings like Slater's had, but he hadn't found the right time.

How did he even ask? What if she didn't?

River crossed to the mini fridge and grabbed himself a bottle of water, chugging half the contents before sitting again. "You know, when I found out I had a sister, I was so thrilled to meet her, to share all the realms with her. To have someone I could confide in, someone who would have my back."

Raven steepled his fingers, leaning in.

"But then Fate told me my purpose was only to ensure Raine fulfilled hers." He let the words flow through him, no longer harboring resentment or bitterness toward his sister for something she had no choice in. "Imagine being told your only purpose is to ensure your sibling is amazing and saves a realm."

"It would fucking suck," Raven grumbled. "Second only to knowing your sibling is hellbent on destroying that realm and you naively gave up everything to save them."

Huh. Guess if one Guardian understood him, it was Raven. "That definitely sucks more, for sure." He sighed, slowly shaking his head. "At first, I resented her and almost refused to leave the Heavens, but then I figured, I'd get to spend a few years in the mortal world exploring, living my best eternity, and all I had to do was be an awesome side-kick." His finger circled the bottle cap, wondering if he should stop oversharing. Surely, Raven didn't want to hear the rest. But when he glanced at the Guardian, the boss gave him a curt nod, and the words tumbled out. "But soon, that's all I was. A sidekick. Raine's brother. A shadow in her greatness. A...hanger-oner."

Raven frowned and opened his mouth to speak, but River held up his hand.

"For a while, I was fine with it. Really, I was. I played the brother and friend role well and had fun doing it. It was freeing. My only responsibility was to ensure Raine fulfilled her destiny. Every other second, I was free to do as I pleased. But then Raine teamed up with Slater and...well, we discovered Slater was the one who Fate planned to help Raine fulfill her path, and I guess I felt cheated. If that wasn't my mission, then what was? I'd spent my entire existence working toward a quest for nothing." He twisted the lid to occupy his hands. Because he wasn't touching that candy again, it must be off given what it was doing to his belly. Or maybe this was his soul's steady decline and he'd only begun to take notice of the signs. "When you say that Ebony is part of your family now, it makes me happy. That you'll include her. I feel like life has robbed her of that, too."

Raven lowered his hands. "You're a part of this family, also, River. You know that, don't you?"

His eyes were suddenly itchy. An allergic reaction to bitter lemon? "Are you...sure?"

Raven nodded his head as he stood to squeeze River's shoulder. "Of course I am, you idiot. I can't be the only one in this house with no fashion sense."

River gasped. "Rude."

Raven laughed, slapping River's back in what felt strangely like a brotherly gesture. "Seriously though, you're more than a sidekick to us. We need you here for more than to keep Raine from stabbing EJ. I value your input on our missions because your mind processes shit on a completely different level. Which more times than not, results in you seeing things from an angle we've missed. And when you stay behind, I know the house's protection is in fucking capable hands. You've become a valuable part of our family and I'm proud to call you a Guardian."

Oh, shit.

He was going to cry. Or suffocate from the tightness in his chest. All this time, he'd felt like an outsider, like the eleventh wheel, hoping someone would want him to hang around, and Raven already considered him a Guardian.

Raven poured them both a bourbon. "Now, tell me

about the trouble my fucking brother is causing and let's figure out a plan to stop him."

After a few deep breaths and a discreet wipe of his eyes, River took a small sip of gross bourbon before pushing the glass aside. Something was wrong. Everything tasted weird, and that swirling sensation in his stomach caused a prickle of sweat to break out at his nape. His heart raced like he was in the heat of battle with urgency pumping through his veins.

"The dreamwalking, uh, it started when Ebony arrived here." He cleared his throat, mouth suddenly dry. "After Slater saved her from Hell. The first time, Blaine—"

"R-River?"

His heart stalled at Ebony's voice in his head. *"Violet? What's wrong?"*

"Help."

He was on his feet in a flash. "They're in trouble. Something happened." The jumbled words fell from his mouth, but Raven caught on, jumping to his feet just as fast. Bolting out the door, he collided with Aric in the hall.

"Fucking Hell." Aric righted himself. "EJ and Slater misted to the bakery. Devoid attack."

CHAPTER 39

EBONY

Had smoke always been that color? Black and ominous? In Hell, hellfire burned almost silently, a deep, fiery orange flickering in every corner of the realm as slate grey flecks of ash fluttered to the sooty ground. Nothing compared to the dark pillars of suffocating clouds billowing in the air before her, blanketing the sky above the bakery. Bright orange fingers burst underneath the eaves, the groaning timber in the roof echoing in her ears as though Ebony stood in the center while the inferno blazed around her. Burned her. A preferred option to standing frozen across the street watching her sister's dreams become a charred pile of wood and melted corrugated tin.

Hailee's sobs sucked the air from Ebony's lungs, as her sister huddled on the dirt a few feet away, EJ consoling her with private whispers.

Dread.

Dread choked her. It seeped into her veins spreading

poisonous inky spiderwebs as it drained her life one heart-beat at a time.

Closer to the blaze, Slater spoke to mortal authorities while two fire engines shot useless water at the remains of the bakery. By now, the damage was done. Water wouldn't save the structure. If anything, it simply prevented the fire from spilling to neighboring storefronts. A tea shop. An old bookstore.

Mortals flocked to the streets in the early morning light, their sick sense of curiosity making Ebony's blood thrum. They whispered to themselves, but she caught every word. *Such a tragedy. I knew they were trouble. I bet she left the ovens on. What will she do now? Julie said the owner was from out of town.* Their voices piled on top of each other, fueling the ones already on repeat in Ebony's head, going around and around until she wanted to rip her hair out one chunk at a time.

She'd thrown the dagger at their father. She'd started the fight. She'd naively thought if she did, that coward would mist away and stop threatening them. Stop threatening Hailee.

She'd been wrong.

So, so wrong.

When she refused his offer to join his sick quest, Asher had instead, directed Devoid to finish what he couldn't be bothered to kill himself.

Them.

Armed with nothing but one retrieved dagger and a weapon on Hailee's finger, they'd fought off four Devoid. But not without injuries. At the reminder, she peered down at her hand, pressed into her side, ebbing the blood oozing between her fingers. The knife wound wouldn't kill her, but it was a stark reminder of what could've happened had she not gone with Hailee this morning.

What if Hailee had arrived at the bakery alone?

What if Ebony hadn't been quick enough? What if their father had ambushed them with the Devoid first?

So many questions plagued her.

She scoffed. The answers didn't matter. All that mattered was her sister's scream a second before someone threw that match.

"Violet?" River shouted from somewhere behind her.

She'd called for his help, but by then, it had been too late.

She didn't bother turning to him. Nor did she acknowledge the frantic pitch of his voice. If she'd told him earlier, if she'd told the truth when he'd mentally asked if something was wrong, maybe the Devoid wouldn't have attacked. Maybe her father would've fled.

Maybe Hailee's bakery wouldn't now be a pile of ash.

Strong hands clutched her numb shoulders, turning her to face him. River searched her eyes, no doubt looking for signs of life, but all she felt was empty. She'd known she couldn't fight the Devoid and walk away without loss. Several times she'd grabbed Hailee, attempting to mist but couldn't concentrate enough to make the shift.

She'd failed.

Sure, they had both survived, but she'd broken Hailee by tearing apart her sister's dream. Destroying all she'd worked for with a flick of a wrist.

This was what Ebony feared. All these years, this was what she knew would happen if she didn't play by the rules. If she didn't do as she was told.

If she dreamed for something beyond her entitlement.

"Ebony, tell me what hurts."

River.

Sweet, sweet, River.

He tried to coax her back to the surface, back to the living, but she refused to return. What was the point when she destroyed everything she touched? Hailee would never forgive her.

"Shit. You're bleeding."

River slowly eased away her hand, replacing it with some form of cloth. She didn't take much notice.

"Can you mist?"

Sure, she had no problem envisaging all the places she could go, but it didn't matter now, did it? What was the use of having an ability when it didn't work in a life-or-death situation?

Maybe Asher wouldn't have burned down the bakery if they'd misted away. EJ had said something to that effect when he first arrived. But what did it matter? They'd never know the answer. All they knew was that someone working with her father had set the bakery alight after she'd thrown the dagger.

Like father, like daughter.

"Hey." River brushed his fingers along her cheekbone, coaxing her to the present. "I'll get Willow to mist us back. She misted me here. You're safe now."

Last night, his smile lulled her into a false sense of security. Today, it proved what she'd always known. He was too trusting. How did he not see that this was her fault? Why was he still being so kind to her? Surely, by now, he'd come to his senses. She wasn't worth the effort. People had told her that her entire life. Now, she understood why.

Everything she touched burned.

She swatted his hand away. "I can mist just fine," she

hissed, right before she stalked behind a patch of dense bushes and left. Without him.

Materializing in front of the Guardian mansion, she stormed inside, not bothering to wait for River and not over-thinking why she came here of all places instead of anywhere else in the realm. The Guardians had weapons she needed. That was all.

Emotion clogged the back of her throat when she thought of leaving River in town, at how she treated him so cruelly when all he'd shown her was kindness and love. But there were things she needed to do without him. And she knew without a doubt he'd try to stop her.

Finding a quiet spot, in an unused coat closet, she tucked herself in the shadowy corner and summoned her powers. Closing her eyes, the magic swirled in her blood, intensifying with her anger, as the dreamwalk took form. An abandoned campsite, in a forgotten forest, in the still of night. The same landscape she used for every dreamwalk with Blaine.

After the landscape stabilized, she sent out a single thread of magic, searching the ether for one Fallen soul through the thousands of pulsing connections. It didn't take long. Blaine's soul blazed hotter and brighter than all the others, and she latched on, dragging him into the dreamscape faster than ever.

In seconds, the Fallen materialized before her eyes. Black ripped jeans, unlaced boots, with that centuries old black leather jacket he was never without. With the twisted crown still gracing his head, his midnight hair flopped over and around the charred bones and shards of obsidian, as though untouched by puffs of hellfire. The flames reminded her of that first spark, the flame that had lit Hailee's bakery on fire.

"Hello, love." A sadistic smirk lifted Blaine's mouth as he assessed her with a stare that made shivers pop up randomly over her arms. "Have you tired of playing house?"

She almost laughed. Playing house? Her feet had barely hit the floor before her father had flipped her realm upside down. No. She had enjoyed her weeks with River, relished rebuilding memories with her sister, but she knew it would all come to an end. Part of her had been conscious of the countdown. Staying, ignoring the dangers, forgetting the consequences of her choices, wouldn't serve anyone. And apparently, it made her father's retaliation worse. As she'd helplessly stood across the street, watching the bakery collapse in flames, she realized her time was up. She needed to choose a side. Needed to cease these games and wistful dreams of happy endings that didn't belong in her world, and face reality.

Choosing between Blaine and her father was easy. At first, she thought hunting down Asher had been the best of two evils, that she could convince him to stop his quest for vengeance. That Blaine wouldn't retaliate if she took down her father for him. But she never had the stomach for it. Not after witnessing those Devoid, locked in cages awaiting their end. After seeing Asher this morning, she realized how wrong she'd been. Her father didn't care how many innocent lives he destroyed. He only cared for death.

Only Blaine could stop him now.

"I know where my father is." She pushed down the spike of fear. Now wasn't the time for doubt or sentimental bullshit. "And I'll help you end him."

CHAPTER 40

Toward the bottom of the stairs, River slowed his steps, though it did nothing to calm the out of beat thrum of his pulse. Quiet sobs from below tore at his heart, but he couldn't rush his approach. He needed a breath to compose himself. Watching Ebony mist away without him, her eyes steeled with vengeance had scared the bejeezes out of him. He'd all but torn Willow's arm off for her to mist him back to the Guardians residence. Hoping Ebony had misted here was a long shot, Heavens, she could've misted anywhere in all the realms, but that tether, the spark of connection between them, had whispered the truth. Never before had he been so thankful.

Now though, in the cool, damp stairwell leading to the basement, he couldn't grasp the difference between his chaotic emotions and hers. Both collided through him, tornados punching the earth, only to dissolve a second later, again and again until he didn't know which way to run.

That wasn't true. He knew. And he would run to Ebony in every lifetime.

Hand trailing along the rough stone, he rounded the last corner of the basement stairs, and his breath stalled. Ebony stood before the armory, her forehead against the closed door, wild violet strands concealing her face. But it was the defeated thump of her fist that punctured his heart. How it weakly banged the door, as though she'd run out of energy and barely had enough to lift her arm. Sobs wracked her body, her shoulders quaking with every sharp inhale. The sight tore a giant cavity behind his ribs.

"Violet?"

He approached with careful steps. The last thing he wanted was for her to bolt again.

"Let me in."

Heavens. Her voice was so broken. So...distant.

Easing beside her, he gently placed a hand on her shoulder, slowly moving it across her back until it reached the other side, where he drew her into his arms. For a moment, he stood there, one arm wrapped around her, and it was enough. Enough to reassure her that he was there, that he wasn't leaving. That he wouldn't abandon her.

He ached to convince her that everyone was okay, would be okay, that everyone she cared for was safe. Material possessions like a bakery didn't matter. But the niggling sensation in his gut warned against it. Those words would only fuel already raw emotions. He'd been at the fire. He'd seen the devastation on her face. Heard Hailee's cries. Nothing he said to Ebony would erase the self-blame he suspected poisoned her mind.

"Tell me what you need," he murmured.

Instead of guessing, he'd let her guide them through

this. If there was one thing he witnessed about soulmates, about relationships that lasted a lifetime, it was that communication and trust were the key. They'd talk it out and when the dust settled and emotions were less heightened, she would see that he'd had her back all along.

"Let me in," she repeated, her voice scratchy and hoarse, tearing a fresh wound in his chest.

As though his brain had suddenly connected all the dots and realized where their bond had led him, the last remaining pieces clicked into place. "Into the armory?"

Ebony lifted her fist once more to bang the door, but it fell flat instead, slipping down the front in a slow, high-pitched squeak. "Weapons. I need to..."

Twisting her to face him, he tunneled his fingers through the tangled mess of her hair until he could see her eyes. "You want weapons from the armory? Who are we fighting, Violet?"

Something snapped inside her. A spark to kindling. In a flash, she jerked away, putting distance between them and with renewed energy punched random numbers into the keypad. Each unsuccessful double beep was met with a yell of frustration.

"Let me in, River," she snapped, baring her teeth at him.

Slipping his arm in front, he punched in the code. The lock clunked, barely disengaging before Ebony shoved open the door and stormed in.

"You need weapons?" he asked, following her. "I'll get you weapons. As many as you want. But first tell me who we're fighting."

"What do you care?"

Oof. Sure, she was in a world of pain right now, but those four words kicked the wind out of him. Her tone lacked venom which reassured him she hadn't intentionally meant to hurt him, only push him away. Which was all she'd ever known. Push away before someone showed their true nature, before they left her in a world of pain. Too bad. She didn't know him at all if she thought those words would force him to leave her. He was a soulmate now. True soulmates didn't run at the slightest grumpy tone.

Holding back by the door, River watched Ebony as she rummaged through the stockpile of spare weapons Raine kept on the far bench. Since he'd broken Ebony free from the cell, he hadn't ventured into the basement because it held nothing but regret. He should've trusted his instincts sooner. Should have rescued her earlier.

He should have gone with her to the bakery.

Air caved in around him, the heaviness making it difficult to drag in a full breath, while his pulse continued thrashing until he thought Ebony would see it fluttering in his neck. When she snatched two more thigh sheaths and matching daggers, he pushed off the door. "Tell me what's going on, Violet. Let me help."

She paused, her free hand curling around the edge of the workbench. "Don't you get it?" She spun, facing him, and the devastation in her eyes almost broke him. "I wasn't meant to be here. This wasn't for me. I was meant to be protecting..." For the second time in a matter of minutes, her voice broke.

He crossed the armory in a heartbeat and reached for her, but she brushed him off. "This is not your fault."

"How can you say that? How can you stand there and tell me this isn't my fault when I threw that dagger?" Her voice rose as she gathered more and more weapons, way more than she could sheath on her body. "I baited him. I may as well have lit that fucking match."

Clasping her wrist, he stilled her hand. "That's not

true." Easing closer, he pressed his front against her back, wrapping his arms around her. "This is not your fault. Hailee knows that. I know that. The only one to blame for the fire is Asher."

Her chest quaked with a silent sob as she stared at the floor. "If I hadn't been here, if I hadn't been playing house, he never would have come for us. He never would have been at the bakery. Hailee would be safe. I wouldn't have ruined all she's worked for."

He rested his cheek on the side of her head, speaking softly in her ear. "But I never would have met you. I never would have discovered the bond between us. I never would have fallen in love with you." When she lifted her head to no doubt argue, he cut her off with a swift kiss on her temple. "I didn't exaggerate when I said I'd do anything for you. That doesn't stop because a new threat has emerged."

This time when she twisted, he loosened his grip, so she turned in his arms. "Right. So, you're going to kill my father with me? Is that what you're saying? Because I don't need you. I already dreamwalked to Blaine. We're meeting tonight to finally end this."

Again, the words hit their intended mark and stabbed his heart a little, but he didn't let it linger. Now wasn't the time to break. To fall to his knees and beg her to stay or convince her to let him in. Now was the time for him to step up. To show her that he was an angel of his word, soulmate material. That he never backed down from a mission, no matter the threat.

Capturing her face in his hands, he bent slightly so they were eye level. "Violet, my entire existence, I thought my only mission was to ensure Raine completed hers. And then, a few months ago, I thought maybe my mission was to save Jemma, to cleanse the darkness in her soul after what Blaine did to her. But you know what?"

She tried to turn away, but he redirected her back to face him and peered into those haunting eyes. The ones that had featured in his dreams long before he knew why or how. The eyes that had pleaded with him to release her, to trust her even when others had warned him not to. The eyes of his soulmate.

"I had a hand in all of that, but none of it was my true mission. Because I realized last night, when you told me about Blaine, that my mission isn't about making sure others live or die, fail or succeed. My mission has always been you. To find you. To love you. To convince you that you *are* enough. That *you* are worth it. And despite the obstacles in our future, I will put my heart and soul into achieving that mission."

A single tear pooled at the corner of her eye, but Ebony harshly swatted it away before it fell. "Just let me go."

"I've never had a mission of my own, a destiny designed by Fate. Heck, I haven't even been wanted enough by anyone for longer than a fleeting moment. I long for that though. I yearn for it. I ache for someone to need me, and I want that someone to be you. With you."

Ebony stared at him for a quiet moment and just when he thought maybe she understood, that she'd let him in, the mask behind her eyes closed him out. "You're too trusting. I've said that all along. You don't want me. You only think you do because you're so in love with the idea of loving someone and having them love you back. You're desperate to make it work. Well, guess what, angel. It isn't going to. I vowed a long time ago that I would protect Hailee at all costs. And that's what I'm always going to do."

"I trust too easily, yes, I admit that, but you need to trust more. Look at me, Violet. Really look. I might not have long left in this realm, none of us know when the darkness will consume my soul. Let me do this. Let me use the last of my time, the last of my light, for you. Let me be the one who protects you. The one who believes in you. The one who puts you first."

Her eyes flared, and his pulse spiked, wondering if he'd overstepped. That maybe he had said too much. The Guardians accused him of oversharing all the time, but now, he felt it was right to push. To break through her barrier so she could really trust him. Had she ever trusted anyone who hadn't betrayed her?

A second later, Ebony's mouth crashed onto his and he stumbled back, taking a second to catch his footing. It was hot and wet and hard. A clash of lips and grabbing fingers, tugging his mouth to hers. And he didn't resist. Instead, he matched her intensity with his own. Her gasp, when he slipped his tongue inside her mouth, set off a detonation in his body, igniting every cell. He wanted to prove to her that he was the one she could trust but more than that, he wanted her to trust him. Trust their connection. The bond that linked them for eternity. Know, that no matter what, he would always be on her side.

A guttural groan rumbled from his chest when her fingers found his pants, tugging and fumbling with the button and zipper. Heavens, he wanted her. Ever since she'd lowered her walls and given him a peek behind her fortified gates, they'd done nothing but chase a deadline and hunt a bad guy, only having slices of time to themselves. Since releasing her from the cell, he envied their time in there, when the world outside their four walls didn't exist. When it was just the two of them, laughing, talking, getting to know one another, sharing candy and secret looks. He wanted those moments back...while also being naked.

Tearing her hands away, he made quick work of his zipper while Ebony frantically shucked off her own pants. Weapons she'd collected clattered to the floor with a clang while clothing vanished in a blur of frantic movements and panted breaths. He took her mouth again, wrapping her legs around his waist as he blindly searched for a place to lay her down, striding back and forth in the armory before settling on the single armchair.

Collapsing into the seat, he positioned Ebony on top, and didn't waste any time driving into her heat. She cried out, her head falling back as he guided her hips up and down on his cock. Nothing had ever felt so good. Not the Heavens, not raspberry candy with a soft, chewy center. Not discovering his true mission. Nothing. Deep inside her he could bask in the light for all eternity and never come up for air.

"Scream for me, Violet." He kneaded the soft globes of her ass. "Let it all out. Let me hear it."

Her fingers dug into his shoulders, punishing and clutching as he thrust inside her. But he needed more. Needed to be closer. Shoving down the fabric of her bra, he growled, mouth watering at her sweet, pink nipples and plump, heavy breasts. For the Heavens, he couldn't get enough. He squeezed and sucked, licking her until her fingers clawed him so hard they'd leave marks. And he was here for it.

In no time, tingles danced at the base of his spine driving him deeper, harder. Sweat slicked his chest, running down the center, pooling at the magic spot where his body sank into hers. Ripples of light bounced between them, streaming back and forth through their bond.

"I'm close...God, River... I'm so close..."

Thank all the heavens because he didn't know how much longer he'd last. Slipping a hand between them, he circled her clit, and his vision went hazy. Ebony moaned, her back arching as she fell apart, clenching and milking him. Millions of stars glittered across the ceiling as wave after wave of heat crashed into him until he lost all control, thrusting inside her as though the realm depended on it. Each time he touched her was better than the last. More intense, heightened somehow, and it became a flavor he couldn't live without. Pleasure took over and the world blacked out. All that remained were he and Ebony, the two of them joined in every way possible, cresting over the ridge to ride out the waves. Her hands clutched his shoulders as she crushed her mouth against his, and he accepted everything she gifted him. Every emotion she poured through their bond, the promises made with her kiss, the commitment secured in the blending of their bodies.

She was his. He was hers. And forever more, they were a team.

When the armory blinked back into focus and their breathing eased, Ebony rested her forehead against his. "I... how do you always know what I need?"

He chuckled, his cock still pulsing inside her. "Violet, you were made for me."

She rolled her eyes and glanced at the cot, all that remained of her old cell now that Raine had permanently unwoven the spelled walls. "You don't have to do this. You can stay."

He cupped her cheek, turning her back to him. "Where you go, I go."

"I guess that means we're off to kill my father."

He kissed the tip of her nose. "When you say it like that, how can I resist?"

She smiled and he silently cheered at having once again broken through her walls. One of these days, she'd feel safe enough to dismantle them forever.

"Okay, Maui. Let's go hunting."

CHAPTER 41

RIVER

He was taking too long.

For the past twenty minutes, he individually handwrote notes to everyone in the Guardian household and hid them around the house, so they'd find them after he left. He wasn't even sure how he convinced Ebony to soak in the tub while he delivered them. But, by some leap of faith, he had. And with her wearing the headphones he surprised her with, and a bag of candy within reach, he'd used up all his time. No more stalling. If he didn't do it now, she'd figure out what he was up to.

Countless times while he ducked in and out of their room with his secret notes in hand, he'd stuck his head in the bathroom to check on her. She'd always wanted to protect Hailee, but who protected Ebony? Who put her first? Who made sure she lived her eternity without danger lurking around every corner?

Him.

In the end, that would be his legacy. His true mission.

Standing by the bed, he peered around the room that had somehow, in the matter of weeks, become theirs. Ebony's shirt hung over the back of the armchair, her brush on the vanity, her boots by the dresser. Was this the wrong path? Maybe. Yet, over the past few months he'd proven she had support, someone to rely on, someone who had her back. More than that, he'd become someone she could depend on.

An immortal she trusted.

If their circumstances were different, he could imagine himself spending the rest of eternity with her. They'd find a cure for his sickness, and they'd live their lives misting from one sunny beach to the next, drinking tropical cocktails. In his fantasy, he'd convince her to wear ridiculous matching Hawaiian shirts, and she wouldn't even tease him about it.

That was a life worth fighting for.

But not a life within reach.

Hovering by the closed bathroom door, he angled his ear for the last time, listening to her quiet, relaxed breaths. His heart sank with what he needed to do. But he'd do it again and again if it kept her safe. Hopefully, the healthy dose of lavender oil he'd drizzled in the bath kept her relaxed for long enough.

He desperately needed a head start.

After placing his final note on top of the bed, he rechecked his quiver and the daggers sheathed to his body while silently moving to the balcony. Most of the other Guardians were still at the bakery fire, but a few had returned, so he needed to be quick and stealthy. If someone spotted him, they'd figure out what he was doing.

Heaviness pooled low in his gut at the thought of not making it back, or worse, Ebony following. If the past few months had taught him anything, it was that she would. Hence, the head start.

Because he needed to do this alone.

While his soul still contained a miniscule of light.

With a stiff nod, he unfurled his wings and took to the dark sky.

Tonight, he didn't take in the scenery or the cities as he flew high above the clouds, only focused on the intended destination.

What felt like hours later, with muscles burning from overuse, River landed between two oversized monuments by the entrance to the tunnels where Asher had caused so much bloodshed.

After nocking an arrow, he mentally rehashed his plan. There were so many weak points, Aric would have a conniption. So, so many opportunities for this to blow up in his face.

Only the slightest chance it could work.

That was the path that held all his hope.

"Enter the cave and destroy everything. Then, kill Asher," he resolved out loud, sounding like the Guardian he'd always hoped to be.

With one hand, he yanked open the door to the crypt and entered the first narrow pathway leading into the main chamber, then veered right down another tunnel to finally emerge in the cave where Asher's sick obsession remained.

Still no sign of that Fallen.

Ebony had told him that Asher had said this was bigger than the three of them. Bigger than Blaine? Fate? From what he knew of the Fallen, his quest for revenge filled his soul with hatred and darkness, twisting him into an evil version of himself. Nothing good ever came from that.

Reaching the intricate runes outside the Devoid farm,

he found the stone wall in rubble on the floor. A gaping hole where the spelled entrance once stood.

He lifted his bow. This was too easy. Why was it unguarded when Asher knew the Guardians had discovered it? Was it a trap meant for Ebony...or him?

For the tenth time, he reassessed the plan. Asher wanted Hailee and Ebony to join him. When they refused, he'd burned down the bakery. Asher had commanded Devoid to kill them knowing that the Guardians were after him.

Was there Devoid waiting inside? *Probably.* What other options did he have? He either faced Ebony's demons or ran from them.

Soulmates didn't run.

He thought back to her eyes as he'd helped her sink into the tub. How the faint blues had washed out all the crimson, and his heart soared with renewed strength.

He was ready.

This was his mission.

The second he stepped over the rubble, a rush of ominous air sprouted prickles over his skin, racing down his spine, branching out in every direction, pooling dread in his belly. Tables, still covered in blood, lined one side of the space, while glass jars containing all manner of flesh and body parts filled the shelves behind.

Still no sign of Asher.

Arrow aimed, he stalked through the space, heading toward the rear where he sensed mortals in the cells. Reaching the first one, he yanked open the bars and beckoned the male huddled in the dark corner.

"There's no time for this," he chastised himself.

He needed to follow the plan and find Asher, but he couldn't turn away. Not when Ebony had wanted to save these mortals the last time. If she were here, she would want to again.

Without further second guessing the twist in his path, River snapped into action. One by one, he released the mortals. Any who couldn't walk, he threw over his shoulder and ferried them to the main tunnel while others hobbled alongside him.

He helped the last mortal to her feet. "Hurry. Get up, damn it." Sweat beaded his temples as he dipped and threw the woman over his shoulder and shouted to her cell mate. "Hurry. Get the fuck out of here. Now."

Thank Fate the mortal listened.

River dashed out of the opening into the main tunnel and bolted toward the cavern with the mortals in tow. Some had escaped on their own, others relied on his aid as they stumbled. Seven in total. He'd saved seven mortal lives today. Seven mortals who had fallen prey to Asher's evilness would now live another day, once he wiped their memories on the outside.

Ebony would be proud.

Light from the clearing gradually approached and he breathed a sigh of relief. He and the mortals would make it. One more tunnel and they'd be outside where he could mind-wipe them and track down Asher.

Ahead, two mortals burst from the tunnel into the main chamber—

In a flash, Devoid swooped in from both sides. The creatures, barely covered in scraps of clothing, snarled and tore at the mortals in a frenzy.

The mortal beside him screamed.

At least a dozen Devoid swung their gazes in unison right at him.

Oh, shit.

CHAPTER 42

"**I** *love you, Violet.*"

Ebony jolted, sloshing water over the side of the glorious tub. How long had she been in here? Given the water-logged wrinkles on her fingers, a while. The noise cancelling headphones River had given her, and the playlist he'd specifically selected had lulled her into a sense of not only security, but contentment. She'd soaked in the tub, listening to eighties power ballads, her mind dancing the fine line between consciousness and dreamscape while River wrote and delivered what seemed like a million notes to each of the Guardians. He behaved as though they wouldn't come home. Although the thought sharpened a near constant pain behind her ribs, she tried to ignore it.

A few times, mainly when a song played that reminded her of Hailee, she'd thought of writing her sister a note. But what would she say? Just when they'd mended their relationship, the fire at the bakery had torn it apart. Even if on some slim chance Hailee forgave her, again, neither of them would ever truly be safe. Not while their father walked this realm. They could reunite countless times, but in the end, Ebony would always choose to leave to protect Hailee. That was the price she'd accepted long ago. A vow she'd taken. Family came first.

Always.

Mood now somber, she carefully stepped from the tub and grabbed a heated towel, mentally cursing River for convincing her to waste time in the bath while he delivered those stupid notes. What did he hope to achieve?

Dry, she reached for her leathers on the vanity when a flash of blue in the full-length mirror stole her breath. Heart pounding, she drifted closer. Blue...

No...it wasn't possible.

Yet staring back in the mirror were her mother's eyes. Sky blue, not crimson. A richer shade than Hailee's, but with the same darker navy, almost black rim.

How?

Before she thought better of it, she unfurled her wings, the tips crashing into the walls on either side of the bathroom. Bits of tile crumbled to the floor as she turned this way and that, fanning them out and retracting them, only to repeat the process. Twisting to inspect the feathers from every possible angle.

"Holy fuck," she muttered.

Her feathers. Instead of wings full of long, narrow crimson feathers with poisonous talons at each tip, her wings had begun to change. Transform. On the left, a patch around the size of her torso had turned silvery-gray. The color of Azrael wings.

Angelic Azrael wings.

And there were several more patches on the right wing.

Her bond with River. The result of the soulmate

connection she'd initially thought was a made-up concept that River had fallen in love with, now stared back at her. It had changed her. Right to the depths of her soul.

Was that what she'd secretly hoped for when River had claimed her? A process, a path of redemption she'd never thought was within reach. Yet now...here she was, living proof.

Excitement replaced her earlier concern. After tucking her wings in, she barged into the bedroom. "Maui, you have to see this."

The bedroom was empty.

At first, she thought River must still be delivering notes, until her gaze landed on the one neatly folded at the foot of the bed. The violet paper burned a hole in her chest. Her name, in River's handwriting, taunted her to open it.

No.

He wouldn't. Why leave her a note when they were about to...*No.*

With a shaky hand, she reached for it.

My Violet,

I have loved you since before I met you, and I will continue to long after I'm gone. Keep your soul and your heart safe for me. This was always my path, my mission. To protect you, to keep you safe. If there is a place for me after this, know that I will wait for you.

Maui.

P.S. The red candy stash is in the drawer on your side of our bed. Devour it.

"You stupid, fucking angel."

She tossed the crumpled note on the bed and stormed back into the bathroom to dress. That idiot. Who did he think he was? That his mission was to protect her? Save her like some helpless heroine? She didn't need protection.

"Fucking martyr," she growled, strapping weapons to her thighs.

If he thought she'd hang out in their room and wait for word on whether her soulmate had lived or died, he had another thing coming. He'd agreed to hunt down Asher *with* her for Hell's sake. Not alone. Two immortals walking away from that fight were slim. One? A suicide mission.

River had confessed how he'd never fit in, that he always felt like an outsider, well no more. He had a soulmate.

Throwing open the glass slider, she stormed onto the balcony about to mist when EJ's car drove up the gravel drive with Hailee in the passenger seat. Instead of disappearing, she paused. She should leave, but would that always be her life? Running when things became too real, too hard, the emotions too heightened. Always taking the difficult path to protect her sister.

Exactly what River had done just now to her.

But things had changed. She wasn't a lone wolf fighting a war she wanted no part in. She was no longer a stranger. A Fallen. An outcast. In the past couple of months, he'd tended to her needs, her wellbeing, her emotions. River had accepted her with open arms and loved her. Now it was her turn to prove she loved him back.

Sure, she could mist to the tunnels and catch up to River, return to the plan they'd agreed on, and maybe survive. Or...she could be smart. Ruthless and cunning. And maybe, just maybe, she wouldn't lose everyone she'd ever cared for in the process.

Maybe, with help from the Guardians, they could all make it home.

Re-sheathing the dagger, she stormed back into the bedroom, yanked open the door, and collided with Aric.

"What the fuck is this note for?" He waved a blue piece of paper in front of her face.

"Call an emergency meeting with everyone in the house. River is fucking gone and we're going to get him back."

<hr>

Less than twenty minutes later, while she paced back and forth trying to devise a plan that wouldn't get them all killed, every member of the Guardian household congregated in the living room. The only one missing was—

"What the fuck happened to my brother?" Raine stormed into the room, flipping a Kiel around her index finger, her eyes narrowed in fury.

Now was the time for trust. For alliances and bonds formed by love rather than blood.

Lifting her chin, she faced Raine's wrath. "I fell in love with him."

The Kiel stilled as Raine lowered her hand. "It's about time." She hooked the weapon onto her belt and crossed her arms. "Then what fucking mess has he gotten himself into?"

Instead of directing it at Raine, she twisted to face the others, spread out on the various chairs and sofas, some standing by the fireplace. "Now that everyone is finally here, will someone explain how an angelic soul like River's, someone with an abundance of sunshine and happiness, thinks that it's his fucking mission from Fate to save everyone except himself?"

No one seemed even remotely shocked at her accusation, which didn't aid her darkening mood.

"I think I might know." A frail looking mortal raised her hand from a chair in the back.

Ebony couldn't stop the protective growl building in her chest. "You're the one he's been cleansing. The one who's destroying his soul."

Gasps resonated around the room. Guess they hadn't predicted that twist. But now wasn't the time for tiptoeing around the truth either. Everyone needed to know what motivated River to dive headfirst into danger alone.

"Destroying his soul?" the mortal repeated, looking as shocked as the others.

Had none of them noticed the signs? Had they all walked around in this big, old house with sunglasses on?

"Yes," she snapped, growing more frustrated by the second. "He believes the darkness he cleansed from you is seeping into his soul and poisoning it, and that he'll soon become a Devoid." She cast her gaze around the faces in front of her. "Surely, you've seen the changes in him? I didn't even know angelic souls could disintegrate."

"They can't," Raven replied. "At least, not without—"

"Affecting the source," Willow interrupted. "Destroying an angelic soul could only happen at the source, where the light pours in."

"Then how the fuck is someone tampering with River's?"

Raine threw her hands on her hips. "He thinks it happened when I healed Slater and unknowingly twisted River's power."

More gasps. Fuck, how little did the Guardians know about all the burdens River had carried? All the burdens and secrets he'd trusted her with.

"No, that might have affected his power, but it wouldn't poison his soul." Raven, the lead Guardian, pushed off the fireplace to address the room. "Regardless of how this happened, we need to step up and fucking help River before it's too late. He always thinks he needs to train harder, to do better, needs to give himself to everyone who needs him to ensure they fulfil their path so that we will think he's one of us. I think he feels like he needs to prove himself worthy. Which is fucking bullshit. He's been a Guardian since the second he stepped across that threshold more than five years ago. It's about time we show him. We don't abandon those we love, especially those in trouble. And we don't fucking leave an angel behind." He slid his gaze to Ebony. "Or their soulmate."

On the balcony, she thought she'd have a fight on her hands, that the Guardians wouldn't help her even though it was to aid River. Yet it turned out that quirky angel made an impact on more than her existence and none of them would let him battle Asher alone.

Hailee stood and grasped Ebony's hand. "Tell us the plan."

As she detailed the strategy her and River had rehashed countless times between the bakery fire and her drifting off in that fucking bath, her sister stood beside her, never letting go.

This. This was what it felt like to have someone's back. Every one of the faces in this room had gathered to ensure River made it home safe, and their trust in her made her feel as though it wasn't only River they believed in. Just like River, they had also accepted and included her in their family.

And she'd tear down Hell to stay.

Chapter 43

RIVER

Fate, what had he gotten himself into? River lowered the unconscious mortal to the ground and propped her up by the tunnel wall. He'd expected a battle, but part of him had hoped to only fight the occasional Devoid, focusing his energy on hunting down Asher. Those hopes sailed out the tunnel, carried on that mortal's scream.

This was the only way out.

He lowered his bow. There were too many Devoid and not enough of him to make it out alive. If he didn't, he was thankful he'd left Ebony a note, telling her how much he loved her. He only wished he'd grabbed her face before he left and kissed the Heavens out of her. But a tiny piece of faith whispered that he might get the chance to rectify that error, and he clung to it like sweet candy.

"Right," he gave himself a peptalk. "Straight for the heart. No fucking around."

Mortals temporarily abandoned, River charged into the clearing. The first Devoid attacked instantly. A male who looked in his early twenties, sunken gray skin, clumps of missing hair, scraps of clothing barely covering his body. The Devoid leaped to attack but didn't stand a chance. River effortlessly dipped, unsheathing a dagger to swipe up and straight in the Devoid's heart. The creature froze, shell-shocked before liquifying into goo. River shook it off his hand but there wasn't time for clean-up. Another Devoid lunged toward him.

He counted ten. No, twelve, but that was on this side of the cavern. On the opposite side, countless Devoid streamed into the space from three tunnels. A steady trail of disgusting creatures, filling the area to capacity.

He'd never make it out alive with so many. Even if he was the most skilled Guardian ever created, he wouldn't be able to fight them all at once.

Too many.

Time seemed to stand still. Every breath depended on what he did next. But nothing would change the outcome. Nothing would alter his circumstances or sway his chances. He'd fall here and the realization calmed his blood.

"*I love you,*" he murmured in Ebony's mind for the final time, unsure with their distance if the words would reach her.

His heart swelled hoping they'd be together in the next life if his soul made it. He'd never stop searching for her.

In an instant, the world snapped back into focus and so did he.

Devoid attacked from every angle. Two approached from his left, one from his right. They weren't as quick as he had expected, nor as agile as the ones who had attacked the Guardian residence, and he ended them without breaking a sweat. Another jumped on his back. He spun, shoving it into the cave wall. The Devoid fell, before he lodged a dagger in the heart.

More poured in from the tunnels.

For every two he annihilated, another dozen arrived. He couldn't fight forever, but he would die trying. Daggers in both hands he swiped left and right, cutting and slashing. Body parts fell, blood splashed his face, but he held it fucking together.

Pain scorched his calf a second before he registered the Devoid's teeth sunk deep into his leg. In the process of trying to kick the female off, he slipped. The cave flipped and air punched from his lungs when he landed with a thud.

"Get up!" He shouted at himself. "Get the fuck up!"

If he didn't, they would end what was left of his soul. He wouldn't find Asher. That Fallen would kill Ebony and his mission would fail.

And he wasn't about to fail a mission from Fate.

He tried to roll, kicking his legs out, but the Devoid latched on for dear life. Screaming in fury, he slashed daggers at every moving body part or approaching Devoid, desperate to reach the arrows at his back. Fire blazed through his leg, flooding his bloodstream in seconds, as the poison seeped into him.

An apparition of Ebony appeared in his mind. Her bright violet strands, beautiful blue eyes, the snarky smirk on her face, snapping him into focus. He grunted, shouting as he stabbed the Devoid in the eye. Rolling left, he lunged, stabbing another in the heart.

He could have all the hope and faith in this realm, but it wouldn't lower the enemy's numbers. It wouldn't aid his battle. There were still too many to overcome. Maybe this was his mission all along. His path set by Fate was to become a Guardian, to fight as one. To learn from them and die protecting all he stood for.

A shitty mission for sure. But like the others Fate had tasked him with, he'd face it head on.

Forcing him back, away from the exit, five Devoid circled him. He swiped left and right, holding them off, but it was only a matter of time. He'd fail at the one mission that meant the most to him and he hated himself for it.

As he tasted the bitter stench of defeat, battle cries rang out. Raine, followed by Slater stormed into the cavern, weapons plowing through Devoid blocking their path.

Help.

He had help.

With renewed energy, he snagged an arrow from his quiver and began firing. One down, three. Five. Ten. Over and over, he shot arrows in all directions, trusting his skill and aim to spear Devoid hearts as they lunged toward him.

More Guardians emerged into the cavern. Aric, Raven, Cole. Hailee and Tayla. But it wasn't until he saw a flash of violet that his world toppled.

"No."

Ebony glanced his way. *"You didn't think I'd sit this one out, did you, angel?"* She plunged a dagger in a Devoid without even breaking eye contact with him. *"Besides, I don't know where to buy those raspberry chews. I need you around."*

He barked a laugh, slicing the throat of the closest Devoid. He could grumble at Ebony for not staying safe or he could be thankful he had such a fierce soulmate who never gave up.

Never gave up on him.

"Heavens, I love you."

Pride and a warm rush of love soared through him at the sight before him. The Guardians. His soulmate.

Next, Evie glided into the cavern, chanting with wild eyes and a dark ominous wind whipping above her head, slowing the Devoid so they could kill them quicker.

Raine's back bumped into his, the two of them performing a lethal dance where he shot arrows and his sister hurled Kiel. "You're fucking ridiculous," she snapped.

If they weren't in the middle of a life-or-death battle, he'd laugh. "How did you know where to find me?"

Raine huffed, flinging another Kiel and hitting the Devoid straight in the chest. "Your note was obvious as shit. And your soulmate over there filled in the rest."

A smile lifted on his face as he and Raine took down twice the amount of Devoid working as a team, gradually moving closer to Ebony. Hailee was at her side, holding their own as they fought three Devoid.

The scene was nothing less than carnage. His boots slipped on the goo coating the ground. Body parts and disgusting things he'd rather not acknowledge splattered his arms and across his face. Remnants of the Fate forsaken creatures were even in his hair.

Thank the Heavens he hadn't worn his favorite shirt.

Despite the Guardians showing up, they still struggled to gain the upper hand, with a new wave of Devoid entering from the tunnels. If Asher's aim was to wipe them out, that Fallen just might succeed.

An older male, lunged toward River. Right as he nocked an arrow, a sword protruded through the Devoid's heart before withdrawing again. The male exploded in a mess of goo, leaving Raven holding a bloody sword.

"Thanks, Boss."

The Guardian wiped his forehead with the sleeve of his

shirt. "When you said you wanted your own mission, this was not what I expected."

"You and me both." River huffed out a laugh. "I need to get to Ebony."

They scanned the expansive space, finding River's soul-mate on the opposite side. "Go. I can handle a few Devoid to cover you."

Clearly, the Guardian couldn't count. Because the swarm of Devoid surrounding them was way more than River's definition of a few. But he took off regardless.

Carving a path through the battle, River kept his gaze on Ebony. His body heaved, arms ached, muscles screamed for an end to their constant use, but he pushed on.

All her life, those Ebony trusted had blackmailed her, promised safety, had even pretended to love her, until some had stabbed her in the back. If they made it through this, he hoped she remembered how many angels, Guardians, friends, had banded together to fight with her. How many allies she had on her side. How many loved her. As his sick-ness progressed, he knew that when the time came for his soul to end, the Guardians would welcome her into their home like they had him.

From the corner of his eye, he spotted EJ on his back, kicking and punching trying to regain his footing, while Aric bounded over the tussle to stab a dagger in one Devoid. Raine and Slater fought off at least a dozen over to his left, Raven taking on two of his own. Hailee still fought beside Ebony with short swords and daggers, while Evie shot black swirling balls of energy, blasting the Devoid off their feet.

All around him, sounds of battle echoed through the cave. Grunts, shouts, swearing and cheering. Was there a chance they could win? The slightest? Not without a miracle. If Fate was looking down from the Heavens, now was the time to aid her angels.

As River nocked another arrow, aiming at a nearby Devoid, a mighty boom rumbled the cave. Dirt and debris rained down from above, shaking the walls. Someone shouted to his right, and River ducked, less than a second before fire streamed in a wide arc, incinerating a handful of Devoid in an instant. Behind the flames, wearing a maniacal smile and a pretentious crown, stood the king of Hell.

Relief swept through him like a dip in a cool pond on a hot summer's day.

Blaine.

He'd come.

Back against the wall, River heaved a breath as Blaine blasted more hellfire at the swarm of Devoid, the scorched remains becoming black sticky goo, like liquid tar, bubbling and smoking in circular piles around the cave.

"Don't say I never help you, brother," Blaine shouted above the roar.

Nearby, Raven threw his head back and laughed. "I wouldn't dare."

Blaine ignited another fireball in his palm, raising his arm—

River's body stiffened before locking into place by invisible restraints. Flames froze midair, hovering inches from their designated target. Devoid halted with scrawny claws raised and teeth bared, some covered in fire. The air in the cavern stilled with an eerie prickling at the back of his neck.

At the far end of one tunnel, forty feet away, he spotted a figure stalking through the lines of Devoid toward the center, golden wings tucked behind their back. The angel lingered at the cavern entrance and even if he didn't have a first-class view, he'd recognize that dress sense anywhere. Though today, it was anything but immaculate.

Gabe.

Fate's most trusted angel. Or more accurately, her advisor.

"Impeccable timing, my man," Raven said, the look of relief on his face was almost comical.

At first, Gabe didn't respond. The Archangel surveyed the carnage before him with a keen, assessing eye. While River did the same of Gabe. Dressed in a three-piece suit, Gabe resembled the same strapping angel he'd interacted with over the past few years in the mortal realm. But something about this version of Gabe, how his eyes seemed cold, darker, how his crooked bowtie was off center, his meticulously styled hair now in array, made River shiver. If he didn't know better, he'd think the angel had walked through Hell.

Raven grunted. "Why the fuck can't I move?"

"It is a necessary precaution." Gabe stepped forward.

As discretely as he could, River tried to lift his arm to reach an arrow but, just like Raven, couldn't move. Gabe had the ability to freeze time, he knew that, but the Archangel usually used that ability to talk with the Guardians, not bind them.

"What is going on?" Raven snapped.

"I came to see what was taking so long. And to my surprise, found this." Gabe's cold, muted golden eyes latched on River. "It was only meant to be you. One weakened immortal, two at most, to prove my point. To ensure it can be done. I must say, because of your interference, the mortal held on for far longer than I expected. But you, you should've been easier." He scanned the frozen occupants in the cavern. "And yet, I hadn't anticipated the king of Hell aiding you. A mistake I won't make again."

"This is cryptic even for you, my friend," Blaine responded, a fireball still hovering and flickering at his palm. "Have you drunk too much of the eternal fountain today?"

Gabe sneered, curling his lip at Blaine. "With you, there is no balance. It's unnatural. She was right to toss you out. You clouded her judgement. Without you there, she listens to me."

A dark and sinister growl rumbled through the cave like an earthquake. Blaine's body vibrated with anger River felt even from the other side of the cavern. A second later, Blaine roared, destroying the invisible bands around himself in one effortless crack.

"If you touch her, I will burn every fucking realm to find you."

Seeming slightly more satisfied than moments ago, Gabe tightened and straightened his bowtie. "How will you find me when you and your realm no longer exists?"

Someone shouted.

Blaine prowled forward.

"It's time to cleanse, to begin anew. To restore the balance. And once Fate sees the error of her ways and that we can correct it, you, Blaine, will be a long-forgotten memory."

Blaine threw a fireball at Gabe but before it made contact, the Archangel simply misted away.

CHAPTER 44

EBONY

The instant Gabe vanished the battle snapped back into motion. Devoid lunged, daggers flew through the air. From her right, Blaine roared, streaming hellfire in a wild arc, wiping out anything in its path. Lava dripped from the ceiling, from the walls, from the flesh of Devoid right before they incinerated. An unstoppable weapon on their side for once.

Unless they stepped in his path.

When the last Devoid sizzled on the ground, Ebony heaved a deep breath of relief. Until Blaine turned his rage on Raven.

"You." Blaine stormed forward, a hellfire ball expanding in his palm. "You fed that bastard information. *You* put her in danger."

Not wanting Blaine's wrath aimed at her, she snagged Hailee's hand and tugged her in the opposite direction. "Let's get out of here."

They darted around the gathering Guardians as EJ stood in front of Aric, holding him back.

Raven raised his short sword, aiming the tip at Blaine's throat. "You were the one who chose to leave."

Nearing River, she spotted a flash out of the corner of her eye and recognized it immediately.

Asher.

She froze, swinging her head toward the space Gabe misted from only minutes earlier, finding her father about halfway down the tunnel, staring back. Crimson wings unfurled behind his back, making him resemble the devil he was.

Hailee must've spotted him also, because she muttered a dark curse before tugging Ebony's hand. "Forget him. He's not worth it."

But he was. It was all worth it.

As though taunting Ebony, Asher stood untouched in the patchy darkness. She couldn't ignore him or forget what he'd done. He needed to pay. She needed to end him for the suffering he'd caused, for the heartache. Did he think they'd fail? Was he waiting to see if his blood survived the battle or watching them fall? The answer didn't matter. She wanted him dead. *Needed* him dead.

She'd kill him for ending their mother's life, for dragging her into this world, for threatening Hailee countless times. For not protecting them as a father should. For burning down her sister's dream. She'd end him for all the times she pleaded to leave, and he never released her.

She'd kill him so he was no longer a threat to anyone she loved.

"Don't," Hailee said, tugging her away.

But she couldn't leave it. She'd never rest with him still out there, with him alive.

When her father turned to flee down the tunnel, she jerked her hands from Hailee's and sprinted toward him. Weaving left and right, she dodged the smoking patches of Devoid, the fire raining down from cracks in the cave ceiling, the Guardians trying to stop her. Hailee shouted. So did River. But she snapped her mental walls shut and palmed a dagger.

If she didn't take this chance, if she didn't chase her father, he'd get away.

She'd always be looking over her shoulder.

Zeroing in on a spot between Asher's wings, she charged through the tunnel, dagger raised, ready to strike. Right before she reached him, Asher spun and smiled. Fucking smiled. As though he'd expected her to give chase. As though he'd somehow foreseen the outcome.

She didn't bother talking, or explaining, or giving him a chance to defend himself, she lunged, dagger in the air, aiming straight for Asher's heart.

Her body jolted, a force slamming into her stomach, halting her mid-stride.

Confused, she peered down at the wide slice through her gut. Her brain took a second to register, before the searing pain took over.

"I wish it hadn't come to this," Asher said, withdrawing his wing.

Blood, red and vibrant, dripped from his talon right before pain like she'd never known tore through her body. White hot flares of fire, consuming her, scorching her flesh and tearing apart her insides.

She toppled forward.

This wasn't the end. This wasn't over. It couldn't be. She'd vowed to protect Hailee. If she let their father live, he'd only come after her next.

Somewhere behind her, Hailee screamed, her voice closing in by the second. River's shouts thundered off the walls. Heavy footfalls descended the tunnel toward them. They couldn't see this.

She wouldn't let Hailee suffer the guilt.

She wouldn't let River think he'd failed.

Black dots danced before her eyes. Shooting agony buckled her legs. Right before her knees hit the dirt, she latched onto the front of Asher's shirt, stumbling into him.

"I'm sorry, daughter." His voice sounded distant, swishing in her brain as the pain took over.

She refused to give in, refused to let him win. Refused to give him her screams when he'd already taken so much from her. Closing her eyes, she thought of a happier memory. Of the times her mother used to bake for Hailee and her. The three of them covered in flour, laughing and singing in the small kitchen, eating their body weight in sugar and cake batter. Their mother selling cookies at the local fair. Mum had never owned a bakery, never chased such big dreams because this monster had stolen her life. Her freedom. He'd awoken nightmares and delusions, hunting her from one state to the next while she'd done everything in her power to protect her two daughters.

Asher swatted her hand, but instead of letting go and toppling to the ground at his feet, she tightened her grip and let the wistful memory whisk them away.

She materialized first, in the kitchen of her old family home. Her father materialized a second later, shocked and disorientated, and she stole the opportunity to strike. Using every ounce of remaining strength, she heaved her arm up and slammed the dagger into Asher's chest.

Right through his black heart.

As darkness swayed her vision, and she collapsed on the linoleum floor, her father's body exploded into mist, in the exact spot where he'd taken her mother's life.

CHAPTER 45

EBONY

Fire that had burned through her for what felt like an eternity finally dimmed until it no longer stole her breath. The lava scorching her veins also tapered off, replaced with a cool rush of light, cleansing and repairing. Each damaged cell slowly knitted back together until her body felt renewed.

The searing pain in her stomach was all but gone. A distant memory where she couldn't quite distinguish between reality or dream state. Had her father gutted her with his talon? Had she misted him to her family home? Had she stabbed him in the heart with a Purah dagger?

As her body gradually came back online, so did her mind. Scenes flashed before her, a carousel of moving pictures, all of them featuring River.

Her soulmate.

Her heart swelled at the memory of his face. How he'd vowed to protect her and never abandon her. How he loved her. How, in the face of darkness, he had her back.

"...and then, you'll never believe what happened."

All five of her senses exploded to life at once. Coconut. The smell of sunlight on her skin, of salt in the ocean breeze, of happiness and laughter. They mingled together, wrapping around her like a thick cozy blanket. Next, his touch, how without even opening her eyes, she knew River's hand held hers. How the rings he wore warmed her skin, his bow-callused fingertips stroked feather-light up and down her arm. Lastly, his voice. It swept her up in a soothing caress, awakening each of her cells and setting them alight. His smooth timbre registered low in her belly. She listened to him speak for a long while, not taking in the words, just remembering the times he'd visited her cell and blabbed on and on about random things she didn't care about. The weather, a new shirt he'd bought, his favorite brand of candy. How at first, his frequent visits and insistent chatter annoyed her, but over the weeks, she'd become addicted to them, much like those raspberry chews he slipped her when she wasn't looking.

Deep inside, their connection, their soulmate bond lured her to the surface until she cracked open her eyes.

"...Blaine went crazy when he—" River gasped, squeezing her hand. "You're awake!"

"I..." she cleared her throat. "You need to start again, Maui. I wasn't paying attention."

"Please don't." The bed dipped beside her, and she twisted her head to find Hailee curled up beneath the blankets like they used to as kids. "He hasn't shut up for days. I was beginning to think he'd never stop talking."

She'd never seen a more beautiful sight than River throwing his head back to laugh. When he laughed, he did so with his entire body, so full of energy and life. His eyes, the way they crinkled at the corners, his wide smile, how his shoulders shook with each exhale.

As she tried to sit up, River darted off the chair beside her bed to adjust her pillows and blankets until she was comfortable, and he was satisfied. She peered around the room, the situation feeling eerily familiar to a few months ago when she'd woken up locked in a cell in the basement of the Guardians' house. Now though, her surroundings were vastly different and in a room she recognized immediately.

River's room.

The drapes were drawn back on the large double windows to witness the moon low and heavy in the distant sky, and contentment bloomed inside her. How could she have ever wanted anything other than to be here with the two people she loved the most?

"Well, my Violet." He placed a jar containing only raspberry candy on her lap. "How about I let Hailee fill you in while I grab you some fresh water?"

He kissed the top of her head before slipping out the door.

"I'm not sure I can do as thorough a job as River, so I'll summarize for you. Our father is dead, Gabe somehow tried to destroy River's soul, and possibly Jemma's, we're still not sure of the details, and River and I found you and brought you back here."

What. The. Fuck?

She tossed a candy in her mouth while digesting that sentence, not sure which part to attack first. She knew her father was dead, she saw his body explode into mist right before she collapsed on the kitchen floor. Her last thoughts were of her mother, and how she had hoped Mum was proud of her, peering down from the Heavens.

"How did you find me?" she asked Hailee.

"You took your bracelet off at the bakery, Eb. Once I concentrated enough to sense you and connect to your signature, I knew exactly where you'd gone. Slater came with us for transport." Hailee laid her head on Ebony's shoulder. "I'm sorry you felt the need to fight our father alone. I would have fought him with you."

She twisted the blanket in her hand. "I didn't want—"

Hailee sat up straighter, shuffling to face Ebony. "I know you've protected me, chosen paths that would keep me safe. I know you made a deal with Blaine so he wouldn't use me to dreamwalk. I'm...I'm sorry you went through all that alone. And just when I thought I had you back, that monster used his talon, and I couldn't reach you before you misted away. I thought I'd lost you all over again. River...I've never seen him in such a rage."

It was over. Her father's threats, the constant danger. The running. It was all over.

Ebony nudged Hailee's shoulder. "We made a good team, you and I. Fighting those Devoid. Where the hell did you learn skills like that?"

"Raine has been training us for a long time. I wasn't about to let you fight alone. This was my battle, too."

When she turned to see Hailee's face better, she braced for another jolt of pain that never came. Her hand drifted to her stomach, absently brushing over the non-existent wound. "How did I survive the talon poisoning if my blood has changed to angelic?"

"The soulmate bond. River's light healed you."

She jolted upright. "He shouldn't. He needs every bit to heal himself."

"Willow thinks—"

Someone knocked on the door before River slipped back in with a bottle of water. "Can I come in?"

"Absolutely." Hailee squeezed her hand before slipping out of the bed. "I should give EJ some attention. He's probably feeling neglected and sulking in the garage with Stella."

Love swelled in her chest, inflating her lungs to the brink as River took Hailee's place on the bed and grabbed the TV remote from the nightstand, plus a new packet of raspberry candy. "There's this movie I've been dying to watch with you. Do you feel up to a snuggle-in?"

"Always."

She nestled closer, rejoicing in the thrum of River's heart beneath her hand, the heat radiating from his body wherever they connected. Which were so many points she lost count because she had practically laid herself on top of him, with one leg draped over his, her arms wrapped around his torso, her face nestled into the crook of his neck.

The movie started but she hardly noticed, too occupied with worry to concentrate on anything but the steady rise and fall of River's chest. Was he healed? Was he still sick? Had ending her father somehow fixed his power?

Eventually, she couldn't take it anymore.

Without loosening her hold, she whispered, "Are you okay?"

River kissed the top of her head and drew her in even closer. "Willow has been working with me to correct whatever Gabe has done. Or started. I guess he didn't finish it. She hasn't had any luck yet, but she's determined and so am I. I have a lot of things to live for, Violet, and they all begin with you." His fingers brushed up and down her bare arm. "Willow thinks it's our bond keeping my soul alive. Or... stable. That's the word she used. So...thank you."

Untangling herself, she propped herself up to see his face. "Thank me? You don't need to thank me, you silly angel. I love you. And someone once told me that regardless of the remaining time, love is worth it."

"Wise angel. You should keep him."

She leaned down and pressed a soft kiss on his lips. "I plan to."

River laughed, coaxing her back into his arms, where the rise and fall of his chest seemed a little lighter, and the swell inside hers seemed a little grander.

Just like that, everything locked into place. The strange feeling that had been lingering on the fringes forever was now within reach. Family. A sense of having people to love, having people love her, caring for her, having her back. Something she'd secretly longed for but never thought was in her future. Yet, it had rushed up on her so quickly she'd barely had time to recognize it.

She had her sister back. She had a soulmate.

She had an extended family with the Guardians.

Maybe, just maybe, happily ever afters weren't only for others. Because this one felt awfully like hers.

EPILOGUE

RIVER

River dug his toes into the hot sand, smiling as he jotted down a song name on a bright yellow sticky note and handed it to the security guy standing near the stage. By now, the mortal didn't bother looking at the paper or asking what River wanted him to do with it. He'd handed the guy no less than twenty notes over the past three days. They were practically BFFs. Not in the sense of him and Tayla, but if Ebony kept this up, he needed to find out Big Joe's surname. Or maybe his real name? Was Big a real first name?

Who in the Heavens knew?

River hovered by the roped off area as Big Joe delivered the paper to Ebony. With headphones over her ears, and her fingers fiddling with the dials on the DJ booth, she was a vision. She'd streaked more of her hair that violet purple he loved, and today she had it down, the wavy strands cascading over summer-bronzed shoulders. After scanning the note, Ebony shot him a wicked grin that made his knees wobbly.

Never, in a million years, had he imagined being so happy. So...in love. He'd loved things before, like that candy from Tasmania with the soft, gooey center. But he'd never loved a female, an angel, quite like he did Ebony. And seeing her in her element, on stage DJing in front of hundreds of mortals, made his chest feel soft-centered and gooey, too. At any moment, it might inflate and lift his feet off the sand, floating him into the clear blue sky.

"Who's ready to switch it up?" Ebony announced through the microphone.

The crowd cheered and screamed, as they did whenever she spoke or played a hit. Which had been every song because her playlist today was epic.

She spoiled him and he didn't even care.

Call him biased but she was the best damn DJ this crowd had ever seen. And considering she had hosted sell-out beach parties for three nights in a row, no one could argue.

One song blended into another, and River weaved his way to the front of the makeshift dance area, losing himself in the beat. The song he'd requested. Ebony played every song he'd requested during her shows and each time one began, he never ceased to be grateful. Not only did the DJ play his song, but said DJ was his soulmate.

How lucky was he?

Over the next few hours, River danced his heart out in the front row. It didn't matter that Ebony wasn't dancing with him, or that he couldn't hold her in his arms, he'd make up for the loss later when they returned to their little slice of heaven in their secluded bungalow.

"Last song, Maui. Make it a good one," Ebony crooned in his mind.

A smile lifted his cheeks as he considered his final request. Tomorrow they'd head back to the Guardian mansion where Raven had put everyone on lockdown until they figured out what was happening with the Gabe situation. Even Blaine, the king of Hell, had visited more often in the past fortnight than ever. Talk about joining forces.

Gabe. The archangel he'd envied for his fancy suits and his ability to mist back and forth from Fate's sanctuary had shocked them all. No one more so than Raven.

But there was time to worry about that later after they returned.

For now, River's soul was still alive, and he'd make the most of living.

He scribbled his last request on a note and passed it directly to Ebony. Without missing a beat, she blended the current song into the one he'd requested, which also happened to be the same one she compelled the DJ to play at SubZero. The crowd went wild for one final time.

At the DJ booth, after Ebony had packed up her gear, he lifted her into his arms. "That was your best set ever." He dotted kisses all over her face, her cheek, her nose, her chin, her lips.

She giggled in his arms. "You say that every night."

"True. But your dance parties keep getting better."

Lowering her toes to the sand, he took her hand in his. "How about we go back to the bungalow and make use of the jacuzzi for our final night?"

"I have something else planned, first." She tugged him toward the north end of the beach. "Walk with me, angel."

They strolled along the cool, wet sand, where the ocean

lapped onto the beach, hand in hand and around the top end of the island. The sun began its descent below the horizon, and he couldn't wait to share another sunset with her. But all thoughts of watching the sun evaporated when he spotted a day bed complete with flickering lanterns, and a table off to one side with a tray containing two creamy white cocktails.

"When did you organize this?"

If he thought his chest would inflate to capacity earlier, that feeling couldn't top now.

"I thought we'd do something special for our last night on Maui."

Jumping onto the pile of cushions, he shuffled back and opened his arms for Ebony.

"Hold that thought. I'll be back in one second."

Before he asked why, Ebony misted away and a second later, returned with a present in her hand. She handed it to him.

"I didn't know we were celebrating. Violet! I didn't buy you anything." He scrambled off the lounge. "Mist me to the gift shop please. This is an emergency."

Ebony laughed and shoved the present at his chest. "Just open it."

Fate. His chest was never going to deflate ever again.

After unraveling the bright yellow ribbon, he lifted the lid of the gift box, then dug through the wad of yellow tissue paper. His heart stalled. Giddiness rose in his blood as he placed the gift box on the lounge and lifted out the... Hawaiian shirt. The coolest Hawaiian shirt he'd ever seen. A white background with hot pink flamingoes, squiggles of cerulean-blue waves, and black glittery palm trees.

In record time, he stripped off his current shirt to replace it with—

"Wait." Ebony stilled his hand. Slowly, she twisted the shirt around so he could read the back.

"*Maui*." River sucked in an excited breath as he ripped the second shirt from the gift box to hold it up and read the back. "*Violet*. Oh, my Fate. Violet! This is the best gift ever!"

Hawaiian shirts forgotten, he cupped Ebony's face in his hands and took her mouth in a searing kiss.

"Just think of all the combinations we could come up with." Ideas popped into his mind in record time. "We could get matching shorts! And pajamas! Do they make Hawaiian shirt pajamas? I don't care. Someone will for the right price."

Ebony laughed and laughed, filling his soul with light and warmth. "Let's not get ahead of ourselves. I'm not wearing this shirt when we get back to the Guardian's house. It's only a treat for tonight."

Now it was his turn to laugh. Snagging her hand, he tugged her on top of him. "We'll see, my Violet. We'll see."

Not ready to leave River and Ebony? Head over to my website and subscribe to my newsletter (www. cassielaelyn.com) to read a bonus dreamwalking scene that will make your heart swoon!

Dear Reader!

First, I want to say a huge thank you for continuing to read the Fallen Guardians series! Without you, this author gig couldn't happen.

Second, if you're reading the series as each book releases, and have waited for a freaking long time for River's story, this book is for you! Back in the very beginning, the dedications for each book began with the Guardian writing a special thank you to their soulmate. Because, really, without him finding her, the book would never exist. And although I still love this concept (and have honored it in Unwavering), this is the first book I really wanted to dedicate to YOU. So, this is my special note! Thank you for sending me your well-wishes during the past 18 months as my family went through the toughest time of our lives, for cheering me on from the sidelines as I returned to writing, for re-reading and recommending my books even though I hadn't released a new one, and for turning up to my table at bookish events to tell me how excited you are for River's story. THIS BOOK IS FOR YOU! I hope you loved reading it WAY MORE than I loved writing it (because let's face it, writing it was a long, tough process! Ha ha!)!

I'm a little sad to enter the last book of this series, but I'm also ready to usher in the end that I envisaged so many years ago when Raven first appeared in my head. The direction really hasn't changed much from that first vision. It's going to be a wild ride to get there, but it'll be worth it.

Much love,

Cassie x

Glossary of Terms

Azrael – Angels of Death who transport souls from the mortal realm to their final resting place in either the Heavens or Hell. Azrael have silvery-gray wings.

Dumahel – Half angel, half mortal, Dumahel possess the power to enter and manipulate dreams. They are rare and always born as twins.

Fallen – Once angels of the Heavens, Fallen now reside in the many realms in Hell and give their allegiance to the current ruler of Hell. Fallen have crimson wings.

Guardians – Fate's warriors, tasked with protecting Chosen mortals, so they can fulfill their fated destiny. Fate exiled the Guardians to the mortal world over three hundred years ago. They have black wings.

Nuriel – Half Fallen Raziel, half mortal, Nuriel possess the ability to cast ancient magic.

Purah – Crystalline water from the Eternal Fountain, found in the Heavens. Purah is toxic to Fallen.

Raziel – Angels who cast magic, commonly used to disguise the immortal world from mortal eyes.

Sarael – the Protector of the Heavens.

ALSO BY CASSIE LAELYN

The Fallen Guardians

Fall for a brotherhood of not-so-angelic angels where the battle between Fate and freewill has never been so twisted. Each book features a different main couple with a standalone happily ever after (no cliffhangers!).

Start with Unforsaken (Raven)

Small Town Packs

Fall in love with small towns, swoony shifters, and unbreakable bonds. Each interconnected story is set in a different small town with a different pack, and has a standalone happily ever after (no cliffhangers!).

Start with Salvation (Wolves of Woodland Falls).

Standalones

Bite-sized paranormal romances with standalone happily ever afters!

Start with The Frost Prince (Jack Frost retelling!).

ABOUT THE AUTHOR

Cassie is an award-winning paranormal romance author living in sunny Queensland, Australia with her husband and two BMX-crazy boys.

She has a passion for crafting stories involving loyal, otherworldly characters in need of love and redemption. She's also a self-confessed chocoholic and a huge sucker for an angsty, gut-wrenching happily ever after.

When she isn't narrating imaginary characters, Cassie loves binging on TV shows, spending time at the beach, and curling up listening to the rain.

Join Cassie's newsletter (www.cassielaelyn.com) to stay up to date with release information, giveaways and access the subscriber's only area for free bonus content to devour between book releases.